Carolina Reckoning

Other books by Lisa Carter

Aloha Rose (Quilts of Love series)

CAROLINA RECKONING

Lisa Carter

a novel approach to faith

Carolina Reckoning

ISBN-13: 978-1-4267-5797-6

Published by Abingdon Press, P.O. Box 801, Nashville, TN 37202

www.abingdonpress.com

Published in association with the Steve Laube Agency

Library of Congress Cataloging-in-Publication Data has been
requested.

Printed in the United States of America

1 2 3 4 5 6 7 8 9 10 / 18 17 16 15 14 13

Dedication

To my mother, Carolyn Rasberry Fulghum, my strongest
supporter and encourager. Her own fictional stories of
adventure involving my brother and me as the main heroes
carried us through many a long family trip as children and fueled
the writer within me. Her life story—of courage, independence,
and faith—inspired *Carolina Reckoning* and is a testament that
God is, indeed, sufficient for every need.

To those who've felt abandoned and betrayed by a spouse, friend,
or family member. You know who you are and so does God.

Acknowledgments

David—Thanks for being convinced, even when I wasn't, that I
was a real writer. Thanks, too, for all your technical expertise.

Corinne and Kathryn—Y'all have made mothering fun. God is
writing your life story—a work in progress—and I'm loving every
minute. I can't wait to see what comes next. It's going to be glorious.

Hope Dougherty—Thanks for being my friend and critique partner. Without you, this journey wouldn't have been half as much fun.

And thanks to Charity Tinnin and Erynn Newman for your
insight into the early drafts of *Carolina Reckoning*.

Tamela Hancock Murray—Thanks for your unfailing support
through this process. And thanks for believing in me and never giving up on *Carolina Reckoning*.

Ramona Richards—Thanks for taking a chance on me and for making dreams come true. You are someone whose integrity of character and deep faith I so admire. I'm blessed to know you.

Cat Hoort, the Abingdon sales and marketing teams, Anderson Design Group (I love the cover)—Thanks for all you've done to make *Carolina Reckoning* the best that it can be.

Lynette Eason—You were the first "real" author I ever knew. You were also the first to tell me *Carolina Reckoning* had a future. Thanks for all your advice and encouragement.

Deborah Raney and DiAnn Mills—You read my first draft and encouraged me to place *Carolina Reckoning* on the path to publication. Knowing you believed in me made such a difference. I want to be both of you when I grow up.

The Blue Ridge Mountain and ACFW writing communities—Because of you, I've learned so much, and *Carolina Reckoning* became possible.

Thanks to my Precepts class for your prayers and support on my writing journey. You all mean the world to me.

Readers—It is my prayer that *Carolina Reckoning* will glorify and inspire you to draw nearer to God, especially if your world has fallen apart. May you find God, who is ever faithful and true.

Jesus—You make all things new. Thank you for placing the dream inside my heart and bringing the dream to fruition. Thank you for second chances. Thank you for your mercy and grace. You know how badly I need them. I love you.

*I'm convinced that nothing can separate us from
God's love in Christ Jesus our Lord: not death or life,
not angels or rulers, not present things or future things,
not powers or height or depth, or any other thing that
is created.*

— Romans 8:38-39

1

October

Part of her wasn't surprised by what she discovered in her husband's coat pocket. In some ways, Alison felt relieved to know the truth.

Her hand tightened on the photo. She took a deep breath, the pain of betrayal stabbing at her lungs. Her chest ached with the hurt searing her heart, the effort not to fall apart overwhelming her.

But in spite of the conflicting thoughts racing through her mind, Alison relaxed her fist, smoothing the crumpled photograph of her husband, his arm around a woman in a black, old-fashioned cloche hat. She squinted in the early afternoon light, trying to make out the details. But the woman had averted her face, burying her head into Frank's chest.

Alison didn't think she knew this woman although it was hard to tell anything about her as she had both of her arms clasped around Frank's waist, pinning him as effectively as a bug on the page of an insect collection.

Make that a worm collection.

She suspected this woman was one in a long line of dalliances in which Frank had indulged, carried on in cities all over the United States, thanks to his job as a pilot with North American Air, based at the Raleigh-Durham airport.

Noting a sign in the photograph, Bay Town Suites, she stalked out of the bedroom to Frank's office. Touching the computer screen, she did a quick Internet search for the location. She wasn't the total idiot Frank liked to believe.

Fifteen minutes later, she had her answer. The hotel was located in a seedy section of San Francisco, away from the more touristy and frequented areas Frank's colleagues might be apt to visit.

Settling into the black leather desk chair, she tried to remember when Frank last made a run to San Francisco. A month ago, he would've needed the raincoat in the photo for the cool, dampness of San Fran.

How could Frank have done this to her? To their children, Claire and Justin? Anger rolled like hot, crashing waves just below the surface. She'd known something was up with Frank. He'd been less cocky, his mind preoccupied, unwilling to make eye contact, his acerbic tongue quiet for a change.

Unable to bear looking at the photo again, she tucked it into the pocket of her trousers. Restless, she made her way to the kitchen. The children would be home from school soon. Taking carrots out of the refrigerator for their snack, she caught sight of the family picture—stuck to the front of the fridge—made last summer on a Caribbean cruise.

Frank, in his favorite blue polo and khaki shorts, leaned against the ship's rail with his arm securely around her like a big cat toying with his captured prey. She'd resisted, trying to pull out of his stronghold. Sunlight glinted off the red tints in Frank's auburn hair. His Arctic blue eyes gazed at the camera intense and as confident as a flag on the Fourth of July. She never allowed herself to vent her anger, but the desire to strike back and punish terrified and electrified her, the violent turbulence stretching her nerves taut. She took a few deep, cleansing breaths and then a few more.

She couldn't fall apart. She had to think. Frank wasn't going to get away with it this time, so help her God.

If only she could believe in God at a time like this.

A key turned in the lock at the front door. Voices called.

Claire and Justin erupted into the kitchen, grappling for snacks at the counter.

As fourteen-year-old Justin stuffed a handful of baby carrots into his mouth, he came around the counter to give his mother a bone-crushing hug. She closed her eyes, smelling the lingering aromas of school, gym socks, and to her surprise, a faint trace of aftershave.

He took a seat at the kitchen island with carrots and dip beside his Algebra II book, his scuffed and worn book bag on the hardwood floor at his feet. "What's for dinner, Mom?"

She rinsed her hands, wiping them with the small hand towel she kept next to the soap. "Probably chicken." She pulled out her wooden chopping block.

Claire groaned, her head falling forward on her arms. "It's always chicken."

Her hair hung long, its color the same auburn hue as Frank's. She'd also inherited that beautiful rose complexion the Irish—or, in Frank's case, the Boston Irish—were prone to.

"Chicken is healthy." She'd reminded Claire so many times, her response felt automatic.

Claire rolled her big blue eyes with great dramatic effect and made gagging noises.

Alison eyed her daughter. "Maybe if you want more variety you should start doing some of the cooking yourself."

Claire frowned, narrowing her eyes. "When's Dad going to be home?"

"His flight gets in at six."

Claire flipped her hair behind her back. "He's probably tired of chicken, too."

Hitting too close for comfort, Alison turned her back on her daughter, chopping the fresh herbs she would put into the chicken recipe. Frank had been tired of a lot of things for a long time.

Better to keep the anger intact for Frank instead of unloading it on her teenage daughter. For the first time since marrying Frank, Alison questioned what *she* wanted to happen next. Could she summon the courage to demand her rights for once and divorce him? Should she?

Divorce was a scary word. Or, was it the thought of being alone? She'd married so young, she'd never been alone.

An image of her younger self, standing over her father's grave, flashed through her mind. Going from her father's house to Frank's, she never had the opportunity to manage her own finances. She had no idea how to file an income tax return or open her own checking account. She'd never held a real job.

"Your real job," Frank would say, "is to be my wife."

She couldn't ignore this by burying her head in the sand. Was this how her dad coped for all those years with her mother's drunken, promiscuous behavior, by pretending *it*, the elephant in the room, didn't exist?

Alison clenched her jaw. Frank wasn't getting off the hook this time. She had her children's future to consider despite the fact she'd like to smack that smug smile right off his arrogant . . .

Gentle-natured like her dad, she walked away from a fight. Most of the time she ran.

She imagined the hurt that would scar Claire and Justin's lives forever, like so much notepaper—once torn into pieces—never easily repaired. She fought the urge to tear the photograph into a million pieces and pretend. Like father, like daughter.

Grinding her teeth, she bore down on the knife in her hand. The pungent scent of basil filled her nostrils.

Not this time.

"How much homework do you two have tonight?" She'd learned over the years not to ask *if* they had homework but simply how much.

Justin shook his wavy brown hair out of his eyes. "About an hour's worth of vocabulary. I hate English." He was a boy who liked to tinker with engines and computers, not words.

Claire rolled her eyes. "Tell us something we don't know."

A tiny smile quivered on Alison's lips, easing some of the tension. "And you, Claire?"

Her daughter dangled the lavender sandals on her feet as she balanced on the stool. "A little English lit and history. Nothing I can't handle. But there's not too much I find I can't handle."

An acrid taste filled Alison's mouth.

Justin responded before she could, patting Claire on the head like an Irish setter. "You know what they say about pride, my ever humble big sister."

"What's that, stinky little brother?"

Justin laughed, walking out of the kitchen with his notebook under his arm. "Pride bites the dirt the moment you trip over it and fall on your face."

She looked at her daughter. Like father, like daughter?

Not this time. Not if she could help it.

Mike Barefoot hated grocery stores. He hated the sight of love-struck young newlyweds too besotted with each other to notice they were blocking the aisle. Grocery stores should be like his former army missions in the Gulf. Get in, target your objective, and get out.

Instead, a preschooler with a miniature-sized cart plowed over his toes. He blinked and clenched his jaw to keep from cursing.

"Sorry." The child's mother wore an expression as overburdened as her cart. A toddler stuffed chubby fistfuls of crackers into a mouth surrounded by a none-too-clean face. The mother also lugged a prostrate infant, slung onto her back, cradleboard-style, like his Cherokee ancestors.

"Tell the nice man you're sorry for hurting him, Billy." She shoved her one mobile offspring forward. The pint-sized cart's back wheels ran over his other foot.

He gritted his teeth.

Billy scowled, his eyes narrowed into slits. "Sorry."

Great. Give it fifteen years. He'd be arresting this one for serial murder.

Mike balanced the green wire basket over his forearm and side-stepped the freak show. All he'd wanted was a TV dinner, the one time he wanted a home-cooked meal and not takeout. Why did the store change up the products on the aisles every time he dropped by? Not that he dropped by often. Fast food was an American way of life for a reason . . . because it was fast.

He dodged a couple of college boys toting large cartons of beer to the cashier—might be wise to let Traffic be on the lookout for that particular frat party. He sidled past a Female with a smile the size of an alligator—and yes, noting those rapier-length nails, a female with a capital F. Did he have "lonely and desperate" tattooed on his face? That Female was a man-eater. He'd stake his grandfather's farm in the Blue Ridge on it.

For crying out loud, couldn't a guy get some dinner and a little peace? After the totally uncalled for and totally unexpected public tantrum of his last so-called girlfriend—he'd forgotten to call and cancel dinner when a murder/suicide thing happened, but he'd been busy at the time—he was wise and wary now when it came to women.

A thin, liver-spotted hand tapped him on the arm. "Young man?"

He gazed down into the cherubic face of an elderly woman.

"Would you be so kind as to hand me a can of green beans?" She gave his arm a playful squeeze. "I don't know why the manager insists on placing items so high on the shelves."

Inbred politeness—the cultural curse of the Southerner—and his granny's former training kicked in. "Yes, ma'am." His 6'4" frame had served him well, whether on the football field or coming to the rescue of elderly ladies. "I'd be happy to help you."

His former sour mood vanished, warmth pervading his being. He could almost hear the echoes of his granny's determined Sunday school efforts. The best way to stop feeling sorry for yourself was to help somebody else. The oneness of humanity—

The old lady rammed the can against his chest, the beatific smile erased. "The French-cut beans. Are you stupid or something?"

"Or something," he growled, handing her another can, French-cut this time. So much for the training of childhood. He wondered as he watched her scuttle away without so much as a backward glance—much less a thank-you—if there was anything he could charge her with.

Obstruction of a police officer on a grocery run? Disrespectful and disorderly conduct toward an officer of the law in North Carolina? Assault against a bona fide Raleigh homicide detective? The sharp metal can against his ribs had hurt.

He'd bet his granny's prize-winning apple pie there were bodies buried in that old broad's backyard. His stomach rumbled at the thought of pie. Where did they hide TV dinners—and pies—in this warehouse they called a grocery store? What he'd give for a slice of granny's pie. Or a glimpse, just one more time, of her laugh-lined face.

Mike needed to go home. His real home, not the apartment where he parked his clothes. It had been way too long. He missed the rainbow quilt of rhododendrons on the mountainside. The silvery flash of trout in the stream. The haunting hoot of the owl that lived in the rafters of the barn.

No home to go back to, gone with the death of the grandparents who'd raised him. His only living relative—his niece, Brooke, whose tuition bills cluttered his home office—would be away at school until summer break.

As he yanked open the freezer door, the air-conditioning hit him in the face like a blast of ice. He reared. He'd been in morgues less chilling.

The cell phone in his front pocket vibrated. Letting the freezer door slam shut, he wiggled the phone out and scanned the number. Dispatch. With the department shorthanded, following his partner's delivery and subsequent maternity leave, he was on call 24/7.

So much for a home-cooked dinner. So much for a quiet evening. Murder never took a night off.

The dinner hour had come and gone. Frank was still a no-show. With their homework done, baths taken, and clothes ironed and laid ready for the early alarm of high school, Justin and Claire were as tucked into bed as you could tuck teenagers.

Frank had done this before. The kids knew they'd see him when they saw him. But if he thought he could outlast her this time, Frank had another thought coming.

Alison jumped at the shrilling of the phone and glanced at the caller ID. It was Val, her best friend and confidante since college, who was never one of Frank's biggest fans. She started to pick it up, then reconsidered, letting her hand fall to her side.

She'd have to fake it or Val would know right away something was wrong. And once Val got a hold of that, she'd be like black spot on roses until Alison cracked and told her everything. She squelched the urge to pour out her soul.

Not just yet. Val might tell her something she didn't want to hear. Like what God would want her to do.

She schooled her features into a mask of calm before she picked up the phone as if Val could see her through the telephone wires. She imagined her thirty-something friend reclining on the sofa in her den, her feet up and over the armrest, running ever-busy fingers through her crop of short brown curls, rumpling them in the process.

"Ali? The house is ours!" Val gushed. "We are the new owners of the two-story brick Colonial only five minutes from you."

She waited a beat too long.

"What's Frank done now?"

They'd known each other far too long for secrets.

"I can't talk about it until I've spoken with Frank tonight, but I promise I'll call you tomorrow." Her voice wavered.

A silence. She used the time to get control of the sudden unexpected tears she hadn't known were hovering on the edge of her eyelids.

"If you need me or Stephen . . ."

Did Val imagine that kind of thing went down over here? Frank preferred to wound with words, not fists. Words weren't as visible

She managed a weak laugh. "No worries. Nothing like that."

"At the risk of your continuing scorn through every crisis of your life," Val sighed, "I only bring this up because I care."

16

"Continuing crises, huh?" She laughed with genuine mirth this time. "You make me sound like Scarlett O'Hara."

"You will be in my prayers all night. If I can do anything for you . . ."

"Whatever works." She replied to Val's gentle prodding. Val never shoved her religion—correction, Val called it her relationship with Jesus Christ—in anybody's face. Val understood all too well why Alison felt so estranged from God. Val had been the only one there with her on the worst day of her life.

"You better not forget to call me when you get a chance. Remember I'm always in your corner and so is God."

Clicking the phone off, Alison wondered why everyone abandoned or betrayed her in the end. Except for Val. And Val would be the first to tell her everyone deserved a second chance.

But a sixth chance, or a twelfth?

The beginnings of a small, secret smile lurked at the corners of her lips. If Frank refused to cooperate, she would make sure the entire community knew every sordid, despicable detail of his miserable life.

She quashed the thought there might be a less brutal, wiser way to handle things.

At first, he would deny her allegations. Then, he'd rage, declaring she didn't have the guts to go public. Frank's problem, she reflected not for the first time, was he never knew when to quit, to leave it alone and fight another day. But she knew what moved Frank, what got him up in the morning. With a certainty grounded on Frank's overweening pride, she had him.

And he would hate her for it.

Alison could hear Val's gentle voice in her ear reproving her.

So what if he hated her?

Kicking off her flats, she curled up on the loveseat in the front room with its excellent view of the street. She was tired—probably what Frank was counting on—but everything that would make life worth living depended on her not giving in this time. She reviewed in her mind the events of the last few months, every put-down, every argument.

Like a soldier preparing for battle, she harnessed the tattered remains of her inner strength—whatever strength Frank hadn't succeeded yet in slashing—gathering the few shreds of what was left of her identity.

What was there about her people found so difficult to love? All her life . . . She winced at the memory of her mother walking away, the smell of the freshly turned loamy soil lingering in the air.

If only she could be like Val. Fighting her aloneness, at this moment, she envied Val her loving God. She wished someone, anyone, would love her like that.

2

CLINGING TO THE TIRE ROPE, BALANCING LIKE THE MONKEY HER DADDY claimed her to be, she crawled out of the doughnut hole of the tire swing. She raised her skinny suntanned legs up until at last, she stood on the top of the tire holding onto the rope with all her might.

She jumped straight out at him. "Watch, Daddy! I can fly!"

And in that split second of time, she knew she was going to fall and he wouldn't be there to catch her. The air rushed past her face, impact seconds away.

With a small involuntary cry, Alison jerked herself awake. Disoriented, she realized she lay on a sofa in a strange room. A clock ticked.

She swung her legs over to the floor. Her heart hammering in her chest, returned to reality. Her dream. Not in Florida. Not seven anymore. Her daddy had died a long time ago. That bitter realization upon waking—time and again—never failed to rend her heart.

Here, in her home in Raleigh, she waited for . . . ? What had she been waiting for? With a rush, the events of what must now be yesterday flooded over her.

She'd fallen asleep waiting for Frank to return. She stood, too quickly for her equilibrium, and swayed, lightheaded. Her brown leather flats lay beside the sofa on the Oriental rug where she had kicked them off the night before.

A streak of pink and gold hovered at the edge of the horizon above the tree line. She glanced over at the grandmother clock in the corner. Early morning. Not yet six.

The children. She must get them up soon for school. Befuddled, she rubbed the sleep from her eyes. She needed coffee.

Where was Frank?

Had Frank somehow slipped past her and left her to sleep undisturbed on the sofa? Or had he come home at all?

She padded on bare feet out of the front room, through the foyer and down the hall into the kitchen to yank open the connecting door to the garage.

Alison rocked back on her heels. His black Corvette did not sit in its usual space beside her car in the garage. With all his secret assignations and late-night partying, he always came home at some point during the night.

The doorbell rang, followed by an insistent pounding. Frank had forgotten his key or, drunk again, had lost it. He'd wake the children. She didn't want them to see him like that.

As she entered the foyer, Justin's tousled head peeked over the banister of the landing. "Someone's at the door, Mom." He stretched and gave a big sleepy yawn.

Claire, in her pink polka dot pajama shorts, popped up behind him. "Do they know what time it is?"

Anxious to divert their attention from their father, she fluttered her hand. "Go back to your room. Get ready for school."

Without bothering to see if they complied, and not pausing to look first through the glass panels on either side of the massive oak door, she reached for the brass handle, throwing the door wide open.

Mike took an involuntary step backward on the porch.

The Uniform, as he liked to refer to them, cleared his throat. "Mrs. Monaghan?"

A tall, painfully thin woman stood in the doorway, blinking in confusion. Whatever she expected to find on the other side of the door, it had not been policemen.

"Mrs. Monaghan?" prompted the officer again.

"Y . . . yes?"

She swallowed, Mike noted, and licking her dry lips, tried again. "Yes, I'm Mrs. Monaghan." Fear sharpened the focus of her coffee-brown eyes. She drew a shaky hand up to her throat.

Interesting. Already dressed at this time of day, yet her attire appeared rumpled, her hair in disarray.

As if she could somehow read his thoughts or the direction of his gaze, she removed her hand from her throat, stroking down the unruly strands of her silver-blonde hair, tucking both sides behind her ears.

He also observed the toenails of her bare feet were painted the same pink as her blouse.

"What's happened?" Her voice heightened in pitch.

He perceived the quickness of her breaths in and out as if she'd just run a marathon. Having delivered bad news countless times in his career, he supposed it was never a good sign when policemen appeared on your doorstep. He remained silent. His role was observer at this point. The Uniform would handle the rest for now.

The Uniform took a small step toward Alison Monaghan. "Ma'am, I'm Officer Randy Ross and this," he gestured to Mike, "is Detective Sergeant Mike Barefoot."

Her lips tightened. "What's wrong?"

Officer Ross wouldn't enjoy this any more than any other cop, but they were paid to do the unpleasant and deal with the fallout.

"We have bad news for you, ma'am." Ross wore his compassion on his face. "Could we come in?"

The lady opened the door wider and motioned for them to follow. A dazed expression on her face, she halted in the spacious foyer.

Ross glanced at the sofa visible in the living room. "Maybe you'd like to sit first."

The woman shook her head.

It never helped to delay. Better to get it over with.

"Your husband, Frank Monaghan." Ross took a quick breath. "I'm sorry to say, ma'am, he was found dead this morning."

Mike's gaze never left Alison Monaghan's face. He caught the split-second flicker of relief flashing across her face, followed immediately by a flush that stained her sculpted cheekbones. Guilt?

She staggered two steps away from them as if she could flee their words. Her hand groped behind her. She started a rapid descent to the floor. Ross caught hold of her arm, slowly lowering her the rest of the way.

"No! You're lying!" screamed a girl leaning over the banister at the top of the stairs.

He, Officer Ross, and Alison Monaghan jerked their heads toward her. A boy tugged her back onto the landing. Ross shot Mike a look.

Mike frowned. He'd not realized children were present. Not the way any kid should find out about their old man.

The girl collapsed to her knees, her face in her hands. The keening arising from the teenage girl sent a preternatural shiver down the spine of the usually unflappable detective.

It was a sound he'd heard once when he was a boy with his grandpa on one of their camping trips in the hollows of the Blue Ridge. Her pain, as ancient as Eve, reminded him of the wild mountain creature they'd discovered mortally wounded in a man-made iron trap. Or, the sound the Ranger—what was left of him—made when the IED—

The boy bent over her, wrapping his arms around her, as she rocked back and forth in a crouch, tears streaming down her face. But thank God, the horrible sound stopped.

Now it was his turn. He scrutinized the motionless woman at his feet.

"Mrs. Monaghan?"

He repeated it twice more before he penetrated her mental cloud and she lifted her face.

Shock? Fear? Defeat? All of which could indicate complete innocence or calculated deceit. He also marked the absence of tears. She'd not spoken since Ross broke the news to her.

If indeed, it was news to her.

As elegant and refined as she appeared, he knew better than to assume the innocence of anyone. He'd been on the investigative team a few years ago, resulting in the conviction of a perky blonde woman, highly educated and successful, who'd poisoned her equally attractive and successful young husband. She'd almost gotten away with it.

Though a cliché, it was true. The spouse usually committed the murder. The one who was supposed to love you the most and forever.

Like that ever happened in real life. Or at least, maybe not to him.

Marriage, he often remarked to his like-minded cronies, was unfortunately the best motive for murder. It's why he avoided it. In his early thirties, he had long ago given in to the rampant cynicism of cops who've seen too much. Too many beautiful women to stick to just one anyway.

Alison Monaghan peered at him. "I don't remember your name." He saw the flash of intelligence and the wariness that followed. "But you are a detective." She started to pull herself to her feet.

Officer Ross grabbed her by the forearm and helped her stand. Mike exchanged glances with Ross. "Perhaps we'd better go into another room."

Alison Monaghan's face constricted at the sound of her sobbing children, but she squared her shoulders and faced him. "My children first."

Before he could respond, she took the stairs two at a time, resting a hand on each of her children's faces. "I need to talk with these officers. I need for you to go to—"

The boy shook his head. "No."

"Please," she whispered. "Just for a few minutes, I promise."

The children trudged up the stairs with a little more prodding, the girl sending a parting scowl over her shoulder at him and Ross.

He pictured the motherless faces he mentored in his off-duty hours at the Teen Center. Alison Monaghan, a loving, devoted mother?

But then again, so were black widows, up to and including, the moment they devoured their spider spouses. The Southern species, in particular, noted for their deadly, sexual cannibalism.

She rejoined the officers. And angling to the open room on her right, she walked on, leaving the policemen to follow her faint fragrance of lavender.

Intelligent and gutsy, somehow she had grasped he was the one in charge and that there was more. More she didn't think the children should hear. He could almost like this lady if she wasn't his number-one murder suspect.

They followed her into the high-ceilinged room. With a frown, he seated himself in the pale blue wingback chair she indicated. Officer Ross continued to stand by the arched entrance.

Mike was astonished this unprepossessing Raleigh housewife had somehow seized control of his interview. He liked to decide where the suspect sat, preferably in strong light, giving him a psychological advantage as the investigating officer.

Squinting as the sunrise made a brilliant splash of light into his eyes, trying to hide his irritation at being upstaged, he removed a pen and small notebook out of his suit pocket. He had a familiar routine he liked to employ in such matters.

Before he could begin, she leaned toward him from the spot she'd taken on the sofa. He realized during his abstraction she'd quietly slipped on some shoes sitting beside the couch.

Armor?

"Now," Alison Monaghan knotted her hands together. "Tell me exactly what has happened to my husband."

3

MIKE CLEARED HIS THROAT. "YOUR HUSBAND WAS FOUND DEAD IN THE early hours of this morning in his parked car."

"At the airport?"

He shook his head. "No. Where Orchard Farm Road dead ends."

"I'm not sure where that's located."

Mike pursed his lips. "A few miles from the airport. It's a rural road used mainly by the NC State University Vet School in their research."

Her eyes widened. "Oh, where the cows graze not far from I-440. But why was Frank there?"

Mike cocked his head. "I was hoping you could tell me."

"I don't have a clue. The road is between the airport and our home, isn't it?"

He nodded. "But you have no idea what he was doing out there?"

Mrs. Monaghan avoided his gaze. "How was my husband killed, Detective Barefoot?"

His eyes narrowed. She'd evaded his question. There was something she hadn't told him yet.

The corner of his lips flattened. "He was shot with a small caliber pistol, a .22. Do you, or did he, own any guns?"

She stiffened. "Absolutely not."

But she leaned against the back of the sofa, appearing relieved about this line of questioning. She definitely didn't want to talk about what Frank had been doing on that isolated stretch of road.

He returned to his original query. "What was Frank Monaghan doing out there on Orchard Farm Road?"

"What time was he killed, Detective Barefoot?"

His jaw clenched. Tapping his pen against the notepad, he waited. Silence unnerved most people into telling things they wouldn't normally say to fill the void.

But stoic, she stared at him. Then apparently reaching some inner decision, she announced, "I'm sure you consider me, as his wife, your primary suspect at this point, Detective Barefoot."

Seeing his upraised eyebrows at her bluntness, she continued. "One only has to watch the nightly news to understand how often it is the spouse."

Most people upon realizing they were suspects in a murder investigation reacted in either fury or fear. Alison Monaghan, however, was as frigid and remote as the icicles that hung from his grandfather's barn in winter.

Too cool?

His eyes bored into her. "Describe the current state of your marriage to me, Mrs. Monaghan."

"I did not kill my husband, Detective." She glanced toward the staircase. "I need to be with my children. They love—" Her breath caught and she lowered her eyes. "They loved their father."

"And you did not?"

She raised her eyes to meet his own. For the first time, he saw a pool of unshed tears well in her eyes. Regrets?

Or, remorse?

"No," she whispered. "Not for a long time."

He fought to maintain his professional objectivity. If this woman was lying, well, she was the best little actress he'd ever come across in ten years of law enforcement. What was it about her that got to him? She wasn't knockout gorgeous by any means. Attractive, but average in his opinion.

Was it her vulnerability? The air of emotional fragility like a taut bowstring? Or was she, too, a liar like most of her gender? Nobody got to him. He'd worked hard to ensure his walls were high and unbreachable. He fiddled with his pen.

Swallowing, she attempted to regain control over her emotions. "I want to help you, Sergeant, in any way I possibly can. If by eliminating me as a suspect, it can speed you on to other lines of inquiry, I will do nothing to stand in your way. Unlike silly fictional heroines, I believe full disclosure saves time."

Alison Monaghan placed both hands upon her well-clad knees. "Frank never made it home." She glanced at him. "It was not necessarily unusual for Frank not to return home right away after completing his flight rotation. He had . . ." she paused, "other interests."

"Other women?"

Her mouth tightened. "Yes."

Mike straightened. "Go on."

"After dinner, the children were in bed, and he still hadn't arrived. I decided to wait for him and I waited here," her arm sweeping across the sofa, "where I could see him pull in the driveway and hear the garage door open."

"Did you usually wait for him?"

She sighed. "No. Usually, I went to bed. Frank always came home eventually, but it would've been too humiliat—" Her mouth pulled downward.

"Why last night?"

"I'd suspected for some time Frank was having an affair. Yesterday, I accidentally found proof, and I was determined to confront him." She shrugged. "I know that gives me a great motive for murdering him, but I fell asleep on the couch while waiting for him and had just woken to realize he didn't come home at all, when you arrived."

The rumpled hair and appearance. The shoes beside the sofa. Perfectly logical explanations.

If they were true.

27

She rose, fishing a photo from her pocket. "This is what I found when I was cleaning out the closets. The photo was in the pocket of the same raincoat he's wearing in the picture."

He took it, catching again a whiff of her lavender fragrance, and examined the image. "Hard to tell who the woman is."

"I want a copy of the photograph."

He wrinkled his brow. "Why?"

"Frank operated in a small, tightly knit social circle. I probably know this woman. I think over the years there were others. To finally answer your question about what Frank was doing out on Orchard Farm Road instead of coming home? I don't know for sure, but I could venture to guess it was part of some preplanned . . ." She struggled for the right word. "Rendezvous."

"The raincoat you mentioned? Could I take it with me for analysis?"

"I'm not doing a good job in clearing myself. After I put dinner in the oven, I took it and the other winter coats to the cleaners' yesterday afternoon. I was in shock after discovering the photo. And yes," noting the questioning look on Mike's face, "angry as well."

"That's a shame. The lady might have left DNA behind. I mean . . ." He flushed.

She leaned forward. "I lost most of my illusions about Frank years ago. I have my receipts from the grocery and dry cleaners I can show you. The children were home after three for the rest of the night."

"But after they went to bed?"

"I see where you're going. I could have left them alone and slipped out. But I didn't. Oh," she blinked. "Isn't there some test for gunpowder you could do on me?"

He tried to hide his amusement. "You read a lot of mystery novels, Mrs. Monaghan?"

For the first time, her tightly gripped facial muscles relaxed long enough for one small fleeting smile. "I do, as a matter of fact."

"Real-life crime isn't like novels or television. But you are correct. There is a gunpowder residue test I'd like to perform on you and your wardrobe."

She waved her hand. "Test away, Detective. And don't worry about a search warrant, if you even need one. Feel free to search everything."

"You're sure I have your permission?" No case would be thrown out of court on a technicality. Not on his watch. "You will need to sign forms to that effect."

Ross coughed and jerked his head toward the foyer. The children had crept back to the landing on the staircase.

"Of course." She pivoted toward the entrance. "If you'll excuse me, I must see to my children."

He cautioned, "We will need to talk more extensively soon."

Pausing at the foot of the stairs, she looked at her children, huddled against the wall, their arms about each other. Taking a deep breath, she placed one hand on the railing and one foot on the first step.

Officer Ross appeared at her side. "Is there any one we should call for you, ma'am?"

Without turning around, she started up the stairs. "Valerie Prescott. I'll call her myself. Just give us a few moments."

He joined Ross at the foot of the stairs. They watched as she kicked off her shoes to sit cross-legged in front of the children. Opening her arms, both children released each other and scooted over to her embrace.

"Why?" the girl sobbed over and over.

At the sight of her children's grief, Alison Monaghan shuddered as tears cloaked her voice. "Someone killed your father." She tilted her head toward the policemen. "They're going to find out who did it."

He prayed her words were true. He almost smiled. How his granny would've loved to see him pray.

"And we're going to do everything we can to help them because no one, no one," Alison Monaghan repeated, "had the right to take your father's life."

Holding her children close, one in each arm, she gave him and Officer Ross a hard look before continuing. "Whatever we learn, never, ever forget how much your father loved you both."

He and Officer Ross turned away, giving the family some privacy. He outlined for Ross the procedural steps to take next. And as he did so, he sincerely hoped the mother would be cleared soon and the real killer apprehended.

Unless Alison Monaghan had killed her husband. Time and the evidence would tell.

A muscle jumped in his cheek. It galled him to realize he wished somehow the Monaghans—all of them—could be spared the soon-to-be public revelations about Frank Monaghan's dirty little secrets.

He ran a weary hand over his head. Sometimes, he hated his job.

It was all Val could do to restrain herself to the speed limit in the twenty minutes it took her to journey from the Prescott home in Cary to Alison's home inside Raleigh's beltline. Steering into Alison's long driveway, she skidded to a stop in her haste.

Getting out of the car, she noted the blue and white patrol car parked at the curb in front of the Monaghan house. Racing up the front walkway, she was about to seize the door handle when a patrolman opened the door. He stood, immovable, halting her headlong flight into the house.

"I'm Valerie Prescott." Her breathing sounded like she'd just finished running a race.

Nodding, the officer ushered her into the house. "They're in the family room. Do you know the way?"

Val tried to quiet her rapidly beating heart. "Like my own." The officer allowed her to proceed while remaining at his station by the front door. She noticed a plainclothes officer in the front room. His back to her as he spoke on his cell phone, he angled at the sound of her passing.

She caught a glimpse of a sandy-haired, barrel-chested man with a small black cell phone pressed alongside a square, iron jaw. His hair, clipped short on the sides and back, was like the state troopers. His eyes—an unusual silver-gray—gave nothing away, neither warmth nor dislike. Trying to ignore him, she hurried past.

God, help me know what to say.

With great foreboding, she found Alison, Justin, and Claire huddled together like refugees in a storm with an afghan about their shoulders on the couch. Justin saw her first and, flinging back the cover, ran into her arms. Claire was the next to follow.

She gazed over their heads to where Alison sat with shoulders slumped, looking defeated. "Ali?"

Alison raised her eyes. "He was shot at the end of Orchard Farm Road."

Val frowned. "Isn't that the back of the Weathersby property?"

Something flickered in Alison's eyes before—like a sliding elevator door shuttering her face—physical and emotional fatigue reclaimed her.

Claire broke from Val's embrace. "The detective is going to search the house. I could tell from his voice he thinks Mom killed Daddy."

"What?" Fear hit Val. "He can't do that without a warrant."

Alison shook her head. "I gave my permission, Val. I have nothing to hide. I don't want anything to stand in the way of apprehending the villain who has done this."

She took a deep breath and tried to think. What damage had Alison already done? "Wait a minute, Alison. You've got to think rationally. We need to call Reese. Don't say anything else to the police before my brother gets here."

Alison shook her head again. "I'm not guilty, Val. The police always suspect the spouse first. It's practically routine. I do not need a lawyer."

"Listen to me. You've got to think of the children and your future. The cops are by virtue of a homicide investigation adver—" She tripped over the unfamiliar word she'd often heard her attorney brother use, "adversarial opponents right now."

"That's good advice your friend is giving you, Mrs. Monaghan."

Startled, she let go of the children and whirled to find the detective in the doorway. A deep cleft in his chin, he was a mountain of a man, not easily trifled with. His cheekbones strongly chiseled and prominently high, his nose a trifle bent. Although his skin was as light as her own, she fancied there was a trace of the Native American in him. Maybe Cherokee, if he'd been born to North Carolina's mountain region.

She was not about to let him railroad her dearest friend. Anxious not to disrespect his position of authority in front of the children, she determined to get them occupied. She had a few questions of her own for this detective.

Val swiveled to Claire. "Your mom and I need you to get dressed and make breakfast and coffee for everyone. We must keep up our strength and," glancing over her shoulder, "I'm sure the officers would appreciate something strong and hot as well."

Claire crossed her arms over her chest. "I'm not hungry."

"Me either." Justin's declaration was unusual for a boy his age, but not surprising given the circumstances.

"We've got a long few days ahead of us. I don't want you or your mom to collapse. Please, children. I know you don't *feel* like it, but it does help your heart a little, if we can keep our hands busy."

Both children looked over to their mother sitting motionless and silent. She nodded to them and, dragging their feet up the back stairs off the kitchen, Claire and Justin returned to their bedrooms to change. She planted herself—feet apart—in front of Alison. With her arms crossed, she faced the stone-faced detective, ready to do battle.

4

Short and feisty, Valerie Prescott glared at him and jutted her jaw. Mike mirrored her stance, feet apart with arms crossed, and gave an aggrieved heartfelt sigh.

He'd known when he got the call that sooner or later he'd have to deal with some high-maintenance women who—in his experience—dwelled in these upscale neighborhoods. Lucky him.

Alison Monaghan placed a restraining hand on Val's arm. "Sit down, Val. It's okay. Detective Barefoot is only doing his job." She pulled a reluctant Val down to her side. "Please, Detective, I have other questions." She gestured for him to take a seat. He lowered himself into a recliner. She flinched.

Had he unknowingly taken her husband's favorite spot? If so, that accidental choice could work in his favor. "I understand your husband was a pilot. Did he seem troubled or concerned about anything before he left for his rotation on . . . ?"

She put a hand to her head. "Monday. He left Monday for Dallas. And no, nothing that I noticed."

"Did he seem moody or . . . ?" His voice trailed off, suggesting nothing, suggesting everything.

She gave him a wry smile. "Frank is, I mean was, a person who experienced a great many moods, Detective. He seemed upbeat. The prospect of flying always had that effect on him."

33

"Are there any other relatives we should notify?"

"No." She sighed. "Like me, he was an only child. His parents were killed a few years ago in a hit-and-run by a drunk. They never found the driver. Ironic, I always thought."

He leaned forward. "How so?"

She dropped her gaze, plucking at the fringe on the pillow cushion. "Frank drank too much. I was afraid one day he'd kill himself and others, too."

Val tilted her head. "Who found Frank's body?"

He flipped a few pages of his notebook. "A Jasper Delaine, caretaker of—"

Alison's breath hitched. "Weathersby House."

"Do you know this man?"

"No, but I've seen him at the House." She shifted toward Val. "That's what struck me a few moments ago when you mentioned Orchard Farm Road was the back property line for Weathersby. I hadn't made the connection before."

"What exactly is your connection to Weathersby, Mrs. Monaghan?"

"I volunteer there as a garden docent in the Master Gardener program once a week. And," she added, "Frank was secretary on the Board of Directors for the non-profit preservation group that runs the historic park, Triangle Area Preservation. TAP."

He scribbled a note. "I've heard of them." Great. A whole bunch of the overprivileged to check out.

Val Prescott bit her lip. "I assume there will be an autopsy."

He glanced at her, glad they were sitting down. "There always is with a suspicious death. Although Mr. Monaghan's driver's license was in his wallet, unfortunately, I'm going to need you, Mrs. Monaghan, to officially ID the body."

What little color remained faded from her face. "You want me to go to the morgue with you?"

He shook his head and removed his phone from his jacket pocket. He scrolled to the photo the medical examiner had sent. "A photo ID of the body will be sufficient." He extended the phone to her.

Tensing, she took the phone. "Thank you, Detective Barefoot."

Val squeezed her arm.

Alison glanced at the photo. Her face constricted. She nodded and thrust the phone toward him. She wrapped her arms around her trembling body.

Shock? Or playacting? He steeled himself not to be a chump.

Officer Ross poked his head into the den. "Your team has arrived, sir."

5

HOLDING TIGHTLY TO THE HANDS OF HER TWO CHILDREN, ALISON MADE the long journey down the center chapel aisle to the front pew reserved for family members. Justin kept his eyes on the carpet beyond the toes of his dress shoes. Claire stared straight ahead.

She tried to make a brief eye contact with each mourner they passed. Stephen, Val, and the boys followed. She'd insisted they sit with them, the only family she and the kids had left. Stephen, with a hand on his sons' shoulders, and Val steered them into the pew.

Alison glanced over to Justin. How grown-up he looked today in his suit and Frank's tie. He sat ramrod straight in the hard wooden pew, his clenched hands over his knees refusing the comfort of the armrest.

"Do you think I could keep all of Dad's ties in my room since I'm going to be the man of the family from now on?" he'd asked this morning.

She'd taken a steadying breath. "Dad would be so proud of how you and Claire have helped out this last week. But he'd also want you to stay a boy a little while longer. Don't try to grow up too fast, please." She squeezed his hand. "We'll be okay."

She'd been saying that night and day to Claire and Justin. Repeating it like a mantra, maybe if she said it enough, she'd believe it herself.

The self-proclaimed new man of the house had selected a vibrant blue tie. "And don't you worry so much either, Mom. Aunt Val is right. God will make sure we are okay."

Where had that come from?

Valerie and Stephen had put their lives on hold for them this week, bringing the boys after school each day and sharing the meals Alison's garden docent friends had dropped off every afternoon. The thought of food made her want to throw up, but under Val's watchdog eye, she'd forced herself to eat something for the sake of the children.

As the organ music soared in the tiny chapel, she realized that over the last few days, her children had clung to the Prescotts like a lifeline. She'd felt too adrift to do more than hold her children when they'd needed to shed some tears.

There had been a fair amount of publicity in the *News and Observer* and on the local television channels regarding Frank's sordid demise. And innuendos regarding her involvement in Frank's death. The neighbors stayed as far away from the Monaghan residence as they could, as if she and the children had suddenly developed the bubonic plague.

But in their world, scandal was worse than the plague.

She'd heard nothing from her so-called country-club friends.

Val's church friends from Jesus Our Redeemer Fellowship had also been a revelation. The church people had been caring and reluctant to intrude upon her grief but sincere in wanting her to feel their support. Not a scandalmonger or thrill seeker in the bunch, much to her relief.

Not what she had expected out of church folk although, in all honesty, her experience with such people was limited. She shouldn't have been surprised. After all, Valerie and Stephen had made the small stone church their spiritual home since Stephen opened his practice in Raleigh.

Neither she nor Frank had ever spent much time on thoughts of the hereafter. But after Frank's murder, here she sat, waiting to bury her dead husband.

The closing chords of the organ brought her back to the present, heartbreaking reality. Val's pastor, Bryan Fleming, left his seat on the platform and strode to the pulpit. The small glasses, pinching the end of his nose, gave him a scholarly and, after knowing him only one week she also suspected, a saintly manner.

"Today we wish to honor the life of Francis Joseph Monaghan, beloved father, husband, and friend."

Valerie and Bryan worked together for days to plan the service. Slightly built, habitually stooping as some tall men are wont to do, with a deep rich voice and thin, bearded face, he'd arrived a few hours after the police left that first day, and he'd been a helpful new friend in the days since Frank's murder.

"I'd like to begin today's service," Bryan continued, "by reading a few Scriptures that over the years have given an enormous amount of comfort to me and will, I hope, give Alison, Claire, and Justin no small measure of comfort as well. From Matthew's Gospel, Jesus said, 'Surely, I am with you always'. . ."

She felt a strange stirring in her heart. Really? Was He here today? This last week? That day, so long ago, when her mother walked away?

If only she could believe the peace contained in those words. But to let Him in, anyone in, was a risk she wasn't sure she could take.

Everyone and everything disappointed in the end. She'd lost most of her illusions about human beings one way or the other through either her mother or Frank. She believed there was a God.

She just hadn't since the horrific day, standing over the grave of her beloved father, believed He believed in her.

"And now we would like to extend God's peace and comfort to Alison and the children through song. Gentlemen," Bryan gestured, "and Mrs. Prescott."

Startled out of her thoughts, she turned to find Val rising out of her seat and going to the platform. Two gentlemen followed her where they formed a trio around one lone microphone on the side of the pulpit.

The pianist played a brief introduction, and the melodious harmonies of Val's strong alto merged with the gentlemen's bass and tenor. She tried to concentrate on the words as the melody line flowed over her like an embrace.

Something about a Father God who was faithful and never changing. Was this God of Val's truly enough for every need she'd ever had or ever would have in the future?

Oh God, make it so.

Surprised, she realized she'd never reached out to Him before. She'd never needed Him while she had her daddy. And after his death, her mother's betrayal had been a gulf her slim to non-existent belief system couldn't cross.

As the last note died away, Bryan returned to the podium. "Claire and Justin put together a PowerPoint presentation they'd like to share with all of you."

When had this taken place? And then, she recalled how often she'd entered the dining room to catch them huddling with Valerie, mysterious objects quickly shoved beneath the table. Their family photograph albums, she supposed. How wise of Valerie to involve them in this project and, in the process, help them face their grief.

God, what would I have done without Valerie all these years?

Praying for the second time within minutes of the first? Must be because she was in a church. Thanks to Val, she'd never, no matter how abandoned by her mother, ever been truly alone. There'd always been Val.

And Me. I am with you always.

She shook her head. Where had that crazy thought come from? Had Bryan read something like that a few minutes ago?

Alison dragged her attention to the large white screen descending from the ceiling where Frank's image appeared, once more larger than life.

To the musical strains of a Celtic lullaby, photos flashed across the screen. Frank, as a boy, grinning mischievously. Frank flanked by Irene and Joe at his graduation from the Air Force Academy. Frank standing next to his brand-new-to-him single engine rebuilt 1953 Piper Cub. And there, at last, in the wedding dress Val's mother made, she stood beside Frank in his tuxedo, their eyes locked on each other.

She released her children's hands, clenching and unclenching her hands in her lap.

Pictures didn't lie. It was there on her face and, in this moment, she could allow herself to believe that, at least for a time, it had been on Frank's face as well. Once upon a time, there had been love.

There were other snapshots. Pictures of Frank holding their newborn children. She joined hands with her children and smiled as wide as she could manage. Those had been happy days.

As the music faded, one last picture remained on the screen, a picture she remembered Frank taking not too long ago. It was a picture of the sunrise as he'd piloted his plane somewhere over the Outer Banks of North Carolina. He'd managed to capture in that split second the orange and pink streaks in the sky as the golden globe of the sun appeared on the far horizon, blazing a molten path to the shore, a highway of shimmering light.

Stephen walked over to the podium. He held the original photo in his hand. "Justin," he nodded over to him, "found this photograph in his father's airport locker this week. The children wanted me to read to you what Frank wrote on the back."

"The photo Frank entitled *Meeting God.*" He cleared his throat. "Frank wrote, 'There's so much I need to change.'" Stephen stared out over the congregation, avoiding her gaze by looking at some vague spot on the far wall behind her at the back of the sanctuary. "So many people I've wronged. With God's help, I intend to try harder to be the man I should be. Like this new day dawning, God wants a new day to dawn for my family and me."

Caught off guard, she jerked in her seat, her heart pounding in her chest. Somehow, from beyond the grave Frank had found a way to ask for her forgiveness. Detective Barefoot had asked her last week how Frank had seemed the last time she'd seen him. She'd attributed his buoyancy to the upcoming thrill of flying. But had that been all there was to his strange, brooding mood? Had there not also been, upon further reflection, a sense of determination and peace?

Now that she stopped to ponder it, Frank had not been his usual bullying, sarcastic self to her or the children since . . . Since when?

Maybe since this photo was taken, making the connection for the first time. What had happened to Frank that day, weeks ago, in the sky?

Frank had never, to her knowledge, been sorry before for anything he'd ever done or said. Had Frank truly connected with God that morning?

Connecting with God? Whatever that meant. Yet Frank, in his oblique way, had asked for her forgiveness.

The question was, could she? She didn't possess the theological knowledge to know what new day dawned for Frank. But he'd surely left them in a mess, and she wasn't certain what kind of new dawn they faced in the turbulent days ahead. Was she ready to let go of the anger that kept her moving and face the stark emptiness that lay before them?

As the music swelled, Val cued her to stand. Justin sprang forward, offering an arm to her and Claire. Facing the congregation, she noticed for the first time Mike Barefoot standing stock-still against the far wall.

He'd been scanning the congregation but at that moment caught her eye. Giving her a slight nod, he slipped into the shadows of the alcove as she and the children followed the flower-draped coffin to the waiting hearse.

What was he doing here?

She tightened her hold on her children. Claustrophobic since she and a childhood friend had tried to dig a hole to China and the sand had caved in on them, the walls of her life seemed to be closing in on her now.

Had he come to arrest her?

Surely not in front of her children? Not at her husband's funeral?

Alison had to do something and soon. Or Claire and Justin could lose her, too.

6

THE MOTORCADE WOUND ITS WAY THROUGH THE EARLY AFTERNOON TRAF-
fic of downtown Raleigh to historic Oakwood Cemetery. Val had
unearthed the cemetery plot receipt from Frank's files. He'd never
asked where Alison wanted to be buried. Not Frank's style. He
made the important decisions.

Actually, he'd made all the decisions.

She could count on one hand the things that were truly her own.
Her garden. Her friendship with Val. Her books. And she'd believed
then he'd outlive her by the sheer force of his personality like the
way the Colorado River had worn away at the Grand Canyon.

But she was still here. And he was not. Funny to realize Frank
was never going to tell her what to do again. Never walk through
the door of their home.

Was she glad or sad about this?

She took a deep breath. She wasn't sure yet.

Leaning her head against the window of the hearse, she observed
the other motorists, who—true to a vanishing Southern tradition—
pulled over to the side of the road out of respect for the deceased and
family. The funeral procession moved off the asphalt and onto the
graveled drive that ran in a grid between weathered gravestones. At
the top of a slight incline, the hearse halted at an open-sided blue
tent.

During the drive to the cemetery, her children and the Prescotts remained silent, lost in their own thoughts. They waited as the funeral director supervised the unloading of the casket and the arrangement of the floral tributes around the site.

The director opened the limousine door, and they all spilled out. She was the last to leave the safety of the car. Of everything this day, this was what she dreaded the most. Car doors slammed as occupants streamed toward the tent, congealing in their dark blacks and blues a few feet behind the folding chairs reserved for the family.

One foot resting on the running board, she gripped the open doorframe, shaking as she gazed across the grassy expanse of graves to the turned red clay that marked the newest grave, Frank's grave. The children hurried forward and paused at the tent.

Val grabbed her, pulling her free of her death grip on the car. "It's going to be okay," she whispered. "Breathe and relax. Claire and Justin need you at this moment more than any other. You must help them to get through this."

A gentle breeze ruffled the strands of hair cupping her face. A caress?

God, is that you?

She glanced through the leafy, saffron branches of the overhanging oak to the dappled sunlight of the sky. Fighting the fog of pain and bitter memories, she came to herself, the rational self none of them had seen much of since the policemen rang her doorbell. She took a deep breath and let it out bit by bit.

Alison disentangled herself from Val's strong clasp. "You're right as usual. I can do better than this. I must do better than this." She shot Val a pointed look. "I will not be my mother today. I will not abandon my children at the grave of their father on the worst day of their lives."

She crossed the distance separating her from the children, taking each by the hand.

⚊✦⚊

Not a bad day for a funeral, Mike supposed, as funerals went. The October afternoon sunshine was warm but without the humid stickiness that hovered over the city less than a month ago. The faint scent of burning leaves perfumed the autumn air. He still missed the ever-present tangy aroma of evergreens from his native Blue Ridge. But Raleigh, as far as his career and murder went, was where it was happening.

From a distance and taking detailed notes, he assessed the attendees. Unless it was a random murder—uncommon in Raleigh—most of his homicide victims knew their killers. Often, like the firebugs that returned to view the blaze they'd set, murderers liked to frequent their victim's funeral. Whether out of a sense of gloating accomplishment, or to make sure the person was truly dead, he wasn't sure.

One day he'd finish that psychology degree he'd started before finances forced him to drop out and he'd enlisted in the army. On the other hand, his criminal justice degree—he had painstakingly finished while still in the reserves—served him well. He'd risen through the Raleigh police ranks due to a combination of ambition, tenacious stubbornness (pigheadedness his granny had called it), and a sharp mind.

He'd tried not to darken the door of any church since he escaped his granny's clutches, leaving the only home he'd ever known. The way the pastor from the Redeemer church presented himself had been outside the scope of his experience. His granny had preferred the hardcore hell and damnation variety in the vain hope of arresting the telltale signs of adolescent wild oats in his younger self.

Pastor Fleming and the Prescotts intrigued him in the way a fascinating and unfamiliar species might intrigue a scientist. Not the usual bunch he dealt with on a daily basis as a homicide investigator.

The autopsy revealed Frank Monaghan died instantly. The .22 caliber pistol pressed against his left temple left a scorched area around the entry wound. Pinpointing a precise time of death in real life was difficult, unlike the depictions on television shows. External parameters could narrow the time frame but rarely proved conclusive.

Monaghan left the airport at 6:15 in the evening, when an airport security camera clocked him leaving the parking garage. At eight o'clock, one of the veterinarian interns—finishing poop duty in the distant cow stalls off Orchard Farm Road—remembered seeing Frank's car pull into the dead-end street. So far, no witnesses to what happened next.

Hurried at the time, the intern was late for a date and hadn't paid the car much attention. Hard to say for certain whether the driver was alone or not. None of his business anyway, he'd explained. Mike had resisted the urge to smack the pimply-faced, smart-mouthed college kid into Sunday.

Where Frank had been in the intervening hour and forty-five minutes had yet to be established.

Mentally, Mike reviewed the evidence he'd gathered thus far. The first responder had noted in his report a faint trace of cigarette smoke hanging in the enclosed vehicle when he reached the crime scene at one a.m. A cigarette stub lay, encircled by a smeared ring of lipstick, underneath Frank's foot. Bright red lipstick.

He'd checked. None of the Monaghans smoked. Nor seemed to own any red lipstick.

A crumpled tissue contained traces of Frank's saliva and a smudge of orange lipstick. As if, he speculated, Frank had wiped it from his lips, wadded it into a ball, and tossed it under his seat. Again, no orange lipstick at the Monaghans.

For him, a picture was beginning to emerge of the lifestyle of the deceased involving multiple liaisons. He was sorry for the kids, but the jury was still out in his mind on the mother.

Despite his unusual lapse the first day, he was back to a professionally neutral opinion regarding his number-one suspect, Alison Monaghan. Doing his job right was all that mattered in the end. The evidence, not him, would prove her guilt or innocence.

Until he'd seen the presentation the children had put together, he hadn't cared too much for the late Frank Monaghan. A jerk if ever there was one.

Generally speaking, there were the "wrong place at the wrong time" victims and victims who for various reasons had broken or twisted relationships resulting in their own deaths. Monaghan was a man who'd invited violence.

He'd interviewed Valerie Prescott the first day when he found her alone in the kitchen. He'd asked her who would want to kill Frank Monaghan.

She'd given a short, incredulous laugh. "The better question would be, Detective Barefoot, who didn't want to kill that—" She'd bitten off her last words. "Not that I'd include Alison in that group . . ."

If Alison Monaghan was the perp, he'd get her one way or the other. He always did.

Lots of mourners at the jerk's funeral. Obviously, he was a pillar of the community, or he owed a lot of people a lot of money.

Mike leaned against a nearby tree trunk, his hands in his pockets, to all appearances a casual observer. But he missed little. He watched from a safe distance at the edge of the historic cemetery as Alison Monaghan, standing under the funeral tent next to the coffin, personally greeted each mourner. The Prescotts and the Monaghan children stood over to the side. The children drooped with fatigue.

The last picture on the PowerPoint left him with a disturbing awareness of his own frailties, aspects of his life he wouldn't have wanted his strict Bible-quoting granny or anyone else to ever discover. Images of desert sands and oxygen-choking oil wells on fire with the flames of hell. A feeling-sorry-for-myself-what-are-you-doing-later-tonight binge at the Wagon Wheel last month with some blonde.

Mike rotated his head from side to side to free the scenes from his mind and loosen the cricks in his neck. Not Granny-rated material. Much less God-rated. And in his line of work more than most, he understood there was no guarantee of tomorrow.

Had Monaghan had a split-second warning or a glimmer of intuition, before the cold steel was placed to his head, that his second chances had run out? What changes would Frank have made had he driven straight home from the airport? What changes would

Mike make if the truth his granny had pounded into his head ever made it down to his heart?

Mike shook the disturbing thoughts out of his mind. He made his own choices, and he lived with the consequences. He enjoyed his life. Most of the time. Frank Monaghan probably had, too.

And he'd ended up dead.

What was wrong with him today? Though she'd been dead for over a decade, he could still imagine the smirk his granny would've given him at the direction of his thoughts.

"God's got big plans for you, son," she always said, her face crinkling with the wrinkles of age and a smile in her quicksilver eyes. "You can run, but you can't hide from Him."

Mike clenched his jaw. Go away, Granny.

His gaze returned to Alison Monaghan. His pulse raced when he thought of her. He clamped his mind shut on the direction of those thoughts, deliberately replacing her image with the image of her dead husband. And relaxed. Murder, a comfortable topic.

Spur-of-the-moment killings were notoriously hard cases to clear. It was premeditated murderers, in their detailed, well-thought-out plans, who unwittingly revealed themselves in some way. The arrogance and egotism that drove them to murder in the first place often trapped them into exposure. His job was a matter of gathering the clues and putting the pieces of the puzzle together.

Easier said than done, of course, but in his five-year stint with the Raleigh police, he'd developed a reputation for figuring out the inscrutable and putting some cold cases to rest. And if this case didn't develop a few more leads, he was going to be in trouble. The first seventy-two hours were critical in solving a crime.

With the clock ticking on this murder investigation, he was long overdue for a break in the case, operating now on borrowed time. Something had to give and soon. Or, this case would go down in the books as unsolved. And as much as his pride hated to admit defeat, his sense of justice demanded recompense for a murderer still out there on the loose in his city, free to strike at will again.

He glanced over the crowd at the gravesite once more.

And recalling his experience as a soldier in Iraq, it was only hard to pull the trigger the first time around.

Her gaze traveled to the detective and then roamed around the cemetery. For inexplicable reasons, the Lawrences were still hanging around, Linda lighting up a Marlboro. Claire, Justin, and the Prescotts stood talking to Bryan Fleming, his wife and their daughter, Sandy. Sandy, Alison remembered, attended the same school as her children, a sophomore like Claire.

A tall, distinguished man approached them, embraced by Val. He appeared familiar, but she was too tired at the moment to place him.

A wave of pungent and exotic perfume enveloped Alison, reducing her to a fit of coughing.

"Darling Alison!"

She found herself overpowered, her face pressed against the large and ponderously displayed bosom of Natalie Singleton. The release was so sudden, she stumbled backward.

The statuesque Natalie had a dark exotic beauty. A stunning brunette in her mid-thirties, with mesmerizing violet eyes, Natalie had already been married and divorced lucratively, four times. The daughter of a retired army brigadier general and an Italian contessa, Natalie was the envy of most women and the desire of most men. And to say Natalie liked men was like saying some cats liked cream.

Natalie, with her multitude of political and social connections in Raleigh, was also on the TAP board. Had she and Frank been—?

What a nerve.

"Dear Frank! How I shall miss him!"

Exactly how much would she miss him?

"What a loss to our whole community!" purred Natalie in that sultry voice of hers.

Did she always speak in exclamation marks? Alison couldn't resist a small smile.

Natalie, apparently not just beautiful, frowned, perhaps suspecting Alison of mocking her. Alison wiped the smile from her face. Time to hunt and gather, not antagonize. Maybe later, she promised herself, if Natalie and Frank had truly been involved.

Just remember, a little voice in her head reminded, it takes two to tango. Frank wasn't exactly innocent in all this. But Frank was dead and beyond the reach of all but God.

Natalie was another matter entirely.

"You and Frank served together on the TAP board at Weathersby, I understand."

In the process of moving along, Natalie teetered on her six-inch stiletto heels to a stop. Natalie smoothed out her puckered brow with one expensively manicured nail. "At great sacrifice to my personal well-being, I came today to offer my respects to dear, departed Frank. Funerals are such a downer." She sighed. "Yes, it is true, as a committee member-at-large, I serve in whatever capacity I can be most useful. Frank and I were involved . . ." She smiled, showing unnaturally white, even, and as perfect as cosmetic dentistry could make them, teeth. "Involved in a great number of projects together."

Alison felt like grinding her teeth. On Natalie Singleton's neck.

Natalie laughed and unsheathed one tangerine-lacquered claw to smooth the resulting frown away on Alison's forehead. She flinched at Natalie's raking touch.

"Stress, my dear. How it does age the face!" Natalie gave one parting shot over her shoulder as she walked away. "That's why I am so careful with whom I associate. How I shall miss those happy times with dear Frank."

Taking enough deep breaths to hyperventilate, she tried to calm her fuming nerves. Why did she care if Frank and Natalie . . . ?

Alison's wedding snapshot from the PowerPoint presentation flashed across her vision, stabbing at her heart. The anger and the hurt were like two faucets turned open at full throttle.

Was it better to get both feelings out of her system once and for all? Which one was the way toward healing? And could she channel them to prove her innocence and uncover Frank's true killer? Weariness engulfed her. She swayed.

A diminutive brassy redhead seized her arm.

"Alison . . ."

In her mid-forties with protuberant light green eyes, Ivy Dandridge was executive director at Weathersby. Her much older husband, a retired history professor, Henry, was writing a definitive work on the history of the house and the flamboyant Weathersby family, an ongoing project. Most of the volunteers, while liking the shy, balding professor, jokingly referred to his always future book as the Ivy's-keep-Henry-busy-and-out-of-her-hair project.

"I was so sorry to learn of . . ." Ivy began, but Henry coughed beside her, one arm looped, possessively or for steadiness, through Ivy's.

"*We* were so sorry to hear of Frank's passing." She gestured to her husband. "I believe as a garden docent you've already met my husband at Weathersby."

Henry inclined his head, and Alison, trying in vain to pluck her arm free of itty-bitty Ivy's fierce grasp, smiled in return.

A human dynamo, Ivy convinced the last remaining Weathersby heir, Ursula, to sell the decrepit house and all that remained of its once lavish estate to the city of Raleigh under the supervision of TAP to restore it to its former glory. She'd single-handedly launched a committee of concerned Raleigh patrons to act as board members to supervise the extensive and expensive renovations on the structure. The Dandridges' painstaking research resulted in the historically accurate showplace that had garnered a multitude of preservation awards.

Her tireless efforts resulted in last year's formal opening of Weathersby House to the public for the first time in its two hundred-year-old history. The five-acre grounds, however, with which Alison had been associated, were still a work in progress, renovations dependent upon massive fundraising promotions.

Despite Ivy's obvious devotion to Weathersby, her intensity to push, push, push did not exactly win friends. There was scuttlebutt, Alison remembered, about the board wishing to oust Ivy from her exalted position and replace her with a more amenable personality.

A motive for murder? She wished she'd paid more attention to gossip for once. What had Frank's stand been on that issue?

"Thank you, Dr. and Mrs. Dandridge, for coming today. I'm sure it would've meant so much to Frank."

Ivy dabbed at her eyes with an antique lace handkerchief. "Frank meant the world to both of us. He'll be sorely missed in our Weathersby family. Such a giving man, sparing neither his time nor his talents for the greater good of our beloved Cause."

Alison arched her brows. Comparing Ivy's passion to a religious fervor, she found Ivy as oddly disturbing as Natalie Singleton.

Interesting mix, this board on which Frank had served for the past two years. Like dynamite and flame.

7

With Claire, Justin, and Val for moral support, Alison faced the stern-faced family attorney, Pete Marrin, across the table. She'd been nervous about this meeting ever since Pete called to arrange a meeting with "Frank's heirs" in conjunction with the family accountant, Gary Jenkins, also across the table from her.

"I didn't realize Frank had a will." Alison fidgeted, unable to stand the tension any longer. "He took care of our legal and business matters."

She'd gathered all the financial documents she could find per Detective Barefoot's request at the beginning of the investigation. She'd managed to find the bank statements for their joint checking and personal savings account, the last seven years of IRS tax records, and the various Roth IRA and 401(k) documents. Frank, thank God—here she was talking to God again—had kept everything meticulously filed and organized in their extra bedroom/office.

It was the first time she'd ever examined those documents. Frank had liked to be in absolute control of everything. She'd made copies and given them to the detective. She had a lot to learn, like an undergrad cramming before the final exam. Except in this case, the exam was about survival.

Alison knew enough to understand the cash reserves she'd expected to find weren't on any document she'd discovered so far. What had happened to their life savings?

She waited with a great deal of trepidation as to what both Pete and Gary had to say. She had a sinking feeling it wasn't going to be good.

Pete cleared his throat, getting down to business. "Frank didn't have a will until a few months ago when he called me. From San Francisco, I believe. Long distance, he told me to draw up certain documents, and when he returned to town a couple of days later, he swung by the office at closing, signed what he needed to sign, and asked me to enclose three sealed envelopes in his estate portfolio." Pete drew from the briefcase at his feet three rectangular envelopes. He fanned them out in front of him on the table like a poker player displaying a winning hand.

She made out Frank's precise no-nonsense handwriting. One addressed to her and the other two were for Claire and Justin.

"Up front, at the time Frank came by the office, he paid to retain my legal consulting services and Gary's." Pete thumbed his finger over to his colleague. "To advise you financially in the event of his unexpected demise."

"What?" Claire grabbed the edge of the table. "Did he suspect he was in danger?"

Alison laid a restraining hand upon her daughter.

Pete ignored Claire, looking straight into Alison's eyes. "Frank told me he'd made a lot of bad decisions over the last few years. Financially and personally speaking. Something had changed in Frank by the time I saw him that afternoon. I noticed it immediately. He told me he had wrongs to right, and he only hoped it wasn't already too late."

Alison frowned. "Too late for what or whom?"

Pete bit his lip. "I asked him that and he wouldn't answer. But North Carolina law is explicit. When one spouse dies, the estate, whatever it is, passes to the other spouse automatically, will or no will." He paused. "In this case, there isn't much to pass."

Alison angled toward Gary. "What does he mean? Nothing? Our IRAs and the 401(k)? What about the children's college funds?"

Gary mopped his forehead with a clean white handkerchief. "I'm afraid, Alison, it's all gone."

"All gone?" A note of hysteria crept into her voice. She twisted a tissue with her hands. "We promised each other we'd never, no matter how bad it got, ever touch that. That was for them and their future."

Pete refused to meet her gaze. "I'm sorry, Alison."

"But how? Why? Where did it go, Gary?"

"Frank withdrew it or signed it over to a third party over the last few years in various amounts."

She pursed her lips. "What third party?"

Gary consulted his records, a manila folder on the table before him.

"Stocks for startup companies. Investment opportunities. I have copies of this for you, Alison." He pushed the folder across to her.

Her eyes refused to focus. She rested her elbow on the tabletop, her head in her hand. Would this nightmare never end? The mess Frank had left them grew larger every day.

Justin leaned over to examine the documents. "Bluestone Real Estate Development." He turned the page over. "CompuVision, the country club's initiation fee—"

"Wait a minute." Claire jerked upright. "CompuVision? Isn't that the name of Mr. Lawrence's software company?"

Startled, Alison grabbed the paper for a closer look. Claire was correct. The multimillion dollar computer company belonged to Bill Lawrence. Anxious to earn "points" with one of Raleigh's key financial players, Frank had insisted they join the Lawrences and their two teenage daughters, Zoe and Heather, on a Caribbean cruise last summer. Now she wondered exactly how he'd acquired those millions.

An investment gone bad and investors like Frank waiting to be compensated? Or had Frank been swindled? Motive for murder? How many murders were motivated by money and greed?

Pete spoke up. "We are here to help you sort through settling Frank's estate."

Her mouth had gone dry. "You mean the creditors that must be paid?"

Pete looked down. Both men were silent.

Later Friday night, with her exhausted children in bed, Alison sat with her bare feet propped on the ottoman after hours of poring through financial records with Pete and Gary. She found herself slumped in Frank's chair in the darkened family room. Her mind reeled with disbelief. Frank, or somebody else, had wiped them out. There was nothing left but bills to pay.

It broke her heart for the children's sake, but the house with its exorbitant mortgage would have to be sold. Which meant they'd also have to change schools.

And her garden? She choked back a sob. She couldn't think about that now. That was the least of her worries.

She and the children would pay for Frank's extravagance. the Piper Cub, she thought as she released a short bitter laugh, would be sold. His car, when eventually released by the police department, sold as well. And considering its history, sold out of state. Thank God, her car was paid for or she'd have no transportation.

Alison felt as if a ton of bricks had landed on top of her chest. Anger and despair engulfing her, she fought queasiness. Had her life been a lie? Even from the beginning? She wasn't sure if Frank had ever meant a word he said to her.

She leaned her head on the soft chenille cushion and closed her eyes. Val and Stephen would never let them starve, of that she was certain. But this test, or trial as Val would call it, was up to her to overcome. If she didn't find the courage to meet this crisis head-on, she'd be as useless and stupid as Frank had always believed her to be. It might be her last chance to prove something first and foremost to herself.

The taxes they owed, the uncertain future ahead . . . Wave after wave of fear threatened to drown her. She shuddered. Every time Barefoot showed up on her doorstep she expected him to hand over a warrant for her arrest.

She remembered the envelopes from Frank. Hers lay un-opened in the pocket of her black skirt. The children opened theirs after Gary and Pete left.

Justin's note simply read,

"I'm sorry for the hurt I've caused you. If I could have a do-over, there are so many things I would change. Think fondly, if you can, of your old man in the many years to come I pray God grants you. All my love forever, Dad.

P.S. Justin, I want you to have my golf clubs. Bud, I see a lot of potential there. Also, I want you to have my camera. God has given you a special gift for all things technical. Use your gifts for Him."

After opening Frank's note, Justin discovered his father's golf bag was not in the garage. Detective Barefoot had given them an itemized inventory of the personal objects the police found in the car at the crime scene that—Barefoot assured her—would be returned to the family in due course. The golf clubs were not among the items found, nor was Frank's briefcase. A subsequent search of the house failed to reveal their location.

They'd cleaned out Frank's airport locker last week in a fruitless search for his briefcase. After Gary and Pete left, Justin had the sudden inspiration his dad might have left the golf equipment in his hitherto forgotten club locker and called Stephen, asking him to drive him over on Saturday. Of Frank's briefcase and the all-important smartphone, there was no sign.

Protective of his phone, which held his business and personal contact information as well as his daily schedule, Frank had never been without it. He left home that final morning with both phone and briefcase in hand. The airport video surveillance revealed Frank leaving the terminal, headed toward the parking garage, with his briefcase in tow.

She could only draw her own grim conclusions, as Detective Barefoot continued to be as closemouthed with case details as the granite rocks of his mountain homeland. Yes, leave it to Val to ask, grilling the taciturn detective every chance she got.

Alison speculated the murderer, after surprising and killing Frank, made off with the briefcase and phone. Those items probably contained incriminating evidence of wrongdoing on the part of the perpetrator that made him or her willing to commit murder to keep them hidden. Now they might never know what Frank had uncovered over the last few weeks in his efforts, as he put it, "to right wrongs." Whatever it was, it had cost him his life.

Claire was next to read her note, though it took her a moment to compose herself after seeing her name written in Frank's familiar handwriting. Her note said,

"Dearest Claire, If you are reading this note, then I failed to fix things, and I want you to know how sorry I am for the hurt I will cause you. I want you to have Grandma Irene's prayer book and Grandpa Joe's little New Testament.

Don't make the same mistakes of pride as your dad. Without God, the flip side of pride is weakness. Remember me kindly, Claire. All my love forever, Dad."

How and when had Frank gotten religion? Irene, a homemaker, and Joe, the dedicated firefighter, had been devout in their faith. Surely, Frank's turnaround, if indeed genuine—she wasn't fully prepared to embrace the new and improved Frank yet—had been the answer to many long years of prayer on their part. Had she been that wrapped up in her hurt and disillusionment she failed to detect this change in Frank in the last few days of his life?

She'd always believed herself to be Frank's victim. Was she, upon the honest retrospection possible only in the dark hours of night, as guiltless as she claimed?

To the day she died, she'd be ashamed her first instant reaction upon learning of Frank's death had been one of relief, like a prisoner who has just received an unexpected pardon. Was she so self-absorbed in her own pain and bitterness to feel nothing beyond a sense of escape upon hearing of the death of the man she'd once sworn—before the God she'd chosen not to acknowledge—to love forever, the father of her children?

Was she any better than her mother, Dot? Or better than Frank, in the myriad ways he'd failed to live up to her expectations? She'd always been quick to compare Frank with her gentle giant of a dad over the years of their difficult marriage. Had that been remotely fair, upon hindsight, to Frank? Perhaps a darker question was how had she lived up to his expectations?

Pain stabbed her temples. Hadn't she, in her own way, been as faithless to Frank as he had been to her? Whose betrayal, her breath caught, had come first?

She'd always, as a matter of personal conscience, tried to be a good person. Where Frank was concerned, she knew tonight how miserably she'd failed. The chance to do better there was gone.

Or was it? Could she pay him one last gesture of respect and love by helping to apprehend his killer? Did there remain enough love for Frank to even try?

It might be all she could do for him now. It might be the least she could do for him.

How to be a better person? Despite her best efforts toward Frank or her children, she let them and herself down continually. Was there another answer? How did Val . . . ?

It was Christ in her, Val would say, that made all the difference.

She was so tired. Soul-weary. Maybe it was time to surrender the control, the reins of her life to Someone who could do an infinitely better job. She wasn't doing so well on her own and it was time she admitted it.

Was that the first step? She winced, thinking of Dot. Like an alcoholic who first has to admit he has a problem? Where did she go from here?

She didn't know Val's God. Was He truly, as Val claimed, the faithful and true God, who was always there, who never changed, who considered her a person of worth despite her failures? A God who would never leave and forsake her?

Was there Someone out there like that? Someone who didn't disappoint or betray or abandon? Someone who loved her, Alison McLawhorn Monaghan?

If there was ever a time she needed Someone, it was now.

Dropping to her knees beside the ottoman, overcome with shame of her own unworthiness before Someone like that, she whispered, "I don't know You, but Val tells me You've always known me. That when Dad died and Dot . . ."

She faltered, unable after all these years to put into words the hurt of that day, her mother walking away, declaring good riddance to bad rubbish.

"Val says You were with me even on that day. And that You've been there caring and waiting this past week, but I've been too stubborn to take Your hand. I don't know how to be what everyone needs me to be. I've been sinned against, but I admit now I've also sinned. I've disappointed and betrayed and abandoned those I vowed to always support. I need Your forgiveness."

Were those the right words? Was there some sort of special formula to this prayer thing?

An image of herself in handcuffs flooded her mind. She lifted her face toward the ceiling. "And God," she whispered, "Help me expose the one who dared to end Frank's life."

A peace penetrated the dark room, filling long-empty places in her heart.

The envelope in her skirt pocket rustled, reminding her of the unread last missive from Frank. Taking a deep breath, she withdrew it from her pocket and, leaning heavily against the ottoman, she pulled herself to her feet.

She walked over to the French doors where the moon gave a gleam of light. Opening it, a small, translucent object fluttered into her hand. Without stopping to examine it, she took out the small ivory paper and read,

"I have sinned against you most of all. You have been the wife I never deserved.

I stared into the Abyss, and I saw myself falling forever. I was forced to examine my life, saw myself for what I was and all I had done, and I fell instead into the outstretched arms of my Savior. If you are reading this now, then I know, despite divine forgiveness, there are always earthly reckonings.

I ask for your forgiveness, realizing I have absolutely no right to expect it.

I wish you joy in the years ahead, and if you do from time to time think on these years we had together, I pray the bad will fade away by God's grace from your memory and that you will remember me as we were in Hawaii. I love you, Frank."

Love? A sob caught in her throat, and she opened her hand, holding the object closer to the glow of the moonlight.

A dried plumeria blossom. Its faint scent rose in her nostrils, bringing sweet memories long buried.

After renting bicycles to explore the island, they'd stopped for lunch. Unhooking the picnic baskets the resort had provided, she and Frank ambled off the beaten path into a grove of trees, next to one of the many waterfalls for which Kauai was famous. As she'd set out the spread, Frank returned from a quick foray into the bush with the most beautiful purple blossom she'd ever seen.

For love, he'd said, tucking it into her hair. After changing for dinner that night, she'd lost track of the flower, never thinking of it until this night seventeen years later.

But obviously, Frank had not forgotten it and had kept it somewhere, tucked in a book perhaps, preserving what for him must have been a treasured memory.

She remembered again the wedding picture from the funeral yesterday. Had there been genuine love at some point in the beginning? Or, was it all a sham? The blossom in her hand testified it was not a sham.

And for the first time in a week, clutching the faded flower petal in the moonlight, she released the tears that had been building not just for the last few days, but also for the years in between. Falling to her knees, her cheek against the cool panes of the glass, she grieved for Frank, for all that once had been, for all there never was, and for all that could never be.

As she crushed the petal to her, its aroma perfumed the air. And crying out in anguish to heaven above for comfort in her saddest hour, she found that, at last, she was no longer alone.

Mike leaned against the headrest of his vehicle, allowing the soft, cool breeze of the October night to fan his face. The hour late, the lights shining from all of the houses on Alison's block had long since winked into darkness. Except for hers. The light on her front porch blazed brightly—a clear indication based on his surveillance over the last week—she was still awake and about. He'd watched the children click out their lights earlier.

From his vantage point down the street, through her unshuttered windows, he'd observed her move from room to room turning out lamps as she went. From a distance, her face shone pale—and scared—in the moonlight.

Scared of being arrested for the murder of her husband? Or, just scared? Scared of being a single parent? Scared of the future? He'd had a long conversation with the attorney and accountant today.

He shifted in his seat, his foot rustling the burger wrapper on the floor. Financially speaking, Alison and her kiddos were in deep doo-doo. Another legacy of the illustrious and dead Frank Monaghan. That guy just kept getting better and better all the time. Val Prescott had been right—it was a wonder no one had killed the jerk before now.

Still, life was sacred. He believed in God. No atheists in the foxhole with his line of work.

But that surrender thing to an all-powerful God? Not there yet. But late at night, when he was alone and staring at the ceiling above his bed, shadows chased him.

Maybe Alison dreaded the dark, lonely nights. Mike, too— when he was honest enough to admit it.

He banged his head, none too gently, against the steering wheel. What was the matter with him? When did he start calling her or any suspect by their first name even in his mind? But something tugged at him at the thought of Alison Monaghan and her fatherless children. Yes, even that prickly pear she called a daughter.

He'd had the oddest sensation as he watched Alison—Mrs. Monaghan, he corrected—turn out the lights. An urge, a wistful longing to belong. A yearning he hadn't felt since his grandparents died.

A wish for home.

Death wish was more like it. "You're an idiot, Mike Barefoot." What kind of fool felt an attraction for a murder suspect?

His hand jerked and came to rest on the slim, black leather Bible with which his granny had sent him off to college. His lips tightened. Whatever had possessed him to dig that out of his army footlocker and bring that along on a stakeout?

"Crazy." He swatted at a passing fly, zooming around his face, and missed.

That pastor must have gotten to him. But his hand returned to the book on the seat beside him. He'd never read the thing for himself. People did hateful things to other human beings out of a zeal for religion. His experience in the Gulf, his study of history, and 9/11 proved that. He'd never attempted to understand that kind of misguided passion before. What made people like that tick?

He flicked on the cab's interior light, dispelling the shadows, and thumbed through a few pages of the book he knew so well from long, enforced vigils on hard wooden pews on his boyish backside: the New Testament.

What prompted people to kill and be killed in the name of some god?

Maybe it was time to find out.

8

Saturday dawned with a crisp chill in the air. A fine mist hung over the yard, obscuring the outer edges of the flower borders, drooping with morning dew. Alison felt empowered despite a sleepless night. She sipped, warming her hands around the piping hot cup of Kona, watching for Stephen's arrival.

An unfamiliar burgundy Dodge SUV pulled into the drive. Stephen emerged from the passenger side. The driver, distinguished and fifty-something, was the same man she'd seen talking to Claire and Justin at the cemetery on Thursday. He seemed, once again, familiar, but she couldn't place where she'd seen him.

Music . . . ?

But the flash of recognition was gone before she could capture it.

Leaving her perch on the arm of the settee in the front room, she opened the front door as the men ascended the steps.

Stephen smiled. "Morning, Ali."

Alison nodded but raised her brows at his companion.

"Oh, I don't guess you've met our friend, Robert Kendall. He's in real estate, an elder at Redeemer, and one of the leaders of the Bible study group. Val and I have known him for years." He stepped away from the door and allowed Robert to step forward, hand outstretched toward her.

She found herself staring into friendly, hazel eyes.

Recognition dawned. "You sang in the trio with Val at my husband's funeral."

Sympathy mingled with the friendliness in his eyes. "Yes, ma'am." His speaking voice proved as warm and deep a bass as when he sang. "I thank you for the privilege of celebrating your late husband's homecoming." His hair, mainly dark, sported bands of gray above his ears.

Alison darted a swift look at Stephen. Wait till she told them the latest about her—well, she wasn't sure what you ought to call it. Connection? Surrender? Relationship was probably what Val would suggest.

She took Robert Kendall's outstretched hand. "You have no idea how much it meant to the children and especially to me. Life-changing, as a matter of fact."

Stephen gave her a quizzical look. She realized she was standing barefoot on the cold slate porch with a coffee cup in her hand.

"Forgive my manners. Won't you come in and have some coffee? I'll call Justin. He's anxious to find his dad's clubs." She ushered the men into the foyer and waved for them to follow her into the kitchen and family room along the back of the house.

She removed two matching cups from the cherry-wood cabinet, pouring the rich aromatic brew into the cups.

"I know Stephen likes his black and strong, but I forgot to ask you, Mr. Kendall, how you like to take yours, or do you prefer decaf?"

"Robert. Just Robert. And I usually need all the go-go juice I can stand. Plain is fine by me."

She smiled. These people from Redeemer were easy to be around. "All right, Just Robert. I'll try to remember next time."

Robert gave a hesitant smile that, once fully ignited, lit his entire face. He had a familiar drawl. Maybe, like her dad, a native of the eastern North Carolina farming region? Robert had the relaxed charm of "country boy come to the city" manner, dressed in Southern country club casual, a golf shirt and khakis.

She'd loved to hear her dad speak with the flat intonations of those from Down East. Our Northern brethren, as Daddy referred to them, often incorrectly assumed slow talking meant slow think-ing. It didn't take long for them, however, to discover their mistake in stereotyping Nate McLawhorn, NASA engineer.

To her ear, the sound of the words on his tongue was like the taste of honey. Slow, but rich. She'd wanted to talk like Daddy instead of like the "nobody from nowhere" speech of the other transplants working at Kennedy Space Center. As a child, she'd practiced the way he said his words, rolling and savoring them like butterscotch morsels in her mouth.

She handed Robert a mug. "Are you a member of the club, too?"

"I am." He sipped from his cup and leaned against the counter-top. "Way too expensive, but I do love my golf."

A guy comfortable in his own skin. A trait she admired immensely.

"Yeah." Stephen propped his elbows on the granite counter. "Robert's one addiction. I'm not a member, so I figured old Robert would be our point man."

Robert laughed. "You forgot about my other addiction—Wolfpack basketball."

Before the men could digress on the one subject most native North Carolinians could get positively rabid about—for hours—she asked, "Just Robert?" He colored but grinned at her. "Did you ever meet Frank before he died?"

"I never had the opportunity to meet him though my late wife, Joan—"

Justin clomped down the back stairs with Claire right behind him. Both their faces lit up when they saw the men. She didn't think all of it was directed at Stephen, either.

What was that old saying about the test of character being chil-dren and dogs? She didn't have a dog, but her children were a great testament to Robert Kendall's kind nature.

"Hey, guys," Robert called out to the kids.

Stephen set down his mug. "Ready to go, Justin?"

Justin hurried over to them. He was dressed in semi-clean denim jeans and a long-sleeved rugby shirt. His hair, though, looked slept in.

She stuck out a hand to smooth some hair out of Justin's face, but sensing her intent, he ducked away.

He frowned. "Mom, please."

Translation—stop treating me like a baby in front of the guys.

She backed off. "Looks like I need to do laundry."

Time to get back into the swing of life. Val, bless her, had coped with everything over the last week she'd been unable to deal with. But life, no matter how unfairly, went on. The trash can overflowed. As did the dishes in the sink and clothes in the hamper.

And murderers needed to be caught.

Back to mothering, she waved a hand toward the book bags piled in the corner. "Homework needs to be done before Monday."

Justin groaned. Claire scowled, her brow wrinkling.

"How you could imagine I care about such trivialities?" Claire drawled out the syllables of *triviality*. Claire liked to use big words because, well, she could.

"Now Claire . . ." No way would she let her daughter start an argument in front of Stephen and Robert Kendall.

Justin laid a quiet hand on Claire's shoulder. "Sandy Fleming collected the notes we missed over the last week. We've got to go back sometime, you know."

"But Monday? It's too soon. I'm not ready to face . . ." Claire glanced around her for the right word, "everything."

Claire meant *everyone*. Facing their peers with all the ugly publicity generated by Frank's murder wouldn't be easy. After a rash of nasty text messages from so-called friends, Claire hadn't looked at her phone in over a week. This from a girl formerly glued to the device 24/7.

Before she could respond, Justin cut in. "Would we ever be ready? But it's something we have to do, and better to get it over with sooner than later."

Alison sighed, struck with how mature Justin had grown this last week.

Behind her, Stephen spoke up. "Putting it off never helps. Only makes things worse."

Claire's face remained troubled. She plucked at the ends of the corded belt dangling from her jeans.

Robert's voice rumbled. "I never knew your dad, Claire, but it sounds as if he greatly admired courage. I think he'd want you to face this, hard as it is, with courage."

Claire, her eyes full of tears, stared at them for a moment, and then she nodded. "It's a little overwhelming."

"Only a little?" joked Stephen.

Claire gave him a wobbly smile.

"We could ask Sandy to come over later and guide us through the worst of it," Justin suggested.

A slight pucker formed between Claire's carefully penciled brows. "Maybe."

This was not the moment to pursue it, but something was going on as far as Claire and Sandy Fleming were concerned.

Justin hung the strap of his dad's expensive Nikon camera around his neck. "We're burning daylight, people."

He was, Alison discerned, afraid something had happened to Frank's clubs like the briefcase. The camera they'd located in the bedroom closet. She made a note to look for the prayer book and New Testament for Claire although she'd not asked for them or commented on Frank's legacy to her.

"Can I come too?" Claire glanced at her mother for permission.

That's a first, Alison thought, nonetheless pleased.

"I'm getting stir-crazy."

Robert nodded. "The more the merrier."

Alison called out to Justin as Stephen and Claire headed for the door. "Did you want to develop those digital prints on your dad's camera?"

"No. I can do it at home later today with Dad's office equipment. I just wanted . . ." He shrugged, embarrassed. "To keep it close to me."

Robert clapped an arm across Justin's thin shoulders. "A comforting idea. When my wife, Joan, died of cancer four years ago, I carried her pink poodle key chain around with me for weeks. Got funny looks, though I can't think why."

Justin laughed as they headed for the porch.

She sent up a quick thank-you to God for the kind people He'd brought into their lives through this tragedy, a vast support network of believers helping them deal with their grief.

Prayer? Who'd a thought? She was getting to be an old hand at this.

Who was that old guy in the Dodge leaving with Claire and Justin? Mike adjusted the binoculars and slid lower into the seat of his truck, grinding his teeth as he replayed the smile that passed between Alison and the man. Mike remembered seeing him at the graveside. His mind teased for the name.

Kendall. That was it. What business did he have with Alison?

And what business was it of his? Mike frowned at himself in the rearview mirror. Everything about Alison was his business until he eliminated her from his suspect list.

Yeah, right. Like in war, everything was fair game.

And in love, too?

Get a grip, dude.

Mike typed the name into the open laptop on the seat beside him.

He'd run a search through the law enforcement records on anyone connected with Weathersby and Frank. Nothing incriminating yet on Bill Lawrence and CompuVision. And no joy so far on any of the rest of those nutcases, either.

Why'd he get all the crazy cases? Bad luck, he supposed. Or, the Chief had a twisted sense of humor where he was concerned.

The Chief would have his head if he knew he'd been spending so much of his off-the-clock time watching the movements of the Widow Monaghan. Murders hadn't exactly come to a standstill in Raleigh after the death of Frank Monaghan. Other cases were starting to pile up on his desk. Fun stuff like gangbangers and deadly barroom brawls.

Yeah, fun stuff. His mouth drooped. But something about this case intrigued him. Engaged unused portions of his mind. Teased at his subconscious. And he wasn't so sure the murder of Frank Monaghan had ended whatever was going on.

He had a bad feeling—and he learned to listen to his intuition—that things were just getting started. Bad things. Dangerous for Raleigh and maybe for the rest of the Monaghans.

Mike's stomach clenched. *Why now, God? Of all the women—*

His head snapped up, banging his forehead against the sun visor. Had he just prayed?

"You and Granny got some sense of humor." He swiped a palm across the back of his neck. "Real funny this little heavenly joke of yours."

Mike called himself all sorts of names. No doubt about it. He was an idiot of the first order.

He grimaced at the ceiling of his truck. "Fine. Have it your way, God." He leaned his head out the window. "Laugh it up, Granny."

Yep. He'd lost his mind. Talking to the air and dead people.

A strange feeling overcame him, starting at the roots of his short-cropped hair and winding all the way to the end of his toes. Peace? It'd been so long since he felt it he almost didn't recognize it.

He sighed deep from the depths of his gut as it ironed out the edges of every fold in his mind. "Okay. I'll trust you on this one." He bit his lip. Not good enough.

"All right. All of it. From now on." He glanced back to Alison's house. "But I'm going to need some real help here proving she didn't murder that jack—her husband."

His answer came with the sighing of the wind through the tree-tops. And for just one moment, he thought—was he certifiable?—he heard the slight, lilting laughter of his granny in the whispers of the breeze.

As the door shut behind them, for the first time since the afternoon she'd discovered the mysterious photo, she was alone in the house. After wiping the counters and putting the last of the break-fast dishes into the dishwasher, she ran up the back staircase to empty their clothes hampers into the laundry room upstairs.

Sorting through the small pile, she started the white load and realized she couldn't stand for her hands not to be busy. The silence, even with the washer sloshing, got to her.

An urge to visit the spot of Frank's murder consumed her. On the heels of that desire, screamed a voice of caution. The rational part of her brain mocked the cautious side as a coward. But the murder happened last week, she reasoned. What was there to be frightened of now?

Besides, maybe God was telling her it was important for some reason to go out there. Squelching her doubts, she ran a distracted hand through her silver-blonde pageboy. Alison changed into a pale blue T-shirt and threaded a wide brown belt through the loops of her jeans. She grabbed the nearest shoes she could find, a pair of old sneakers she kept by the steps between the kitchen and garage for her gardening.

She felt the stares of many eyes boring into her as she backed out of the garage and down the driveway. She passed several joggers on the sidewalk. A dog walker. Her neighbor trimming the hedge between their properties.

Her mouth tightened. Funny, she'd never seen him doing any of his own landscaping before. Nosy, gossipy old—

A new, strange feeling tingled at the edges of her mind. She darted a glance skyward through her sunroof.

"Okay, God. Sorry for that, but You and I both know the Monaghans are the hot topic of the neighborhood right now and likely to remain so until Frank's murderer is behind bars." She grimaced. "Or I am."

As she drove down the street, the sense of well-being she experienced last night returned. Seven minutes later, she reached the end of Orchard Farm Road.

Seven minutes. Frank had been seven minutes from home.

Which direction had his car faced? Inward toward the dead-end sign? Or pointed out toward home?

She stopped the car halfway down the small rural road where the asphalt ended and the gravel began. Faint traces of yellow police tape tied to electric fence posts marking the property belonging to the NC State Vet School Research Lab fluttered in the breeze. Over there lay pastures, deserted except for a few cows. In the distance, the morning mist dissipated, revealing red dairy barns.

Across the street, a band of thick forest edged the back of the Weathersby House Historic Park. She wasn't sure how close or distant the house was from this point. She'd always parked at the front entrance and ventured only as far as the vegetable and cutting gardens.

"No time like the present." Again, that voice of caution tried to make itself heard, but she jumped out of the car before she lost her nerve. She walked the remaining twenty feet to where she supposed Frank's murder had occurred.

Leaning down, she spotted a shiny oily patch. It had been a dry autumn. No rain since the murder. She remembered Frank commenting on needing to take his car in for repair.

Feeling the need to touch something of Frank, she dabbed one finger into the oil and rubbed it between her thumb and forefinger. The sound of the wind moaned, picking up in strength. The sky overhead had turned a dark, ominous gray, a portent of a coming afternoon shower.

The isolation of her location struck her, the loneliness. Depending upon the timing of Frank's death, there would've been the dusky half-light of twilight at best or complete darkness at worst. There were no street lamps. And the shadows cast by the trees on the opposite side would've slowly lengthened, engulfing the car with Frank inside.

Spooky. She shivered.

And sad.

What had been the last sight Frank beheld in those final moments of life? The peaceful, bucolic pasture? The dense undergrowth of the forest? Or a face, familiar yet full of evil intent?

She jumped as the sound of a pop hit the ground beside her shoe and a puff of sandy smoke flew into her face.

"What was—?"

Another whining pop struck the gravel on her other side. Small chunks of rock bit into her ankle.

Someone was shooting at her from the cover of the trees across the road.

At first, she was unable to move, paralyzed in her crouched position.

There was a sudden roar of tires accelerating and spinning on gravel. A hunter green pickup truck barreled toward her. What was she doing out here? Did the murderer have an accomplice? She was trapped. Claire and Justin . . .

God!

The truck did an almost out-of-control three-point turn and pulled along beside her. The passenger door flew open.

Over the steering wheel, she glimpsed a furious, white-faced Detective Barefoot.

"Get in," he commanded as another whizzing pop careened over the cab of the truck, slamming into the fence post behind her.

Move! Now! an inner voice yelled.

Alison hesitated no longer. Leaping forward, she hurled herself into the truck cab, winding up on Barefoot's lap. He reached over her to slam the door shut and, hitting the accelerator, surged toward the main highway off Glenwood.

Shaking, she started to sit up.

"Keep your head down!" He slammed on the brakes and reached for the police transmitter on the dashboard.

"Shots fired," he shouted into the mike. "Officer needs assistance. Orchard Farm Road. Backup requested."

He flung open the driver's door and hopped out. As he bent over, she noted his blue jeans and brogan work boots. Not his usual suit and tie. He stuck his hand inside the bulky beige Carhartt jacket. She glimpsed a shoulder holster and the glint of gunmetal.

"Stay here and stay down."

He crouched alongside the truck and in a sideways crablike maneuver made it as far as her abandoned vehicle.

"Police," he yelled. "Come out with your hands and the weapon in the air."

Through the open window, she heard a rustling followed by the heavy crashing sound of feet running away through the underbrush of the forest. Away—thank God—from their position.

Braver now, she poked her head up to the back window of the cab. Would he pursue or remain and protect her until backup arrived? Balancing on the balls of his feet, his eyes scanned the woods for any sign of movement. Both hands clenched and unclenched around his firearm, his forefinger extending along the side of his gun.

In the distance came the whirring sound of multiple sirens. Three blue and whites screeched to a halt beside the truck. Barefoot ran over to the officers.

Alison wasn't close enough to hear their conversation, but it was terse and quick on Barefoot's part. Four officers drew their weapons and started down the dead-end road for the woods. Fanning out, they disappeared from her sight.

Sighing, she swiveled in the seat, disconcerted to find Barefoot leaning in the cab through the open window, fighting mad.

"Are you stupid, Miz Monaghan?"

She knew he was almost beyond the limits of his self-control in the way he drawled out the Miz in a too-soft voice.

"Or do you have a death wish?"

Feeling it a rhetorical question, she chose not to answer.

Alison lowered her eyes, as docile as a child before the headmaster. She'd learned long ago with Frank, the tirades ended faster if you kept your mouth shut and didn't add any fuel to the fire raging within him.

She heard Barefoot mutter something under his breath and tried not to listen too hard. She doubted it was complimentary.

He thrust the pistol into his holster. Stepping onto the running board, he leaned over the roof of the Ford F-150. "He scratched the paint." He groaned, scrambling higher for a better look.

"Or she," Alison added in the interest of fair play.

"You," he growled from his perch, "be quiet."

Alison noticed how he stroked the wounded vehicle as if it were his girlfriend. Guttural moans came from up top. She wiped the grin off her face when he poked his head into the cab.

"Surely now, you believe I had nothing to do with Frank's murder."

"Why, in the name of all that's holy, were you out here?"

She hesitated, unsure how to explain the intense urging. In hindsight, she realized it was probably not from God. This relationship business was still so new to her. She was going to have to learn about distinguishing His voice from her own desires. She heard Val's voice in her head. She should've prayed about it first.

"Well?"

Alison refused to meet his gaze. "I don't know. I just wanted to be here." She sighed. "To be where Frank was last."

Silence.

Alison lifted her head to see a strange mixture of compassion and wariness in the detective's eyes. Maybe there was more to this tough guy than he wanted most people to see.

He gripped the edge of the cab, taking a deep breath and blowing it out slowly.

She bit her lip. "Which way was Frank's car pointed when you found him that morning?"

The detective pushed back from the truck door.

"Facing home, Mrs. Monaghan. Facing home."

9

"THANKS FOR COMING TO MY RESCUE, DETECTIVE."

Mike poked at the dirt with the reinforced toe of his boot.

"You came just in the nick of time." She shivered. "How did you know I was in trouble?"

He shrugged. "I've been tailing you for several days now whenever I was off-duty."

"You've been what?"

The corners of his mouth tilted up. "You heard me. I had a feeling you were going to do something . . ."

She narrowed her eyes. "Stupid?"

He grinned.

She blinked, flushing.

A policeman came out of the trees and reholstered his gun.

"No sign of him, Sarge."

She sniffed. "Or her."

Mike ignored her. "Witnesses?"

"The park opened at ten so not many people about yet," the officer informed him.

"You're getting their names and addresses so we can interview them."

It wasn't meant as a question.

The officer swallowed. "Yes, sir. According to procedure."

Mike nodded. "Good work. Continue to secure the perimeter. I'm going to scout the scene for any leads. And," he glanced over to her. "I'd like one of you to escort Mrs. Monaghan back to her residence."

"I don't need a—" She stopped after he donned his "I'm spoiling for a fight" look, the bane of every rookie forced to work with him in the department.

Having more than its intended effect, the officer took a step back. "Sure, Sarge. I'll send one of the men." He took off again across the road.

"Are you going to dig that bullet out of the fence post and check to see if it matches the bullet that killed Frank?"

Standing in the middle of the road with his hands on his hips, he towered over her. "I plan to if you will get back to what you're supposed to be doing and let me do my job. Which I happen to do well."

He retrieved his cell phone and snapped several photos of the crime scene from all angles. Pulling out a Swiss army knife from his jacket, he strode to where the shots hit the ground. He scrutinized the tree line, easing down to where she'd crouched when he rescued her. Marking an invisible line from behind with his eye, he crossed over the drainage ditch to the electric fence post.

"Figuring the angle and trajectory of the bullet, Captain?" she asked at his elbow.

He whipped around, knife extended. "Not a good idea to come up like that unannounced on a guy with a knife in his hand. And you know full well, I'm a Sergeant. Flattery will get you nowhere."

She gave him a wide-eyed, who-me? stare, not as intimidated as the rookie. He donned his poker face to show her how unimpressed he was, but the scent of lavender she wore floated by his nostrils. He shifted his feet at her close proximity, his pulse galloping.

Bending down, he examined the wood for splintering, running his forefinger along the grain. "Gotcha." He took a quick photo of the post with his cell phone.

He pulled out a plastic bag and, after digging the bullet out, removed the tiny pellet. He labeled it and stuck it in his pocket.

She cleared her throat. He glanced her way. "Frank left notes to be given to us after his death. I'm not sure how useful they are to your investigation, but you're welcome to look over them, if you'd like."

Her face contracted, a frown marring the skin between her brows. He resisted the urge to smooth the frown away. Maybe something in his face betrayed him for she stepped back.

Mike chewed the inside of his cheek. "I've got interviews to conduct, but afterward, I'd like to come by and see them."

"Sure. I'll be home all day."

He'd believe that when he saw it. Why did the elegant Alison Monaghan make him so . . . ? He wasn't sure what she made him feel. Maybe that was the trouble. Since Fallujah, he'd been real careful about feeling anything.

She's a suspect, he reminded himself for the thousandth time.

He needed some air. He needed space away from her so he could think. Or maybe he was doing too much thinking these days when it came to a certain Alison Monaghan. What was wrong with him?

God, help me . . .

As soon as her "babysitter" arrived to escort her home, Mike muttered an excuse before rushing away—as if the insurgents from hell were hot on his heels—into the tangled undergrowth that led to Weathersby House.

Alison shook her head, trying to dispel the image of that dazzling grin of Mike Barefoot's from her mind.

Megawattage. It was fairly blinding in its intensity.

She bet he had quite the way with the ladies. Been down that road. Her dad had an old saying he used to quote, "Fool me once, shame on you. Fool me twice, shame on me." One Dot or Frank was enough for anybody in one lifetime.

No way. No how. Never again.

Willing her heart to return to a more even beat, she thanked God that as a widow, those days were behind her.

She returned home only minutes before the children arrived. She'd just parked the car—the garage door still open—when Robert's truck pulled into the driveway. Justin grinned from ear to ear. Stephen helped him unload the bulky golf bag from the truck bed.

"Hurray!" Alison called, clapping.

Robert stuck his head out the window. "Got to get going. But mission accomplished."

Stephen hopped into the passenger seat and waved. Claire helped Justin pull the bag into the garage.

Alison leaned against the open door frame and waved in return. "Thanks, guys." Claire and Justin waved good-bye.

"I'm going to hit some balls." Justin headed for the side entrance to the backyard.

Hunger pangs reminded Alison of the time. "Lunch is soon. Want to help, Claire?"

As soon as the garage closed and they were in the kitchen, a pall settled over Claire.

"Let's do grilled cheese." Choosing a favorite comfort food of Claire's, Alison hoped to distract her daughter from her depression.

Claire shrugged but dragged out the skillet.

As she sprayed the pan with cooking oil, Claire retrieved the bread from the pantry and Muenster cheese slices from the cold box in the fridge.

"I told Detective Barefoot about Dad's notes. He's coming over this afternoon. It could be important."

Claire, normally hard to shut up, said nothing.

Alison decided to keep the events of her morning adventure to herself. Out the window, she watched Justin putting to an imaginary hole ten feet away. "Why don't you like Sandy Fleming, Claire?"

Claire stiffened. "She's not—oh, I don't know. I don't want to sound mean, but she's just not—our kind of people."

Frowning, Alison eyed Claire. "What do you mean? She and her whole family seem nice to me."

"Oh, they are." Claire pursed her lips. "But they're . . ." She struggled for the right word. "You know, unsophisticated." She bent her head to butter the bread. One shoulder rose and dropped. She focused on layering the cheese slices. "Sandy doesn't dress well. Her clothes come from discount stores. She doesn't wear much makeup, and she's sort of plain. None of my crowd would ever hang out with people like her."

Alison's mouth opened and closed. The spatula clattered against the cast-iron skillet. Shame followed indignation. Had she modeled this to her daughter?

Change Claire's heart, God. And mend mine as well.

"You mean you think you and your friends are better than her because you have more money?"

Red splotches dotted Claire's cheeks. "When you put it that way, it sounds so ugly. We just have nothing in common with her."

Alison pivoted to the skillet in time to flip the sandwiches and avoid burning them. "News flash." She threw a glance over her shoulder at her daughter. "We're not rich. Or at least we're much poorer than we were."

Claire huffed around the kitchen, dragging out the plates and cutlery. "You call me a drama queen. I think you're exaggerating. Tons."

Alison turned off the range and put a tentative hand on Claire's arm. Claire shrugged it off. "Claire. Look at me."

Claire, her lips bulging, obeyed, but under duress.

"We're going to have to sell the house. And when the club membership expires, we will not be renewing."

At that, Claire's eyes filled with tears.

"I'd cancel it now, except they won't give me a refund. The days of maid service are over. Life will be different and difficult. Until we pay off the debt, we're going to have to drastically change our lifestyle. There'll be little shopping in our future, I fear."

"But that's not fair!"

Alison wished she could turn back the clock to impart somewhere along the way that things and money weren't everything. But she and Frank had done a pretty good job of raising Claire to believe otherwise. One more example of her failed mothering skills. Time for all of them to grow up.

"I'm sorry, honey. Time for a reality check." She made a mental note to contact a realtor on Monday. Maybe Robert.

Through the window, she observed Justin take a practice swing into the net Frank had set up to perfect his own drives. Life was going to be hard, but in its hardships, they—with God's help— might become better people. Adversity built character depending on how you responded to it, but those kinds of lessons, while essential, were never fun.

Claire turned silent again, and this time Alison left Claire to her own thoughts. She scooped up the paperwork she'd been poring over from the breakfast nook table and set out the sandwiches as Claire poured the drinks.

In the background, Justin manically drove one shot into the net after the other. Thud after thud. Followed by a curse. Something that didn't sound like Justin.

She and Claire, glancing at each other, watched tears roll down Justin's twisted face. He slammed shot after shot as fast as he could, and upon reaching the end of his strength, he slammed the club into the ground.

Alison started for the French doors, but Claire grabbed her arm.

"Don't." Claire shook her head. "Let him get it out of his system. He can't keep pretending to be strong all the time. Don't embarrass him."

She bit back her own tears at Claire's compassion for her brother. Maybe she hadn't been a perfect parent, but God would hear her prayers for her children. He wasn't done with any of them yet.

With Alison's arm around Claire, they returned to the kitchen to give him some privacy, but there was a shout.

"Mom!" Justin yelled. "Mom!"

Her heart in her throat, she ran across the family room. This time, Claire was right behind her. They met Justin at the door.

"Look what was stuffed in the bottom of Dad's golf bag." He waved a small black object in front of their faces.

It was Frank's missing smartphone.

10

OVER THE NOW-COLD GRILLED CHEESE SANDWICHES, ALISON SCROLLED through the calendar feature entry by entry, while the children looked on, eating their lunch without a word. She noted the days in September highlighted in red that she believed he'd met with the cloche hat lady in San Francisco. He'd entered the date he'd last taken the Piper Cub out on a day off. Probably when he took the picture of the sunrise. She found the note Frank had written to call Pete and Gary. A few weeks later there was a reminder to drop by Pete's office.

Flipping ahead, she saw Frank's flight schedule recorded— flights he would never fly. The only other notation, color-coded orange, was the date of every Weathersby House board of directors meeting for the next year. Almost as an afterthought were a series of numbers.

4155557654	7719208120
6489317176	0922012

Puzzled, she searched her memory for important family dates like birthdays and anniversaries. She left the children to brainstorm for ideas while she retrieved her telephone/address book from the kitchen desk. She checked the numbers against the numbers of friends and acquaintances.

Claire pointed out the seven digits, plus three contained in all but the last set of numbers. "Maybe they're out-of-state telephone numbers."

"I could run a check through the Internet and see what comes up," Justin volunteered.

"Maybe it's a secret code." Claire's mouth drooped. "But we don't have the key."

Alison sighed. "I do think it's something important. Something your dad wanted to remember."

"Something Dad wanted Justin to find, in case something kept him from completing his mission." Claire's voice rose with excitement.

Alison wasn't sure she'd go that far, but seeing the bright, interested look on Claire's face, she decided anything was better than the apathetic, alternately angry Claire they'd seen for the last week.

"Go ahead, Justin. See what you can find out before the detective gets here. Claire, would it be possible to make copies of every calendar notation? We'll need to hand the phone over to Barefoot."

Claire reached for the phone. "I'll select the calendar items, e-mail them to the home computer, and print the file." She looked at Justin for confirmation. "Right?"

He nodded. "Don't worry, Mom, we've got this." Both of them jumped up, eager to do something.

As she cleared the table, she questioned her early morning impulse to venture out to Orchard Farm Road. Was she like the children? Wanting to do anything to keep from thinking, from grieving? Looking for any distraction to keep busy?

I need to remember I'm not alone, God. I don't have to figure this out by myself.

She picked up the wireless phone from the kitchen, and taking a deep breath, she dialed Pastor Fleming's home.

"Bryan? I'm sorry to bother you on a Saturday."

"No problem. Most of my congregation thinks us pastors only work one day a week anyway." He chuckled to let her know he was kidding.

"I did something last night, and now I don't where to go from here." She rushed to tell him about her prayer before she lost her nerve.

"Oh, Alison. I'm so glad you've come into a relationship with Jesus Christ." He went on to ask her if she owned a Bible.

Feeling like a heathen, the impulse to lie struck her, but she ignored it. "No."

As if somehow guessing her thoughts, Bryan reassured her, "No reason to expect you would until you were a believer. I'd like to give you one, if I may. The only way to get to know someone is to spend time with them, and God has graciously provided us His Word— His love letter to His children—so that through its pages we might come to know Him better. You can also get to know Him through prayer. Spend time with Him and let Him speak to you—and you to Him—in the quietness of your heart."

"I don't know the right words to pray."

"There are no 'right' words, Alison. You'd never refuse to listen to one of your own children if they didn't speak just the 'right' words. It's the same way with God. He's your Father, and He delights in whatever you say to Him. All you have to do is talk to Him openly and honestly from your soul."

She closed her eyes as she held the phone to her ear. Peace washed over her like a gentle low tide.

Her Father. How grateful she was to be His child. But she had so much to learn. "I'm planning to attend services in the morning."

"That's an excellent place to start. I'll see you then and mark some verses for you to look over in the next few days."

"Thank you."

"Congratulations, Alison. You've embarked upon the most exciting journey men and women are permitted to experience in this life—the journey of faith."

Placing the phone into its receptacle, she found Claire standing stock-still in the doorway, the copied papers in her hand. How long had Claire been listening? She hoped one day Claire would share in this life-changing experience.

She waited for Claire to say something. She didn't have to wait long.

"If you think I'm going tomorrow to that bunch of hymn-singing, boring, badly dressed, prayer—"

Justin appeared behind his sister. "I'd like to go. Those people have something. I see something different about you, too, today, Mom. You don't seem so scared. You always seemed afraid, even before Dad's murder."

He was right. Until today, she couldn't remember a time, from the earliest days of her childhood, when she'd not felt fearful. God had already changed her.

She told the children as simply as she could about finding the petal in Frank's note. Without going into details they didn't ever need to know about their dad, she told them how alone she'd felt and how she was tired of struggling by herself.

Alison told them about her prayer. "I'm trying to forgive all the hurt your father caused me. I'm not there yet, but I know I need forgiveness, too, and so I have to forgive others. God has given me a peace and a joy I can't begin to explain."

"God?" Claire threw the papers onto the kitchen floor. "Where was God when someone put a gun to Dad's head? If He's so great, He could've stopped all this from happening. He could save our house, so we don't have to move. Why didn't He stop Dad from sleeping with—?" Claire clapped a hand over her mouth.

Alison wrapped her arms around Claire and Justin.

"I don't know the answers to your questions, Claire," she whispered. "I wish I did. There's so much I want to know. Some things, I have a feeling, we might never know until we see God face to face, but I'm going to keep on praying and asking God. Tomorrow, I want us to go to church together, as a family."

Claire pulled away, but Alison held on.

"I wasn't doing so hot by myself before. I don't know about you, Claire, but I was desperate for help, for strength. Being with God's children is the best place I can think of to start."

"I think it's a great idea." Justin placed one arm around his mom and the other arm around his sister. "Claire, after everything those people have done for us and for Dad over the last week, it's the least we can do."

Claire lifted her head and sniffed, but she could tell Claire was mulling over that thought.

She reflected Justin was as wise in dealing with his sister as Claire had been with him earlier. Thanking God for them, she sent up another quick prayer for Him to continue to move upon their tender, grieving hearts.

Claire nodded slowly. "When you put it like that, I guess that's the proper thing to do, to thank them, I mean."

A start.

Justin gave them both a hard squeeze. "It's the right thing to do." He smiled. "And I got a hit with one of the numbers. Claire was right. 4-1-5. That one was an out-of-state phone number, a hotel in San Francisco, California."

Alison grimaced. Thanks a lot, Frank.

Mike rang the doorbell at the Monaghans' mid-afternoon, the large manila envelope balanced in the crook of his arm. While he waited, he glanced at the dark sky. He'd come to an unorthodox decision—one that, if he turned out to be wrong about Alison, could cost him his career. But he'd learned over the years to be as well informed as he could be and then to act on what his gut was trying to tell him.

Life was all about taking chances. Carefully calculated risks had propelled him thus far in his meteoric rise within Raleigh's police ranks. He'd learned the hard way in Iraq that ignoring his hunches was at his own peril.

Claire answered the door. Unsmiling, she let him in.

An image of a high-strung filly came to his mind when he thought of Alison's daughter. Or that nervous feeling he'd gotten when trying to disarm land mines in Fallujah.

In that cool, grown-up voice he'd come to associate with Claire, she dropped a bomb of her own. "We found Dad's smartphone and made some discoveries. We have a lot to show you."

We?

In the family room, he found Alison and Justin seated at the farmhouse table in the breakfast area, poring over the display screen of a smartphone. Pink polka dot flip-flops rested beside Alison's chair. Her feet, tucked under the table, were bare. Mike noticed again the comfortable mixture of contemporary and antique furnishings. Homey.

Alison looked up when they entered. "Good. You're finally here."

He gritted his teeth. And people thought he was single-minded? "Sorry to have kept you waiting. I didn't realize I was on your clock."

Justin laughed and Ice Princess Claire cracked a smile.

The corners of Alison's mouth twitched. "Forgive me. We're just excited about finding Frank's phone." She explained about the golf bag at the country club and how Justin had found it.

"If you want my opinion," Claire examined her fingernails with a studied nonchalance. "And I know you probably don't—"

"But," he sighed. "You're going to tell me anyway."

"I think," Claire ignored the interruption. "Dad knew he was in danger and left home that last morning, dropping the phone off at the club to retrieve later. Or maybe for one of us to find. In his note, he practically instructs Justin to go get it."

Mike rubbed the back of his neck. "Speaking of notes?"

Alison gestured for him to pull out the chair beside Justin.

She placed three ivory note cards on the table, smoothing them for him to examine.

He picked up the one addressed to Claire and scanned the note. "Interesting." From the inside pocket of his jacket, he pulled out two small black books. "These, I believe, belong to you." He handed them to Claire, hovering over her mother's shoulder.

Claire inhaled. "It's Grandma Irene's prayer book and Papa Joe's Bible."

Justin flicked a glance toward Mike. "Where did you find them?"

"They must have been inside Frank's briefcase. We found them tossed with North American flight schedules in his car. Whatever our murderer was looking for, it wasn't those. Now, what's this about a phone?"

"Read Justin's note." Alison pushed the paper toward him. He read it.

With the air of entrusting Mike with the crown jewels, Justin handed him the phone. "We were wrong to think Dad's phone went missing with his briefcase. He'd hidden it for safekeeping."

Justin told him about the numbers and his successful Internet search. Mike listened as he thumbed through the contents of the calendar.

"Good work, young man."

Justin flushed with pleasure.

Alison smiled at her son. "Justin is a computer whiz."

Mike scrutinized the list of numbers. "Any idea what these other numbers refer to?"

Justin shook his head. "But I'm not giving up yet. They could be bank account or passport numbers, computer file codes, etc. . . ."

"If you don't mind, I'd like to get my people working on this, too." He smiled at the boy. Justin grinned back.

He well remembered fourteen. Its pain. Its awkwardness. Its confusion. He'd already lost his father, too, at that age. Though not to murder.

Alison and the children exchanged a look. "The kids are going upstairs to finish homework while you and I, Detective Barefoot, finish our talk."

He figured this was a prearranged signal because the children cheerfully bid him adieu and went upstairs to their rooms without arguing.

"Now that we're alone"—Alison folded her hands on top of the pine table—"there are issues you and I need to discuss. Why don't you read the note Frank left for me?"

Mike picked up the remaining letter, and with a quick glance over to Alison's now shuttered face, he bent to read.

"Hawaii?" he asked after a minute.

"We spent our honeymoon there."

A feeling of great sadness came over him as he finished reading the short note. Sadness for Alison, surprisingly, for Frank. What a waste of what should've been. But he was convinced more than ever he was doing the right thing. Alison wasn't guilty of her husband's murder.

He laid the note in front of her. "Let's stop tap dancing around this issue of mutual trust. I think we've reached the point of full disclosure. I'm willing to trust you're not the killer we're both looking for."

She grabbed the edge of the table, leaning forward. "Do you mean it? We can work together?"

"Whoa there." He held up a hand. "As my granny used to say, 'Don't go hog wild on me.'"

Alison laughed. It was a little rusty, he decided, but pleasant.

"Sorry. Most of my friends would be shocked for anyone to think I—of all people—would go off half-cocked over anything. I'm usually the quiet, cautious one."

Drawing the manila envelope from his lap, he laid it on top of the table. He upended the contents until they slid out of the envelope to rest in front of her. "The personal effects we found at the crime scene. I'll need to take some of this back with me to the station."

With a shaky hand, she reached for the wallet. Flipping through it, she studied Frank's driver's license and counted out the credit cards and cash. "Everything appears to be present and accounted for." She leafed through the North American Air documents. "Nothing unusual here." Fingering the plastic baggie, which contained a lone cigarette butt, she frowned. "Frank didn't smoke."

"Frank, I assume, didn't wear red lipstick, either."

She examined the red ring. "I still believe his murder is connected to Frank being on the board at Weathersby."

"Why?"

Her teeth tugged at the edges of her lip. "Because of where he was murdered. Because of the significance he attached on the calendar to the board meetings. Because you and I were shot at over there this morning."

"Good reasoning." He nodded. "I tend to agree with you though I do think the shots this morning were a way of warning us off. If the killer had wanted to kill you, he or she," acknowledging her motion of protest, "could have done so twice over before I got there. Our killer definitely knows how to handle a gun."

"Have you questioned the other board members at Weathersby?"

"Extensively and repeatedly." He rubbed his chin. "The investigation is at a dead end, but I'm still working a few angles."

"Frank was either duped, or someone cleaned us out of most of what we had." Her mouth tightened. "CompuVision is a subsidiary in Bill Lawrence's computer empire."

He took out his small notebook and jotted down the information. "Linda Lawrence is the only one I've observed so far who smokes and has a connection to Weathersby or Frank."

"You noticed that, too, at the funeral, I mean."

He gave her an appraising look. "Very observant aren't we, Miz Monaghan?"

"And she wears crimson red lipstick. But what was the motive behind Frank's murder? Greed or . . . ?"

"Or a woman scorned." He finished for her. "Look at this." He handed her another small baggy containing a crushed tissue with a smudge of tangerine lipstick.

"Oh, Frank." Her shoulders slumped. "Multiple rendezvous?"

Mike tapped his pen against the notebook. "I don't think so. It appears Frank wiped this off himself with his own saliva."

Her mouth twisted. "Getting rid of the incriminating evidence of adultery."

"Don't be so sure. He could've been removing an unwelcome intrusion. I think Frank was well-acquainted with his killer. So well-known to him, in fact, the killer could put a gun to his temple and pull the trigger before Frank knew what was happening."

"You think he never saw it coming?"

"Not until it was already too late. I have found such life and death moments—the few I've experienced myself—to be surreal." He ran a rough hand through his short sandy hair. "Seconds morph into slow motion, and then real time rushes back in double time with all its horrific consequences."

She gave him a quizzical look. "Your bad guys?"

He shrugged. "The ultimate in bad guys. War." His military background and its painful disillusionments weren't topics he chose to discuss with just anyone, much less a comparative stranger.

"Natalie Singleton wears tangerine lipstick."

"You noted this at the funeral, too?" He smiled, relieved at her willingness to change the subject and put him at ease. "I had your cell phone company provide a list of calls Frank sent and received over the last two months. He got a call after he landed that afternoon. The call issued from one of the Weathersby extensions. That's why he didn't come straight home."

She squared her shoulders. "Somebody lured him to his death."

"Exactly. The murderer is clever, and you could be putting yourself into danger by getting too close to the truth. I want you to stay away from those people at Weathersby. I promise I'll keep you in the loop on any new developments."

"I need to do something, Detective Barefoot. For my own sake and for Frank's. Can you understand that?"

"Yes, I can. But you've got enough to deal with right now with the kids and settling Frank's estate—"

"You mean his debts and getting a job to put food in my children's mouths."

Mike flushed. "That, too. But watch your back." No way would the Chief authorize any drive-by protection on department time. Better get used to long nights in his truck until Frank's killer was behind bars and Alison and her kids were safe.

"You'll make a praying man out of me yet."

Hearing him as he'd meant her to, she smiled. His gut twisted.

And he realized his granny used to say almost the same thing about him.

With a great deal of secret pleasure, Alison watched Val's eyes almost pop out of her head when she caught sight of the Monaghans straggling down the middle aisle. She gave a tiny wave to Val, seated in the choir loft, the delighted shock on Val's face worth a thousand words.

"Our text comes today," said Pastor Bryan from the pulpit, "from Romans 8. *Who will separate us from Christ's love? Will we be separated by trouble, or distress, or harassment, or famine, or nakedness, or danger, or sword?*" She shivered. Evil had reached out its hand to engulf the Monaghans. It had been victorious with Frank.

Or had it?

"*But in all these things we win a sweeping victory through the one who loved us.*"

What a concept. What a God.

"*I'm convinced that nothing can separate us from God's love in Christ Jesus our Lord: not death or life, not angels or rulers, not present things or future things, not powers nor height or depth, or any other thing that is created.*"

He closed his eyes, and when he opened them, she felt he gazed directly at her little family. "For those who belong to Christ, death is not the end. But even in death, evil cannot win against those in Christ Jesus. For in Christ, though we die, we live. We've already won. Because, my beloved brethren, God *is* enough."

Pastor Bryan closed the service by inviting all who wished to make a public profession of faith or who needed prayer to come forward.

Shaking like a beech leaf in the wind, she nevertheless found herself surging forward with others to the front of the sanctuary. She and Bryan had discussed this on the phone yesterday. Tears streaked down Val's face as she went. Stephen squeezed her hand before she rose. Justin and Claire stared, mute.

Bryan put an arm around her for support. He introduced her to the congregation and told them she was a brand new child of God. He welcomed her and her family to their body and encouraged the congregation to greet her after the service.

She felt as light as she'd always felt swinging high above the treetops as a girl.

As people made their way out of the church, she caught a quick glimpse of the back of a man with sandy-colored hair. She couldn't see his face, but he reminded her of Detective Barefoot.

Surely not? Mike Barefoot wasn't the church-going type.

You weren't, either, she reminded herself, until today.

He was probably doing more off-duty surveillance on her family, believing they were in danger.

But instead of fear, she experienced comfort. A flutter in her stomach of something she didn't wish to examine too closely.

Not only did she have an all-powerful heavenly protector, but she had an earthly one as well. Mike Barefoot, she realized, was not your run-of-the-mill guy.

Outside the church, fluid cluster groups gathered on the steps and on the lawn. Justin gave her a smile and moved away to speak with some boys his age whom she recognized from school. She hadn't known their families were members of the Redeemer church. They were, she remembered, nice young men. She was glad Justin had a positive peer group in his life.

Claire brushed by her without a word. She reached for her, but withdrew her hand. Now was probably not the best time. Claire was confused and angry. It might be better to let Claire make the first move. But she resolved to use what she now knew to be the best tool in her arsenal for Claire. Prayer.

She watched as Mike's truck pulled away from the Redeemer parking lot. She had an uncomfortable feeling she'd be needing prayer a lot more from now on.

For more than one reason.

11

April

ONE OF THESE PEOPLE SHAKING HER HAND AND MURMURING THEIR CONDO-
lences killed her husband. Of that, Alison was sure. She was also
certain beyond rhyme or reason the murderer was the woman in the
photo she'd found last October.

How long ago that seemed, like another lifetime ago. When
Hilary Munro, TAP President, had suggested planting a memorial
oak to Frank, she'd almost refused to attend the ceremony held on
the lawn at Weathersby. This was the first time since Frank's murder she'd set foot on Weathersby property. She'd been busy trying
to sort through the financial and legal mess Frank had left for her
to deal with.

Paying the bills by selling the Piper Cub to Frank's pilot buddy,
Dennis, had temporarily given her the time and space she needed to
help her children begin the healing process. But that grace period
had ended. It was time to get a job and move on with life. She was
also sick of the pointed, accusing looks from the neighbors and living in limbo. Frank's murder investigation had grown cold despite
Mike's best efforts. He'd long ago gone on to other more pressing
investigations. But his presence in their lives had gradually increased
over time, not lessened.

The thought of Mike Barefoot brought a blush to her cheeks.
She schooled her features into the mask of calm she'd learned to

wear early on in her marriage to Frank. And today was about Frank. Not for impossible dreams that could never come true.

Dreams of starting her own landscape design business. Dreams of the warm shelter of strong arms, arms that resembled one police detec—

Bill Lawrence, dragging Linda behind him, barreled his way toward her under the new apple-green foliage of the oaks where Hilary had insisted she hold court. Grimacing, she allowed herself to be enfolded in the immense bear hug that threatened to snuff the life out of her.

Trying not to shudder, she endured Linda's red-lipped society air kiss on both cheeks that, oh, so conveniently, never quite touched the recipient's face. She'd been distressed to see Claire drawn into Zoe and Heather's shallow circle of friends at school this year. Like mother, like daughters. Linda scanned the crowd over her shoulder, searching for someone more important to talk to.

"So sorry for your loss," boomed Bill.

Her eardrum throbbed.

"We miss old Frank at golf. Never found another player like him to fill our foursome." He touched his knotted silk tie.

She reached out, snagging Bill's coat sleeve. "I understand you both served together on the Weathersby restoration project."

Bill, a big guy, tugged at his shirt cuff before abandoning the attempt as awkward. His eyes flicked away, evasive. "So?"

"What capacity do you and Linda fill as members of the board?"

In a blitzkrieg move, Linda yanked her husband's sleeve free, glaring daggers at her. "Bill is the treasurer, and I serve as the fund-raising chairperson." She fluffed the ends of her bottle blonde hair, resembling a preening bird. "We, like Frank, are proud to serve at Weathersby for the greater good of Raleigh by preserving our proud Southern heritage."

Our proud Southern heritage?

The Lawrences transplanted from California five years ago. Alison resisted the urge to roll her eyes.

"Let us know if you and the children need anything, you hear now?" Bill and Linda beat a hasty retreat.

Where had they been six months ago?

Hilary stumbled up behind them. "It's not much but we on the board wanted to honor Frank's faithful service to Weathersby." The former beauty queen, with her over-the-top brunette bouffant heavy on the teasing and hairspray, sometimes resembled a near-sighted raccoon sporting too much black eyeliner and makeup.

Short, chubby Hilary was everything the Lawrences were not. She gazed at Alison with those dog-like brown eyes of hers, sincere in her concern. A slight crease between Hilary's carefully tweezed eyebrows marred the usual sunny disposition for which Hilary was renowned.

However, the friendly exterior Hilary portrayed to the world seemed designed to keep at bay a lonely marriage to a neglectful high-powered attorney and a nest now empty of children. Nearing the half-century mark, Hilary threw herself into all kinds of charity projects to fill the long hours of her days and nights.

"Are you and the children okay for . . ." Hilary, leaning in closer, whispered, "for money?" A question Hilary had repeatedly asked over the winter months. Hilary had taken the time to help Alison fill out insurance claim forms. She'd personally rented a condo at Carolina Beach during Thanksgiving so Alison and the children could retreat from the television reporters camped out on her street, dodge the creditors pounding night and day upon her door, and find some space to breathe.

A true friend. Alison had discovered who her real friends were. Not the society matrons or her tennis foursome. But Val and Stephen, Hilary, and Robert Kendall. Her garden mentor at Weathersby, Polly Grimes. The people at Redeemer.

And don't forget Mike Barefoot, too.

As if she could. She'd tried.

She wiped suddenly moist palms down the sides of her white linen dress. She dragged her attention back to Hilary.

And at that moment, a terrifying idea entered into Alison's head. Fighting feelings of guilt for taking advantage of her friend's kind nature, she threw a quick glance over her shoulder to see if anyone was standing close enough to eavesdrop. "Actually, Hilary, now that you mention it, I'm embarrassed about it, but I . . ."

Alison flushed. "I appreciate all your help this past year, but it's time I made a new start for myself and my family." She took a deep breath. "Is there perhaps some position for which I could be hired at Weathersby?"

She'd said it, the thought that tugged at her mind in the wee hours of the night. A chance to clear her name and bring Frank's killer to justice.

Hilary's eyes rounded. "Don't you worry, my dear. I will not allow you or your children to drown in this economic cesspool of fear."

Her talent had been dramatic presentations in the beauty pageants.

Hilary jutted her chin. "As President of TAP, I can assure you in the course of our restoration there is much that could be accomplished by an educated, organized, and creative person such as yourself."

"I'm not—"

Hilary shushed her, one carmine-tipped finger against Alison's lips. "You leave it to me, dear heart. It will be handled. I must speak to someone first though." She craned her stout neck about, searching. "I will be in touch. Aha!" She strode off like a great white hunter tracking his quarry on safari.

Professor Dandridge and Ivy appeared, her hand outstretched toward Alison. She winced as Ivy's bony fingers wrapped around her wrist.

"I'm so sorry, Alison." Ivy's voice hitched. "When I think of how awful it must be for your children to lose their father in such a way . . ." She glanced at Henry. "We married too late in life to have children, but what a comfort they must be to you now, a link with Frank that nothing—not even death—can ever sever." Pain streaked across Ivy's face. "I've asked the board to consider setting up a scholarship in Frank's memory for your children."

Alison swallowed, blinking away the sudden moisture in her eyes. "Why, Ivy . . . I don't know what to say." Just when you had

Ivy pegged as obsessive-compulsive over all things Weathersby, she surprised you with an unexpected kindness.

"Th-thank you." Her voice wobbled. Who knew the manic Ivy had a soft spot for children? But her claws dug into Alison's flesh. Alison tried tugging free.

Henry grabbed hold of Ivy's hand. "Ivy's passionate about her Weathersby family." He pried his wife's fingers loose from Alison's arm. "Not so tight, my dear."

Passionate? Odd choice of words.

Alison rubbed at the marks Ivy left on her wrist. "I didn't realize Ivy worked so closely with Frank."

Ivy Dandridge and Frank? Alison toyed with a new thought. Ivy, not Natalie, the woman scorned? Henry, the outraged, cuckolded husband killing the rival for his beloved wife's affections?

Na-a-ah.

Maybe Mike was right. Maybe she did read too many Gothic whodunits. The scholarship would be a godsend and one she wasn't too proud to accept.

Ivy straightened, a hurt look appearing in her agate green eyes. Henry put a protective arm around her shoulders. "Ivy, like me, has endured a lot of loss in her life. She's very tenderhearted and considers everyone at Weathersby her extended family." Ivy huddled against him, sheltering in the crook of his arm.

A stab of jealousy, of which she quickly repented, raced across Alison's heart. The lonely evenings after the children had gone to bed flashed through her mind. Was it God's will for her life to be lived alone? At this point, she reckoned the only way to move on might be to bring closure to Frank's memory by apprehending his killer.

Robert had made no secret of his admiration for her. She'd yet to take him up on his weekly invitations to dinner. Mike Barefoot, however, hung around the house a lot, but most of his attention appeared directed at her children.

As the Dandridges prepared to move on their way, Hilary rushed forward, her ruffled orchid purple caftan fluttering in her locomotive wake. With both arms outstretched, she captured the Dandridges, forcing them to remain in place. Ivy's lip curled.

"Ivy! I'm so glad I caught you," Hilary panted, trying to regain her breath from her ungainly sprint among the oaks. "I had a quick impromptu meeting with the other board members. And . . ." She paused for dramatic effect.

Alison winced with a dread foreboding of what forces she might have unwittingly released.

"Ivy's assistant, fourth one this year, left our employ last week."

Henry stiffened. "Ivy's drive and vivacity," in an endearing attempt to defend his wife from the implied criticism, "are often misunderstood. Not everyone is able to keep up with the greatness of her vision."

Ivy flashed Henry a fond glance.

Hilary kept her gaze focused on Alison. "Anyway, how fortunate the timing of events. Orchestrated, one might say."

"Please." Ivy fidgeted. "Before bedtime, Hilary."

Hilary pursed her lips before adding, "We've hired Alison as your new personal assistant."

Ivy's eyes widened. Alison rocked back on her heels.

What on earth had she gotten herself into now?

Val rounded on Alison. "What on earth possessed you to do such a stupid thing?"

Bristling, Alison slammed the coffee mugs onto the granite countertop. "Stupid?" she repeated in a dangerous voice.

"What else would you call it, since you believe one of those loony people is also the murderer of your husband?"

"Exactly."

She measured the beans into the grinder, pressed the button, and counted to ten. The rich, sensual aroma of Kona coffee filled the air. Mike and Claire would be back from Claire's driving lesson any minute now.

"The police are at a dead end. I can do things they can't."

"Like get killed?"

"Just stop with the negativity. I know what I'm doing."

"Do you?" Val set out the saucers and spoons. "Did you stop and think about the ramifications of what could happen if you stick your nose in too deeply?"

Gritting her teeth, Alison tore into the cookie tin. "If you're going to say pray, I've done nothing but pray over our situation. I need this job, and I need to bring closure for the children and myself. I start work on Monday morning."

"I know it's not been easy living with the suspicions hanging over your head. I'm just not sure this is the right direction for you to take in easing your grief and clearing your name."

She gave Val a quick hug. She hated it when they fought. "I mean to see Frank's murderer brought to justice before I'm arrested for the crime." Clutching the cookie plate, she marched into the dining room.

Val followed her out of the kitchen. "Justice? Or revenge?"

"Whatever it takes." She set the plate onto the table with a clink of china. "I'm going to make it happen if it's the last thing I do."

Val corralled her against the curved mahogany edge of the Duncan Phyfe table. "Why, Alison? So Claire and Justin can lose their mother and father just like you did?"

She shoved Val back, and they glared at each other, faces red, chests heaving.

"That's not fair! I'd never do what Dot did to me."

Val closed her eyes. "I'm sorry, Alison. You know I only want what is best for you and the kids. I get too protective and my mouth runs ahead of my brain."

She swallowed and managed a tiny smile. "Yeah, that mouth was always way bigger than that pea-sized thing you call a brain."

Val laughed. "Forgiven?"

"As if—to quote Claire."

Val's voice brightened. "Let's talk about your love life."

Flushing, she twisted the damask napkin around her fingers, stalling at Val's abrupt change of topic. "Love life? What love life? I have good friends. Nothing more."

Val smirked. "I'd say from the look on both men's faces when you walk into a room they'd like to change that to something else."

Alison gripped the back of a chair. "That's the problem. One of them is safe and the other . . ."

"The other is like stepping off a cliff into nothingness." Val returned to the kitchen to grab her purse off the counter. "You got to take a chance and jump, if you ever want to fly."

She shot Val a surprised look. "You could always read my thoughts. Spooky. And irritating."

"Don't ever play poker, dear friend. You've got a face that gives away your hand every time. God is in control, and what will be will be." Val giggled. "I'm starting to sound like Doris Day, aren't I?"

She smiled. "Doris who? Claire would say." She sighed. "But that kind of dangerous didn't work out so well for me and Frank."

"Mike's nothing like Frank. Not where it counts."

"He's not a believer, Val."

Val rested her hand on Alison's shoulder. "He and I have had some deep conversations over Sunday lunches about life. And death. He's seen more than his share of death. He's not as far off from faith as you think." She gave Alison a penetrating look. "If that's even the real reason you hold back."

"What do you mean by that?" Her tone sounded hotter than she intended.

"I think you know what I mean." Val darted a quick glance at her watch. "And all I know is, I don't want to be around when you break your plan to trap Frank's killer to Mike. He's going to go ballistic." She headed for the garage. "Let me know how that works out for you."

"Coward," Alison called after her. She was a grown woman. She needed this job, and she wasn't scared to stand up to Mike Barefoot.

She squared her shoulders. And if all else failed, like all Southern girls, she'd learned in the cradle that a little sweet magnolia went a long way.

At the sound of truck doors slamming, she glanced out the window overlooking the For Sale sign glimmering in the bright glare of the morning. Claire was home.

And Mike. Her heart picked up a beat.

He waggled his fingers at Val as she backed out of the driveway, his casual off-duty T-shirt stretching across his broad shoulders.

Averting her eyes by force of will, Alison slipped her feet into a favorite pair of flip-flops, a paisley coral and brown. After all these months on the market, the house had not yet sold. The delay in selling their home allowed Justin and Claire to continue at Stonebriar High, much to their delight.

Reaching for the brass handle of the door, she realized how thankful she—make that the children—were to have Mike Barefoot in their lives. Claire, the intrepid one, had developed an inexplicable aversion to driving after her dad's murder. Mike had made it his personal mission to ease her out of her fears and prepare her for the all-important driver's exam next month.

Not that they could afford a car for Claire. It was all Alison could do to put gas in her own. Money worries cast a pall over the brilliant spring day. She shook her head. Where was her faith?

A new believer, she was still getting the hang of this faith thing. She thought of her Bible tucked into her capacious handbag on the breakfast table, beginning to show the evidence of wear. Taking a deep breath, she flung open the door.

"It wasn't that bad." Claire placed her hands on her hips.

Mike, a deathly white, clutched the region of his heart. "Water," he croaked and reached for the steadying structure of the door frame. "My life flashed—"

Alison laughed. He always made her laugh.

Claire cuffed him on the shoulder with her fist. "He's exaggerating, Mom. I never went over the speed limit once." She flipped a long strand of auburn hair, ironed straight this morning, over her shoulder.

Mike swallowed convulsively, his silver eyes wide with fear. "That was the trouble. My dead granny drove faster than that when she was ninety-two. The shame, oh the shame—"

Claire licked her pink-tinted lips and shook her head. "We passed two of his cop friends on St. Mary's. Officer Ross said to say hello." She shouldered past her mom in the doorway. "I'm hungry. Lunch started yet?" She laughed at her own joke. "Silly me. Of course not. If it is to be, it's up to me," she quoted, heading for the kitchen.

Alison hauled Mike inside the house. "Are you trying to air-condition the whole outdoors? My bill to pay until we move or get foreclosed on." She winced.

Mike reached toward her face, as if he was about to touch her, but instead ran his hand through his sandy hair till it stood on end and resembled a Mohawk. A sign with him, she'd noted, when he was perturbed. The Mohawk, though not traditional with the Cherokee—she fought the urge to grin—might be a genetic throw-back to his larger Native American roots.

"Claire and I stopped off at the grocery—"

She made a face. "You know I don't like it when you—"

"Miz Monaghan, I was hungry and tired of eating lunch alone, and since you got a child that gets her kicks from feeding people . . ." He coughed and turned away as if ashamed of his admission of vulnerability. "Could use some help bringing in the groceries."

Once a mountain boy, always a mountain boy. He was not, by any stretch of the imagination, Mr. Manners. Yet, on the upside, he never treated her as the weak, unable-to-cope widow that some irritating—bless their hearts—souls tried to pin on her. For what it was worth, in his mind at least, she was as capable as the next guy.

Hope he still felt that way after she informed him about her new job.

She meandered over to the cab of his truck, her flip-flops slapping against the pavement. She dragged a cardboard box of canned goods across the seat. She grunted at its weight. "Could use a little help here."

Was chivalry dead?

He balanced three jugs of milk in his arms. "Don't tear the upholstery."

Yep. Dead and buried.

Mike snagged two cookies from the platter, pausing at his lips. "Quite the list of suspects at the memorial ceremony." He eyed the cookies and cocked an eyebrow at Alison.

She stuck out her tongue. "Not to worry. Chef Claire made those." She shoved the platter toward him. "All of them. For you."

He relaxed, settling back into the chair in the dining room. Usually he sat at the kitchen counter and shared a cup of joe—that expensive coffee he was starting to acquire a taste for—with Alison. Kona, she called it.

Not the only thing he'd started acquiring a taste for, either. And after a day chasing down the filth of humanity, her conversation highlighted his week. He shoved both cookies into his mouth, the sound of pots clanging in the kitchen. He'd not been so well-nourished since Granny died.

And he wasn't just talking about his stomach.

In his quest to find out the truth about this God to whom Alison was so devoted, he'd taken to attending Redeemer every Sunday he wasn't working a case. But sitting in the back.

Wa-ay in the back.

And, if he was honest, also attending so he could catch a glimpse of Alison.

He realized he was pathetic.

If he played his cards right, he was usually able to wrangle an after-church dinner invite from Claire. Along with the Prescotts.

And Robert Kendall.

He'd forgotten how touchy Alison was about her independence. But if he was going to eat their food every Sunday, he wanted to make sure they had plenty more the rest of the week. He'd become a regular and informed grocery shopper.

What a laugh. On him. God had a strange sense of humor.

But he didn't want Alison to need him. Needy women weren't attractive to him.

He didn't need her or anybody else. Okay, maybe he needed Claire and Justin and his niece, Brooke, in his life to keep him sane and human. The stirrings in his heart during the worship time—

Alison called it God-stirrings—maybe he'd add God to that list of what he needed, too. But that's not what he wanted from Alison.

He wanted her to want him. The way he wanted her. And he wasn't talking about only the obvious.

Wiping his fingers on the fancy napkin at his plate, he shuffled his feet under the gleaming mahogany table. Kendall was too old for her. Ancient. He had to be pushing fifty-five if he was a day. She said she and Robert were just friends.

Yeah, he had no pride. He'd asked. He could feel the back of his neck redden at the memory.

Friends.

That's what Mike supposed he was to her. And he thanked God—the one he wasn't willing to publicly admit to yet—for her friendship. He was realistic enough to know that was probably all he'd ever be to her.

People like Alison from the highly stratified air of Raleigh's social elite married people like Robert Kendall. Suave, handsome, glib of tongue, socially connected, and rich. She'd never have to worry about paying the bills with Robert. Robert was everything she was looking for—security.

And he was everything Robert Kendall was not. His lack of social accomplishments could fill a book. His bank account almost as empty as Alison's.

He glanced around. What was with all the high-society touches today? His gut knotted.

Unless she had an announcement to make.

About her and Robert? He inhaled sharply before realizing she was still speaking, giving him a blow-by-blow description of her impressions of her "suspects."

She gave him a funny look and pushed the cookies at him again. Was he that obvious? "Help yourself to as much as you want."

If she only knew. He shoved another whole cookie in his mouth to keep from saying things she wasn't ready to hear. Yet.

"I plan to do more digging . . ." Her eyes fastened on the napkin she twirled in her lap. She took a deep breath. "When I start my new job on Monday as personal assistant to the executive director at Weathersby. I'll keep you briefed on what I discover."

Choking, he came out of his chair. It fell against the Persian carpet with a thud. "Now wait a minute." He sputtered bits of cookie on himself and struggled to swallow the rest.

She'd timed that slingshot well. He'd give her that.

"Didn't getting shot at teach you anything? The perpetrator doesn't like you and next time might decide to do more than warn. Killing is always easier the second time around."

Recoiling, she wrapped her arms around her too-thin body, a shiver ricocheting all the way to her coral-tinted toes. Fear clouded her face.

Unable to resist, he reached over the table and cupped her face in his hand. For a moment, she closed her eyes. Melting into his hand, her lips brushed his palm sending an electric tingle up his arm and to his heart. Her eyes flew open, realization of what she'd done shadowing her face. She drew back.

He clenched his jaw, angry at his clumsiness.

Got to go slow. He'd spent the better part of a year watching that always-scared, when's-the-other-shoe-going-to-drop look fade from her eyes. She needed to make the first move. Not him.

After her abusive marriage to Frank, she'd been like an easily spooked filly. Trusting no one but her God, her children, and Val. He worked hard, one step forward two steps back, an inch at a time, to be included in that circle of strays she gathered around herself and called family.

He was a stray, a castaway from life and love, and he cherished the circle of warmth found only within her orbit. He'd not realized how lonely his existence had become until she'd opened the door and granted access to friendship, belonging, and those kids of hers whom he adored.

Mike let his breath trickle out, the way a balloon released the air inside if only a tiny crevice opened.

Something in the sound brought her attention to his face. He felt her searing, searching look upon his broad face—courtesy of his beloved Cherokee grandfather. She stopped when she reached his eyes.

"Mike?" she whispered. "Try to understand. I owe this to Frank, and before I can start my life over, I have to . . ." Tears welled.

"Don't cry, honey." He thrust both hands into his jean pockets to keep himself from touching her. She'd be his undoing.

Already his undoing.

The little-girl-lost bit in her voice wrung his heart. He wished he'd known the bright, suntanned girl from Florida. The one trapped inside the grown-up Alison. Known her before her mother's downward spiral and her father's death. Before Frank Monaghan had done his number on her.

Some days, he found it hard not to hate Frank Monaghan.

"We're partners." She laid her hand, soft and warm, atop his clenched fist. "I'll pray and be careful. I'll keep your cell number on speed dial."

He hardened his heart. If anything happened to her . . . "It's not a game."

A mulish expression crossed her face. She withdrew her hand. "You don't get to boss me around, Mike Barefoot."

She stood quickly, her own chair crashing to the floor. Leaning over the platter of cookies, her face inches from his own, she jabbed a finger into his chest. "And you can't stop me."

He scowled. "Watch me."

Their noses almost touched.

Her nostrils flared. "How?"

"I'll . . . I'll arrest you."

A gleam of triumph darted in those Kona-brown eyes he loved. He caught a whiff of her lavender fragrance. He tried not to inhale.

Catching him in the act, she smiled and relaxed, folding her arms across her chest. "I don't think so."

He ground his teeth. Of course, she'd be aware of the power she had over him. The power that began in the Garden with Eve—if he remembered his Sunday school lessons.

Blast Eve, Alison Monaghan, and all their kind.

A new tactic was called for. Two could play at this game.

"Please, Miz Monaghan . . ." He turned the full power of his lost little puppy dog look on her, coming around so nothing stood between them.

Alison blinked. Rapidly. Gulped.

Score one for his side.

Alison tucked a strand of hair behind her ears and licked her lips. "When are you going to stop calling me Miz Monaghan?"

When I can start calling you Miz Barefoot.

He sucked in a breath. Turning purple, he coughed. Had he said that out loud? He watched her face.

No, thank God, not this time.

She knelt to right her chair, apparently feeling her question rhetorical. Bending to help her, his fingertips met hers on the lyre back of the chair. Electricity bolted from her hand to his heart.

He stifled a groan. "Can't keep away from trouble, can you?"

She squeezed his hand and twined her fingers through his. His insides puddled.

"I promise to be careful and keep you in the loop."

Defeat staring him in the face, he knew when to beat a graceful retreat. "If you get yourself killed, I'll never forgive you. Keeping you alive—what a lifetime occupation that's turning out to be."

Her eyes crinkled, fanning small lines courtesy of her gardening avocation to the outer contours of her face. "Wanna help me transplant some seedlings before lunch?"

Practically love talk coming from a horticulturalist like Alison. "Sure."

A sucker born every minute.

Still, she hadn't let go of his hand. And hope springs eternal.

He was pitiful.

But with her fingers braided through his as she led him out the French doors to the patio, he didn't care.

Okay, he'd officially lost it. His heart and his good sense.

12

THE PHONE RANG AFTER SUPPER. LIGHTNING STREAKED ACROSS THE EVENING sky. Thunder, once a distant sound, boomed, creeping closer. Alison, wiping her hands on a dishtowel, hurried to pick up the receiver. She snatched up the phone, thinking it might be Val who'd been out of town all day with Dillon's soccer tournament, but she didn't recognize the number on her caller ID.

"Hello? Monaghan residence. Alison speaking."

She heard heavy breathing and then silence. Uneasy, she tried again.

"Hello? Is anyone there?"

This time there was a faint hissing sound like a snake followed by high-pitched insane laughter.

A prickling sensation spread up and down her arms. She yanked the phone away from her ear and crashed it into its receptacle.

Something loathsome and evil.

"Who was it, Mom?" In the den, Justin leaned over his putter, attempting to chip a shot into an empty, clean tub that once contained margarine. "Wrong number?"

Shaken, she ran a trembling hand over her forehead and then lowered her hand back to her side, afraid to alarm the children. "Very wrong number."

Justin returned to his putting, no longer interested in the mundane in light of the glory of golf. Claire lay sprawled on the couch as she had for the last few months, mindlessly watching one cooking show after the other.

Alison never closed any of the blinds or curtains except for the ones upstairs in their bedrooms, but tonight, she closed every one in the house and checked three times to make sure each door was locked and double-bolted. There was a deafening crack, followed by a blinding flash of light as showers poured from the sky with a vengeance. Her garden needed the rain, but she hoped the fury of the storm wouldn't flatten her tender plants in the process.

Returning to the den, she noticed the Testament and prayer book gathering dust on the end table where they'd sat all these months after Claire had tossed them there with only a cursory examination. Seeking a distraction, she carried them over to Frank's chair under the glow of the floor lamp.

Kicking off her flip-flops, she lifted her feet to the ottoman and thumbed through the contents. She was surprised to find certain verses underlined in blue pen with comments in the margin. In Frank's handwriting, not the spidery handwriting of Papa Joe. As she read, she marveled at the apparent change in Frank from these truths that had been on his mind in his last days.

One in particular Frank dotted with three extra exclamation points after writing *Wow* in the margin. It read,

Therefore if anyone is in Christ, he is a new creature; the old things have passed away; behold, new things have come.

Wow, indeed. Forgiven, cleansed, and a new creature. Sitting there in Frank's chair with the television blaring and the children involved in their own activities, she sent a swift prayer of gratitude to her Savior.

She jumped as the windows rattled, like a gunshot, in the wake of a particularly loud peal of thunder. Holding the Testament close, she rechecked the doors one more time.

What had her interference into Frank's murder set into motion? Mike was right. She was out of her league.

Mike . . .

It had not escaped her notice in her verbal duel with him he'd called her honey. The feel of his fingers in hers twining like honeysuckle around a post . . . The warmth of his palm against her mouth . . . She blushed, glad the children were occupied in the family room.

She flicked the porch light off. She was out of her league with Mike, too. Drowning, truth be told.

And then, there was Robert.

The doorbell rang. She jumped two feet into the air.

Peering through the glass sidelights, she gasped and flung open the door. Speak of the . . .

"Too late for a friendly visit?" Drops of water beaded the gray streaks above Robert's ears.

"Never too late for you." This night was turning into a regular *Twilight Zone* episode. "Come in." She pulled him inside. "Claire. Justin. Look who's here."

Robert gave her a slow smile. "You mean look who the cat dragged in on a dark and stormy night."

She smiled. "A mystery lover after my own heart."

Time for a little perspective on the raging hormones and Mike department. She was way too old for that kind of foolishness, wasn't she, God?

One could do far worse than Robert. Especially on nights with spooky crank calls.

"I think you're the excuse I need to start a new pot of coffee." She laughed at the pleased expression on his face. "Decaf, I promise. Or at this time of night, I'll never get to sleep."

Robert brushed the moisture from his hair, a sheepish look on his face. He leaned toward her. "After spending time with you, sweetheart, I always have trouble falling asleep."

She took a half-step back as Justin and Claire edged between them to welcome Robert. Sweetheart? Part of her infused with a sudden, glowing warmth. The other part of her felt a little panicked. Moving into the kitchen, she ground the Kona beans and filled the coffeemaker as Robert chatted at the kitchen island with the children.

A mature, Christian man. Beloved by children and dogs alike. Well-respected in the community. Her children's future secure.

Did that sound too mercenary?

Robert, she instinctively knew, wasn't a man prone to wander like Frank. Robert could prove to be her tower of refuge.

She frowned over the coffee mugs. Wait . . . Wasn't that supposed to be God?

"We'll give you two some privacy." Justin exited the kitchen.

She whirled around after placing the rest of the coffee beans in the freezer. "What?"

Claire gave her a tight smile. "We'll put ourselves to bed. 'Night, Robert."

Robert winked at Alison. "'Night, kids." Easing off the barstool, he closed the distance between them.

Whoa. What just happened here? Things between them were rushing along—it seemed to her—at breakneck speed.

He tugged her toward the family room, the only sound the plinking of the brewing coffee. "How is it you always look so lovely at any time of the day or night?"

And after years of put-downs by Frank, it did feel incredibly nice to have someone so openly appreciate her attributes. Good ole Robert. Never a worry—

She pursed her lips. Old? Where had that come from? She could wager a guess.

Alison gave a quick shake of her head to clear the cobwebs from her mind.

Mike, get out of my head.

"Cold?" Robert trailed his arm across the back of the loveseat behind her. She looked down at her hands locked together in her lap.

Awkward. She didn't know what to do with her hands.

Robert solved her dilemma by slipping a hand between her locked fingers, cupping her hand with his own. Feeling like one of her staked hollyhocks, she surrendered to the pull of his weight against her.

All in all, murder and mayhem seemed diversionary at this point.

She cleared her throat and told him about her new job.

He received it in about the same spirit as Mike. Not well.

"Whatever is going on, I think you need to steer clear of it. At your age and with your children to think about . . ."

She jerked. Her age?

Robert held up his hand, palm out. "I'm only saying this because I care. Let that Barefoot guy handle this. It's his job. Though how he gets anything done when he's always hanging around here . . ."

She stiffened.

Robert released her hand and captured her chin with his thumb and forefinger. "Ali, he's not one of us. A believer. I know Stephen's befriended him, but as your mentor in the faith, I feel it my duty to warn you. He's dangerous to someone like you."

Her eyes widened. Someone like her?

Robert leaned in, a hint of expensive aftershave preceding him. His hazel eyes scoured her. "You must've guessed how I feel about you. And the children. What place do the Mike Barefoots of the world have in your new life?"

What place indeed? All the old insecurities, all the old inadequacies—courtesy of an alcoholic mother and a faithless husband—rose to the surface.

She swallowed and studied the wall beyond Robert's shoulder. A mature Christian man. Beloved by children and dogs . . . One could do far worse.

She already had once upon a time.

13

ALISON WAVED AS STEPHEN BACKED THE FAMILY MINIVAN DOWN THE DRIVE on their way to the youth meeting. On board were Justin and Claire with the rest of the Prescott family. After an afternoon of mindless Food Channel television, even Claire had been ready to escape.

She went into the garage and lowered the door. Remembering she needed to stake her roses, she grabbed a few wire hangers she kept for that purpose from the workbench and some eco-friendly green twine. After church and lunch, she'd changed into comfortable denim capris and an old yellow T-shirt. Mike, working a drug-deal-gone-bad case he'd been investigating all week, disappeared from church right after the music and was a no-show for lunch. She patted her pocket to make sure her cell phone was there in case the children needed her while she was in the backyard.

Leaving the side door locked, she walked inside the house and through the family room to exit out the French doors into the backyard. She picked her way in her yellow and white striped flip-flops around a few low-lying spots still muddy from the rainstorm the night before.

It took only a moment to prop and tie the plants. She relished the feel of the loamy soil in her hands. The waning sunshine felt good on her face. She decided to stay outdoors a while and enjoy this small sliver of the spring season before the mosquitoes arrived en masse come summer.

Heading over to the huge oak tree in the corner of the yard, she sat down on the black wrought-iron bench. Late afternoon tended to be her favorite part of the day, when, after a day well spent, man and beast prepared to rest once more from their labors.

Only the occasional birdcall and the droning of bees enjoying her verbena broke the stillness. She kicked off her flip-flops to run her toes through the silken feel of the grass. This time of year, she loved the green caress of the grass between her toes, never wearing shoes if she could help it. The large fence and evergreen hedges screened her from the neighbors. She leaned her head against the back of the bench and closed her eyes to let her other senses soak in the garden. When she opened them again, she realized it was much darker than when she had closed them. Had she dozed off?

Jumping up, she stuffed her feet into her flip-flops. In the fading light of twilight, she could barely make out the time on her watch. She'd been out here over an hour. She pulled her cell phone out of her pocket to check for any missed calls she might have slept through as she walked through the French doors.

With her phone in hand, she entered the darkened living room. The first thing she noticed was the blinking light from the wireless phone on the telephone stand in the kitchen. She hoped it hadn't been the children needing her. The caller ID box said "blocked call." Afraid it might be the insane caller from last night, she turned on the table lamp and hit play.

It was surreal to hear Frank's voice on the recorded message say, "This is the Monaghans. We're unable to come to the phone at this time. At the beep, you know the drill. Leave your name and number and we'll call you back. Bye."

She frowned. Another matter she should've taken care of a long time ago. Time for another recorded voice. She'd ask Justin.

There was the beep, then a silence, and the caller disconnected. Probably a wrong number. She'd decided to fix a pot of tea and a sandwich when she heard a small thud overhead.

Were the children home already? Getting spooked, turning on lamps as she went, she checked the front door. It was locked and bolted.

She shook herself trying to get the kinks out of her neck. Her overactive imagination was no doubt at work again. Houses creaked all the time.

There was the sound of a door shutting upstairs.

"Claire?" Her voice croaked like a frog. "Is that you or Justin?"

Silence.

Alison glanced again at her watch. Only 6:30. The kids shouldn't be home for another hour.

But someone was prowling around her house.

The shock like an electric current running through her body, she took the stairs two at a time and stopped at the top only to catch her breath. Had Frank's killer returned? Was he or she searching for something? The phone they'd turned over to Mike? Something that now belonged to her children?

Her hand shaking, she dialed 911 and whispered her emergency to the dispatcher who promised the police would be on their way. The dispatcher also advised her to vacate the premises until help arrived.

But was this her one chance to make sure Frank's killer didn't get away with murder and succeed in ruining their lives? What if the intruder left before the police arrived? She was sick to death with being victimized.

She stuffed the phone into her pocket, keeping the line open with the dispatcher just in case. But she was done with being a doormat. She stalked to Claire's room and shoved open the door. Searching the closet, she also peered underneath the bed. Tiptoeing into the Jack-and-Jill bathroom Claire and Justin shared, she flung back the shower curtain like a character in an Alfred Hitchcock movie.

Nothing.

Creeping into Justin's room, she grabbed one of the drivers out of Frank's golf bag. Finding no trace of an intruder, she exited into the home office and discovered papers strewn across the carpet. The drawers of the desk and cabinet rifled. Her home invaded, her children in danger, her husband dead.

Blind, irrational fury overcame her good sense. Shrieking, she raced into the master bedroom with the driver held high over her head like some Viking warrior. She ran headlong into a tall masculine figure—dressed completely in black, outlined by the fading light from the Palladian window—pawing through the nightstand.

It would've been tough to say who was the most surprised, the intruder or Alison.

The prowler made a grab for the club as she swung it inches from his head. Too late, she attempted to wrest it back. Fearing the intruder would beat her to death with the titanium steel club, she hung on for dear life. A tug-of-war ensued until the burglar's superior force wrenched it free of her grasp.

"Get out of my house!" She lunged for the black ski mask hiding the burglar's face.

The prowler reared, but her fingernails slipped underneath the edge of the mask near his collar, drawing blood. Reacting in pain, he shoved her away.

Caught off balance, she fell, the back of her head smacking the footboard. The prowler loomed over her, the golf club raised. Stars spiraled before her eyes. Her last thought before the darkness claimed her was a plea for God to protect her children.

14

ALISON ROTATED HER HEAD AND MOANED. HER EYES FLEW OPEN, AND SHE realized she was alive and lying on her back. The darkened room, thank God, stood empty except for her. Gingerly, she tested her hands and arms, checking her legs carefully to see if anything was broken. So far, so good.

A police siren blared, the volume increasing with proximity. Grabbing hold of the edge of the bedspread she winced as she fought her way to an upright position.

Too fast. Slow down. The world spun.

Leaning against the side of the bed, she squinted at the clock on the nightstand. She hadn't been out long. The closet door stood open and piles of clothing littered the floor. The driver lay where the prowler had dropped it.

Surprised although grateful he hadn't brained her with it, she rubbed the back of her head and flinched at a tender spot. But as she examined her hand, she was relieved to find no blood. She took several deep breaths, willing the nausea to subside.

Trying to avoid any sudden moves, she wrestled her cell out of her pocket and hit Mike's number.

⚬━━◆━━⚬

Thirty minutes later, Mike and another policeman circled the perimeter of the Monaghan home dusting for prints. With the house lit up like a Christmas tree, Alison, assisted by a female officer, lay on the sofa in the family room with a blanket tucked around her. The woman took samples from underneath her fingernails to see if they could trace the intruder's DNA to any criminals in their database.

Mike stalked into the family room. A palpable fury radiated from him like steam off a hot Southern pavement.

She lifted her chin. "It wasn't my fault. He came looking for me this time."

To say Mike looked grim would've been the understatement of the century. "And you didn't hear him enter?"

"No, I told you. I was out in the backyard gardening, and I fell asleep."

He gestured to the telephone. "The intruder called from a burner phone to see if anyone was home. We found the phone in the garbage can. And when he didn't see any lights on, he broke in through the side door in your garage."

She shrank into the cushions. "That door was locked when the children left. I checked it when I closed the garage."

"Well, the lock's busted now, and you better get it replaced tomorrow." A muscle jerked in his jaw. "What in the world made you go upstairs after you heard the noises? Why didn't you call me then?"

She hung her head, her chin to her chest. He could make her feel like a disobedient schoolgirl. Rightly so, she supposed, in this case.

"I know it was stupid," she whispered. "I didn't stop to think. I was just so tired of feeling helpless and out of control."

He shuffled his feet at the foot of the couch.

"I'm sorry." She sighed. "I guess I saw red and charged up there without stopping to consider the consequences."

He perched on the edge of Frank's chair. "Alison . . ." He folded and refolded the bottom of his tie. "Our intruder, if it is the same person that killed Frank—"

"You don't think it's the same person?"

"I'm not ruling out any possibility. But we could have one *or* two motivated individuals who are looking for something they believe you have in your possession. You've been shot at and attacked. I think it's time you gave the sleuthing a rest and let us handle the investigation from here."

She struggled to sit taller. "I didn't do anything this time."

"No, but you've somehow set in motion a chain of events that has caused the perpetrator to get nervous. You could've been killed."

She shook her head. "But that's the funny thing, if the guy wanted to kill me—and I do think the burglar was a guy—why didn't he hit me with the club? He had the perfect opportunity to get rid of me once and for all."

He rubbed his chin. "I agree. All he did tonight was to shove you away. And it was an accident, you believe, that caused your head to strike the footboard. It was definitely a male. We found what looks like a size-twelve shoe print in the mud off your side door entrance. We'll take a casting of the print. Can you tell if anything was taken?"

"I don't believe he found whatever it was he was looking for. Nothing is missing as far as I can tell."

He relaxed in the chair. "I'm just glad you won't be able to go to work at Weathersby tomorrow."

She crossed her arms. "Oh, I'm still going."

He frowned. "What? After all this? Are you crazy?"

"Yes." She tilted her head. "I realize now, I am."

He ground his teeth. "You're not funny."

She curled a tendril of hair behind her ear. "Missed you at lunch today."

The silver in his eyes gleamed. "You did?"

"I mean Claire and Justin . . ." Her voice trembled to a stop.

An emotion she couldn't read flickered across his features. His eyes went opaque.

Shrugging, he rose, ready to end the conversation. She'd noticed he tended to walk away from topics he didn't want to discuss.

"Yeah? So what?" He stuffed his notepad and pencil into his jacket. "Take the afternoon off to have a quick game of pool with a buddy and what happens? You get yourself knocked out in your own home. Can't win for losing." Avoiding her gaze, he drifted toward the kitchen.

She flushed. Her mistake to assume he'd been working a case. She was an idiot. Of course, he had a life that had nothing to do with the children.

Or her.

She bit her lip. "Sorry I messed up your date, Mike."

His eyes darted to hers, but the strain around his mouth eased. "A buddy I said. Don't worry about me. You worry about keeping yourself alive tomorrow." He headed for the kitchen, muttering under his breath. "Some people's guardian angels should get combat pay."

"Ray." He pressed the cell phone to his ear, grateful for Stephen's offer to maintain a watchful vigil at the Monaghans' through the coming night. "It's Mike."

"Yeah, long time no see." From his parked truck down the block from Alison, he'd called an old army buddy who'd managed to do well for himself in the DEA.

Ray Jarrod he'd trust with his life. Or, with someone more precious to him than his own life.

Like Alison and her kids.

He listened, drumming his fingers against the steering wheel as Ray caught him up-to-date on the social and professional whirl of a federal agent based in the District of Colombia. He turned back to answer Ray's question.

"Doing well." A curtain fluttered in Alison's bedroom upstairs. "Better than I have in a long while. And hoping for better things still." He smiled into the darkness at Ray's remark. "You got it, ole buddy. Definitely a woman involved."

Time for the whole truth. He cleared his throat. "I've also been getting myself reconnected to God like you and Karl nagged me to do all through our tour."

He laughed as Ray responded. "'Bout time, I know. But some of us are slow learners. Speaking of Karl, I could use a professional favor from both of you."

In less than a minute, he summed up for Ray a concise picture of the events since Frank's death and the players at Weathersby he suspected.

"Proof's the problem." Ray said something, and Mike laughed again. "Ain't that the truth? And if Karl with his position at the IRS could—*ahem*—stir the financial waters a little, if you get my drift . . ."

Ray promised to give Karl a call in the morning. Mike didn't suspect any drug involvement on the part of the starched collars at Weathersby, but multiple federal inquiries into people's lives had an amazing unsettling effect.

Which he hoped would rattle the killer into doing something stupid to reveal his identity.

"Thanks, buddy. I knew I could count on you." He smiled as Ray gave one more parting shot to his manhood. "Like you weren't a basket case till Serena had mercy on you and put you out of your misery? Took a good woman to agree to marry a loser like you . . ." Grinning, he pulled the phone away as Ray's voice barked with laughter and threats of retaliation.

He sobered at Ray's next remark. "I appreciate the help and the prayers. I'm doing a lot of that these days for Alison and myself." He flicked a glance toward the Monaghan residence. "Tell Serena I'm also praying baby Jude ends up looking like his mother."

At the whoop from the other end of the line, he smiled, flipping his phone shut. He glanced at the dashboard clock and repressed a sigh. One phone call down. Quite a few to go. Another long night ahead.

God, any help You'd like to give on this cold case, I'd appreciate.

The light in Alison's bedroom went out. He sighed.

And with Alison, too.

15

At breakfast, Alison tried not to show any ill effects from her bout with the burglar. A bout, from the throbbing of her head, she'd lost. Stephen had insisted she go to the emergency room last night when he and Val returned with the children. X-rays revealed she'd sustained no concussion.

Val hadn't been pleased with this latest turn of events and Alison's brush with danger. "Maybe this will knock some sense into that hard head of yours."

The children had been nervous, so she hadn't protested when Stephen decided to spend the night on the couch in the family room. She'd kept the driver, dusty with powder from the fingerprint kit, beside her bed. Stephen dashed out the door at 7 a.m.—an English muffin between his teeth—for an early morning angioplasty at Rex Hospital.

Somehow, the burglary managed to make the early edition. Front-page headlines. She groaned before stuffing the entire newspaper into the recycling bin.

"You better take a look at this, Mom." A Facebook page glimmered from Justin's laptop on her kitchen desk.

Claire leaned over his shoulder, gasped, and closed her eyes.

"What is—?" Peering past Claire, she saw snapshots of their house cordoned off by rolls of yellow crime scene tape. A host of blue and white police cruisers surrounded their property. The photos posted to every FB friend Justin and Claire possessed incorporated the catchy title "Murder at the Monaghans. Again?"

Alison clenched her fist. "Who took these pictures?"

Claire's eyes widened. "Who would want to humiliate Justin and me at school?"

Alison had thought—hoped—that the media sensation had died a natural death. She winced. Bad comparison.

Who was trying to make her life and her children's so difficult? And why now? Was the new job worth this renewed scrutiny?

Grim, but determined, summed up the overriding mood at the Monaghans. It was back to school for Claire and Justin after spring break, and now both were clearly dreading the encounter with their peers. Over the break, Justin had been in touch with many in his circle of friends through Redeemer. But Claire, the cheerleader, the darling of the high-school hierarchy, had yet to hear from any of her so-called best friends who'd dropped her one by one over the last months.

Today, Claire wore more eyeliner and blush than usual. Alison supposed it was her way of putting on a brave face. Justin hunched over his cereal, slowly chewing each bite, as if by drawing out the meal he could postpone the inevitable reckoning at school.

"I'll drop you guys off on my way to Weathersby this morning." She took a steadying sip of her coffee, her version of Dutch courage. The liquid warmth with its caffeine jolt trickled through her veins.

Claire cut her eyes at Alison. "I thought you didn't have to start work till nine o'clock?"

"I want to get there early on my first day to check out my responsibilities."

Claire pursed her lips. "You mean you want to get a jump start on grilling the suspects." She went back to her methodical buttering of her toast, row-by-row, stroke by stroke.

"Now, Mom . . ." Justin shook his head. "Remember what Mike said."

"I'll be careful, I promise." She took another sip of coffee. "I'm just going to nose around and get a sense of who knew Dad and if anyone had a grudge against him."

"A grudge?" Claire snorted. "Is that what you call what happened to him? What happened to you last night? What—?"

"I told you I'd be careful." She pressed a hand to the back of her head, the pain becoming acute. "I'll be home around five o'clock. Do you think you can walk home from school?"

Justin carried his bowl and glass over to the sink. "Sure we can. We've done it before lots of times."

"Any after-school activities or will you be home by 3:30 at the latest?"

Claire followed Justin, frowning. "At least cheerleading is over for the year or it'd be more torture having to explain *ad infinitum* about . . ." She gestured toward the laptop.

Ad infinitum. It always had to be the last, and biggest, word with Claire.

Rinsing out her cup, Alison called up the stairs as the children went to brush their teeth. "Your transportation—that would be me—rolls out in ten minutes. Be there. Don't make me late my first day of work."

She brushed her hands down the length of her skirt. She'd chosen a soft denim twill skirt and a butter yellow crinkle top. It'd been years, after Claire's birth, since she'd worked part-time as a horticulturalist with a local nursery. She hoped her business and people skills weren't too rusty. Like her children, she was anxious about what the day would bring.

She ran up the stairs to finish her own morning preparations. In the bathroom mirror, her gold bangle earrings continued to sway from her forward momentum. She stared at herself in the glass and took a few deep breaths.

I'm so afraid, Father.

She closed her eyes and willed her heart to a steady beat.

I need you today more than ever. I pray for Claire and Justin as they face their own trials. And don't let me do anything stupid.

Taking one last look in the mirror, she whispered, "Courage."

She grabbed her keys, cell phone, and purse. "I'm leaving now," she threatened, calling down the hallway toward the direction of Claire and Justin's rooms. But when she came down the back stairs, Justin and Claire were waiting for her by the garage door.

She paused to pick up her Bible and stuffed it into her handbag. "Everything but the kitchen sink," she joked.

On a sudden impulse, she gave each of her children the bear hug she used to give them on the first day of elementary school. Neither pulled away.

"Seriously, Mom," whispered Claire into her ear. "Watch yourself today."

Alison nodded. "I will. I'll be praying for you both. I know it's not going to be easy, but it will get better."

Claire rolled her eyes. "Like when?"

Her daughter shouldered her backpack. "Don't worry about dinner. I'll handle it."

Tears welled in Alison's eyes, the culmination of a long night and aching head. "Thanks, honey."

If it wasn't God working on Claire, then she didn't know what would account for the attitude reversal in the previously rebellious, mouthy child Claire had been since adolescence.

She'd missed that sunny-natured, butterfly-kissing little girl with the auburn ringlets. But maybe, in God's timing, she and Claire could reconnect. She was discovering God was all about hope. And she needed a lot of that commodity, especially today.

Alison squared her shoulders. "Okay, guys. Let's do this."

Claire snagged the coveted front passenger seat. "For Daddy."

Justin scrambled into the backseat. "For Dad." Then he tuned them both out by putting in earbuds and turning on his iPod.

Alison glanced at him in the rearview mirror. Everybody, she reflected, had his or her own brand of Dutch courage.

16

WEATHERSBY HOUSE STOOD TALL AND PROUD ON A HIGH KNOLL ABOVE the parking area. Alison admired its white-columned Greek Revival splendor as she climbed the wide stone steps through the gap in the seven-foot yew hedge to the sandy graveled path.

She paused at the fork in the path at the cornerstone of the historic home. To the right of the fork lay the deep wood-planked porch with its overhanging second-story portico. The bright, brave rays of the sun poked defiantly through the green canopy of stately oaks and maples.

Alison followed the meandering path alongside the house, past colonies of pale pink evening primrose nestled next to the hand-mortared foundation stones from nearby Crabtree Creek.

"*Oenothera*," she whispered the Latin name, savoring the sound of it on her tongue. "Pink ladies."

Beyond the detached kitchen, a pleasing hint of wood smoke hung in the air. She rushed past the tempting vistas of the cutting garden and the mass of heirloom roses. No time today to stop and smell the roses, or anything else for that matter.

She kept her hands clamped to her sides lest she yield to temptation and touch the fuzzy lamb's ears in the curve of the path or stroke the velvety petals of the old-fashioned early-blooming Bourbons.

Their spicy fragrance accompanied her brisk strides, luring her with their siren call. But duty's strident voice hastened her on her way.

At the end of the path lay the overseer's office, not open to the public but renovated as a modern workplace for the director and her assistant. Mounting the front stoop, she pushed open the door and was immediately disappointed to find she wasn't the earliest bird at Weathersby after all.

Ivy Dandridge, in a trim Ann Taylor suit, sat perched on the edge of the assistant's desk waiting for her. Her black leather sling-back pumps dangled, swinging like a child's. Ivy smiled. Or bared her teeth.

Sometimes it was hard to tell the difference with Ivy.

Ivy jumped to her feet and rushed over, tugging Alison into the room. "At last! We have so much to accomplish today."

At last? She was forty-five minutes early.

Towering over the diminutive Ivy, she allowed herself to be propelled to her seat and pushed into it. Ivy swiveled the chair—and her—around to face the computer monitor.

Ridiculous, but she'd just been manhandled by, comparatively speaking, a five-foot midget. She counted to ten in her head, reining in her attitude.

Ivy was . . . forceful? Bossy? Or crazy? Take your pick.

Four assistants in a year? She gripped the chair arms. What had she gotten herself into?

Ivy inserted her scrawny chicken neck between Alison and the screen, tapping at the keys on the keyboard. Alison wrinkled her nose at the overpowering scent of Shalimar.

"There." Ivy announced with a flourish. "I assume you can do basic Word documents. We're not too techno-driven yet. We're all about the past here at Weathersby." She laughed, a shrill little sound, showing her teeth again.

Alison leaned as far back as she could, struggling to be charitable. Ivy, obviously, had no sense of personal space. Or as the boss, maybe she felt it was her right to invade Alison's at will.

Ivy opened a drawer and drew out a small recording device. "Letters. A dying art." She indicated the earbuds and demonstrated how to turn on the sound. "The correspondence with our sponsors." Ivy sighed dramatically. "The state and federal bureaucracies alone are a full-time job."

She whipped around so suddenly Alison jumped in her seat. Ivy thrust one earbud into Alison's right ear and hit the play button. A tinny Ivy rattled her eardrum. Alison threw a beseeching glance toward the ceiling. These people were nutcases.

God, help me.

Ivy bent her bright, red head close, as if suspecting a less than ardent devotee of Weathersby lurked in Alison's rebel heart. She fastened her horn-rimmed chartreuse reading glasses to the bridge of her nose and looked over them, inspecting Alison's reaction.

"I hope it's not too much. When my last assistant left so abruptly there was much left undone. You shouldn't have any trouble sorting through it."

Ivy glanced at her equally chartreuse wristwatch. "I think a good six hours will knock it out." She smiled.

Alison was beginning to hate that smile. As far as she could tell, never boding well for the recipient.

"I'll set aside time this afternoon to proof and sign the final copies." Ivy pumped her fist into the air, not unlike the football coach at Stonebriar High before a big game. "Are we ready?"

Alison smiled through gritted teeth. "Ready as I'll ever be."

Three hours later, Alison was three-quarters of the way through the dictation. Piles of laser-printed copy lay in neat stacks upon her desk.

She hit the save button and paused to roll her shoulders to release the tension. Ivy had been in and out all morning. Though for now, she'd decided to hover somewhere else.

More like torture someone else.

Whatever or whomever, Ivy had moved on to her next victim, and for that, Alison was profoundly grateful.

With a soft knock, Val poked her short brown curls around the door frame. "How's it going?"

She smiled. "I'm surviving, but just barely." She rose, scooting back her chair. "Ivy is a human dynamo. It's exhausting to watch her, much less to try to keep up with her."

Val pulled two white bags from behind her back. "Lunch is served."

She smoothed her skirt and followed Val outside. They'd arranged to meet for a quick on-site, first-day lunch.

Alison pointed up the path to the far left side of the house. "Let's sit on that bench overlooking the cutting garden."

Sitting down, she leaned against the old Osage orange tree— a *Maclura pomifera*—reputedly brought by a Virginian Weathersby family member back from the famous Lewis and Clark expedition. Large green balls as bright as Ivy's glasses littered the lawn at their feet.

Val spread out the deli sandwiches. "No Kona," she joked. "But I brought you the next best thing, a Pepsi Cola."

Alison sighed, heartfelt and guttural. "You are the best friend a girl could ever ask for. If ever I needed a jolt of caffeine, it would be now." She stroked the rough texture of the Osage bark.

"Here." Val thrust a sandwich at her. "If you can quit caressing the plant life, I have a turkey on wheat for you and a corned beef on rye for me. Unless . . ." Val smirked. "Unless you want to trade."

Alison grabbed the turkey. "You know I hate corned beef." She shuddered.

"Yeah, yeah. Ever since you threw up after eating one in the eighth grade. Or so you keep telling me." Val took a bite out of hers. "Yum, yum. You have no idea what you're missing." She laughed. "Except all the extra calories you, of all people, could afford."

Alison took a long, satisfying sip of the cola and smacked her lips. "I needed that. Ivy could work somebody to death."

"Any breaks in the 'case'?" Val asked around a mouthful of corned beef.

She could tell from Val's tone she was being gently mocked. "Not so far, Miss Smart Mouth, but Ivy's had me cooped up in the office all morning."

"At least it keeps you out of trouble."

She furrowed her brow. "Trouble? All I want to do is talk to the people Frank worked with at Weathersby."

"That's what I'm afraid of." Concern lined Val's face. "People tell you stuff they shouldn't or wouldn't tell anybody else."

She shrugged. "Exactly."

"But that's the problem. Then they regret revealing so much, and the fallout this time could be deadly."

Alison rounded her eyes. "I can't help it if I have one of those homely faces that inspire confidences."

"Homely?" Val wagged her finger. "If I ever hear you utter such an untruth again, if God doesn't strike you with lightning, I just might."

That mental image caused Alison to snort a small, unladylike stream of Pepsi up and out her nose onto the grass as Ivy marched by.

Ivy stopped to glare, her hands on her bony hips. "There's simply no time for lunch." One finger tapped at her watch. "I have learned instead to sublimate those appetites into the greater work to be done for our noble Cause." She made a chopping motion. "Return to your station."

And expecting resistance to be futile, She-Who-Must-Be-Obeyed sallied forth to the office.

"Is she for real?" Val raised her eyebrows. The corners of Val's mouth twitched. "Has she also been able to sublimate her urge to pee?"

Alison fought to control an adolescent desire to giggle. "Must be." She fluttered a hand. "She's sublimated the need to pee."

Val chortled. "You rhyme." She crunched down on a chip. "Remind me to ask Dr. Stephen if females can suffer from Napoleonic complexes, too."

"Mrs. Monaghan . . ." bellowed Ivy from the path. Alison dropped her chin in resignation.

"Good luck with that—that—," Val gestured toward Ivy's retreating figure. "Words fail me." She took a swig of her Mountain Dew.

Alison's lips quirked. "Well, that's a first."

Val shot a stream of yellow Dew out of her nose, and the both of them gave way to the giggles. Alison prayed Ivy was too far away to hear them.

Because Ivy did not—she'd decided about 10:30 this morning—have any sense of humor.

17

CUTTING HER WELL-DESERVED BREAK SHORT BY TEN MINUTES, ALISON BID Val farewell, promising to update her by phone that night. As she rounded the curve in the path, she caught sight of Ginny Walston, head staff docent, slipping into the office.

Loud, arguing voices arose immediately. Mostly, Ivy's.

Due to the open windows—another example of Ivy's cost-cutting measures, that is, no air-conditioning—she clearly discerned Ivy's half of the conversation. Ginny's quieter tones were less audible. Alison pressed her back against the exterior office wall. Maybe, at last, she could get to work on her real purpose for being at Weathersby.

"It's unacceptable, I tell you, Ginny," screeched Ivy. "The docents are talking about your slipshod management. We'll soon be the laughingstock of Raleigh."

She couldn't make out Ginny's soft-spoken murmur.

Ivy spoke at her usual high decibel level. "I've tried to be as patient and understanding as humanly possible after your tragedy."

There was a low-voiced rejoinder as slight as the breeze ruffling the curtains at the window.

Then Ivy. "But I cannot tolerate your inebriation any longer. You almost tumbled down the steps of the porch as you led a group of visitors to the gift shop today. You are officially on notice, Ginny

Walston. Despite our families' long-standing friendship, one more incident and I'll be forced to terminate your employment at Weathersby."

"But with Leo gone, I need this job, Ivy." This time, Ginny's wail of protest could be heard at least a block away.

A pause. Had Ivy smiled at this point?

"Be that as it may, consider yourself warned. And now . . ." There was a rustling and staccato-like footfalls.

Alison decided it would be prudent to disappear for a moment around the side of the building.

"I have important work to do at the House, and you need a pot of strong coffee, Ginny." Her boss burst through the door and hurtled up the path.

Alison waited until she was sure Ivy was gone for good on another of her crusades before stepping across the threshold. The sound of disconsolate sobbing floated through the open door of Ivy's adjoining office.

She shifted from one foot to another, not eager to intrude on a painful and embarrassing private moment. But she decided she'd better take advantage of every second she wasn't under Ivy's eagle eye. Squelching any personal feelings of distaste, she strode into the room more confidently than she felt. Huddling in the visitor's chair, Ginny's face was in her hands.

"Ginny?" she whispered, trying not to startle the woman.

Ginny lifted her head and stared at Alison. It took a moment for recognition to dawn.

"Oh, yes," she swallowed convulsively. Her pale, elegant-looking face hardened. "You're Frank Monaghan's widow."

Alison flinched. No one had called her that until now. But, she supposed, that's what she was. She remembered the front-page account in the *News and Observer* of Ginny's husband's death before Frank's murder. Of a self-inflicted gunshot wound last summer.

"Yes." She licked her lips. How to begin? "I'm Alison Monaghan."

Ginny folded her hands in her lap. "I know who you are. I've seen you working in the garden every week with Polly Grimes for several years."

With her stylishly coiffed ginger-colored hair and patrician face, Ginny was well respected and well liked at Weathersby, a volunteer until she'd come on staff shortly after Dr. Walston's suicide. Tears lingered like dew on a lily's petals, but she sat ramrod straight with her feet regally crossed at the ankles.

Ginny tilted her head. "No doubt you overheard."

She ignored that remark for courtesy's sake. "Did you know my husband, Ginny?"

Ginny clenched her hands together, but she answered in the same languid tone as before. "Unfortunately, I did."

Alison stiffened, smelling the liquor on Ginny. This wasn't the Ginny she remembered from docent teas and garden club. Had she and Frank become drinking buddies?

Ginny stood and scrubbed the tears from her cheeks. "He was a bully. Overbearing. One of the most conceited men I've ever had the misfortune to meet."

Alison retreated a step.

Ginny scowled. "And he unfailingly propositioned me at least twice a month." She glared at Alison, unblinking. "I thought you should hear it from me first. I turned him down each and every time, several times publicly. I believe I was, what your husband would term, a challenge."

Alison's mouth tightened. "And was this before or after you became a widow, Mrs. Walston?" As soon as the words were out of her mouth, she would've done anything to call them back.

A spasm of something crossed Ginny's face. "It's nice to know the media," she said the word like one said *vomit*, "have a new target to pursue."

Ginny tossed her head. "But good for you, Alison Monaghan. There's hope for you yet. Maybe you won't turn to booze, like I have. I would've taken you for a mouse. But you can roar, I see."

She brushed past Alison to the outer office and stopped beside Alison's desk. "A year and a half ago, Frank caught me at a weak moment. Leo had been out of town for a couple of days at a conference. We'd argued ferociously before he left."

Alison's eyebrows arched.

Ginny sighed. "I wanted him to retire. I was lonely. His passion, I believed, had always been his patients. I was a distant third, or so I'd convinced myself. I blame myself for the argument. I was trying to force him to choose, trying to cause a showdown between his work and me. After the board meeting that week Leo was gone, Frank asked me out for a drink. I went."

Clamping her lips together, Alison grabbed hold of her chair.

Ginny's shoulders slumped. "We had one drink, and I realized what a fool I was being. I got into my car and drove as far away from Raleigh as I could go on a half tank of gas. When I came to myself, I was somewhere between Burlington and High Point. I spent the night at a Motel Six." Ginny leaned over the desk. "But nothing happened between Frank and me. That night or ever."

"Not for any failure to try on Frank's part," Alison whispered.

Ginny glanced toward the window. "Leo picked that night to try to call me to apologize. Of course, I wasn't there. All night he called without success. When he got home the next day, I told him a lie, that I'd been called away to a seminar for Weathersby. He, trusting man, believed me, and he promised to resign and wrap up his practice in the next six months. I'd won, you see."

She laughed, but the sound echoed with despair. "I'd won, all right. Two weeks later, on the night I was facilitating new docent training, someone paid Leo a visit at our home. The police were unable to identify fingerprints. He left a note on his computer explaining what this evil person had revealed about my alleged affair with an unnamed someone. He drew out his shotgun from the display case behind his desk, put the gun to his mouth, and pulled the trigger."

Ginny shivered and wrapped her arms around herself. "It had to have been Frank. I'd rejected him, and in his conceit, he couldn't let me get away with that."

Alison's fingers clutched the chair. "But you don't know that for sure."

Ginny sniffed. "I know everything I need to know about the monster that destroyed my life. Don't worry, though, there's plenty of blame to go around."

What did that mean?

Ginny cast her gaze to the floor. "Why do you think I drink? I'm not as brave as Leo. I'm a coward. Maybe I deserve to go on suffering."

She couldn't believe Frank had been responsible for Leo Walston's suicide. Frank was all about the easy conquest. This wasn't his style.

Alison jutted her jaw. "Leo should've trusted you and not jumped to conclusions without hearing your side of the story."

Ginny shook her head. "Don't try to absolve me. I'll end my purgatory someday, the only way I know how."

The door ajar, Alison observed Ginny's mournful figure wend her way to the main house. A shadow flickered at the corner where she'd eavesdropped earlier.

Drawing a quick breath, Alison stumbled to the porch. She caught a flashing glimpse of dark clothing rounding the corner to the back of the office and the safety of the woods beyond.

Goose bumps broke out on her arms. She hugged herself, cold despite the growing midday humidity. Someone was watching her. A feeling of exposure and vulnerability swept over her.

She hadn't realized until now her new working environment was so remotely located. It backed up to the dense, tangled undergrowth that led to the same dead-end road where Frank had met his death on Orchard Farm Road.

18

IT HAD BEEN AS AWFUL AS CLAIRE HAD FEARED. SHE WALKED INTO THE building with her head held high, past clumps of students, groups she normally would've been included in BWWC.

Before the world went crazy.

Today, there were whispers and quick looks in her direction and glances that darted away. Snickers and smiles half-hidden behind hands. She was used to being one of the whisperers.

Now, she was on the outside. Friendless. Alone.

By virtue of the rigid caste system that ruled high schools, she'd always been one of the golden ones. An arbiter of all that was cool and fashionable. But today, she'd receive the subtle cruelties of which she had once been the chief inflictor.

Giggling, Heather and Zoe Lawrence arched their bodies away from her in the hallway as if she had a disease. She opened her locker to find a crude drawing of a dead man in a car with his head blown off. Smashing it into a ball, she crammed the paper deep inside her backpack.

Reaching the comparative safety of first-period honors English, she prayed for the teacher to start class and kept her head buried in her textbook throughout the next ninety minutes.

Prayed? Claire Monaghan?

What a joke.

As if that could make a difference.

But by third period, she was ready to try anything. Whatever works, she figured, though she wasn't sure if the prayer thing worked that way or not.

And so went the day until lunch. Dreading lunch with its virtually unsupervised arena of peer torture, she hid in the back of the line with the hope of getting lost by intermingling with the freshmen.

Carrying her tray, she assessed the scene as a soldier might survey a field of land mines. Getting through the day was all she could hope for at this point.

"Where have you been keeping yourself, Claire?" Ellen, head cheerleader in her too-tight skirt, grabbed one of her arms, and Kaitlyn, tenth-grade homecoming court representative, grabbed the other. "You must join us and tell us every luscious detail about your family."

They dragged her across the cafeteria to a table loaded with jocks and their janes. A table she would've picked out herself and been welcomed to BWWC. Her cheeks flaming, she tried to halt their progress by planting her feet with the sheer force of inertia. But Ellen and Kaitlyn proved an irresistible force.

Out of the corner of her eye, she watched Justin rise from his own circle of lowly freshmen friends, victims of social apartheid. He'd never reach her in time though, and she surrendered to her fate. It was payback.

Payback in the biggest and most humiliating way.

Ellen smirked. "Like a soap opera, isn't it, Kaitlyn?"

"If you're into trailer trash, I suppose." Kaitlyn's sycophantic laugh grated against Claire's nerve endings.

She squirmed, trying to loosen their hold on her arms. But both girls put their backs into it, lugging her across the floor.

Sandy Fleming, appearing out of nowhere, stumbled into Kaitlyn, knocking them both off balance. Green Jell-O flew off Sandy's tray to land in a squiggly jumble all over Ellen's fuchsia pedicure.

"Oooh," Ellen wailed. "My sandals."

Sandy threw both hands to her face, dropping the now-empty tray on Kaitlyn's similarly vulnerable feet.

"You imbecilic moron." Kaitlyn hopped up and down, bunny-like, rubbing and massaging each throbbing foot, first one, then the other. Bent over double, she lost her balance and stumbled face first into the moss-green muck at Ellen's feet.

"Get off me." Ellen gestured to Tad Ewell, who was gawking with the rest of the jocks and janes. "Tad! Get some napkins and help me."

He rose but started to laugh. Soon the rest of the table were laughing themselves silly.

"Stop laughing at me!" screamed Ellen. A crowd formed. The kind of crowd that bands together to watch school-yard fights or that rubbernecks at traffic accidents on the Beltline.

The kind of crowd that enjoys public executions.

"Quick." Sandy grabbed Claire, stunned into paralysis by the unfolding drama. "Now's our chance." She jerked Claire out of the melee as two teachers rushed to investigate the commotion.

Sandy brought her over to her own table, occupied by three other girls she recognized from the Redeemer youth group. With an anxious look, Justin returned to his guy friends.

Claire sank onto the bench. "What did you do?" She loosened her death grip on the lunch tray. It landed with a clang on the Formica-topped table.

Sandy shrugged. "No big deal. Can someone share their lunch with me?"

"What did you bring *her* over here for?" Three pairs of hostile glares pointed in her direction, laserlike.

Claire gulped. No safe harbor here. "Have my lunch, Sandy. You deserve it." She slid the tray over to her. "Way beyond the call of duty."

A girl Claire vaguely remembered from English jabbed a fork in Claire's direction. "Duty? Like Sandy or anybody else owes *you* anything."

She hadn't been aware before now that girl could speak. Was her name Ethel? Or Wanda?

Maybe Phyllis? It didn't matter, did it? She was one of those brainy, boring girls.

She sighed. How low had she fallen? God help her, she was sitting with the geeky girls.

Was this her life post-BWWC.?

Sandy stuffed a French fry into her mouth. "That's enough, Anna."

Claire pursed her lips. Okay, so her name was Anna. Big whoop.

Sandy twirled another fry between her thumb and forefinger. "I did what I thought was right. Has nothing to do with you guys."

"Nothing to do with us?" Another girl weighed in, staring daggers at Claire.

She glared back. Weighed in was right. Somebody should put that one on a diet. Ever hear the word *exercise*? How about *self-control*?

Hefty, Claire dubbed her, shifted her bulk on the bench.

The table moved.

"You put a target on each of our backs. Like we need more grief from that crowd."

Sandy fiddled with the burger. "Lily . . ."

Lily? Claire's brows arched. Interesting. Definitely not typecasting.

"I mean it, Sandy." Lily poked a chubby finger at Claire. "She's as arrogant and obnoxious as they are. She deserves everything they dish out and more."

Claire scrambled to her feet. She hadn't realized there were people out there who hated her this much. Had her dad realized that, too, in that last split second?

"It's not about deserving, Lily." Sandy angled toward the other girl. "I got this crazy idea. You know I can't stand to see anything suffer, a bug or an animal. Much less a person God created in His own image."

Sandy held up her hand before they could voice any protests. "I'm not trying to get preachy like my dad. But right is right." She rose to stand beside Claire. "Wrong can't be tolerated. Somebody has to take a stand or we become like them and her."

Claire winced.

She shot Claire an apologetic look. "We'll go. I don't want to force anyone to fight my battles."

"Wait, Sandy." Her slanted black eyes huge in her wire-rimmed glasses, the hitherto silent third girl placed a restraining hand on Sandy's arm.

Claire was beyond guessing names at this point.

The girl squeezed Sandy's hand. "I just wish I had half your courage." She stuck out her hand to Claire.

It hung there in the air for a second. Then Claire had the good sense to take it.

"My name is Julie. We're in—"

"clothing apparel and design together," Claire finished for her. Thank God, she'd remembered that.

Anna stood next. "Anna." She didn't offer her hand. "You're right, Sandy. It's what Jesus would've wanted you to do."

Claire's brows rose almost to her hairline.

Wow, there were people who took that stuff seriously? Not just on Sunday?

Lily moved awkwardly to her feet. "Grace. Isn't that what your father talked about a few weeks ago? How none of us deserve anything but death. Yet God . . ." Tears peppered her eyes.

For the first time, it occurred to Claire that other people in the world carried wounds, too.

Julie laughed, her cheeks lifting and her eyes turning into half-moons. "I wish I had Sandy's imagination. Did you see the look on homecoming queen's face?"

19

Take that, Ivy!" Alison piled the last of the correspondence on Ivy's neatnik desk. Looking to her left and right to make sure she was unobserved, she searched the long middle drawer.

Her fingers fumbled through paper clips and sticky notes. She moved on to the side drawers. Office supplies. Nothing personal or revealing. She gazed about the director's private office. No photos of children. Ivy and Henry married late in life after the death of his first spouse. No photos of Henry, either.

Plaques covered the walls. Awards and achievements in the field of historic preservation dotted the surface of the side table. A lovely watercolor of Weathersby House, perhaps an artist's rendition of its past glory, hung proudly over a four-drawer filing cabinet.

Aha!

She knelt, grasping the handle of the bottom drawer.

"What, may I ask, are you doing in my office, Alison?"

She jumped, jamming her thumb in the process. Standing so quickly she saw stars, she spun around to face Ivy. "Dropped a paper clip." Panting as if she'd run the Raleigh Marathon, Alison removed a paper clip from the pocket of her denim skirt and held it to Ivy's face, inches from her own.

Willing her nerves to steady and feigning a nonchalance she didn't feel, she forced herself to move past Ivy. She clipped an envelope to its corresponding letter. "There. All ready for you to inspect and sign."

Ivy peered at the stack, bearing page after page of the Weathersby letterhead. "All of it?" She examined the first copy. "Well, I must say I'm pleased at your efficiency." A genuine smile of relief on her face, Ivy waved Alison out of her office. "Let me read over these, so we can get them out with the afternoon mail."

She beat a quick retreat, closing the adjoining door. Exhaling, she leaned her forehead against the wood-grained panel. Too close. She must be more vigilant if she was going to make a habit of snooping. She'd come back later and search the file cabinet.

Alison bit the inside of her cheek. She must also remember to thank Val's son, Trey, for teaching her that sleight of hand trick when he was in his magician phase a few years ago.

The stack should keep Ivy occupied for a while. Time for her own toilet break. She, unlike her illustrious boss, had not learned to sublimate that particular urge.

Her lips twitching, she started for the main house. True to its historical nature, the overseer's office had not contained washroom facilities. And wanting the house to remain historically accurate, Ivy had seen to it that it still did not.

She trotted up the path. "Maybe that's why she makes so many trips to the Big House?" She was all for historical accuracy, but please . . .

Alison dashed up the back steps of the "new" addition, circa 1940, giving a quick wave to Erica Chambers, the educational director and Jill-of-all-trades at Weathersby. On the phone in what served as the reception area/ticket office, Erica engaged in a heated verbal battle with someone on the other end of the line.

On her way out of the tiny bathroom provided for the docents' use, she snagged a "Help yourself" oatmeal cookie from the center of the conference table. This area served as the headquarters for board meetings. She didn't know how she was going to work it, but she intended to be in attendance tomorrow night for one of the all-important board meetings color-coded on Frank's appointment calendar.

Erica, a wiry strawberry blonde, came out of the ticket office. "Alison, just the person I needed to see. I just got off the phone with Ivy."

Uh-oh. Alison bit into the cookie. Here comes trouble.

"Natalie Singleton, who's supposed to be chairing our spring costume ball fundraiser, cancelled on me. Again." Erica muttered something unpleasant about parts of Natalie's lineage. "Ivy insists I set up the display mannequins tomorrow so the board can get a preview of the fashion exhibit that opens the ball on Saturday."

Alison chewed. Wait for it . . .

Erica planted her hands on her hips. "Like that has to be done tomorrow with all I've got to do to get ready for the Open House this weekend. Not to mention the six school groups traipsing through here the end of this week with their grubby little hands."

Alison swallowed. Hard.

Erica cocked her head and smiled. "Ivy said you were caught up with the paperwork and could help me tomorrow."

Okay. "What do you want me to do?"

"First thing, we have to get the mannequins we're borrowing from the history museum. I'll pick them up on my way to work. Then, we need to unpack the garments from their archival storage in the attic and dress the mannequins in their period clothing. I have the layout on my computer."

Alison frowned. "I don't know anything about handling such fragile items."

Erica dismissed her concerns. "No worries. I'll do the major stuff. I just need an extra pair of hands."

She nodded. "Sure. I get here about nine."

"Great. It'll be fun. Like playing dress up."

Except, she grimaced, some of the garments were museum quality and priceless in their own way.

"Ivy must have a lot on her mind to let me do this."

"What do you mean, Erica?"

Erica laughed. "Usually for special exhibits, she allows no one to touch the family heirlooms except for her." She leaned against the door frame, sticking one hand in her back jean pocket. "You'd never know I graduated last year with a degree in textile preservation. To Ivy, I'm just a kid, too inexperienced to handle the sacred Weathersby treasures."

Out on the porch, Alison bent to stroke the resident feline, Miss Patty, a Siamese. Around the back corner of the house, a stooped, elderly black woman huffed up the path, waving her broom like a jousting knight, fighting mad.

She stalked past Alison.

"Miss Lula?"

Lula Burke swung full circle. A scowl contorted her ebony features, as lined and creased as one of Alison's gardening gloves. She leaned the broom against the porch railing and rubbed her arthritic elbow. "Gots to remember my age. But that woman does beat all."

Miss Patty entwined around Alison's ankles.

"That cat's a good judge of character. Forgive me, for ignoring you, Alison. I just got so worked up. That creature, and I'm not referring to Miss Patty, will be the death of me yet."

Alison disengaged herself from Miss Patty, careful not to trip down the steps. "I wanted to thank you for your sympathy card last October."

"Humph," Lula grunted. "I lost my man forty years ago this week."

"You couldn't have been more than a girl yourself."

A brief smile flickered on Lula's face, revealing the smooth, even facade of new dentures. "I reckon I wasn't much more than that. We married young in those days. Nothing else to do. Not like today."

Lula lifted her chin. "My two grandbabies—one in law school at North Carolina Central and the other graduating as valedictorian from high school this year." She sighed. "But I do remember what it's like to be left alone to raise young'uns. I don't envy you that task in this hard world."

She touched Lula's arm. "You're an inspiration."

Lula patted her hand. "You were always one of the kind ones, a real lady. Not like some"—she dropped Alison's hand and gestured down the path toward the office—"who think they is somebody and treat those they consider beneath them like dirt." She kicked the gravel to underscore her point.

"And I'm not just talking about Herself." Lula clenched and unclenched her fists. "Telling me to get a move on and clean up that, and I quote"—Lula's deep contralto, pitched itself an octave higher, in a near-perfect imitation of Ivy at her prissiest—"that pigsty of a conference room you were told to clean last week."

She knew better than to laugh.

"Humph." Lula grunted again. "I'd like to clean her clock. Told to clean, my . . ." She glanced at Alison. "Makes me forget I'm a Christian woman sometimes." She wagged a finger. "Somebody on the board complained, Herself said. Like I said before, some people think they is somebody and the rest of us are just trash to do their bidding."

She'd always been amazed at how immaculate the seventy-year-old Miss Lula kept the historic structure.

Lula placed her hands on her still-ample hips. "Told me I better mind my p's and q's or she'd have to let me go. Like she was Miss Ursula Weathersby resurrected." She tossed her tight gray curls. "She can't fire me. Said in the will old lady Weathersby left when she transferred the deed of land and the house over to the city, I was to have a job as long as I wanted it."

She bent on creaking arthritic knees to stroke the cat sitting between their feet. "And Miss Patty was to have her home here for as long as she lived. Isn't that right, Miss? Just two old girls left, you and me." Miss Patty gave a low, contented purr as Miss Lula ran her fingers through Miss Patty's sable-colored coat.

"It was good of Miss Weathersby to look out for you."

Lula straightened, adjusting her housedress, careful to look Alison right in the eye. She wasn't smiling. "Nothing good about it. It's payback for keeping the family secrets all them years."

Alison stared. "What secrets?"

Lula smiled sphinxlike. "You're hoping to find out who killed your man, aren't you?"

Alison's lips parted. "How did—?"

Lula laughed. "Don't look so worried. You're not obvious to anybody but me. 'Cause that's what I would've done in your place." The old woman's gaze drifted to the gardens and orchards in the distance. "The secrets I could tell . . . Don't matter anymore. The living that cared is all dead now, except for me."

She crossed her arms over her ample bosom. "There's a lot of blood covering this Weathersby ground. But I warn you," Lula retrieved her broom. "Be careful. Like me, you got young'uns at home to raise. What's done is done. And some things are best left alone." She commenced to sweep the steps as if personally trying to scour out the wickedness, past and present.

Alison sidestepped the flying debris. "You think someone connected to this place murdered my husband, Frank?"

Lula shuffled her feet. "I don't rightly know who, but after the po-lice questioned everybody, I got to thinking about that night. I was working late, doing the cleanup that lazy hound of a caretaker, Jasper, failed to do after the Harvest Festival." She shuddered. "I ax you, whose bright idea that was to let loose three hundred rip-roaring young'uns to do a scavenger hunt all over the property? Candy wrappers everywhere."

"And what exactly did you see?" Alison prompted, knowing Miss Lula's penchant for getting off topic.

"It was plumb like a parade the folks caterwauling through here and none of them up to any good or any better than they ought to be, including your Frank." Lula stopped. "I shouldn't have said that to you, I reckon, but it was the truth."

How much of the truth did she want to know? Was Miss Lula right? Were there things best left uncovered?

But steely determination stiffened her spine. Her children's future depended on putting Frank's murder to rest. "I'm under no illusions as to what Frank was like, Lula. It's okay. I faced it long ago. Tell me, if you can, who was out here that night."

Lula leaned on the broom, the handle tickling her second chin. "Your Frank was out here a lot, especially those last few weeks. Early in the morning or late in the evening. He had keys as all the board members do. He wasn't his usual self. Cocky, I mean. He actually spoke to me that last night."

Her breath caught. "You mean he was here in the house before going to Orchard Farm Road?"

"Not at first." Lula shook her head. "He was coming out of your office." She waved the broom away. "He followed me into the house."

She twisted her fingers in the folds of her skirt. "What was he doing in there?"

Lula harrumphed. "Not my place to question Mr. High and Mighty Airplane Pilot. I've survived and sent three children to college 'cause I know when to keep my mouth shut. I went upstairs to dust. He stayed downstairs. I looked out the upstairs window later and saw that high-heeled hussy, Natalie Singleton, wheeling out of the parking lot. I can't say for sure when your man left the premises."

"Who else, Miss Lula? Please."

"Best I can recollect, 'cause despite rumors to the contrary," she hissed with a glance down the path. "I do have work to do."

Alison leaned forward. "Who?"

"Linda Lawrence slunk by here like the alley cat she is, not to mention Jasper was around here somewhere up to no good as usual. And Ivy was here, there, and everywhere like she always is."

"Ginny Walston?"

Lula sighed. "Now I feel like a tattletale. Yes, she was closing the house and setting the alarms. Winnie was in the gift shop, tallying the day's receipts, and Little Miss College was right here on these steps, yakking into her cell phone."

Alison frowned. "Gracious, was the whole city here that evening?"

Lula chuckled. "Just about, Alison. Just about."

20

Claire stuck close to her new friends—make those protectors—for the rest of the school day. One of the girls would save a seat for her at the front of the class.

She sighed, martyrlike. Such suck-ups.

Though they obviously didn't trust her any farther than they could throw her—except for maybe Lily who could throw her, that is—they stood by her and escorted her on a sort of rotating sentry duty through the congested hallways to class.

Figuring there was something to be said for safety in numbers and liking them no better than they liked her, she nevertheless accepted their physical support. Surrounded by the geeks, her usual crowd left her alone, avoiding her as if she had the plague. No one, least of all her, wanted to be seen associating with this group. Not unless she had to.

But beggars couldn't afford to be choosy.

Claire fought tears off and on all day. Who knew you could be so lonely in a crowded high-school chemistry lab?

At last, the three o'clock dismissal bell rang and surging masses of teens hurtled through the doors to buses, the parking lot reserved for juniors and seniors, or to begin the walk home.

As soon as her feet hit the bottom step, her current guardian, Anna, slipped away without a word. Claire stood motionless like one lone salmon attempting to stop the headlong swim upstream.

"Claire."

She pivoted to see Justin waiting for her at the corner. He waved her over. She all but ran to him.

Breathless, she fell into step beside him. "I hope your day was better than mine."

Justin adjusted the strap of his book bag to a more comfortable setting on his shoulder. "Good to see you've still got your sense of humor."

"Barely."

"My day was okay. My friends had a few questions but . . ." He shrugged. "It'll be better tomorrow."

She panted with the effort to keep pace with Justin's long strides. He'd soon be taller than Dad. Her mouth drooped. Than Dad had been. "Maybe for you."

Justin rounded the corner toward home. "I see you made some new friends."

Claire rolled her eyes. "Yeah, right. That's me, Miss Congeniality, and my so-called bosom buddies."

Justin stopped mid-sidewalk. "Don't make any more ene-mies, Claire. I know those girls' brothers. They're good people."

"If you say so, brother dearest."

"Claire, listen to me, please—"

At the sound of honking and yelling, they wheeled around. A black BMW, creeping over the curb, headed straight for them. Zoe Lawrence, a junior, drove. Hanging out of every window were at least two jocks and janes. In the backseat, Heather Lawrence leaned out the window over the roof of the car anchored in place by Tad Ewell.

Claire tapped her foot in sudden fury against the pavement. How high some had risen upon the occasion of her social demise. Tad had been her date at the February Sweetheart Dance, much to Heather's chagrin.

The car pulled alongside her and Justin. "Claire. Wait up! Want a ride home?" Tad hollered.

Justin tugged at her arm. "Let's go."

"Look at me! Look at me!" Heather cocked two fingers to her temple and pretended to pull the trigger. "Bang! Bang! I'm dead! Just like your old man!" Her former BFF threw herself onto the top of the car with a thud. Shrieks of laughter erupted from inside the vehicle.

"Come on." Justin positioned himself between her and the car. Grabbing her elbow, he hurried her down the street only to be followed as relentlessly as death by the BMW.

"My turn! My turn! Let me be the dead guy," Tad hooted.

She felt a choking sensation as her chest tightened and the contents of her stomach rose.

"Don't you dare let them see you cry," Justin hissed in her ear. He hustled her past the neighbor's house. Her baby in her arms, Mrs. Lambert stepped onto the porch as music blared from the radio of the BMW.

Catching sight of an adult, Zoe floored the gas pedal, almost dislodging her passengers clinging for dear life to the sides of the car. With a squeal of her tires, she rounded the corner out of sight and earshot at last.

The tears, hot and wet, cascaded down Claire's cheeks. She kept her head tucked into her chest and allowed Justin to pull her into their driveway to the safety of the porch.

His hands shaking, he dropped the house key on the step where it bounced into the grass. Leaving her sobbing by the door, he scrambled on his hands and knees to find it. "It's going to get better, Claire, I promise."

But she knew he had no power to make it so. Because this was her new life after the world went crazy.

21

At five o'clock, after a fruitless wait for Ivy to leave the office first, Alison surrendered and went home.

Pulling into her garage, she noticed Mike's truck roll in beside the curb. He thrust open the door amidst much dinging and swung his long, blue-jean clad legs over the side.

She glared at him through the open garage door. "Are you following me again?"

"Yes ma'am, I am. Spill your guts. What did you learn from your highbrow friends today?"

Her shoulders slumped. "Not as much as I wanted to. That Ivy's a slave driver. But come in and I'll fill you in on what I do know." She stepped out of her flats as soon as she entered the kitchen and pushed her feet into a pair of tie-dyed flip-flops.

Claire had dinner on the table when she dropped, exhausted, into her chair. Justin looked up in surprise when Mike followed her through the kitchen.

"Oh." Mike stepped back. "I forgot normal people eat dinner at this hour." He backpedaled. "Just call me later, Alison."

Claire was already laying out another place setting. "There's plenty. Sit down, Mike. You have to keep up your strength if you're going to catch my dad's killer."

Mike raised both hands, palm up. "No, I couldn't intrude." His Adam's apple bobbed up and down in his throat. A flush of red crept up the back of his shirt collar.

Alison had never seen Mike so flustered.

Getting out of her chair, she grabbed hold of his shirtsleeve. "Sit down and eat. I can tell you're hungry." And she inhaled the fragrance that was part pine-tree outdoors, part sweat, and part Mike.

Today—okay, any day with Mike Barefoot in it—was turning out to be not so bad a day. She gave him a timid smile. "Please stay and eat with us."

Claire and Justin added their pleas for him to stay. "New recipe . . ." Claire coaxed.

Alison locked eyes with Mike. The stark longing she found there took her breath. She sank into her chair. "Stay . . ." she whispered.

His eyes never leaving her face, he seated himself in the chair across from her. "Problem with stray cats is if you keep feeding them, Alison, they'll never leave."

Alison's heart hammered. She put a hand to her throat.

"Tea or water?" From the kitchen, Justin clinked ice cubes out of the dispenser and into a glass.

Mike broke eye contact and shifted his gaze to Justin. "Is it sweet?"

Justin laughed. "My mom's parents were from Down East. Is there any other way to make it?"

Mike nodded. "Same way we make it in the mountains. Tea, it is then."

His nose twitched, reminding her of the pet rabbit Justin had as a child. "Smells good." He looked at Claire, caution on his face. "What is it?"

She made a face. "Don't worry. I'm not going to poison you. It's shepherd's pie. With a twist."

He poked out his lips. "It's the twist that worries me."

Justin clapped him on the back as he made his way around to his own place. "Don't worry. The twist is something she picked up last week from that Italian lady cook on TV. Makes it look sophisticated, that's all."

Alison waited until she had everyone's attention and bowed her head. She murmured a quick and sincere prayer of thanks for the food and the hands that prepared it. She knew better than to test her children or Mike with a longer one.

Anything other than short and sweet would've resulted in mutiny as Justin and Mike had their forks poised in midair over their plates. The sight of the four of them around her kitchen table warmed a deep place in her soul. Her breath hitched.

When had Mike Barefoot become essential to her well-being?

Mike took a small, cautious bite. At the look of surprised delight on his face, Claire clapped her hands.

"You've got a way with the grub, Claire girl." He sighed and rolled the next bite around in his mouth, savoring the peppery stew.

Alison smiled across the table at him. "She's a much better cook than I am. One of the many things my mother failed to teach me. Frank was good enough to teach me everything his mother had taught him or we would've starved those first few years."

She gripped her napkin in the sudden realization Mike was seated in Frank's customary spot. The Sunday lunch crowd usually sat in the dining room. She darted a quick look at her children to see if they'd noticed. But as Justin began spinning a whopper size of a golf tale on Mike, she saw only open pleasure on their faces at his company.

He was a bit rough around the edges, but a nice man to listen to their adolescent prattle. No—she could see it on his face—he loved them. She blinked back tears and took a quick sip of her tea to hide her emotion.

Claire scraped back her chair and opened the freezer, retrieving an ice cream extravaganza fit for a king. Curls of chocolate artfully graced the three-layer creation.

Her eyes widened. Mike and Justin salivated. "Claire, when did you have time to make this?" Suspicion laced her voice. "Did you do your homework?"

Claire rolled her eyes. "Mother, please stop being such a M-O-T-H-E-R." She punctuated each letter, in case Alison missed her meaning. Claire cut a tremendous, Southern-sized helping for Mike.

Throwing back his head, he groaned in sheer pleasure. "Girl, if you were twenty-six, instead of fifteen? Lord, have mercy. I'm going to start showing up here for dinner every night." His face flushed. "I mean . . ."

He'd slipped into his native Blue Ridge burr unlike his usual clipped, professional cop voice. She'd noticed it months ago the first time he said her name—Alison. She took another sip of tea. Mike kept his eyes averted as he stabbed his fork into his dessert.

"I'm doing the dishes, Mom." Justin all but licked his plate clean of the last puddles of ice cream. "You and Mike go talk."

Claire gave her an audacious wink. Alison sighed, but a smile leaked from the corners of her mouth.

Her children—a couple of matchmakers.

Mike swiped a finger across his plate. Elbow on the table, her chin on her hand, she flashed Mike a smile.

Caught in the act with his finger halfway to his mouth, he gulped. She was pleased to note the tips of his ears burned. She stood to gather the dishes.

He scrambled to his feet to help her round up the remaining silverware. "How was school today, kids?"

A smile tugged at her lips. Raised right by someone. She would've loved to have met that granny he talked so much about.

Claire and Justin exchanged glances.

"Fine." Claire avoided her eye by taking the last of the plates and shooing her mother out of the kitchen. Claire's fist clenched the side of her chef apron.

Alison drew her brows together. Something was up with those two. She'd question them later.

Mike cut his eyes over to her. "I feel bad leaving you guys to clean this up."

Like her, she reasoned, he probably wondered why they were so eager to get rid of them. A little more than matchmaking maybe?

Justin gave them a gentle shove. "Go."

Sinking into the recliner, Mike listened closely as Alison filled him in on the discoveries of her day concerning her chat with Lula and on Ginny's accusations.

He wrote copious notes in his notepad. "I'll check out Ginny Walston and her husband's suicide."

And, discover what was going on with those kids.

She lowered her voice to a whisper with one eye cocked in the direction of the kitchen. "I don't for one minute believe Frank was responsible for what happened to Ginny's husband." She dropped her eyes to her skirt. "I won't believe even then Frank was capable of such cruelty."

He remained silent. The jury was still out on the spiritual reformation of said Frank Monaghan. In his professional experience, leopards never changed their spots, much less became new creatures, but more often than not became more unbalanced and malicious.

"I know how to prove it." She jumped up and rescued her handbag from the sofa where she'd tossed it before dinner. "I have the copies of Frank's flight schedule you found in his car."

She kept that stuff with her after all these months?

He clenched the pen in his fist. Some guys had all the luck with love and devotion. Devotion to which Frank Monaghan had proven totally unworthy. An image of Calvary's cross on the wall of Redeemer flitted across his mind. He swiped his hand across the top of his head.

Okay, a devotion and love he'd up to now proved unworthy of, too.

Alison flipped through the pages. "It was last August as best I can remember. Look." She shoved the laser-print copy at him. "That week, Frank was out of town Monday through Saturday on one of his rare international flights to Japan." She gave him a dazzling smile that made it hard for him to breathe. "I knew it couldn't be Frank."

Mike forced himself to focus. "But still a motive for murder if Ginny Walston believed it *was* Frank who had driven her husband to suicide." He scribbled a note. "Time to interview the illustrious Widow Walston more thoroughly this time."

"You've already interviewed her?"

"All the staff at Weathersby has been interviewed by me at least once. Mrs. Walston was also on the premises the day someone took a shot at you."

She knotted her fingers together. "And the result of that ballistics test?"

Consumed by her children's grief and their overwhelming debt, she'd never asked him before. And if he'd been smarter and solved her husband's murder by now, she'd never have felt the need to take this job. She and the children could've moved on.

Maybe he and Alison could've even . . . What? Acknowledge the possibility of a future together? Just once, he'd like to take her out to get ice cream. She looked like a cone kind of girl to him. Not the cup sort at all.

Wondering if she'd order vanilla or something more exotic, he smiled over the top of his notebook. "My, my. Don't we sound professional? Been watching *CSI* again?"

She arched an eyebrow at him. "And what if I have?"

"For your information, it was the same weapon used in Frank's murder. At the range from which you were fired on, aim is inaccurate and imprecise. More likely meant as a warning. And no, before you ask," he stuffed the notepad into his pocket. "We never located the gun."

His cell phone shrilled. "Barefoot here," he barked into the mouthpiece. He cocked his head sideways and sighed. "Be there. ETA ten minutes or less." He flipped the cover shut and closed his phone. "Gotta go. Hooker shot and killed by her pimp for refusing to give up the cash." He flushed, realizing what he'd said.

She walked him to the front door. "I'm not that delicate. I've heard of hookers and pimps before."

Leaning against the door frame, he grinned over the threshold at her. "Betcha haven't met any, though."

"No, but I do watch a lot of *CSI*."

22

Alison set off the next morning determined to get into Ivy's file cabinet before Herself could arrive. But she was seduced by the Heavenly Blue morning glories entwined along the white picket fence of the kitchen garden, their glorious faces lifted to the sky.

"Makes you want to cry for the sheer beauty of it, doesn't it?" Polly Grimes rested her flannel-clad arms along the top of the gate, her enormous man-size gardening gloves dangling over the side. The knees of her overalls were encrusted with dirt, the pant legs tucked into her Wellingtons.

Alison smiled at her elderly gardening mentor. What Polly didn't know about plants wasn't worth knowing. Utilizing the original garden designs housed in the Southern Historical Collection at the University of North Carolina, Polly had organized a team of garden docents. She enlisted the expertise of the Master Gardener division of the NC Cooperative Extension Agency and put Weathersby gardens on the NC Board of Tourism map.

Polly leaned on the gate. "Getting too old for this bending and weeding. Time for new blood like you. You've got the horticultural degree and plenty of experience with the Master Gardener program."

Alison shook her head.

Polly caught her eye. "What's more, you've got a personal investment in Weathersby. After all, your husband, Frank, was involved
in the fundraising for restoring the orchard."

Alison rocked back on her heels. This was news.

Polly nodded. "Bill and Linda chaired that committee, but they
mainly wanted the effort to fail so they could build restroom facilities or parking or some such nonsense. Frank 'invited' himself onto
the committee at the last board meeting he attended. I was there
to oppose the Lawrence plan to divert the money and land to other
purposes. Frank and I made a vocal team."

A smile flitted at Alison's lips. She had no trouble imagining
that, what with Frank's Irish temper and Polly's plain outspokenness.

"Didn't sit too well with those high and mighty Lawrences, I
can tell you."

Alison crossed her arms. "So Frank made enemies that night.
How did the rest of the board react?"

"It was news to them—the Lawrences' so-called study of best
land use. Bill had copies from geologists and engineers. Feasibility
studies. You name it. Ivy was beyond livid that sacred Weathersby
land might be desecrated. She still hates old lady Weathersby for
selling off the Orchard Farm Road parcel to the vet school in the
1960s."

Alison shrugged. "I didn't realize Ivy was around then."

Polly dusted the dirt off her knees. "Ivy's mom was the cook here
when the Weathersbys were still in residence. She's got a bigger
stake than most of us, I guess, in seeing Weathersby succeed as a
premier historic preservation destination. She'd like nothing better
than to see Weathersby restored to its antebellum glory, orchards
and all."

Bending, Polly poked her forefinger into the dirt. "We need
more rain." She straightened. "Last thing Frank said to me? That
he was going to do some fishing around to see what was up with the
Lawrences. Shady business, those people." She cocked her head and
grimaced. "Not from around here, you know."

Alison grinned.

That was one of worst things locals could say in the backhanded, eternally polite Southern way about someone they didn't particularly like.

"Think about what I said, Alison. I'm not going to be around forever." She snipped off a faded morning glory blossom and stuck it in her pocket. "Not forever here, anyway."

Alison slung her purse across her desk in her hurry to get into Ivy's office. Glancing from side to side, she slipped in feeling like a cat burglar.

She scanned the files in the bottom drawer. Nothing remarkable. Accounts payable. Accounts receivable. Personnel files. Travel documents and invoices. Files on the Harvest Festival in October, upcoming Fourth of July Bash, and docent teas.

Personnel files might bear looking into if she ever got Ivy out of the office for any length of time. Nervous, she kept stopping to peer out Ivy's side window, which offered a view of the path leading to the house.

What she beheld stopped Alison mid-search and sent her rushing toward the house to the docent porch where Ivy, all five feet of her, wrestled featherweight, eighty-year-old head quilter, Velma Jones, to the ground. Each jerked on the end of a king-sized, pastel-colored, feed-sack quilt in a textile tug-of-war.

"Let go of that quilt, Jones."

"Get your grubby vermin paws off, Dandridge."

Ivy's mouth hardened. "I'm the director here, Jones. You quilters will put that quilt where I tell you to put it."

"I'll tell you where to put something, you . . ."

Breathless, Alison reached the tumbling forms rolling over and over, gravel and freshly mown grass lodged in Ivy's bright-red do and Velma's equally vivid blue rinse. With a headless mannequin under one arm, Erica emerged at the top of the steps next to the yew hedge. Her eyes rounded with alarm. Hilary followed right on her heels. Docents lined the steps of the porch.

Holding onto a railing, Lula Burke hee-hawed so hard she sent herself into a coughing fit. Ginny crossed her arms. A strange, self-satisfied smirk adorned her face.

Curiouser and curiouser.

Winnie Allen, the gift shop manager, a fifty-something Greek-American, pushed through the knot of docents. "Stop it. Ladies, I beg of you." She wrung her hands.

Alison remembered enough about school-yard brawls to be hesitant to intervene. Bystanders often got hurt.

"Alison." Hilary panted from the effort of climbing the parking lot steps. "Do something."

Alison pointed to herself. "Me?"

The oak leaf hydrangeas rustled at the corner of the house. Jasper Delaine materialized, a paint bucket in hand. He extended the bucket—filled with water—to her.

Alison frowned. "Why me?"

He shrugged, thrust the bucket into her arms, and slunk away.

Stalling for time, she swiveled to Winnie. "What's going on? What's this about?"

Winnie put a shaky hand to her scarf. "Ivy insists the quilters are taking up valuable space needed for this weekend's fashion exhibit, and she's trying to kick them out of their meeting room on the second-story sleeping porch."

"Over our dead bodies," called a voice in the crowd. "Hit 'er where it hurts, Vel!" She pumped her fist into the air *à la* Black Panthers.

Alison recognized her from among the dozen or so Weathersby House quilters. None of the quilters would ever see seventy again.

"This is beyond ridiculous, Winnie."

Winnie clasped her hands in front of her. "Ivy had already dismantled the quilting frame when Velma and her cohorts arrived. I knew there'd be trouble. I knew it." Winnie moaned.

Ginny joined them on the fringe of the melee, a note of misplaced delight in her voice. "A regular bloodbath. If only Ivy had discussed this with them first. I'm sure a compromise could've been reached. But we know Ivy's motto on such matters."

At Alison's quizzical look, Winnie nodded. "It's easier to ask forgiveness than permission."

Hilary huffed over to them. "Well, if you're not going to do something, I will. Visitors are starting to arrive for tours." Grabbing the bucket, Hilary threw the bucket's contents on top of the combatants' heads. Shuddering and gasping, they instinctively released their hold on each other.

"Ladies . . ." Hilary pursed her lips.

Velma smoothed her bedraggled white locks from her eyes with one blue-veined hand. "That word," she grunted, "is thrown around entirely too loosely these days."

Ivy surged forward, her chest heaving. "What? You want some more, old biddy?" The golden specks in her catlike green eyes glowed like sparks in a fire.

Hilary inserted her considerable bulk between them. Rivulets of water tracked through the dense face powder on Ivy's cheeks. Her mascara dribbled streaks to her chin, leaving her resembling some hideous gargoyle.

With the ruckus over, the other quilters rushed to Velma's side. "Is the quilt ruined?"

The quilt lay in a crumpled, sodden ball at their feet. Velma emitted little moans.

Alison stepped forward. "Let me help you, Velma. It's such a beautiful day. I'm sure the visitors would love to see the quilters in action under the shade of the big oak on the lawn. I'll help you reset the frame." She placed the quilt in Velma's arms. The other quilters gathered around, stroking the fabric as if soothing a sick child.

Winnie patted Velma's shoulder. "We have the marquee tent in the gift shop we use on sale days. I could erect that for the quilters as a special outdoor exhibit for the weekend festivities."

Alison smiled at Winnie. "Like an old-fashioned fete."

Velma sniffed, but she could tell Velma was thinking about their offer.

"It would be nice to be outside for a change." Velma whirled around to Ivy. "But not permanently, mind you." She folded the quilt in thirds. "We could string a clothesline to air-dry this one and display a few others."

A silver-haired dowager with rouged cheeks lifted her index finger. "How about that Double Wedding Ring from the 1920s?"

"And my Grandmother's Flower Garden?" Another quilter offered.

She watched the possibilities taking hold of Velma.

Velma nodded. "Might work. Quilting is an art form, you know. It's about time we had our own exhibit."

Hilary mouthed a sincere thank-you over Velma's head as Alison took Velma by the arm to help her up the steps into the house. Winnie bustled away to retrieve the tent from her gift shop domain. Hilary herded Ivy in the opposite direction of her office. Ginny had slipped away.

Alison plucked a blade of grass from Velma's hair. "We'll get you set up right away. Erica?" She called over her shoulder. "I'll be with you as soon as I can."

Erica nodded, the mannequin stashed at her feet. "What a way to begin a day. Better than roller derby."

23

Several hours passed by the time Winnie and Alison restored the upstairs room. Located above the front door, such rooms were known as "sleeping porches" by decades of Southerners enduring hot summer nights without the benefits of modern air-conditioning. They resurrected the wooden quilting frame, haphazardly torn apart by Ivy, placing it amid the oaks of the side lawn. Winnie managed to capture the elusive Jasper into setting the tent pegs and erecting the red-striped canvas. It lent a *Mary Poppins*-like carnival air to the grounds.

Velma and the rest of the quilters were thrilled with their temporary new digs. Alison sent up a quick prayer for no rain till the spring festival was over this weekend.

She poked her head around Ivy's open door. "You wanted me to help Erica set up the fashion exhibit this afternoon, right?"

Huddled over her computer, Ivy didn't bother to look up. "Go ahead." She flicked her hand toward the door. "I've got to get ready for the board meeting."

"Sure thing." Alison half-turned.

"One more thing, Mrs. Monaghan."

Alison bit her lip. What was with the Mrs. Monaghan?

Ivy's eyes, like those of a bug-eyed tree frog, blinked. "I realize you're a special friend of Hilary. But, in the future, let me handle personnel disputes. I had the situation under control. After all," she smiled. "You mustn't forget your place. If I need your assistance, I'll ask for it."

Alison fumed all the way to the main house. If she'd been Velma, she would've walloped Ivy right in that big mouth of hers.

She gave a swift kick to the gravel at her feet. "Mustn't forget my place?"

Puh-leeze . . .

Reaching the gardens, she stopped to take a deep breath of the rose-scented air and tried to hold on to her temper.

She needed to focus and not allow Ivy or anyone else to sidetrack her from her real mission. One of these people she worked with on a daily basis at Weathersby committed murder. Someone, maybe more than one someone, was lying.

Alison found Erica in the third-story attic, the former house servants' quarters. Layers of archival parchment tissue littered the wooden floor. Hatboxes and shoes were strewn about.

Erica's face contorted. "Will you look at this mess?" She waved her arms. "No one is supposed to touch the linens, except for Ivy or me."

Alison rubbed her forehead, feeling a headache coming on. And, another crisis.

"What's wrong?" She stopped on the threshold, afraid to venture more than a foot into the room for fear of trampling priceless heirlooms.

"They've not been put back according to their ID tags." Erica lifted a shirtwaist blouse circa 1900 off the floor. "Someone's been playing dress-up here in the attic. They're out of order."

Alison reached for a taffeta crinoline skirt.

"Wait—" Erica extended a pair of white archival gloves.

"Sorry." She slipped them onto her hands. "Who could've done this?"

Erica shook her head and scrambled to her feet. "Ginny locks up and sets the alarm most weeknights. And she's been . . ." Erica glanced toward the attic window. "She's not been herself lately. Or it could've been Natalie." She gestured at the mess around her. "It'd be just like Natalie to borrow from the collection for her private use."

"Do you have the only key?"

"No. All the board members have a universal key to the doors."

Alison busied herself, tidying up the room. So where was Frank's key?

Mike hadn't found it on Frank's body, and she hadn't been able to find it after searching the house.

Had the key been what the burglar had been looking for?

Under close supervision, she followed Erica from room to room, dressing the mannequins set up earlier in the costumes representing the various historical eras in Weathersby history. In one bedroom, they dressed the mannequin in a brown wedding ensemble.

Alison straightened the brown lace collar around the mannequin's smooth, alabaster neck.   "Brown? For a wedding?"

"White is a modern wedding notion from around the turn of the twentieth century. A symbol of high social status if a girl could afford a white, to-be-used-one-time type of gown." Erica nudged her chin at a portrait hanging above the fireplace mantel. "The bride, Prudence, married into the Weathersby family before the Civil War. Brown and bleak was a pretty good omen for her future married state."

Alison draped a set of ocher beads around the mannequin. "Why do you say that?" As a garden docent, she hadn't bothered to learn the family stories the tour docents memorized for their guests.

"Her husband, Oliver Weathersby, was a rake and a scoundrel by all accounts."

Alison smiled. "A regular Rhett Butler?"

Erica tweaked the faded brown bonnet, tying the frayed ribbons in place. "That and more to hear Miss Lula tell it." She shot a look over the mannequin to Alison. "You can learn a lot from old people like her. If you've got the time to hear them out."

Remembering Robert's admonition to act her age, she ducked her head so she didn't have to stare at her own profile in the wavy antique glass of the vanity. Where exactly did the hip, young Erica categorize her?

Probably in the same category as Miss Lula.

"Not that Ivy allowed that in the official version." Erica adjusted a sleeve cuff. "But you know, in those days, how some men who owned plantations viewed their property." Erica clamped her mouth shut in distaste.

Alison's eyebrows rose as comprehension dawned. "Oh."

Erica smirked. "Oh, yeah. He's that fat, pompous guy over the mantel in the front parlor. He gives me the creeps. I always feel like his beady green eyes are watching me no matter where I am in the room."

"An artist's trick?"

"Whatever." Erica fluttered a hand. "He got what was coming to him during the War."

The War—all good Southerners knew—referred to the Civil War, not the more recent global conflicts.

They shifted their attention to a smaller child-size model set up inside an elaborately carved wooden crib. Erica buttoned the tiny calico blue pinafore. "They had one daughter, Opal, and her husband, a carpetbagger, took the Weathersby name to preserve Fatso's posterity."

Alison bit back a laugh. She'd hate to think what Herself would think of Erica's youthful euphemisms for the scions of the Weathersby clan.

Erica moved into another bedroom, laying out glittering flapper-era costumes and feather boas. "They had one son, Malcolm, but the Yankee didn't last long, either. Then, it was just a bunch of old women and the little boy."

"Sounds healthy," Alison noted with dry humor as she helped Erica pin garnet and amethyst brooches onto the mannequins.

Erica grinned and shivered. "Sounds positively gothic to me."

She smiled. "Southern gothic."

"Are you coming to the ball on Friday night?" Erica secured a boa in place. "You're supposed to wear a costume from an era of the Weathersby house."

Alison shrugged. "I hadn't given it much thought, what with . . ." She angled away, struggling to control the tremor in her voice.

"Oh, I'm such a dope. I forgot about—" Erica peered into her face. "And here I am chattering on about crazy people dying."

Except for the body piercing in her navel, Erica reminded Alison of Claire with her youthful exuberance and naïveté. She sent a swift prayer to heaven that body piercings and tattoos were not in Claire's future. With Claire, one never knew . . .

Alison squared her shoulders. "Don't worry, I'm adjusting. I keep busy so I don't have too much time to think about how much my life has changed."

Erica fisted her hands on her hips. "Well, you should come then. To the ball, I mean. Do you good to get dolled up. Probably what our mysterious intruder was doing, looking for accessories to add to their costume for the ball."

Alison nodded. "Could be."

Like all the board members, Frank had pre-purchased two tickets for the ball, but she'd not given her attire a second thought after Frank was killed and her entire world went off-kilter. Was it too soon for a widow to appear out in public? Or was that too old-fashioned?

"Did you know my husband, Frank?"

Averting her face, Erica bent to sort the box of bead-encrusted slippers on the bed. "A little."

Alison narrowed her eyes.

Twenty-three-year-old Erica was a lovely strawberry blonde with a willowy build. The old Frank couldn't have helped but notice her.

"How little?"

The rustling stopped and Erica stilled. "I have a boyfriend. He's a drummer in a band."

She gently rotated Erica. "How well did you know Frank, Erica?"

Erica refused to meet her gaze but blushed a becoming rose pink. "I'd rather not say."

Alison lifted Erica's chin with her thumb and forefinger. "I'm under no illusions about my late husband, Erica. You can tell me the truth. I promise I won't be angry at you."

Erica's eyes filled with tears, twin blueberry pools. "When I graduated and got this job last year, after a board meeting one night, Frank invited me out to celebrate. He was so friendly and cute. In an older way." Erica sank onto the bed. "I was flattered. I swear I didn't know he was married, Mrs. Monaghan."

Back to Mrs. Monaghan.

Did she want to hear this? The old weariness and defeat settled upon her. Was she doomed to spend the rest of her life encountering the lurid remnants of Frank's betrayal?

But this might be important. She pushed the darkness from her mind. "Of course you didn't, Erica."

Unlike Ginny's story, this tale sounded like Frank's *modus operandi*. "How did you learn the truth?"

Erica sniffed and drew one gloved finger under her eye, swiping at a tear. "After dinner, I invited him to my apartment. While he was getting the car, Ivy and Henry showed up at the restaurant. She'd seen Frank in the parking lot and guessed the rest. She set me straight, and they took me home." Her mortification radiated off her even after all these months.

Alison's temples throbbed. "That must have been embarrassing for you. Ivy can be—"

Erica touched her arm. "Oh, no, Mrs. Monaghan. She was so kind to me that night. Like an older sister, looking out for me. I'm ever so grateful she prevented me from doing something in ignorance I would've been ashamed of the next day. And then a week later, I met Travis, my boyfriend, and we fell in love."

Alison sighed. "On behalf of Frank, I apologize for his deceitful behavior. Thank you for telling me." She traced an imaginary circle with the toe of her shoe.

Erica grasped Alison's hand. "Oh, Mrs. Monaghan, it's not your fault. Nothing of what happened was your fault." Glints of anger—was there something else, too?—sparked out of her baby blue eyes. "I deserve better than that from him or any guy. And so did you."

24

Alison wheeled to hide the surprising tears that sprang into her eyes. She was finding that despite her new faith, some wounds ran so deep that it didn't take one supreme act of forgiveness on her part, but daily resolutions continually to forgive Frank.

Erica surveyed the exhibit. "Just about done. Oh," she clapped a hand to her head. "I forgot. The Museum of History is loaning us military uniforms. Revolutionary, Civil War, and both World Wars to interest the guys among us. I'm going to have to go downtown and pick those up." She gathered hangers and boxes.

Alison retrieved a hatbox hidden under the frame of the mahogany four-poster rice bed. "What about this?"

"Hats?" Erica frowned. "What's it doing in here? I didn't remove that from storage. Hmmm . . ." She wrinkled her forehead. "How about you arrange a hat display in the foyer downstairs? Be creative."

Erica piled her up with the rest of the boas and half-empty hatboxes until she could barely pick her way downstairs. She got to work on the antique coat tree as Erica set off on her errand. The house was quiet in the early afternoon, except for the steady ticktock of the still-functioning 1830s grandfather clock.

She had the public areas of the house to herself. Faint whispers arose from the closed docent room behind her as the volunteers sat down to a late, makeshift lunch in a lull between tours. The electrified crystal chandelier, converted from its original gas, cast a small pool of light at the front of the 1820 addition to the house. The hardwood floors gleamed, a tribute to Miss Lula's housekeeping.

The last box she uncovered was the one she'd found under the bed. Brushing aside the archival tissue, at first she couldn't believe her eyes.

A black cloche hat.

If not the same one as the one in Frank's photo, then identical to it.

Trembling, she fingered it, turning it this way and that, examining it inch by inch. Inside hung a single strand of hair, caught in the label. In the wavering light cast through the dimpled glass of the window, she could just make out its color, a reddish hue.

She fell back onto her heels.

This had to be the hat the mysterious woman wore in the picture with Frank. Who among her Weathersby suspects was the redhead?

Erica was more strawberry than blonde. Ginny was ginger-headed. Ivy's hair was copper-colored, and Linda ascribed to a rotating variety of bottled hues.

Had Erica's wide-eyed ingénue confession been an act? Ginny certainly had a reason, in her own mind, to do away with Frank. Mike was checking into the myriad of financial pies Linda and Bill Lawrence had their fingers into. And what about Ivy?

The front door banged open. She dropped the hat like a hot potato. A cloud of patchouli, wafting like a prelude, filled Alison's nostrils even before Natalie Singleton strode into the house.

Natalie wore knee-high white go-go boots and a vivid orange sheathlike dress, provocatively short, revealing tanned and muscled thighs. There wasn't much fabric at the top, either.

Feeling decidedly flat-chested and at a disadvantage, she scrambled to her feet.

Natalie pointed to the cloche hat. "That's my hat."

Swooping, Alison grabbed the hat. "This hat belongs to the Weathersby collection."

Violet sparks assessed her. Was another wrestling match about to break out inside the house this time? Alison tightened her grip on the hat.

Natalie extended her manicured hand. "I need it for my costume. I'm on the board. And I want it now."

Alison shook her head. "No."

Proud of herself for standing up to this Barbie-doll bully, inside she quaked at her own nerve. Inch for inch, she figured she could take Natalie down if she had to, although those nails of Natalie's gave her pause. She didn't figure Natalie for a fair fight.

Natalie touched one finger to the hat. She stepped back a few paces to rest her hand on the stair rail.

"Fine." She tossed her jet-black hair over her shoulder. "I'll go upstairs and pick another one that shows off my red wig." She laughed, placing one foot on the stair. "Frank always did prefer redheads, you know."

Grinding her teeth, Alison hurled the hat across the space, clobbering Natalie in the back of the head. Caught off guard with one foot already lifted to ascend the next step, Natalie stumbled and crashed with a loud bump against the wall. A door opened to a gaggle of voices. "What's going on out there?"

Ginny's voice?

Alison flushed, ashamed of her outburst. "Nothing." She retrieved the hat from under the stairwell where it had bounced and offered her hand to help Natalie to her feet. "Just a wardrobe malfunction."

Natalie looked at her outstretched hand and sniffed. The first one to look away, though, Natalie accepted her help, and she heaved Natalie to her feet.

With her hand inside the cap, she handed the hat to Natalie. "Here you can have it, if you want it so badly."

Suspicion dotting her eyes, Natalie grabbed for it before Alison changed her mind. Alison slipped her hand behind her back. She'd snagged the hair strand between her thumb and forefinger for Mike to get analyzed.

Alison lifted her chin. "I'll note on the inventory to Erica you borrowed it for the ball." It was petty, but she was pleased nonetheless to observe those expensive tangerine nails of Natalie's would have to be redone.

Clutching the hat to her expansive bosom, Natalie and the evocative patchouli leaned closer. "Be careful, my dear. Not everyone at Weathersby is as forgiving as I am. It's wise not to make enemies of people who are smarter and more powerful than yourself."

Natalie's face twisted. "It'd be a shame for those lovely children of Frank's to lose their mother, too." Lurching away, she slammed the front door behind her.

The heavy, overpowering scent hung in Natalie's wake. In two strides, she flung open the door, releasing the stench from her nostrils. Inhaling, she filled her lungs with deep, clean breaths of the lilac-scented air. The docent room closed behind her with a soft click.

Ginny spying? What game was she playing?

A movement, a shadow on the column, caught in the periphery of her vision. She shrank back as she recognized the gnomish form of Jasper, clad in the ubiquitous black hoodie he wore. He stared, unblinking and unfriendly.

Shivering in the warm April breeze, she retreated into the shelter of the house and shut the door on her *voyeur*.

Perhaps Natalie was right. Perhaps she'd already made one too many enemies.

25

CLAIRE DODGED BETWEEN OTHER BODIES HURRYING TO EXIT THE BUILDING. Heather, Zoe, and their gang had dogged their walk home from school again on Tuesday. Closeted in their bathroom at home, she and Justin had discussed the situation. Mom didn't need any more worries added to the financial mess Dad left. They'd fight this battle on their own.

Mom had arrived home from work yesterday too quiet. In an uneasy silence, they'd eaten the dinner Claire prepared. Mike rang her several times Tuesday evening, but Mom hadn't picked up.

Her head ached with worry.

Worry about her mom in danger. Worry about moving and a new school next year. Worry about ever having a real friend again.

But maybe, she'd never had a true friend.

She dashed down the steps and out to the parking lot, scoping the area for the black BMW. She hoped to get a head start home before the harassment began. Justin motioned to her from his usual lookout spot. They set off at a brisk pace, not exactly running, but on the fast side of a walk.

Sure enough, as they rounded the corner out of sight of the campus, Zoe and her pack moved in for the kill. The engine revved, accompanied by catcalls. Jeering turned to profanity when she and Justin refused to acknowledge their presence. The BMW crept for-

174

ward, braking and accelerating in an attempt to startle them into a response.

Reaching their street at last, Justin gripped her elbow. She darted a quick sideways glance at his face. A vein in his cheek pulsated with suppressed anger. He'd taken to driving golf ball after golf ball into the net each afternoon while she fixed dinner.

She feared he'd explode one day. In the cafeteria. In the hall. Or out on the field if he ever caught Tad or any of the others outside the safety of their pack.

Claire picked up her pace as they rounded the final curve toward home and stopped abruptly. Justin bumped into her.

His head snapped up. "What's—?"

She pointed at Mike's truck, parked sideways across both lanes of the street. He leaned casually, his arms folded across his massive chest, against the cab door. The BMW screeched to a shuddering halt.

Unwinding like a timber snake she'd once seen on a Girl Scout campout, he strolled over to Zoe in the driver's seat and flashed his badge.

"I think I'm going to have to see your driver's license, ma'am." He drawled out the ma'am, bending to within inches of her face.

Zoe reared. There was a furtive click of seat belts from the backseat because North Carolina is a Click It or Ticket It state.

She fumbled for her purse, in her hurry dumping its contents into the lap of Tad. A burning cigarette hung midair in his hand.

Mike cocked his head and gave Ewell a slow, menacing smile like the timber snake that'd just caught sight of his dinner.

You could almost hear the crickets chirp with the sudden stillness of the passengers.

Zoe timidly extended the plastic card through the window to Mike. He made a show of scrutinizing it. She jumped as he whipped out his notepad and pencil.

"I believe I'm going to need to see everyone's ID." He smiled. Again.

There was a rush to grab backpacks and a search through pockets until eventually Zoe handed over four other ID cards. With excruciating precision, Mike pronounced each syllable of every name as he painstakingly wrote them down.

"I'd sure hate to have to haul you kids downtown to jail."

Someone whimpered from the backseat.

"But you see, I've had complaints from the neighbors about excessive speed and noise on this street every afternoon." He paused to let that sink in.

He leaned the entire upper half of his body through the window. Zoe recoiled over the gearshift and into Tad.

Mike's face went granite hard. "I don't want to see any of you so much as put a toe on this street ever again. Do I make myself clear?"

"Y-yessir." Tad and Zoe stuttered in unison with a chorus of agreement from the backseat.

Claire's lip curled. What had she ever seen in Tad Ewell? What a weasel.

Mike straightened, flipping his notepad shut. "Good. Now get out of here." He slapped one hand against the door frame. "But take it slow and legal."

He watched as Zoe did a careful one-eighty and returned from whence she'd come. Claire and Justin stood rooted like statues on the sidewalk. Mike gave a slight nod to someone behind them. Swiveling, Claire noticed Mrs. Lambert rocking her baby on her own front porch.

Inclining her head at Mike, Mrs. Lambert scooped up her baby and disappeared into her house.

"She kept my card when the uniforms and I interviewed her after your dad's death." Mike shifted toward his truck. "I'll meet you in your driveway." He gripped the door handle. "And both you kids have some explaining to do."

26

WEDNESDAY HAD BEEN A LONG DAY. ALISON WAS SLOWLY GETTING USED TO the daily blitzkrieg of paperwork Ivy torpedoed her way every morning. Which Alison dutifully completed. Ivy had been impressed despite herself, even bringing Krispy Kreme doughnuts today. Ivy's version of a peace offering?

Alison managed to carve out a few moments alone, usually first thing in the morning, to sit in the garden and think over the scanty information she'd acquired thus far.

Employing a favorite device of Mike's, she brought a pad and pencil with her to make a list of her prime suspects and possible motives for murder. She'd also seen Jessica Fletcher do this on TV.

She topped her list with Natalie Singleton's name. How she hated—no, that was wrong—disliked that woman.

Motive for murdering Frank?

Alison chewed the pencil's eraser. Perhaps he'd refused to leave his family for her. Frank had been all about dalliances but steered clear of commitment and scandal. She removed the eraser from her mouth when her teeth cleaved off a chunk. She spit the piece onto the ground.

She'd read somewhere that murder was most often committed for one of three reasons: love, money, or revenge. Not necessarily in that order, either. And, they didn't say hell hath no fury like that of a woman scorned for nothing. So, back to her list she wrote:

1. Natalie Singleton—love scorned

2. Ginny Walston—revenge

3. Bill and/or Linda Lawrence—money

There was also Erica Chambers's story, if you believed it. Perhaps she'd done more with Frank than dinner before she'd realized he was married? She jotted down Erica's name.

4. Erica Chambers—love/revenge

5. Ivy Dandridge—???

She added Ivy's name to the list because she seemed to be so universally disliked, but she wasn't sure what connection Frank and Ivy had with each other. And Ivy did have red hair. Had they crossed swords over Weathersby?

Alison pursed her lips. Not to be mean, but Ivy didn't possess the right attributes to have drawn Frank's attention otherwise. She struggled not to allow her personal feelings to influence her reasoning. Was Ivy too easy a suspect with her "my way or the highway" approach? Was Ivy a killer or just fingernail-on-the-chalkboard annoying?

In her gut, she was convinced Frank's murder was tied to that illicit trip to San Francisco, and therefore, his murderer was a female. However, the burglar had been decidedly male. Mike had suggested—she jabbed herself none too gently with the lead point at the thought of what that man did to her insides—the burglary had been a random and separate crime. So to be thorough, she added Jasper Delaine's name to the list.

6. Jasper Delaine—???

Alison scrubbed her chin in case the pencil had left marks. Why would Jasper murder Frank?

She wasn't sure. But he gave her the creeps, and he always seemed to be hovering somewhere close by. If she could muster the courage, she needed to question him about his knowledge regarding Frank. She shuddered. She'd have to dragoon him somewhere public.

Add Miss Lula to the list?

She decided not.

Winnie or Polly? Hilary? None of them were redheads. And her gut pulled away from them and toward the names on her list.

Since four of the seven were employees of TAP, she resolved to go through those personnel files in Ivy's office as soon as possible. Maybe some detail from their background would give her the clue she sought.

And, many of the suspects would be assembled in the conference room at six o'clock sharp for tonight's board meeting. She jumped to her feet. Time to get to work.

Ivy spent most of the day harassing Winnie and Erica, so between quick sorties to check that Alison was indeed earning her keep, for once Alison had the office to herself. And the personnel files. She started with Jasper.

He was twenty-three, the same age as Erica, but a high school dropout, a ne'er-do-well. Perusing his file, she sipped her third cup of the morning. She'd brought her own single-brew coffeemaker to the office.

Jasper listed no permanent address. At the small snapshot attached to his folder, she shuddered again at the sight of his stringy black hair, the unibrow, and the perpetual jack o'lantern leer on his face.

A face maybe not even a mom could love.

She felt a twinge of guilt upon reading further. The victim of a broken home and abusive father, Jasper had been shuttled from one foster home to the other. He'd disappeared from social services' records until he turned up at Weathersby at the legal age of eighteen.

Ginny's file was brief, with the newspaper clipping of Dr. Walston's suicide clipped over her photo. Ivy had recently updated the file with notations about recurring inebriation. The file indicated Ivy and Ginny had met in college at the University of North Carolina. A letter was also enclosed, written by Ginny. As the wife of an affluent doctor, she'd recommended Ivy to the board to serve as executive director of Weathersby.

Erica's file was equally slim. A copy of her historic preservation degree from UNC lay in the file. As well as an interesting grainy photo of a radical student rally proclaiming their undying support of legalizing so-called recreational drugs. Banner aloft, Erica's face shone with fanatical fervor from the front of the crowd.

"Not quite the thing to go over with our ultra-respectable board." Ivy's relationship with Erica by Erica's own account appeared cordial enough, but why had she included this photo?

The door banged open, caught by a late afternoon breeze, and Alison jerked. She slid the folders into her top drawer.

Her breaths labored, Winnie thrust the pile of receipts and reimbursement forms at her. "Sorry, Alison. I'm three steps ahead of Herself, on her broom, no less. I came to turn in my travel reimbursement forms from the buying trip for the gift shop at Atlanta's trade show last month." She fanned herself with the end of one of her elaborate scarves. "I know, I know. I'm always late with it. I've missed this month's payroll again."

She took it from her as Ivy burst through the door.

"Winifred. If I've told you once I've told you twelve times, you must turn in those receipts according to the payroll schedule."

Winnie didn't respond.

Ivy threw up her hands. "With all I've got to do before tonight, I'll be incommunicado for the rest of the afternoon while I finish my report to the board. Hold my calls and make yourself useful, Alison."

Alison considered saluting but restrained herself in time.

Once Ivy disappeared into her director's cave, Winnie relaxed. "She's nervous as a cat on the day of the monthly board meeting." Winnie leaned closer, whispering on the off-chance of being overheard. "She serves as director only at their pleasure, you know."

As a former garden docent, she hadn't interacted much with Winnie. But the gossipy Winnie could be a treasure trove of information on the rest of her suspects who didn't have personnel files at Weathersby.

She lowered her voice. "You've been here almost as long as Ivy. What do you know about Natalie Singleton?"

Winnie made a face. "Nothing pleasant. Never met a man she didn't consider fair game." She glanced at Alison. "Sorry."

Alison reddened. Was there anyone on the planet who didn't know what a louse of a husband Frank had been? Had Frank and Winnie—?

She shook her head. She'd never clear her name and bring Frank's killer to justice if she started imagining murderers behind every . . . gift shop manager.

Alison squared her shoulders. This was going to hurt. "Did you ever see Frank and Natalie together?"

Winnie pleated the edge of her scarf, a translucent Aegean turquoise that created a bright glow upon her Mediterranean complexion. "I stopped by the shop on my way to the airport for a buying trip the day he was killed. I parked next to where Frank and Natalie sat in his car. They appeared to be having an intense discussion." She sniffed. "But the windows were rolled up, and I couldn't hear their conversation."

Not for lack of trying, she'd be willing to bet.

"What time was this?"

The woman crinkled her forehead. "I was in a hurry so I wouldn't miss my plane. I rushed to the shop to grab the inventory I'd left. I couldn't have been gone more than five minutes. When I returned to the parking lot, I saw Natalie all over Frank with her arms around his neck, but he shoved her away. Natalie slammed the door and got into that Maserati thing of hers. She spun gravel as she wheeled out of the parking lot." She tapped her finger on her chin. "Maybe about seven o'clock?" Winnie's black eyes widened. "I may have been the last person to see Frank alive."

"Other than the killer."

Winnie shuddered, but Alison could tell she was enjoying her starring role. Winnie fluttered the scarf. "None of us will feel safe until your husband's killer is caught."

Alison leaned forward on her elbows. "Who do you think murdered my husband, Winnie? Do you believe Natalie came back and killed him in a jealous rage?"

Winnie put a hand to her throat. "I can't believe it was someone we know and work with like Natalie. It was probably a homeless person, and Frank was in the wrong place at the wrong time." Her eyes gleamed. "But Jasper, I could believe."

Hilary stepped into the office carrying a sheaf of papers. "Need to make copies of tonight's agenda." She moved her bulk with surprising grace over to the small copier. "How's our director doing?" She shot a glance over to Winnie. "Is someone manning the shop right now, Winnie? The docents just finished a tour with a group of eighth graders who have money burning holes in their pockets."

"Oh, my." Winnie waved her scarf. "I must be off." She sped off down the path.

An expletive followed a thump from Ivy's office.

Hilary cocked her head. "Not so well, I gather." She placed the original on top of the glass and closed the top. "Did Ivy remind you to order dinner from Angelo's for the meeting? It's a working dinner."

Alison shook her head and thumbed through the assorted menus she'd found stuffed in one of her desk drawers. "How many of what?"

Hilary pressed start on the copier. She counted on her fingers. "We have a standing order with them for board meetings. Just call and remind them for eight as usual." Distracted by the flashing toner light, Hilary grimaced. "I hate these things."

Leaving her chair, Alison fiddled with some buttons and took out the cartridge toner and shook it. She slammed the drawer and the light faded. "Voilà!"

Hilary grinned. "I love people who are mechanically gifted."

Her lips twitched. The kindest remark Frank had ever made about her skills was to call her all thumbs.

A green thumb definitely.

She needed an angle to get her foot in the door tonight. "I'll pick up the order and set everything up for you guys."

Humming a Broadway tune as she scooped her copies out of the bin, Hilary readily agreed. After that, it was easy to distract Hilary into leaving the original on top of the glass. Forewarned was forearmed.

27

On her lunch break, Alison decided to confront Jasper in his own lair. She'd seen him disappear several times into the labyrinth that used to be the orchard and head toward the woods where a cabin/toolshed still existed.

As she crossed through the dense undergrowth, the gardener in her was distressed to see gaps in the tree line where stumps rotted. She was glad she'd worn her brown flats, as it was relatively easy to trip over the exposed roots and craters in the earth. Yet again, she reviewed the circumstances surrounding Frank's final hours.

There'd been no evidence at the murder scene of another vehicle. Possibly the murderer had picked his or her way to and from murdering Frank using this exact route. In the dusk of that autumn evening, the killer was either familiar with the terrain or careful not to turn an ankle.

Reaching the edge of the woods, she spotted the roughhewn, windowless shack. Cautious, she crept forward, tiptoeing in case Jasper was holed up inside. A hush descended as the trees closed around her. Glancing over her shoulder, from here she could no longer view the large comfortable refuge of the main house.

Not even a bird's call broke the overpowering silence, the absence of sound deafening. With no traffic noises from nearby Glenwood Avenue, it was easy to believe she'd stepped into Weathersby's antebellum past. She rattled her twenty-first-century keys in her skirt pocket for reassurance.

Beginning to regret the impulse that brought her here in the first place, she shivered. Her nerves unsettled, she might have retreated at that moment, except she caught sight of the door swinging open on its hinges in the springtime breeze. Pulled along by curiosity, she stepped across the threshold.

If the vast canopy of trees outside had dimmed the light, the inside of the cabin was even gloomier, but empty. Rotting leaves littered the wooden floor.

She wrinkled her nose at a musty smell, reminiscent of mildew, hanging in the air. A stronger more pungent scent mixed and mingled with the earthy aromas. "Pot," she whispered as the odor triggered images of college dorms.

Certain smells never left you. Her thoughts drifted to Erica. Erica and Jasper?

There was no accounting for taste.

As her eyes adjusted to the gloom, she surveyed lopsided rakes, hoes, and a chain saw hanging upon pegs protruding from the wall. Cobwebs festooned the tools, and the one-room shack exuded an air of neglect. She'd never ventured this far off the beaten path at Weathersby. She preferred the open nature of sunlight in the gardens.

Something skittered in the corner, and she recoiled.

Alison crinkled her nose. Of course, there'd be mice. Maybe even rats. She gave the workbench in the center of the room a wide berth.

There was no other furniture. No other drawers or shelves to inspect. Yet there were signs of habitation. Under the bench nestled a grungy, stained sleeping bag and haversack.

Was this Jasper's permanent address? Did the board or Ivy know about this?

She reached for the bag and hesitated. Should she stick her hand in there? Something might bite.

Dragging the bag by its long strap from under the table, she flipped it open and upended the contents, jumping back in case something did decide to bite. Or explode. Then, she felt silly.

Nothing. A comb, toothbrush. Toothpaste. A pile of papers, drawings.

Squatting with her back to the door, she smoothed out the first one, crudely drawn with a combination of colored pencils and crayons, like something a child would do.

But unlike the innocent kindergarten drawings her children once proudly displayed upon her fridge, it was the image of a woman bound in a chair, a noose draped around her neck, and blood dripping from various bodily injuries. Her open, drawn mouth reflected a scream, silent in two-dimension.

Alison rocked onto her heels, repulsed.

Fascinated and horrified at the same time, she unfolded the second, which was more of the same, except thematically sicker. Small tool-like objects surrounded the woman in the chair.

A sinking feeling in her gut, Alison noticed the workbench sported identical sets of pliers, screwdrivers, and bolts.

Was this the work of sinister fantasy or a historic rendering of an actual event?

Either way it didn't matter. This had been a bad idea.

Rattled, she stuffed the horrific depictions into the haversack. Jumping to her feet, she nudged the bag underneath the workbench with her shoe. A trickle of warm, moist air tickled the top of her foot. Her gaze locked onto a small gap between two of the floorboards.

A shadow fell across the threshold.

"Were you looking for something, Mrs. Monaghan?"

Alison spun around, digging into her pocket for her keys as if for a weapon.

Standing with a maniacal leer on his face, Jasper blocked her only way of escape.

28

LOOKING FOR SOMETHING? OR JUST SLUMMING?"

Alison swallowed hard. "Ivy sent me to find you."

When in doubt, always blame Ivy. Besides, it couldn't hurt to let him know somebody knew where she was.

Jasper raised his one brow.

He didn't believe her.

Perhaps the best defense was a good offense.

Alison arched a foot at his haversack. "Are you camping out here, Jasper?"

He crossed his arms. "So what if I am? What's it to you? Haven't you got enough on your plate these days with your old man dead? Bang, bang."

Alison quivered. He was vile, like every creepy crawly thing that lived underneath rocks. She resisted the urge to brush imaginary cockroaches off her skin.

He inched closer. "Maybe you're getting lonely?"

Keeping the workbench between them, she backed farther away from him—and from the door—moving in the wrong direction for escape.

Jasper slithered over to the tools hanging from the wall. "Ivy and I hooked up a few years ago. I was sleeping underneath a bridge. She made me an offer I couldn't refuse."

Ivy and her soft spot for children . . . Alison bit her lip. Bless Ivy and her tender heart. Not in his case.

He ran a finger lightly over the razor-sharp blade of an ax. "This place is a palace compared to where I come from." He tilted his head over the blade, rapt. "Not that a fancy lady like you would know anything about such things, but I'm a good teacher." He smirked. "Or so Ms. Singleton says."

Bile rose in her throat. Was he a stooge for Natalie? Her second string?

With a whack, he slammed the ax into the workbench. The table shuddered and so did Alison. The reverberations continued through the floorboards.

Jasper gazed about the room. "Not much, but it's home. And you know what they say, there's no place like home."

If those drawings were any indication of his former life, she didn't want to know. And if he was trying to scare her, he was succeeding. She gauged the distance and time factor it would take to race around the bench and out the door. Despite her best calculations, she wouldn't get far if Jasper decided to pursue.

Jasper caught her eye. He laughed.

"Got an appointment somewhere, Mrs. Monaghan? Well, don't let me keep you." He came around to her side of the table, and just as fast, she skedaddled around the other side and out the door.

She hated to run, but hearing his mocking laugh, she forgot about decorum. She raced toward the house.

Tripping in the orchard, she fell facedown. Leaping up, she didn't stop to brush off the decomposing leaf mulch. With a frantic glance over her shoulder, she burst upon the path of civilization and smack into Henry Dandridge. The force of their mutual collision landed both of them on their backsides among the primroses.

With the breath knocked out of her, Henry was the first to recover. "My dear Mrs. Monaghan."

Seventy-five if he was a day, he propped his arms on his knees, wincing with the effort. Leaning against a handy tree, he hauled himself to his feet.

"I'm so sorry—"

"I wasn't looking where I was going."

She and Henry laughed.

"Fine." He rubbed his back. "We're both a couple of inconsiderate, tunnel-vision nincompoops." He held out a deeply veined, liver-spotted hand to where she sat on her rump.

Grasping his hand, she was careful not to rely too much upon Henry for support. She made it look good, though. A man like Henry, especially an elderly man, ever the gentleman, had his pride.

She squeezed his hand before releasing it. "Thanks."

"I've come to take Ivy home." He removed a small gold pocket watch from his waistcoat. "I fear board meetings are rather much for her delicate constitution. I simply insist she nap on such days."

One thing she'd always admired about Henry was his unswerving devotion to Ivy. In her mind, the least likely candidate on the planet for a delicate constitution. But she envied the brassy tyrant her devoted husband, who lived to ensure Ivy's comfort. Not many were loved like that.

Not her, anyway.

Alison retrieved his hat from behind the oak leaf hydrangea, brushing it free of debris. "Ivy's lucky to have you in her life." Ducking her head to hide her moist eyes, she pretended to inspect his hat.

Such a crybaby these days . . . Probably a reaction from her near-death experience with creepy Jasper.

Henry covered her hand to stop her fretting at his hat, "No, I'm the lucky one." He flicked a single finger on her cheek, and a tiny tear trembled on its tip.

"After my first wife of thirty years passed on," he took a deep breath. "I never believed I'd find love again." He squeezed her hand. "It seems hard to believe now, my dear, but one day, I pray you'll find love again, too."

She shook her head. "That's behind me." Her voice wobbled. "The burned child dreads the fire, Mr. Dandridge."

"Call me Henry, and fire, my dear Alison, if properly cradled, warms rather than burns." He snagged a stray leaf from her bangs.

"Did I do all this to you, or have you been wrestling an alligator today?"

She laughed. "It was something just about that nerve-wracking, I'm afraid." She took his proffered arm, and they strolled toward the office.

"Jasper Delaine, I bet." At her surprised look, he shrugged. "You were running from that direction when we collided. Nasty young man, that one."

"He scares me."

The professor snorted. "He ought to scare any right-minded person."

"But didn't you and Ivy adopt him from the streets?"

"I'm afraid Ivy has bitten off more than she can chew. Prison or the army, I suspect, may be the only thing that can reform him."

Alison cut her eyes at him. "Or a psychiatric ward."

He threw back his head and laughed. "My sentiments exactly. But Ivy, with her big-hearted generosity, doesn't see the wickedness. Isn't that such an old-fashioned word, Alison? Do you believe in such things?"

She sighed. "I do, Henry. I believe whoever murdered my husband is evil. And I mean to expose Frank's killer."

He stopped. "Be careful, my dear. Never underestimate evil. Remember what I said about the fire that warms. Evil is also a fire, a fire that burns the perpetrator as well as those set on revenge." He gestured to a bench. "Mind if I sit a spell? These knees aren't what they used to be."

Alison clutched his arm. "Oh, I hope our collision hasn't sidelined you, Henry."

"Not to worry. Only old age can do that. I'll be as fit as a fiddle for the Spring Ball on Friday night. Ivy and I have been practicing. We plan to cut a rug."

Ivy was a lucky—make that a blessed—woman.

She smiled as she helped Henry lower himself onto the bench. "I'll look forward to it."

He took off his hat and swiped his sweating brow with it. Clapping it back on his head, his eyes twinkled. "A man has to stay young to keep up with Ivy."

Truer words were never spoken. She'd probably aged ten years working for Ivy this week.

She settled herself beside him. "How long have you and Ivy been together?"

"Five years come June. Ivy and I met when she was caring for my invalid wife, Doris."

"I didn't realize Ivy had a nursing background."

Henry nodded. "She was a godsend. Doris had gotten to be more than I could handle. I wasn't retired yet. With the MS, her body was the first to go." He cast his eyes down. "When her mind went, it was more than I could cope with. If Ivy hadn't already been there for us, I don't know what I would've done." He was silent, lost in remembered pain.

She patted his hand. Sometimes, as she knew far too well, words were out of place.

Henry's mouth tightened. "But after I stepped down from my teaching position, I was depressed. Nobody believed I'd live much longer." He looked at Alison to gauge her reaction. "Ivy urged me to write a historical account of the Weathersbys, distant cousins of Doris, and their home. The book and Ivy gave me new life. Soon after, we married."

"That's terrific."

He shrugged. "Some people said it was too soon after Doris's death. Unseemly." He spat on the ground. "What do they know about two souls knit as one by shared adversity?"

"What do they know," she sighed, "about loneliness?"

His voice shook. "I see you, too, have trod that dark valley. You understand. I knew somehow you would. I've sensed from the beginning what a remarkable woman you are."

"What's going on here?"

They jumped at Ivy's strident voice.

He leaped to his feet—as much as a septuagenarian could leap—like a naughty puppy caught piddling in the corner. "Just resting, Ivy. On my way to collect you."

Ivy ran a claw through her hair. "I don't have time to rest. Not with the board meeting tonight and the festival this weekend. And you, Mrs. Monaghan . . ." She rounded on Alison.

She fought the urge to roll her eyes. Too childish for a mature woman of her age. Too Claire.

But it would be so-o-o satisfying.

"You." Ivy jabbed a short little finger at her. "I have more correspondence for you regarding federal grants we're trying to secure. You need to get to work right away. No more lollygagging."

Alison tossed her head. She'd never lollygagged in her life.

It was a miracle no one had tried to murder Ivy.

Yet.

Rising, she gave Henry an affectionate pat. "See you later, Henry."

Henry, stooped as he was, towered over Ivy and gave Alison an insolent wink of conspiracy over Ivy's head. "Nice bumping into you."

He laughed and she giggled. Ivy muttered something about the senility of the aged and the weak-mindedness of the young.

"Well, come on, Henry," Ivy whined. "If we're going home, let's go." Grabbing his arm, she yanked him toward the parking lot.

Doing his best to keep his balance, Henry allowed himself to be jerked along. He'd probably learned long ago there was no point in resisting a force of nature like a hurricane or a tornado.

Or Ivy.

29

In the office, late afternoon shadows reached like sinewy fingers across Alison's desk piled high with application forms and papers. Her shoulders slumped.

Retrieving her purse from the bottom desk drawer, she checked her messages. There were two from Mike and one from home. She'd deal with him later. She replayed the message from home.

Claire's voice echoed in the office, enhanced by the twelve-foot vaulted ceiling. "Mom, Mike wants to talk to you. Now. He wants to know why you're not returning his calls."

She frowned. Who was the mother here? Obviously, Mike was giving Claire her marching orders. What was he doing at her house?

"He says you better call him im-me-di-ate-ly." Claire stretched out the syllables.

Who did he think he was?

Claire's voice choked. "Something happened after school today."

She straightened. Claire didn't cry easily and never much at all until her dad died.

Her daughter's voice quavered on the message. "Can you come home now? Please?"

She scrambled to her feet, knocking her shin against the open desk drawer. Grabbing her keys and purse, she shut down her computer.

What on earth had happened? And why was Mike involved?

The crank caller rose to her mind. And, Jasper's drawings.

"Oh, dear God," she whispered. In her haste, she dislodged a few papers from Ivy's stack. She stopped, watching them flutter to the floor. Ivy had wanted this done today.

A not-so-nice phrase flitted through her mind about what Ivy could do with her paperwork. Irrational visions streaked through her mind as well of Justin and Claire, hurt and in trouble. She had to get to them.

Now.

On the way to the parking lot, she whirled past Ginny and a group of tourists. Spinning gravel, she put the car into drive and flew out of Weathersby as if the demons of hell nipped at her heels. She slammed on the brakes, almost hitting a car as Winnie turned into Weathersby. Winnie's mouth hung in an open O.

Alison's hands shook on the steering wheel.

Too close.

"Oh, God," she prayed. "Help me get home in one piece." Taking several deep breaths, she managed a weak wave of apology to Winnie and then, trying to maintain a more sedate and legal pace, hurried home as fast as she could.

Pulling past Mike's truck parked in her driveway, she raised the garage door and screeched to a halt mere inches from the wall of the house. Leaving the car door open and the keys in the ignition, she dashed into the kitchen.

"My, my, Miz Monaghan." Mike leaned against the granite counter, watching Claire brown hamburger in the skillet.

Did the man ever stand up straight?

"What's happened?" She touched Claire's head. "Are you okay? Where's Justin?"

Claire exchanged a guilty look with Mike. "We're okay. Justin's hitting balls in the backyard."

She grabbed a handful of Claire's hair.

Claire's eyes widened. "Ow, Mom. Let go."

She tugged harder. "Do you mean to tell me, young lady, you scared the life out of me and made me leave a pile of work at the office for nothing?"

"Mom! Please. Mike's going to think you're violent or something."

She glared over Claire's head at him. "I feel violent."

Mike backed away from the counter, both hands up in surrender. "Hey, don't shoot the messenger. I figured as their mother you needed to know what was going on."

She released Claire's chunk of red hair. Claire scooted out of arm's reach.

"What exactly has been happening, Claire Irene Monaghan?"

Claire flicked her gaze to Mike, a plea for help in her eyes. He shrugged and strolled off toward the family room.

"I'll get Justin," he called over his shoulder. "I've done my duty."

Five minutes later, two subdued children in fits and starts explained what had been going on after school this week. Mike leaned against the chair railing.

Anger and fear warred for supremacy within her. She was a terrible mother. She should've known that after the bad publicity, this week would be difficult. She should've asked more questions, only she'd been caught up in her own little detective drama.

Who did she think she was, Miss Marple?

She was their mother, first and foremost. Nothing else in life could or should ever take priority over that.

Alison gripped her stomach with both hands. "I should've been there for you guys. I've let you down."

"It's not your fault, Mom." Claire shot an angry look at Mike. "This is why we wanted to handle it ourselves. Mom doesn't need this on top of everything else."

Justin's eyes dropped to his sneakers. "I should've taken better care of Claire."

Mike laid a hand on Justin's shoulder. "Not your job, bud. This was way out of your league. I just wish I'd found out sooner."

Falling to her knees in front of them, Alison took each of their hands in her own.

This was her fault.

And Frank's . . .

The anger at Frank, as lava hot as the day she'd found that cursed photograph, kept her tears at bay. Just when she thought she'd forgiven him, something happened to show her how far she still had to go. She could almost forgive him for her own hurts, but her children's?

"Not there yet, God," she whispered.

Justin touched her hair. "What'd you say, Mom?"

Alison changed the topic. "Remind me, kids, to take Mrs. Lambert some of my roses. We owe you a great deal, Mike. Who knows how far this could've escalated by the end of the week?"

Claire shrugged off her mother's arm. "Are we done here? I've got to put dinner on the table." But she stumbled over Justin's feet, dumping her schoolbag. All of them bent to retrieve the contents.

A familiar paper covered in bright lurid crayon colors caught Alison's eye. She gasped and straightened.

Claire snatched at the drawing but wasn't quick enough.

Feeling sucker punched, Alison wasn't sure she could continue to breathe with her stomach hurting so badly. "Where did this come from?"

Claire tried again to grab it from her, but Alison had the height advantage. She passed it over Claire's outstretched hands to Mike. "Where did you get this?"

"I found it in my locker that first day after break." Claire lowered her eyes to the floor, studying the carpet. "I stuffed it in the bottom of my bag and forgot it was there. Stupid Zoe and Heather up to their tricks."

Mike looked at Alison, his eyebrow cocked like a question mark.

"It wasn't them." She closed her eyes. "Not Zoe and Heather." She licked her dry lips and coughed to clear the bile from her throat.

First, Frank. *Please, God. Not her children, too.*

She told Mike about the drawings she'd found that afternoon in the toolshed and about her scary encounter with Jasper. "How could he get into the school and do this? How did he know about my children? Why is he doing this to us?"

"Whoa." Mike held up a hand. "I realize you're freaked. Let's not panic and jump to any conclusions."

Her nostrils flared. "Not panic? He's threatened my children."

Claire sat on the sofa, her face white. Justin collapsed beside her. They huddled tense and frightened shoulder to shoulder.

Mike whipped out his cell phone. "I'll deal with that psycho son of—sorry for the language, kids." He squeezed Alison's arm. "I promise you I'll make this okay. I'll be right back." Hitting speed dial, he stepped into the kitchen out of their earshot.

God protect us. She squeezed her eyes shut, willing the nausea to subside.

A few minutes later, Mike returned to find her on the sofa sitting between the children, with an arm around each. Glints of fire sparked in his eyes. Anger darkened his features, and for the first time, she felt a little sympathy for Jasper Delaine.

A little, but not much.

"Patrol car will be stationed on the street till we locate and detain our suspect for questioning. Officers are being dispatched as we speak to search that shack at Weathersby."

He waved the drawing in the air. "This gives us all the probable cause we need. An officer will follow you kids home from school every afternoon." At Claire's quick motion of protest, he added, "Discreetly, Claire, I promise. I remember what it's like to be in high school, believe it or not."

Justin gave a long sigh. "I guess this nixes my plan to go to youth group with Aunt Val tonight."

Alison put tonight's board meeting out of her mind.

Mike shifted his weight. "I'm not about to let that slimebag ruin your lives. If you want to go, I'll escort you myself."

Justin perched on the edge of the sofa. "For real?"

"Might be interesting. Haven't been to one of those since my granny stopped being able to drag me there." Mike searched Alison's face. "If it's okay with your mom. A patrolman will be right outside the house all night for you and Claire."

"Please, Mom? Can I go?" His eyes pleaded for her approval.

This group had become important to Justin. They were his support network, helping him work through the maze of his father's betrayal and death. Was this the hand of God working in her son's life as she'd prayed?

She sighed. "All right, since Mike will be with you. But come straight home."

Justin nodded his head in quick agreement. With a quirky, lopsided smile, Mike gave her a smart salute. She grimaced, feeling like both of their mothers.

"Could I come, too?" Claire leaned forward, her hands gripping her knees. "I need to thank Sandy and the other girls for their support at school this week." She darted a look at her brother's grinning countenance. "As Mike said, it could be fun." She pursed her lips. "Although I doubt it."

Alison resisted the urge to laugh. *Good luck, Lord, with that one.*

Claire would be Claire come hell or high water, as Alison's daddy used to say. He'd have gotten a kick out of the granddaughter he never met.

All she usually got was a headache.

She surrendered to the inevitable. "Homework?"

Justin patted her arm. "Mike stood over me while we were waiting for you to come home and helped me finish my essay in English."

Mike winked at Justin.

She raised her eyebrows, trying to suppress a grin. "And what, pray tell, was the topic?"

Mike turned all sheepish and coughed. "How to Win Friends and Influence People."

She gave him a sideways glance. "And what did you suggest to my son, Detective Barefoot?"

Ducking his head, Mike followed Claire into the kitchen. "What time did you say dinner was going to be ready?"

Justin laughed. "Talk softly, but carry a big stick."

30

Alison peered around the damask drapes. On the street, a cop sat in his car. Gathering her courage, she exited the house and strolled over to him. Sighting her, the officer lowered his window.

"Hi." She fluttered her fingers. "You're going to watch the house all night, correct?"

The patrolman nodded. "Yes, ma'am. I'm staying put right here in this exact spot. Don't you worry."

She smiled. Big. A little sweet magnolia . . .

"With you guarding the house, I don't have anything to worry about."

She handed him a plate of the chocolate chip cookies Claire had taken out of the oven before she and the guys left for church.

Back inside, she grabbed her purse and keys. But she turned off her cell phone. Mike would have them home by nine o'clock. The board meeting started in about thirty minutes. It should finish in plenty of time for her to get back to the house before he arrived with the kids.

She grunted. As if she had to sneak into her own house. She didn't answer to him. She would've stayed home, but since the kids wanted to go to their meeting, she had one of her own she definitely needed to attend.

Raising the garage door, she backed out onto the street. As she passed the patrolman with his mouth full of cookie, she waved at him and got out while the getting was good.

She blessed Mike and his literal-minded pals on the force who strictly followed the letter of the law. Mike told the officer to watch her house, and watch it he would.

Mike never said to watch her.

Semantics. She'd learned a long time ago with Frank it was all about semantics.

No doubt the cop was frantically calling Mike right now. She only hoped Mike had turned his phone off as a courtesy while within a house of worship. That should buy her enough time to pick up the food at Angelo's, serve it, and gather intelligence on the board of directors.

A sliver of doubt niggled at the back of her mind like a rat terrier with a bone. Mike would call her all kinds of names, the least of which would be obsessed. But at this point, she'd decided, like Ivy, it was easier to ask forgiveness than permission.

Later, with gyro and souvlaki boxes piled to her nose, she raced up the stone steps through the yew hedge to the docent porch at the back of the house. Using her hip to prop open the door and balancing the boxes, she erupted into the conference area.

Nothing like making a grand entrance.

Her eyes rounded, and she dropped the boxes. "What are you doing here?"

Was there no one she could trust? She'd imagined the people at Redeemer to be her safe haven. And for the first time, she wondered at the timing of him showing up to her house right after . . .

Robert, in a teal golf shirt and casual khaki chinos, hurried over to help. "Here, let me." He scooped up the boxes.

She glared. "What are you doing here?" Noting they alone occupied the room, she gave an involuntary shiver.

Unspoken accusations vibrated the air between them.

Robert's brow furrowed into a V. "Joan, my wife, was one of the charter members of the board at Weathersby before she became ill.

When she stepped down, Frank was elected to take her place." He dropped his gaze. "Hilary asked me to finish Frank's term."

He shuffled the boxes in his arms. "I tried to tell you the day Stephen and I took Justin to the club, but we were interrupted."

"And you never saw fit to rectify that error since?"

He stiffened. "Error? It never came up."

"Even when I told you I was taking the job here?"

Did she have *stupid* tattooed on her forehead?

Robert threw the boxes on the floor between their feet. "Perhaps I didn't realize we had progressed so far in our relationship where I had to account to you for my every movement. My mistake."

Her breath hitched. She took a step backward, tensing as he drew closer.

Robert's eyes drooped. "I'm sorry, Ali. I shouldn't have said that. My temper . . ." He caught hold of her arm. "It's just you sounded so . . . You don't honestly believe I was involved in Frank's . . . I would never betray you like Frank did." He tugged at her sleeve.

Wrapping one arm firmly about her body, with his other hand underneath her chin, he urged her mouth closer to his lips. She let him kiss her, his cheeks smooth against her flesh, a faint scent of an expensive aftershave filling her nostrils.

It had been a long time since she'd been kissed. Life with Frank those last years had been anything but sweet and tender. Robert held her tight, both arms around her. She could feel his yearning for her. Her heart beat as wild as a bird in a cage.

What did she feel for Robert? Fear? Or desire? Why was she so confused?

She didn't really think of Robert as one of her "suspects," did she? What possible motive . . . ? Not Robert, beloved by children and dogs. Her safety net.

Perhaps obsessed would be a correct description of her behavior lately.

That and paranoid, too. Not that she didn't have good reason to be, after the day she'd had so far, but it wasn't fair to take out her angst on Robert.

Still . . . something didn't feel right to her.

Her lips broke free of his. His chest heaved, and her breath came in short spurts.

"Don't shut me out, Ali," he whispered into her hair. "I know it's too soon. But give us a chance. Give yourself a chance. I love you, and I would dedicate my life to making you the happiest woman on earth."

And she believed him.

"Forgive me? I should've told you about taking Frank's place . . ." He looked away at the awkward pause. "At Weathersby."

"No." She smoothed the silver tendrils that had escaped from their usual place behind her ear. "I'm the one who's sorry for snapping your head off. It's been a bad day." She lifted one hand and dropped it to her side. "Actually, it's been a bad year. Forgive me, please?"

The twinkle returned to his eyes. "And us? Will you promise to consider my offer?"

Offer? That sounded so . . . so like real estate.

Which, to be fair, was his area of expertise.

"Only God knows the future, Robert." She bent once more to retrieve the boxes, praying the board dinner was salvageable. "And the future, as I'm learning, is best left in His hands."

"I'll take that statement with cautious optimism." He made a move as if to touch her.

"Good. The food's here." Lumbering in, Hilary tossed her stack of papers on the table.

Alison sidestepped Robert's extended hand. "I'll get the plates." She slipped into the kitchen before Ivy could arrive and throw her out on her ear. Time to get busy or at least act like it.

When she returned, she found Hilary seated, as were the Lawrences. A young man wandered in with Erića. Bill frowned at the sight of Alison. Linda put a tissue to her nose as if smelling something unpleasant.

Alison puttered around, setting out the place mats and dishing out the individual orders.

"So nice of Alison to offer to take care of the food for us." Hilary favored her with an approving glance. "Now we can get started on the last-minute details for this weekend's Spring Ball and festival fundraiser."

Alison headed to the kitchen to retrieve the tea pitcher Lula had left in the fridge for the meeting. She also placed enough glasses on a white tray for everyone.

Hilary had begun to fidget when she returned to the conference room. Several chairs remained empty. Though Hilary gave every appearance of being laid back, she liked to get down to business on time. As Alison poured tea or water as requested, the young man seated beside Erica introduced himself.

"Todd Driver." He offered a limp hand.

Juggling a pitcher in each hand, she nodded.

"Oh," Todd retracted his hand. "I guess you do have your hands full." He was cadaverously thin, about Erica's age, but pale. The beginnings of male pattern baldness on his high forehead gave him a windswept look.

Erica took a glass from Alison. "Todd is our city council representative. He tries to keep us on the straight and narrow, budgetwise, that is."

At the sound of his name on Erica's lips, Todd lit up like a firefly in July. Erica patted his hand and then blushed, becomingly.

Hadn't Erica mentioned a boyfriend, a rock 'n' roll band drummer?

Who was the real Erica? Demure textile conservationist or a pothead wild child? Interesting, though, how Erica could switch personas at will for her own purposes. It never hurt to have friends in high places, especially on the city council, Alison supposed. What exactly was little Miss Erica's agenda?

The sound of angry voices filtered in from outside. Natalie and Ivy emerged, locked in verbal combat.

"I don't care if you're the director," Natalie shouted. "I'm family."

"Just because your father was related—distantly," Ivy pursed her lips, "to Ursula Weathersby does not give you the right to make decisions without my approval."

Natalie sneered. "Daddy and I don't know how you bamboozled the old lady into handing Weathersby over to you and the city, but I'm not going to let you get away with it."

Hilary cleared her throat. Loudly.

Apparently realizing for the first time she had an audience, Ivy's eyes narrowed as she caught sight of Alison trying to disappear into the safety of the kitchen, pitchers still in hand.

Ivy jabbed a finger in her direction. "What is she doing here?"

Robert shuffled his feet under the table. Bill buried his head in his laptop.

"I asked her to help with the meal." Hilary rose. "Now, I suggest the two of you calm down or take your dispute elsewhere. We've already waited long enough for the both of you. I call this meeting to order." She banged a gavel on top of her file folder, careful not to mar the antique finish of the oval conference table.

Natalie flounced into her seat. Ivy gripped the top of her chair, not ready to surrender the fight. "Board meetings are not open to the public, and you, Mrs. Monaghan, left your post early this afternoon."

Linda Lawrence heaved a dramatic sigh. "For the love of preservation, Ivy, sit down so we can get started. Some of us have other things to do tonight."

Hilary leaned forward for emphasis. "Alison is not the 'public.' She's a member of our staff and," with a sly look at Ivy, "she had every right to leave early today since she's working for Weathersby tonight per my instructions. I, for one, assumed Weathersby lacked sufficient funding to pay overtime. Isn't that correct, Bill?"

Hearing his name, Bill buried himself further into his computer. "Yeah, right," he mumbled.

"So, Ivy, I repeat," Hilary grimaced, "if you have no other issues," in a tone that indicated how much she doubted the likelihood of that, "let's get down to business."

Ivy fumed, looking long and hard at Bill's bowed head. Alison realized he'd taken the seat Ivy preferred, the one at the other end of the table opposite Hilary. Bill ignored Ivy. Rattling the chair to show her displeasure, Ivy sat down.

Alison retreated to the kitchen to give Ivy time to cool off. She spread her pirated copy of the agenda on the countertop with one ear figuratively pressed against the open threshold into the conference area and one eye peeled around the door frame.

Functioning in Frank's role as secretary, Robert read the minutes of the last meeting. Six months ago, she realized with a pang, Frank had been alive, probably sitting in the same chair Robert occupied, reading the minutes.

Hilary flipped through her folder. "Old business?"

Erica, in the sweet, schoolgirl role she was playing tonight, raised her hand. "Excuse me, but I want to remind everyone being on the board doesn't give anyone the right to meddle with archivally preserved textiles that have been carefully stored and tagged."

"I second that." Ivy nodded. "It's ridiculous how many people have keys to this complex. Only the president," with a nod in Hilary's direction, "staff, and of course, myself as director should have that kind of access for security and liability reasons."

Linda took umbrage and fluffed like an angry, molting bird. "Are you accusing someone, Miss Chambers, of wrongdoing?"

Erica flushed. Todd stood, sending his chair back with a crash. "Now see here, Mrs. Lawrence. No one said anything about you."

Natalie laughed. "My daddy used to say the 'bit dog always barks the loudest'."

Ivy rounded on her. "Exactly, Ms. Singleton. I forget, is it still Mrs.? Or after four failed marriages, do you prefer to revert to Miss?"

Natalie reached across the table for Ivy's throat.

"Ladies!" shouted Hilary.

How much of this was Robert bothering to record in April's minutes? He looked over the top of his laptop and winked at her.

Hiding a smile, she ducked into the depths of the kitchen to prepare after-dinner coffee. At the rate they were shouting, she'd have no trouble following their conversation during her preparations.

"Let's move on," Hilary encouraged, striving to regain some semblance of order. "And Mr. Driver, please resume your seat."

A chair scudded across the floor.

"Please . . ." Ivy moaned. "Those floors are two hundred years old. Were you raised in a barn?"

"Some of us were," Linda hissed with meaning.

Hilary sighed but brought their attention to several committee reports: the garden committee report prepared by Polly, the gift shop proceeds from Winnie, docent training from Ginny, and a report of educational outreach in the Wake County public schools, this one read by Erica herself.

During the seeming lull in hostilities, Alison set out the rest of Claire's cookies and, with the tray full of coffee mugs, offered decaf or regular. The rich coffee aroma floated above the table. She'd brought her own stash from home. The stuff they kept here for the docents tasted plebian to a coffee connoisseur like her.

Bill took a cautious sip. "Mmm. Good stuff," he mumbled around another mouthful of cookie.

Was Bill coming down with something? He'd been unusually quiet, and he wore a navy blue turtleneck, more than a little unseasonable for April in Raleigh.

Ivy puckered her lips. "Brackish."

Talk about winning friends and influencing people? She'd just made Ivy's you-know-what list. She removed herself without comment to the kitchen.

"New business?" Weariness colored Hilary's voice. Hers was a thankless job. "How are the plans proceeding for the ball on Friday night?"

Natalie rested her sun-kissed bare arms on the table, showing just enough cleavage to intrigue. Todd blushed. Robert kept his nose in his laptop. Bill appeared transfixed until a not-so-subtle jab from his wife brought his attention to the present.

"The caterers have been confirmed." Natalie recited the menu. She tossed her dark tresses, whiplashing Erica in the face. "Erica and I set up the fashion exhibit in the upstairs' rooms." She favored each of them with a languid smile. "I encourage all of you to preview the collection tonight before you leave. Friday will be hectic, to say the least, for those of us acting as hosts and hostesses for this soiree."

Ivy jutted her jaw. "As director, I should be the hostess."

"Oh, dear me. Ivy's jealous," Natalie mocked. "Must I remind you—yet again—that you are an employee?"

Ivy sizzled.

"And how are the ticket sales going for the ball?" Hilary swiveled to Linda.

Hoping to distract the combatants? Good luck with that. Alison dumped the coffee grinds into the trash.

Linda cleared her throat. "At five hundred dollars a ticket, our attendees will be the cream of Raleigh society. Sales are brisk, and I expect this ball to be a resounding success for Weathersby at sellout capacity."

"Outstanding."

"Great job."

Linda preened. Bill said nothing.

Ivy crossed her arms. "Are we done yet?"

Hilary gave her a pointed look. "Not yet. I don't believe Bill has given us the monthly financial report."

"Bill's been under the weather this week." Linda laid a wifely hand on his sleeve. He coughed. "He got behind with the paperwork what with the ticket sales, too. He'll e-mail everyone the report."

Hilary sighed. "This is most irregular, Bill. If you'd told me earlier I could've pitched in."

Bill kept his head down.

Alison chanced peering around the door frame. He must be sick. He looked terrible. Shadows pockmarked his face, especially under his eyes and his right cheekbone.

Ivy squirmed. "Are we done now?"

"Where's the fire, Ivy?" joked Robert.

She gave him a nasty look. "I make a motion this meeting be adjourned."

Natalie, bored now her time in the spotlight was complete, played with a fingernail. "I second."

Hilary threw up her hands. "All right already." With a much-maligned expression, she banged the gavel on her folder.

Did Hilary ever wish she could bang this crowd's head instead?

"The meeting is adjourned."

Natalie leaned over the table. "Anyone want to accompany me on a tour of the exhibit? I hate to go up there in the dark all by my lonesome."

Chairs scraped.

"Come, Todd. *I'll* show you the collection."

Alison watched Erica grab his arm. She bit back a smile. Keep it up, love; you'll turn him into another Henry.

Robert and Bill shut down their computers. Linda and Bill were the first out the door.

"Thanks so much, Alison." Hilary caught hold of Robert's arm as he moved to join Alison in the kitchen. "A question for our secretary, Robert?"

Frowning as he bent his head to listen, Robert gave Alison a wave good-bye as Hilary pulled him out the door toward the parking lot.

Ivy marched straight into the kitchen. "Yes, so considerate of you, Mrs. Monaghan. Don't forget you'll have a lot of work to catch up on bright and early tomorrow." She smiled.

Wait for it.

"And," Ivy gestured around the kitchen, knocking Alison's cup across the counter. "Be sure and clean this mess before you leave."

31

Footsteps creaked overhead as Natalie and company roamed through the exhibit. Alison stuffed paper plates in the trashcan.

Thankful Lula had insisted on the board installing a dishwasher for such events, she loaded the cups and utensils and set it on the wash cycle. Its humming drowned out further sounds from upstairs. She glanced at her watch. 7:45 p.m. She had plenty of time to get home before the kids returned.

Not about to wait for the others, she turned off the lights in the kitchen and conference room. Her senses ratcheted up a notch in the darkness. Old houses, how they creaked and groaned.

Out on the porch, she locked the door behind her. Natalie could set the alarm when she left. Darkness wrapped around her like a cloak.

Thunder rumbled in the distance. Polly would be glad of the rain. So would her thirsty roses.

Leaving the shelter of the porch, she noticed the security light affixed at the top of the stone steps had blown out.

Probably be her job to call the utility company tomorrow and report it.

As she walked away from the house, bushes rustled. She picked up the pace with a glance over her shoulder toward the house. She stutter-stepped to a halt.

The house lay dark behind her. Not a light shone from the upstairs. Goose pimples broke out on her arms. Had Natalie and crew somehow managed to slip out before she did?

The dark pressed in upon her. A sound again from the bushes. Small, nocturnal animals?

Or, remembering the drawings, nocturnal human monsters?

She clutched her purse, her keys in her other hand wedged like a weapon between her first two fingers. Should she go back and set the alarm?

Lightning flashed, and in that instant as she pivoted, she detected a shadowy form in the deep recesses of the porch she'd just vacated. "Who's there?" Her voice sounded quavery and scared. Her heart drummed in her chest.

Silence.

Freaked, she decided the heirlooms were on their own and bolted through the sinister darkness of the yews, down the steps to the parking lot. The parking lot was deserted except for her lone black Lexus. She'd deliberately parked underneath a street light, but as she reached the safety of her car, glass crunched under her feet. And she realized the streetlights here were dark, too.

Spooked, she jabbed the lock release on her key chain. Light flooded the interior of the vehicle.

Grabbing the door handle, she caught sight of a flash of silver where her tire should be. A knife protruded from the vulcanized rubber of the tire. Deflated, the tire listed heavily. Her car was going nowhere fast.

She gripped the frame of the door, its solidity a small comfort between her and the darkness. Panting, she threw herself into the driver's seat and slammed the door, locking it.

The thunder boomed closer and lightning zinged across the sky. Something moved at the top of the stairs. She grabbed for her phone.

Idiot.

She'd turned off the power. It would take a minute to charge up. Coldness despite the muggy April evening enveloped her.

Evil approached. She could feel it deep in her bones, a prickle rising on the back of her neck. The age-old reaction of the prey in response to the predator. Menacing her in the darkness, it was coming for her. Gravel crunched, closer and closer.

Oh, God, help me.

There was a sudden flash of light as another car swept into the parking lot.

Savior or accomplice? Why hadn't she listened to Mike? What was she thinking stirring up trouble . . .?

The headlights revealed a pair of black-jean-clad legs on the steps. A man's legs.

Robert jumped out of his SUV. "Hey, you," he shouted as footsteps pounded up the stairs. "Stop!"

Her suspicions from earlier returned. Robert? Savior or accomplice?

But if she couldn't trust Robert . . .

She released a pent-up breath. She undid the locking mechanism and got out of her car. As the adrenaline seeped out of her body, she took a few wobbly steps toward Robert where his SUV stood running, lights ablaze. Robert met her halfway and held her upright as he supported her weight.

Her teeth chattered. "Y-you saw him?"

"I saw something." He peered into her face. "You're in shock. What happened?"

She shuddered. "My tire." She gestured.

Leaving her propped against his truck with its still-running engine, he examined her vehicle, taking a handkerchief out of his chinos and prying out the knife. Wrapping the cloth around the knife, he leaned into his car, tucking it under the seat for safety. "For your detective."

"He's not my detective."

Robert gave her a funny look. "Are you sure?"

No, she wasn't sure about anything. But she didn't voice her doubts to Robert.

Taking a look at her frozen face, Robert fumbled at his back pocket. "I'm calling him. He gave all of us his cards. Guess he knew you needed all the guardian angels you could get." In the faint light of the SUV, Robert withdrew a card from his wallet and dialed the number. No one picked up. Robert left a terse message on Mike's voicemail.

"He took my kids to Redeemer. I have to get home."

"I'll drive you home. Someone made sure your car wasn't going anywhere tonight." He helped her into the vehicle.

Always the gentlemen. Beloved of dogs and Bible study teachers.

She shook her head. No, that wasn't how it went. She suppressed a giggle. Was she hysterical?

If she could only stop shaking.

With a final ear-splitting crash of thunder, the rain cascaded in torrents from the night sky.

"Got any of that great coffee at home? I think you need a strong cup of joe with a lot of sugar. Best thing for the nerves, my friend Dr. Stephen would say."

She heard the smile in his voice. Beloved of children—that was it. A nice man. Who were, in her experience, an endangered species.

"I'll have you home in five minutes."

Once home, she gave him her house key. Her hands shook too badly to do the honors. In the kitchen, he ushered her into a chair.

Thank God, they'd beat Mike and the children home. There'd be hell to pay when he heard about her latest adventure. But a niggle of joy at the thought of his comforting presence filled her, warmed her. Better than the Kona.

"Just show me where you keep everything. You relax."

She pointed to the cupboard. "Do we have to tell him?" meaning Mike.

Robert, filling the carafe with water, laughed. "Yes, we do. He needs to know."

As her decaf brewed, he pulled out a chair.

Truck doors slamming, the cavalry returned. She heard Mike shouting from the street at the patrolman.

She winced. She'd not meant to land the officer in hot water.

As he stormed into the kitchen, a subdued pair of teenagers on his heels, she knew her reckoning had come.

32

She held up a hand, halting Mike in his tracks. "You never said I couldn't go out."

His eyes narrowed at the sight of Robert, his elbows on the table, smiling at him, cozy over a cup of coffee. "Nice try, but no dice. You," he pointed at her, "never said you wanted to go out and certainly not back to that den of psychos."

"It was job related, a board meeting."

"You were sizing up the suspects and you know it."

Robert picked up his mug and started for the sink, trying to disappear.

Mike jabbed a finger in Robert's direction. "What's he doing here?"

"Doing your job for you, Detective. Protecting Alison." Robert broadened his chest, a smirk on his face.

Mike took a step, clenching his fists at his side. He'd wipe that . . .

Alison scooted between them. She caught hold of Mike's balled fist. "What is wrong with you?" she hissed with a meaningful glance over to her children.

He shrugged free of her hand.

Robert, still smiling that Cheshire cat smile of his, jiggled his keys. "I'll call you tomorrow, Ali."

Irritation bubbled to the surface. "Not so fast, Robert. I'll need a statement from you about what went down this evening."

Justin and Claire exchanged a look.

The corners of Claire's lips tilted. "Mommy's in trouble."

Alison put her head between her hands on the table. "Act your age, Claire."

"Don't you kids have school tomorrow?" Mike growled.

Alison pointed at the back staircase.

Justin rubbed her shoulder. "I'll pray for you, Mom." Then he laughed.

"Everybody's ganging up on me." She groaned as Justin climbed the stairs two at a time. Claire snickered all the way upstairs.

"Unattractive in females," she called after Claire's retreating figure. Reducing Claire to loud, raucous laughter silenced only by the closing of her bedroom door.

Mike leaned in his favorite position against the counter.

Yeah, he had a favorite position.

From the looks of this cozy sit-down, Robert did, too. Which only stoked the flames of anger licking at his craw. Robert at least had the good sense to keep his mouth shut. Perhaps remembering Mike had a license to carry?

And boy, did he feel like killing something.

"It wasn't my fault," Alison stammered.

He crossed his arms. "Not buying it 'cause that's what you always say."

She stiffened. "Now before you go on the warpath—"

He locked eyes with her. "Are you slurring my ethnic background?"

"What?" She stared back, frowning in confusion. "Oh." Her eyes widened. "I forgot about you being Native."

He laughed outright. "You make it sound . . ."

Robert looked puzzled. "Native?"

Mike gave Robert a measured look. "It's Cherokee. I'm proud of the one-quarter Native American blood that runs through my veins. But enough of that." He shook his head. "For such a quiet-mannered lady she can sure play some fancy word games. Better than some lawyers, I've met."

He fixed his steely gaze on Robert. "Almost as good, wouldn't you say, as a mutual friend of ours? I believe you know Tom Richardson."

Robert's face lit up. "Indeed. Son of an old college friend." His smile faded. "But then I guess you already know all about me and everyone else at Weathersby. I'd have been disappointed to hear otherwise. You and Tom met at college, right?"

He nodded.

Robert examined him. "He speaks highly of you. Says you're a good guy and first-class brain. I didn't realize at first, you were that Mike."

"How did you happen to rescue Alison?" He laid a particular stress on the word *rescue* as if it seemed a little too opportune to suit him.

Robert shrugged. "Your reputation precedes you, Detective. As a man of reason and science, I don't think you're going to believe me."

"Try me."

"I left with the others. I didn't realize Alison was still in the house until I pulled out of the parking lot and noticed her Lexus. I got as far as three blocks. Someone," Robert lifted his eyes toward the ceiling, "told me I needed to check on her. I debated for a few more minutes." He glanced at Alison. "I didn't want to look like an old fool, but I eventually listened to that voice telling me to go back."

Mike thrust his jaw forward. "How convenient."

Robert bristled.

Alison grimaced, a glint in her eye. "It certainly was for me, Detective Barefoot."

So it was back to Detective Barefoot when the eligible Robert Kendall was around, was it? He glowered at her.

Alison pounded the table. He and Robert both jumped. "Could we get back to the real issue here? Like how I was stalked and scared witless twice today? Is Jasper Delaine in custody?"

Mike dropped his gaze, fumbling with his notepad. "Not exactly."

"Yes or no?" She narrowed her eyes. "Either you are in jail or you are not. Which is it?"

"We searched the toolshed again."

"Again?"

He lifted his shoulders and let them drop. "We searched it the day someone shot at you. The shed backs up through the woods to Orchard Farm Road."

Robert's eyes rounded. "Someone shot at you, Alison?"

"Where Frank was killed." She fluttered her hand. "I promise to tell you about it later."

Mike ground his teeth. "He'd already cleared out. We've got a BOLO out on Delaine all over the state."

Alison tilted her head. "What's a BOLO?"

"Be on the lookout." Mike gripped the pen. "But he's gone to ground for now."

"Like the vermin he is." She knotted her hands together. "It was definitely a man stalking me tonight. Probably Jasper. Revenge for ratting him out?"

Robert cleared his throat. He'd been quiet, watching the two of them slug it out, verbal tennis balls launched back and forth across the kitchen. "That reminds me of the knife I pulled from your tire. With your permission, I'll get it out of my truck." He looked at Mike.

He nodded. "Fine by me."

As Robert exited, she set her jaw. "He wrapped it carefully in a handkerchief. Maybe you'll be able to pull prints off it."

Mike shook his head in mock despair. "Have you ever considered a second career in law enforcement? I can give you a good recommendation, if you want to apply to the police academy on Old Garner Road."

She snorted. "Aren't you the comedian?"

He leaned across the table. "Are you sure you're okay?" He should've known she'd try something like this on her own. He should've been there for her.

She gave him a wobbly smile and reached for his hand. "I'm—"

"Here you go, Detective." Robert returned, laying his package in the middle of the table, forcing Alison and Mike to drop their hands back into their laps.

Seething, Mike stuffed his hand into one of his plastic bags and shook the knife free of the hanky. "Maybe we'll get lucky with the fingerprints."

Alison shuddered.

His heart thudded with the possibilities of what could have happened to her tonight. "You need to take this as a warning to back off, Alison."

She swallowed, her eyes fixed on the knife. "A warning or a promise of murderous intent?"

Terse, Mike led Robert once again through his eyewitness account of the crime scene as he remembered it. She filled Mike in on the board meeting.

Alison angled toward Robert. "I didn't realize Natalie's family was shut out of the inheritance of Weathersby."

Robert nodded. "Worth a lot on the open market for developers."

Mike's lips tightened. "Your area of expertise."

Robert shrugged. "With Raleigh mushrooming the way it is and one of the hottest spots for business and lifestyle, a sizable chunk of land close to the heart of downtown could've made someone a billionaire."

Alison nearly choked. "Seriously?"

"Easily."

Mike pursed his lips. "And how did you come to be on the board, Mr. Kendall?"

Robert explained his late wife's connection from the beginnings of the historic park.

Alison reached for her purse. "I've made a list of suspects and their possible motives. This just points more strongly than ever at Natalie."

Mike's eyebrow arched. "I get it, Alison. You don't like that lady."

She sniffed. "Under no stretch of the imagination could she be called a lady." She dug through her handbag. "Here it is." She smoothed it out on the kitchen table.

He jerked his head over to Robert. "What about him?"

Robert scrambled to his feet. "I'd better leave you two to your detecting."

"No, wait, Robert." She put a restraining hand on his arm. "There's nothing here we can't discuss in front of a friend. Please stay. I think your long association with Weathersby could provide us with valuable insight."

So it was like that between them, was it?

"Whatever." Mike swallowed down more than just his pride. "You've known these people longer than either of us." He scanned her notes.

Alison filled Robert in on what she'd found yesterday and of Natalie's suspicious behavior. "Was forensics able to determine anything from that strand of hair I found in the cloche hat?"

Mike eased into Justin's seat. He flicked a resentful look at Robert, who occupied his usual seat. "It wasn't synthetic. Its shade is inconclusive without another sample to match it to."

"So that rules out a wig."

Robert tilted his head. "Which would rule out Natalie as being the lady in the hat in San Francisco?"

"Humph." Alison crossed her arms and glanced away.

"And do not," Mike pointed a stern finger at her, "take it into your head to go around snatching hair from other women's heads. I'd have to arrest you for assault."

She straightened. "As if I would. Do you think I'm an idiot?"

"No comment. We've run these people through our databases with no luck." He flipped through his notepad. "However, your educational director, Erica . . ."

"Chambers."

"Yeah, her. She does have a record. One prior from her days in Chapel Hill. Arrested for assaulting a police officer and disorderly conduct following a protest march."

"For the legalization of marijuana, I'll bet."

He heaved a sigh.

Robert looked at her. "How'd you guess that?"

She avoided their eyes. At her soft-spoken admission to rifling through Ivy's personnel files, Mike restrained a grin.

Robert's lips parted. "Alison . . ."

"I don't normally act like this." She ran her finger around the rim of her mug. "I'm usually a law-abiding citizen."

Mike rolled his eyes.

"Of course, you are, Ali." Robert patted her hand. "I'd never doubt that for a minute."

Suck-up.

"Anyway . . ." He stared pointedly at Robert's hand until he dropped it back into his lap. "I've had the genius computer lads trying to crack this code of numbers from Frank's phone. San Fran's finest interviewed the staff of that hotel. But—" Mike glanced over at her.

"Not the greatest accommodation in the first place." She frowned.

"With not the most observant of employees." He ran a hand through his hair. "Half of them were afraid we were there to deport them as illegals, if you get my drift."

"So nobody remembers Frank, and San Francisco is pretty much a dead end?" Her voice sounded as hopeless as those early days after Frank's murder.

"I'm afraid so, but now that you"—he favored her with a small smile—"have a few female suspects, I'll fax over the photos and see if they can jog anyone's memory."

She sighed, weariness leaking from every pore. "We're no closer than we were the day someone murdered Frank."

"We?" Disapproval coated Robert's voice.

Mike bit the inside of his cheek. This guy was insufferable. What Alison saw in him—?

Discouragement etched her features. "The burglar was a man. My stalker tonight was male. Maybe you're right, Mike. Maybe I'm letting my emotions cloud my better judgment about Frank's killer."

Robert, as if sensing he was backing the wrong horse, abruptly changed his tune. "You've got good instincts, Ali. I say trust your gut and no one else at Weathersby." He glanced over to Mike. "Between you and Raleigh's finest, I'm sure you'll figure this puzzle out eventually."

"Tomorrow is going to be nightmarishly long." Just making the observation brought a tired look to Alison's face.

Mike darted a glance at the kitchen clock. It was going on eleven.

"It'll be chaos with the docents and staff scrambling to get ready for the ball on Friday. The entire weekend looks to be out of control at this point."

Robert's eyes gleamed. "Are you attending the ball?"

Mike fidgeted, a muscle jumping along his cheek.

Alison looked at him.

First, he noted. But before he could savor the small victory, she shifted toward Robert.

"I guess. Frank had bought two tickets. Although what society will say about a widow . . ." She drew herself up. "But at five hundred dollars a pop and a no-refund policy, you bet I wouldn't miss it for the world."

"And I'll plan on being your escort and use Frank's ticket." Mike stuffed his pencil and pad into his pocket. Nothing like a preemptive strike.

Her eyes widened. "Well, don't mind me." Her eyebrows rose almost to her hairline. "Feel free to invite yourself."

But he detected a pleased note in her voice.

Robert glared.

Mike smiled at them, barracudalike. "I won't mind you. I'll be there to keep a watch on our suspects and keep you from doing something foolhardy. Again."

She sputtered.

"And perhaps, because I'll be on official police business, I can recoup some of your ticket by filing for reimbursement with the chief."

She swallowed. "When you put it like that . . ."

Mike rose and waited for Robert to do the same. "A woman after my own money-grubbing heart. Shall we, Mr. Kendall? I think it's time we let Alison get her beauty sleep."

Robert gestured to the door. "After you."

"You first." Mike grunted.

"Both of you," Alison pointed. "Get out."

33

VAL DROPPED ALISON OFF AT A CAR RENTAL AGENCY. ALISON ZOOMED along Glenwood on her way to Weathersby, feeling sporty and carefree despite last night's harrowing adventure.

She put the top down on the red Chrysler Sebring, enjoying the sun and the wind on her face. Val, plus a generous insurance policy, convinced her to rent the convertible.

And the color?

Well, she felt like red today. It was bolder than her normal palette of choice. But despite a lack of sleep the night before, she had a feeling something was going to happen soon to break open the case, and she was determined to remain optimistic.

That pile of dictation still waited for her, and if she knew Ivy—and she was beginning to know her all too well—she'd be cooped up in the office all day despite this glorious April weather.

And true to her prediction, the typing did take all day, but by five o'clock, she'd managed somehow to catch up with Ivy's frenzied dictation and correspondence. Justin and Claire reported a quiet day at school when she quizzed them over the phone.

Officer Ross had trailed them—discreetly to Claire's satisfaction—home. Dutiful Justin called his mom when they walked through the door and on the hour every hour per her instructions.

She walked in to the enticing aromas of chicken and wild rice soup. But with a kick, as Claire pointed out. She ditched her purse and her shoes, slipping into her favorite pink polka dot flip-flops.

"Twenty minutes," Claire cautioned. "Justin is upstairs on the phone with Mike. They're working on Justin's new 'How to' essay."

Go figure. Mountain-man Mike—English tutor.

"What?" She mimicked Claire, drama-queen style. "Mike's not planning on joining us for dinner?"

Claire stirred the soup. "Not tonight, but I invited him over for dinner Saturday."

She blinked. "You what?"

"You'll both be busy tomorrow night at the ball."

She placed one hand on her hip. "Now wait a minute, Claire. You make it sound like it's a date."

"Oh, Mom. Give me a little credit. He already told Justin and me about it on the phone when we called him after school."

They had phone instructions from him, too?

"He wanted to make sure Justin and I understood he was there to protect you and gather intel."

"You make me sound like Mata Hari with her dance of the veils."

Claire clanged the lid on the pot. "Puh-leeze, Mother. Now I have to live forever with that image of you burned into my delicate young mind."

She swatted at Claire's behind.

Claire clasped her hands together. "So . . . I've been working all afternoon on your ball gown."

"My what?"

"You heard me. Have you for one moment considered what you're going to wear tomorrow night?"

She bit her lip.

Claire threw up her hands. "Exactly. That's why I took it upon myself to make sure you didn't disgrace our family with something you yanked out of the closet at the last minute. Justin and I have to live in this town, you know."

Taking hold of her shoulders, Claire steered her into the family room. "Men have it so easy. A tux and they're done. I've been advising Mike on accessories to tweak his ensemble."

Imagining that conversation put a smile on Alison's face.

Claire dragged her mother over to a heap of fabric lying helter-skelter across the sofa. She draped a swath of shimmering gold lamé over Alison's shoulder. Claire stood chin in hand, surveying the result. "Yes, just as I thought. Gold is definitely your color."

Alison fingered the material. "It's a little clingy."

"Silhouette-revealing, Mother. You're thin, and you've got great, long legs which I intend to show off with a slit in the side up to about . . ." Claire's hand moved up the outside of Alison's thigh.

She grabbed Claire's palm and pushed it down. And down. And farther down still.

"I'm not in the market, young lady."

Claire raised an expertly penciled brow. "Oh, really?"

"Yes, really, and I'm not trying to advertise my assets or lack thereof, either."

Claire skewered her with a look. "You must try and develop a little more self-confidence." She grinned and tossed her head back with her hand across her brow. Her golden hoops quivered. "We artists are so little understood. But as you wish, Mother dear, if you don't mind being boring. And lame."

Smart enough to know when she had been roundly insulted, Alison decided to drop it. "Where did you get all this fabric?"

Claire folded the luscious lengths of spangled material. "Aunt Val took me after her doctor's appointment. I left Justin with strict instructions to start the soup. He taught Officer Ross how to putt while I was gone. Aunt Val and I had to dash through Fletcher's Fabrics to make it home in time. She just left, as a matter of fact, right before you got home."

Through years of experience in dealing with Claire, she seized on the most important piece of information. "Why was Val at the doctor?"

223

Claire shrugged as she wrapped the black feather boa around her neck. "How should I know? Female stuff, most likely. I'm not as nosy as you are, Mother. I respect other people's privacy."

As Claire made her grand exit amidst much flouncing up to the bonus room where she had her own sewing corner, Alison stopped resisting her urges. She rolled her eyes.

"And the good Lord alone knows what getup she's going to have for me." Alison pressed the phone against her ear.

"It's going to be lovely. She showed me her design drawings. I'm so jealous. The costume I bought is going to pale by comparison," Val commented on the other end of the line.

Alison tucked her feet under her, the pillow cushion propped between her and the armrest.

"I'm looking forward to the ball. Stephen and I don't usually attend these sorts of society functions. But Stephen's boss, the head of cardiology, was pushy about the whole thing. Stephen felt pressured to buy a ticket. Two, to be exact. The entire department will be there."

"Yes, Dr. Reynolds has always been a generous supporter."

"He's certainly a generous arm twister," said Val. "Nothing wrong with Weathersby and historic preservation, mind you, but it's a lot of money, and we tend to lend our financial support to our church."

"I know, but I, for one, will be glad to have your presence there tomorrow night. It will be my first official outing since Frank's death. People will stare and point."

"Now you sound like Claire," Val chided. "It will be far less dramatic than you imagine. There've been no follow-up articles since Monday."

"That's because there have been no developments. But I'm working on changing that."

Val heaved a deep sigh. "I thank God every night for Mike. Lord knows he's got his job cut out for him, if he hopes to restrain you from rushing in where angels fear to tread."

"You sound like him. Have you guys been conspiring against me?"

"No, just trying to keep you alive. Consider Stephen and me your backup. We plan to take our jobs seriously," Val joked. "Speaking of the handsome detective, you know I expect you to spill your guts about your big date after the ball."

Alison bolted upright, almost dropping the phone. "It's not a date, Val. We're working the case."

Val gave a short bark of a laugh. "You two are working something all right."

She fretted at the zipper on the cushion. "He's too young for me, Val."

"Hah! He's all of what? Three years younger? Or is that just your latest excuse to stick your head in the sand this week?"

She gripped the phone. "I do not—"

"I always say, 'Get 'em young and train 'em right.'"

Alison giggled—despite herself—as Val had intended.

Skirmishing broke out on Val's end.

"Got to go," yelled Val over the noise. "Stephen's on call tonight, and World War III just erupted in the living room between Trey and Dillon over the remote. It's a guy thing apparently."

She laughed. "Sure thing. I'll see you at the ball." As she clicked off the phone a tiny flicker of excitement ignited within Alison.

The ball. That sounded so—so outside her usual life, so full of enchantment.

She darted a glance at the ceiling, toward the steady hum of the sewing machine. If it were up to Claire—her own personal fairy godmother—she wouldn't only feel like Cinderella going to the ball, she'd look like her, too.

And on Mike's well-muscled arm. Her toes curled in delicious anticipation.

Whoa . . .

Better not get carried away. Because deep down, despite the excitement of ball gowns and dancing, she refused to give herself over completely to fantasy. Reality had hit fantasy head-on a long time ago.

No handsome prince awaited her. Not now. Not ever. In fact, she didn't believe they existed anymore. She hadn't believed for a long time.

Not since Hawaii.

34

ALISON HUNG UP THE PHONE. MIKE PROMISED THE POLICE WOULD BE FIN-
ished with her car by Saturday. He'd pick her up tonight in time for
the ball.

She frowned.

That sounded way too much like a date for her peace of mind.
Not to mention what other people would think. She shook her head.
Too late, though. They were both committed to this investigation
now.

Maybe thinking of this evening at the ball as part of her investigation would help her get through it. Like Val, she wasn't so big
on socializing with these society movers and shakers. Some of them
were nice, regular people, like Hilary. Many of them were not. A
picture of Natalie rose in her mind.

"Ugh!" She shook herself free of the image.

Even before coming to know Christ, and she was faithfully
working her way through the Bible, she'd known it was wrong to
value or devalue someone because of the house they lived in or the
car they drove.

Or, the color of their skin.

Glancing out the window, she caught sight of Miss Lula raising Cain with the party rental deliverymen. If anyone should be
on the Weathersby board, it should be Lula Burke, whose family

had served the Weathersbys and knew more about its history than anyone else living.

Nate McLawhorn had taught his daughter one thing if nothing else—to see beneath the surface. Miss Lula, the housekeeper, was "good people," he would've said. But in this world, housekeepers, white or black, didn't serve on boards.

They scrubbed them.

Goodness—as she was learning over and over in these last troubled months—had little to do with money or position and everything to do with the heart.

She smiled as she watched Miss Lula directing the traffic of tents, tables, and chairs. The rental company had erected an open-air outdoor dance pavilion along the side lawn. Another nearby tent was being set up to accommodate the caterers who would serve food to Raleigh's glitterati. White wicker chairs and tables sprinkled the landscape.

Ginny marched her little troop of fourth graders, their eyes as round as saucers, past the hordes of docents stringing white lights around the bushes and the perimeter. "Like Christmas!" one little boy shouted.

Erica corralled her restless grade-school charges past Polly and the garden docents creating colorful garden centerpieces for each table of eight.

Alison pushed her bangs back with one hand. And here she was, stuck inside with Ivy's to-do list. How she wished she were part of their fun.

But no rest for the weary. Ivy, like the wicked stepmother of Cinderella fame, seemed determined to keep her nose to the grindstone. She smiled at her own whimsy. She must stop with the Cinderella analogies. A psychologist would have a field day with that one.

Humming the theme from *The Wizard of Oz*, she replaced the Cinderella folktale with another one. The image of Ivy in a witch's hat distracted her for at least five minutes until she heard the tiny peal of her cell phone.

Leaving her happy contemplations of houses landing on Ivy or better still, the possibilities of water melting Ivy altogether, she dived into her desk drawer and caught it on the last ring.

There was a hesitation before the caller realized he was live and not on voicemail.

"Alison?"

It was Dennis Scott, Frank's flying buddy and sometime copilot. The last time she'd heard from him was when Dennis had bought the Piper Cub.

"Yes, Dennis."

His voice warmed. "I'm so glad I caught you. I wanted to thank you for introducing me to the Lawrences at Frank's funeral."

Dennis had been one of Frank's pallbearers. In the haze of that mournful afternoon, she didn't remember doing any introductions, but whatever.

"It's been a hectic week since Bill asked me to take over Frank's job. He's already deposited that chunk of change in my account. With our daughter, Savannah, off to college next fall, I appreciate all the moonlighting I can get. And I wanted you to know I'm going to write you a check as a finder's fee in memory of Frank."

She frowned into the phone. "Frank's job? What job are you talking about, Dennis?"

"I'm taking over Frank's contract to fly the Lawrences to Grand Cayman on Saturday."

The Grand Caymans had been one of the stops on their cruise with the Lawrences last summer. Going again so soon? How nice.

For them.

She was amazed at how petty she seemed to be lately. Still, it was sweet of Dennis to think of her and her current financial need.

"That's generous of you, but not necessary."

"I insist. Frank had already done the legwork. I'm just fulfilling the rest of the contract."

Intrigued, she frowned into the phone. "What legwork?"

"He'd completed all the paperwork preparatory to filing a flight plan. I kept Frank's call sign. So it'll be Piper-seven-seven-Charlie-

Papa from RDU. Final destination Grand Cayman. I found the flight details stuck in the cockpit."

Piper 77? That number rang a bell. Her eyes widened and she scrambled in her purse until she retrieved the pile of papers Claire had copied from Frank's phone.

They were at the bottom of her purse, of course.

"Dennis? Could you hold on one second?"

She turned page after page until she found the photocopy on which Frank had recorded four sets of numbers. The first, 415, had been the sleazy motel where he'd conducted his out-of-town affairs.

Just as she thought, the second number began with 77. A crazy idea took hold. "Can you hang on a few minutes more, Dennis?"

"Sure." He sounded puzzled by the urgency of her voice. "Are you okay, Alison?"

Alison typed in a question in the search engine on her computer. Five seconds later, she had her answer to one part of the puzzle. "When are you scheduled to fly the Lawrences out of the country?"

"Saturday morning, 10 a.m. I told Linda this evening would be a better time to travel. Meteorologists are calling for a storm front to sweep the Southeast tomorrow. Strong winds, maybe isolated tornados. But Linda was insistent they couldn't leave till after that fancy-schmancy ball you folks have got going on tonight. I guess they're heavily invested in its success."

Suspicious now, she was beginning to question how invested they were. And what exactly was Grand Cayman's extradition policy with the United States?

"When are you flying them back, Dennis?"

He laughed. "That's the funny thing. Just the one-way trip. Bill told me their plans for returning were in limbo at the moment, and they would fly commercial or give me a call when they got tired of vacationing. Must be the life. I, for sure, wouldn't know."

"Or me." She grimaced. "But if I have my way, you and I won't know life inside a jail cell, either."

"What jail?" A slice of fear trickled through his voice. "What are you talking about Alison?"

"You need to tell Detective Barefoot everything you just told me, Dennis. He's the lead investigator in Frank's murder."

"Wait a minute." Dennis's voice caught. "You think these people killed Frank? Why would they do that? They were counting on him to fly them out tomorrow."

"I'm not sure about all the details." She gripped the phone. "But lots of things about the Lawrences are too good to be true. Maybe Frank discovered their plans to leave the country permanently and they silenced him."

"I don't know, Alison. Sounds far-fetched to me. All of this could be perfectly innocent." She could tell he didn't want to believe his cash windfall was a hoax.

"Wait, Dennis. Let me read to you a number Frank entered into his appointment calendar." She read him the number.

"Okay, suspicious maybe," he conceded, "with the first two numbers the same as the aircraft number, 77."

"I looked it up, Dennis. The latitude and longitude of Owens International Airport in George Town on the Grand Cayman Island is 19°20'North by 81°20'West. 1-9-2-0-8-1-2-0." She repeated the numbers to him.

Dennis groaned. "Oh, man. Alison, you may have saved me from making the worst mistake of my life. I'd be charged as an accessory to whatever they've done. I should've known. If it sounds too good to be true . . ."

"It probably is," she finished. "I'm sorry about this, Dennis."

He sighed. "Not your fault. I was dazzled by the cash and not suspicious enough."

She gave him Mike's cell number. "Give him a call and tell him everything we discussed. He can do a more thorough check on their background and advise you on how to proceed."

Tears stung her eyelids. Had she managed to solve Frank's murder by Dennis's inadvertent phone call and a few computer searches?

"Don't tip off the Lawrences to what we suspect." She sucked in a breath. "Or you and I both could end up as dead as Frank."

Mike tried hard not to grin. His face was beginning to hurt. But every time he thought about his date with Alison tonight . . .

His cell phone jangled on top of his desk. Caller ID denoted his friend, Ray, as the caller.

"Hey, buddy," Mike kicked back. "How's it going? Any news on the case I—"

He frowned, listening. "Sounds like an opportunity. Six months ago I'd have jumped at the chance."

Ray filled his ear with the details.

"I know. Big city. D.C. Chance to work with the Feds . . ."

Ray interrupted.

Mike whistled. "Big salary jump, too. But, man, I—"

He listened again. "I know, I know. With my language skills, it would be right up my alley."

He went silent as Ray gushed on about the career move of a lifetime.

"Okay. I'll think about it and let you know in the next couple of days. But, I've got another opportunity of a lifetime right here in Raleigh . . ." He flushed, surprised at himself for revealing so much.

"Will do." He ended with a promise to call soon. "And tell Serena once again I'm praying Baby Jude takes after her not you. Wouldn't wish that kind of ugly on any kid."

Laughing, he flicked the cover shut but quickly sobered. He glanced to the fluorescent lighting of the police station.

He'd been angling for a career change like this for ages. Was God trying to tell him something about his future or lack thereof with Alison? Or was this some kind of test?

Why now, God?

He'd sensed in these last few days, a crevice had opened in the door of Alison's heart. Or was he kidding himself? Did he have a chance with her?

Should he stay and find something that until now he hadn't realized he'd been looking for all his life? Or should he go and use his God-given abilities in the cause of justice? What if Alison didn't feel the same way he did? What if God wanted him to sacrifice his feelings for her for a greater good?

He thought of her smiling at him over a cup of Kona. Her flip-flop collection—all of them her favorites. The special warmth—he told himself—in her eyes just for him. Was he imagining all that? Surely not.

But the idea of declaring his feelings for her left him more afraid than facing down a street gang. Not good with words, he'd attempted to tell her what he felt but got all tongue-tied and instead told her something totally inappropriate describing his latest case involving multiple homicides.

Yeah, that was him. Mr. Smooth-talker with the guts and gore.

Nobody would ever mistake him for a prince to be sure. But tonight?

Maybe the magic of a real, bona fide ball . . .

"God, I'd be most grateful," he muttered under his breath as his phone rang again, "if You could see fit to bestow a little charm this way." He frowned, a vague memory of a fairy tale playing through his mind. "Or at least help me not to be a frog."

35

AFTER SHE HUNG UP WITH DENNIS, ALISON DID A SEARCH FOR SCHOOLS IN George Town in the Caymans. Perhaps this explained Heather and Zoe's bizarre persecution of Justin and Claire. The girls had only been in Raleigh about five years and from all appearances had settled nicely into Stonebriar's high-school life.

If they knew anything about the events of the last few months, maybe in some irrational way they blamed the rest of the Monaghans for "forcing" their mom and dad to relocate.

The Caymans were in the same time zone as Raleigh, Eastern Standard Time. If she was lucky—scratch that, make that if God made the way—she'd catch somebody at one of the high schools and verify Heather and Zoe Lawrence were enrolled, pointing to a longer stay than that of mere tourists on vacation.

Please, God, make someone pick up.

She'd start with the top boarding schools in the George Town area. That sounded about right for Linda Lawrence's style.

It was scary how easily any and all information could be obtained via the Internet. She gazed out the window, stalling.

Ivy, as was her leadership style, personally supervised the setup of the orchestra pit and technical wiring of the speaker's podium. She wanted to make sure all and sundry heard her opening speech.

At least, it would keep her out of Alison's hair long enough to make a few phone calls.

Taking a deep breath, she dialed the first number. It rang four times, but as she was about to hang up and try the next number, a brisk British island–accented voice answered. "Hullo? St. George's Preparatory. How may I be of service?"

She straightened. "I'm calling from the USA to verify you received Heather and Zoe Lawrence's transcripts this week."

A computer mouse clicked and keys typed. "We have no record of any students by that name. Who did you say was calling?"

She hung up. *Thank you, God, for island helpfulness.*

Two phone calls later, she had her answer. Heather and Zoe Lawrence were enrolled beginning Monday morning at St. Bertha's Preparatory School of Learning for Young Ladies.

"Gotcha." She dialed Mike. Would he think her theories worth checking into, or would he tell her to stop imagining she was Poirot?

Mike answered on the first ring. "Miz Monaghan . . ."

She got goose bumps at the sound of his voice.

Focus . . .

"I spoke with Dennis Scott," Mike drawled into the phone.

"And?"

Get on with it, man.

"I think you are a genius. Good detecting."

She slumped against her chair. "You think it's possible?"

"I do indeed. It's not only possible, but your conclusions are logical and reasonable given their highly suspicious behavior of the past few weeks."

She released the deep breath she hadn't realized she was holding until now. She quickly brought him up-to-date with her information about the permanence of the Lawrences' vacation.

Another horrifying thought occurred to her.

"Do you suppose Frank was going to . . . ?" Her voice trembled. She wasn't sure she could say it out loud.

Mike remained silent for a moment. "No. As a policeman, I don't ever suppose. But if I had to make an educated guess, the evidence points more in the opposite direction of Frank gathering evidence, not to collude with their crimes, but to expose them."

She cradled the phone. "You think so? Really?"

"My gut tells me so. But we'll know more after the Lawrences are brought in for questioning. I intend to rattle their cage as hard as I can. They're up to their necks in something illegal."

She told him about her suspicions regarding the Lawrences and the ticket sales from the ball.

"That would certainly explain their insistence on not leaving town till Saturday morning."

"Bill was sick or something, Linda claimed, at the board meeting on Wednesday, and although he was sitting right there at the table with his laptop, she did most of the talking. She said Bill had been unable to get the monthly financial reports ready in time for the meeting."

"Suspicious," Mike agreed. "And I find his silence interesting."

Alison perked in her seat. "So what's the plan?"

"The plan is for you and me to attend the ball tonight, and we'll keep a close surveillance on the sticky-fingered couple. I'll have a plainclothes officer watching their house, too."

"But when are you going to pick them up?"

"At the airport."

"Isn't that calling it a little too close for comfort?"

He growled. "You know, Miz Monaghan, I have done this kind of thing at least once or twice in my career."

She could tell he was getting irritated.

He took another deep breath as if she tried all the patience to be had in the world. "The banks are closed by the time the ball is over. I've been checking the Weathersby accounts, and so far, no recent deposits have shown up in terms of that amount of cash. So if the Lawrences arrive at the airport terminal with that much cash on their person . . ."

"You've caught them red-handed."

"The smoking gun." He rustled some papers on the other end. "A colleague is checking into their background before arriving in

Raleigh, but so far, no William or Linda Lawrence has shown up on any tax records or in any criminal cases."

"You think they changed their names when they moved to North Carolina?"

"It's a possibility I'm checking into. Do you have any idea where they were from in California? California is a mighty big state."

She had a sudden hunch. "Try the San Francisco Bay area first."

"You're thinking of Frank's last trip to that city?"

"Perhaps Frank was gathering evidence, as you suggest, in addition to his extracurricular tryst with the mysterious woman."

"Alison, hon—" He took a deep breath. "Why don't you let me handle this case from now on? These kinds of reminders can't be too comfortable for you."

Sudden tears winked in her eyes. Kindness always got to her. She had experienced very little kindness in the last few years from Frank. And Val was right. Mike wasn't anything like Frank.

"No, Mike. I need to see this thing through. I want to be there tomorrow morning when you arrest them at the airport."

He snorted. "No way. No how."

"Why not? I'm the one who connected the dots that led you to them."

"Because you are a civilian, and you're not going to get hurt on my watch."

"Please, let me come. I'll stay far back in the hangar. I won't say a word. I'll be as quiet as—"

"A mouse?" He chuckled. "Alison, you are anything but a mouse."

She smiled into the receiver. Time for a little Southern magnolia.

"Puh-leeze, Mike. It's important."

"Now you sound like your daughter. You and that red-headed kid of yours are a lot alike."

"Claire and me?"

"Yeah, when the both of you get an idea in your head, heaven help the rest of us. Do you have any idea what she's badgered me into wearing tonight?"

"Stop changing the subject."

"Like I said, two dogs with a bone."

"Are you going to let me come tomorrow or—or do I have to sneak into the airport terminal and run the risk of alerting the Lawrences?"

Silence on his end. Then, "Are you blackmailing me, Miz Monaghan? I sure would hate to have to arrest you for threatening an officer of the law."

Alison smiled. She could tell from his voice, he was going to let her tag along on Saturday. She'd won this skirmish. No need to rub his nose in it.

"What time are you picking me up tonight?"

He sighed, letting the air out slowly.

She imagined him leaning back in his chair, hands locked behind his head and his feet up on the desk. Goose bumps broke out all over her skin. Again.

"Alison . . ." He lingered over the syllables of her name, a strange hitch in his voice.

Did he have any idea what the sound of his voice did to her?

"Seven o'clock." He cleared his throat. "Be ready. I'm not hanging around waiting for you to make a grand entrance. The word for tonight is *inconspicuous*. Got it?"

"Inconspicuous." Her face hurt from smiling. "Got it."

36

"THERE. ALL DONE." CLAIRE STOOD BEHIND HER MOTHER AS THEY EXAMined her handiwork in the mirror.

Alison's eyes widened. What magic had her daughter wrought? Was that her, Alison McLawhorn Monaghan, glamorous and sophisticated?

"What have you done to me, Claire?" she whispered.

"Don't you like it? You're . . ." Claire searched for the right word.

Alison tilted her head. "Almost beautiful."

"So you do like it." Claire finger combed a few hair strands behind her mother's ears, smoothing them in with the rest of her silver-blonde hair, styled in a 1930s Art Deco chignon. Claire reached for the hairspray.

She grabbed for the can as well. "Whoa there, Hairdresser Extraordinaire. It's plastered to my head."

"Oh, Mother. It's perfect." Claire twirled several short strands of hair into a curlicue and layered them on each of Alison's cheeks.

Alison turned this way and that trying to get a fully rounded view of the new and improved Alison Monaghan. "I look so different. Not like myself at all."

"It's not supposed to be you. It's a costume ball, and you are a starlet, a Hollywood glamour girl from the silver screen."

She raised a hand to her face. "I don't usually wear this much makeup." Her brown eyes appeared twice as large thanks to Claire's lavish application of eyeliner and lash-lengthening mascara.

Claire slapped her hand away from touching her rose-tinted cheeks. "Stop being such a prude."

"Where did you get this stuff?" She swept her hand across the top of the dresser where piles of eye shadow, foundation, and mascara littered the surface. She peered at herself in the mirror. "And would you look at my cheekbones?"

"I sculpted them, emphasizing the assets you already possess. You look gorgeous, Mom. Relax. I've been watching that makeover show on cable. You have to put the makeup on with a trowel for an evening event." Claire's tone implied, don't you know anything, Mom? "Turn around. Let's get the full effect."

Alison pirouetted in slow motion. Claire, like an anxious mother hen, plucked at stray threads only she could see.

The form-fitting gold lamé hugged every curve of her body. Where she didn't possess the right degree of curve, Claire had cleverly augmented her mother's lack of cleavage by inserting a built-in push up bra.

Claire had also chosen—after listening to her "client"—to place the slit in a wide V in the front of the floor-length dress. Its peak slightly above the knee gave the mysterious illusion of more than was actually revealed. She'd sewn a black feather boa into the top of the off-the-shoulder bodice.

Alison kept hoisting the straps onto her shoulders. Claire kept pulling them down and off her shoulders.

Claire nodded. "You'll do. Oh." She grabbed the dangly diamond pendant earrings from the bureau. "Don't forget Grandma Irene's earrings. Vintage to the period," she noted with satisfaction. "I do so love, as the TV guy used to say, when a plan comes together."

From her elbow-length ivory satin gloves to the faux diamond bracelet, unsure how to take in this transformation, Alison glanced over her shoulder at her backside. "Do you think this dress makes my butt—?"

"No, I do not think this dress makes your butt look big. Get a grip, Mom."

She tried to get adjusted to the vision in front of her eyes. The dress was beautiful. Claire had used her eye for color, texture, and line to create something out of the ordinary.

Maybe if she closed her eyes, she could believe she was actually some screen siren. She certainly looked like she belonged in an Agatha Christie costume drama. "Thank you, Claire. You outdid yourself."

The doorbell rang downstairs. Her hands convulsed at her sides.

"I'll get it, Mom," yelled Justin from the foot of the stairs.

"Showtime." Claire pushed her mother toward the stairs. "Let's not keep Mike waiting."

Alison dug in her heels, but it was a losing battle. "Are you sure," she hissed over her shoulder to Claire, "that I look okay? That I look my age and not like I'm having a midlife crisis?"

Claire put her back into it. "You look great. Mike's going to love it."

"That's not what I meant." She reached the landing and peered over. Justin and Mike stood in the foyer.

Wearing a double-breasted, pinstriped tuxedo, like some 1920s gangster, Mike carried a small white box in his hand.

Alison fell back onto Claire. "I'm not ready for this."

"Stop stalling, Mother. You'll hurt his feelings. Don't panic. He brought you a corsage to match your dress per my instructions."

A corsage. Classic Claire.

She squared her shoulders and started down with Claire lagging a few steps behind. Claire was determined to let her have her so-called Big Moment.

The guys were probably going to laugh their heads off at the sight of her. She looked ridiculous in this getup. She was more of a flip-flop, casual sort of girl than steamy sex symbol.

But, perhaps the outfit would give her the courage she normally lacked. She wanted to get this entire evening over with as soon as possible.

About halfway down, the guys stopped talking and looked up. Justin grinned from ear to ear. A crooked smile hovered on Mike's granite face, a frown between his eyes.

She swallowed. He didn't like—

"Wow." Justin high-fived his sister. "Way to go, Claire. You look beautiful, Mom."

She gave everyone a tremulous smile and patted Justin's cheek with one satin-covered hand. "Thanks, honey. You know how to make a girl feel special."

"Here." Mike thrust the box at her, landing a small blow to her stomach. A spot of color darkened each of his sharp, high cheekbones.

She took the box and, with trembling fingers, removed the corsage from the packing. "You shouldn't have, Mike." She slipped the purple-tinged orchid over her wrist and shot a pointed look at Claire. "You shouldn't have, but thank you. It's beautiful."

The refracting light of the chandelier lent a shimmering, rainbowlike quality to the entryway. Claire handed her the gossamer gold stole, again from the wardrobe of Grandma Irene—a prominent Irish city councilman's daughter.

Mike cleared his throat. "Justin's right. You look stunning." He appeared distracted, glancing about the foyer. "We'd better get going. Officer Ross will be outside as usual all night."

Claire took the empty box from her mother and handed her mother a small, ivory-beaded clutch purse. "And what time do you plan to bring our mother home, Detective Barefoot?"

Alison gasped. "Claire."

Justin laughed. "Yeah. About what time should we expect you?" He crossed his arms across his chest and tried to look stern.

Her children were having way too much fun with this situation.

Mike leaned against the railing of the stairs. "Whatever time you say, Mr. Monaghan, sir."

Justin pretended to frown. "I think before midnight sounds about right to me." He opened the front door for them. "We'll be waiting for you both."

Mike jiggled his keys. He winked at the kids as he passed, and she attempted a wobbly smile.

Midnight. Wasn't that when coaches turned into pumpkins anyway?

Weathersby glowed with life when Alison and Mike arrived. Every room in the three-story house was alight. The grounds, thanks to hundreds of Chinese lanterns and small fairy lights, had an air of magic, full of romance and possibilities. They paused at the top of the stone steps between the gap in the yews to take in the scene.

The scent of lilacs hung in the April night air. The sun, almost below the horizon, created its own spectacular show with luminous streaks of pink, purple, and smoky blue.

The ride over in Mike's truck hadn't been uncomfortable, though he kept glancing over to her as he drove.

Feeling self-conscious, she put a hand to her chignon. "I know I look . . ."

"You take my breath tonight." He reached over gently flicking one of her earrings into motion and placed his hand beside hers on the seat. "But I also have a fondness for girls who wear flip-flops and drink exotic coffee."

She could feel him smile. She didn't know how she could, but she could.

Driving into the packed parking lot, she realized this fundraiser ball was shaping up to be The Event of Raleigh's social season. Everybody who was anybody was bound to be here tonight. The question was, what was she doing here?

She shivered with sudden nerves.

"Are you cold?"

She shook her head. "No, just . . ."

Mike squeezed her hand. "Me, too."

His hand sent a tingle up her spine. It made her feel dizzy.

"You don't look it," she hastened to assure him and distract herself from the direction of her treacherous thoughts. "You clean up pretty good." He did, rugged yet debonair, thanks to Claire's efforts. Like a cowboy all dressed up.

He smiled, one of those rare, genuine moments of warmth reaching all the way to his eyes that he only occasionally displayed when he let his guard down. "Shall we?" He held out his arm.

She took a deep breath and slipped her arm into the crook of his elbow.

He patted her gloved hand. "Can we eat first, before we start casing the joint?"

She laughed.

As they made their way into the catering tent, she noted Natalie and Erica over by the dance pavilion. Natalie, true to her word, had on the cloche hat with a designer-quality fringed black flapper dress that showed off her tanned, muscular legs to perfection. As intended, no doubt.

She kept her eye on them through the open flap of the tent entrance as she picked up a glass plate. Mike piled his plate as high as gravity would allow, the variety and amount of food not often enjoyed on a cop's salary.

Erica, true to her more modern inclinations, was dressed as a psychedelic flower child, her go-go skirt revealing as much leg as Natalie's. Gel spiked Erica's strawberry blonde hair, and a matching tie-dyed headband encircled her head. Erica pointed at Natalie's hat. Natalie had added an artfully placed black feather on the side of the hat.

Erica had recognized the cloche hat from the Weathersby collection. Alison noted this with satisfaction as she dived into the Caesar salad. From her vantage point, it was obvious the two were engaged in a shouting match. Only the discordant strains of the nearby orchestra tuning up kept their battle skirmish from attracting more attention.

Mike gazed at the dessert table with undisguised longing. She could tell he was calculating whether he should defy gravity or get another plate and then, if he could carry two plates successfully out to the tables near the pavilion. She buttered a wheat roll before adding it to her plate.

The shouting match escalated. Both women waved angry arms and pointed fingers in each other's faces. Out of the corner of her eye, she watched Hilary—at least she thought it was Hilary in a farthingale—on her way to intervene.

She found it hard to tell who was who among the cleverly disguised doctors, lawyers, and politicians partying tonight as Civil War generals, World War I flying aces, and what looked like a roll call of debutante fashions through the ages.

Apparently deciding he possessed enough balance and fine motor skills to juggle two plates at one time, Mike heaped great tablespoons worth of cheesecake, German chocolate cake, and French silk pie onto a smaller plate.

Leaning over the almond-slivered beans, Alison observed Natalie give Erica a mighty shove. Erica would've fallen right on her keister had Todd Driver not appeared in the nick of time to save his princess from public humiliation and a sore behind.

Erica fell into Todd's waiting arms. A dream come true for him. All of his expectations of playing the handsome prince and rescuing his damsel in distress from the fire-breathing dragon were becoming reality at last.

The romantic analogy broke down for her as she surveyed the wild 1970s Afro cleverly concealing his receding hairline coupled with a heavily fringed leather vest and matching skintight pants. The psychedelic shirt made her eyes cross. No question who'd planned their little ensemble. It had Erica written all over it.

Hilary reached the tableau, and from body language, she surmised Hilary told them to calm down or take it off site. Erica, suddenly the fragile, ethereal creature, clung to Todd's masculine—*ahem*, make that skinny—arms. It was probably the proudest moment of his life. He unsuccessfully tried to control his glee by frowning ferociously at Natalie.

"Can we find a table now?" A sheen of perspiration glistened between Mike's brows. He balanced a plate in each hand.

Enjoying her upper hand with him for once, she sailed forth from the tent like the *QE II* on her maiden voyage. "Certainly." He took careful, mincing steps, struggling not to capsize in her magnificent wake.

She found the perfect spot, a table close enough to the dance floor to enjoy the view yet not close enough to the orchestra to make conversation difficult. It was also perfect because Stephen and Val were already there and saving places for them.

"At last," cried Val. "We saw you two go into the tent and were afraid you were never coming out."

Stephen kept chewing.

With a sigh of relief for not having disgraced himself and the entire Raleigh Police Department, Mike took a seat across from Stephen, clad in a vintage World War II army staff uniform. "My granddad served with Eisenhower in London before D-Day," said Stephen in between bites at Mike's upraised brow.

Mike grunted. "Why couldn't Claire dress me in something more masculine like Stephen? I'm even an army vet. I feel like Alison's fancy man bodyguard."

"I think you look sophisticated." Val took a sip from her crystal goblet. "A man with the right amount of confidence to carry it off."

He grunted again, more satisfied this time, though, and adjusted his bowtie.

She winked a thank-you across to Val. "I love your costume, too, my friend."

"This old thing?" Val waved a hand. "After getting a preview of that luscious number Claire was making you, I ditched the costume and borrowed from my mom's old trunk in the attic. This is from the one time Mom and Dad attended the governor's inaugural ball in Raleigh when Jackie Kennedy was all the rage in Paris and Berlin." The pale pink floor-length gown was as classically chic as the former First Lady herself.

"You sure look different, Ali." Stephen glanced at her. "Ow!" as Val kicked him under the table. "I mean that in a good way. Ow!" as Val with a fierce smile landed another blow on his shin. "Okay, I'll shut up now," and he shoved a stuffed mushroom into his mouth.

"Don't mind him." Val gritted her teeth. "You can dress him up, but you can't take some people anywhere. Forget he's a top cardiologist. Most people don't realize how dim Stephen is because I've been covering for him for years."

They all laughed, Mike around a mouthful of beef Wellington. Night had fallen, revealing a crescent moon. The stars blazed high overhead. The orchestra played a series of waltz numbers. People, like on the ark, paired up two by two and filled the dance floor. Hurricane lamps on the tables imparted a flattering old-fashioned candlelit glow.

"Care to dance, Alison?"

She jumped as Robert appeared—as if out of nowhere—by her side. Mike choked, caught with a chicken wing in his mouth.

Putting a hand over her rapidly beating heart, she gave Robert her other hand. "Sure." She glanced sideways at Mike.

Robert drew her onto the floor, and she was amazed at his skillful leading as he steered her between the dancing couples, making a full circuit of the pavilion.

"You're a good dancer," she said, not altogether surprised.

He had a natural grace. Robert had the dapper, distinguished air of Cary Grant in his elegantly cut full evening attire.

"You, Alison Monaghan," he smiled into her eyes, "are beautiful, inside and out." He squeezed her hand as he whirled her about the floor.

She couldn't remember the last time she'd felt—maybe never—this lovely. Robert held her as if she were an exquisite piece of porcelain. As a gawky teenager and adult, who often towered like a giraffe over many men and boys, Robert somehow managed to make her feel petite.

But instead of finding herself lost in Robert's admiring gaze, she found herself looking surreptitiously over Robert's shoulder to Mike glowering at their table. And as Robert whirled her around the pavilion, she wondered if and when Mike would ever ask her to dance.

Why did it always seem to come back to Mike?

Maybe it was time to start listening to God and her heart.

37

As the last strains of "The Days of Wine and Roses" faded into the twilight, she removed her hand from Robert's shoulder.

"I'd love to have another dance with you this evening," whispered Robert as they walked off the dance floor together. His gentle hand on her arm guided her through the throngs of couples.

"Oh-kay." But she hoped her dance card would be filled by a certain detective.

At their table, Val wore a bemused look. Stephen was still eating. Mike scribbled notes in his ubiquitous notepad, keeping his eyes glued on the paper.

She sighed. Just another work night for Mike. She'd managed to build this evening into way more than it meant to him. How stupid could you be? Robert nodded to everyone and asked Val for the next dance.

Val jumped to her feet as the band started a tango. "Great. My husband, the cardiologist, is still stuffing his face. If I wait on him, I'll be waiting all night. I'm itching to get out there and show off my moves."

"Now you're in for it," hooted Stephen at the look of mock horror that crept across Robert's face as he recognized the tune and its sultry beat.

Val grabbed Robert's hand and pulled him out onto the dance floor. "I intend to get my five hundred dollars' worth."

Mike jammed the notepad into his jacket. "So do I. Or the department's money, that is." He grabbed her hand. "Shall we, Miz Monaghan?" Dragging her out of her chair, he propelled her onto the floor.

"I don't know how to tango."

"All I know is, they say it takes two," he drawled.

With a suddenness that stopped her breath, he dipped her.

As he led her in the formal dance sequence, she had several simultaneous thoughts: (1) Mike had done this dance before; (2) thank God Claire had foreseen this kind of situation when she hemmed her dress; and (3) where had this Cherokee mountain boy learned to tango so well?

"If I haven't said so lately, I like your friends." He arched his brows. "Makes a nice change from the psychopaths and drug-crazed killers I usually get to spend Friday nights with."

She was having trouble talking and concentrating on her steps at the same time. "They decided to like you once they were sure you weren't going to charge me with murder."

He held her hand in a vise, and under his expert guidance, she did a twirl under his arm. It was a maneuver made possible by his six-foot, four-inch height. She smiled at the sheer pleasure of the movement.

"Don't smile," he growled, low in his throat. "The tango is meant to be fierce and passionate and intense."

She rolled her eyes. "Oh, puh-leeze. Where did you learn to dance like this?"

"My niece, at the School of the Arts in Winston, majored in dance performance. You wouldn't believe the number of dance recitals I've attended over the years. Not to mention," he said with a sheepish expression, "that I watched a YouTube video all day per Brooke's long-distance instructions to brush up on my cotillion skills." He dipped her again and lunged over her with a menacing glare.

"Well, stop it."

He brought her back to eye level. People were starting to stare, amused. Val grinned over Robert's shoulder. Robert, when he turned, did not.

"You're making a spectacle of us. I thought the word was *inconspicuous*?"

"Can't help it." He negotiated a tricky move. "Some of us are born to dance."

Alison laughed loud enough to be heard over the orchestra. Heads turned in their direction again. She blushed but continued to chuckle when she regained her breath.

She couldn't remember the last time she'd laughed so much. It felt good. Correction, Mike always made her feel good. And alive.

Tugging at her hand, he pulled her off the dance floor and into a shadowy alcove under an enormous Southern magnolia. Away from the lights and the people, the distant, muted music created its own ambience.

Her pulse staccato-stepped. "Mike, what are you doing?"

Faintly, she heard the music wind down to a stop.

He gave her a wolfish grin. "I'm dancing with the prettiest girl at the party."

She quivered, but not because she was cold. "The music has stopped."

He pulled her toward him. "Didn't notice. How about dancing a little shag?"

"You know how to shag?"

Mike broadened his chest. "Hey, I may not look that smart, but I did attend college in North Carolina. Who doesn't learn to shag in the Carolinas?"

Her lips parted. "What about the music?"

"We'll make our own." He sang a stanza about Carolina girls.

Repressing the urge to laugh, she let him lead her through the familiar 1-2-3, back 2-3, rock step.

"You don't like my singing?"

Actually, he had a nice, if rusty, baritone. No need to let him know it, though. Would go straight to that large, already oversized ego.

He twirled her through an elaborate pretzel move. His left arm around her shoulders, his right hand holding hers, he led her in a half circle step-kick maneuver before returning to the basics. She giggled.

Ignoring her, he belted out a faster-paced tune about "Kokomo" and something to the effect of getting there fast and then taking it slow, alternating between a froggy bass and a clear-as-a-bell falsetto.

She laughed right in his face as he pulled her toward him at the 1-2-3. "This is ridiculous. What are we doing?" She stopped laughing at the look on his face in the moonlight.

His eyes met hers, traveled to the vicinity of her lips, and then meandered back to her eyes once more. "What *are* we doing, Alison?"

She fondled the necklace at her throat. "I . . . I don't know, Mike."

He tightened his hold. "What do you want us to do from here on out, Alison?"

She moistened her lips. "I don't know that, either." She craved the touch of his lips upon hers. Wanted it badly, but longing warred with fear.

He tilted her chin, his thumb caressing her jawline. "Why are you so afraid?"

Dropping her gaze, she studied the toes of her shiny shoes. What was she afraid of? Mike? the "us" part? or herself?

Maybe all of the above.

Cupping the sides of her face in his hands, he drew her face toward his own. Stopping just short of her mouth, he allowed her the chance to pull away if she wanted.

Instead, her arms slid up his back, and she pressed him toward her, closing the gap. Her lips parted. His mouth descended.

As the stubble of his five o'clock shadow scrape against the smoothness of her cheek, their lips touched and fused. Incredible sweetness like a barely remembered dream. A tenderness. She moaned.

And on her part at least—this shocked her to the depths of her soul—a hunger. Not for anything necessarily physical, but for so much more. A realization of what she now only glimpsed might be possible with this man. She deepened the kiss, and he made a sound in the back of his throat.

He pulled away first, leaving her skin suddenly and achingly cold. She shivered and brought two fingers to rest against her now bare lips. Feeling bereft of him, she blushed, thinking of her forwardness. So not Alison Monaghan.

She was pleased to note he seemed to be having as much trouble as she was in regaining his breath. They stared at each other, unsure what to say or do next.

He opened his arms, and she came, resting her chin against his shoulder. He ran one hand underneath her hair against the back of her neck, cradling her. "I need to tell you—"

Tensing, she saw Bill and Linda Lawrence arrive.

"What?" Mike asked as she squeezed his shoulder.

"They're here." The spell broke.

He swung her around so he could get a better view. He snorted. "Bonnie and Clyde? Give me a break."

"How arrogant and appropriate considering *their* eventual fate."

"Don't make me search you for a weapon, Miz Monaghan." He grinned. "Although in that there getup, I have no idea how you'd conceal a firearm."

That was as backhanded a compliment as she'd ever heard. Typical Mike. Eloquent he was not. But she was finding his other attributes more than made up for his lack of a silver tongue.

"No worries." She stepped out of the circle of his arms. "I'm more than content to leave the fireworks to you."

"I'm hoping it won't come to that. Real-life police work isn't like the TV shows with guns ablazing." He steered her toward their table. "Best definition of police work is 'days of absolute boredom followed by moments of sheer terror.' I hope for the best but train for the worst."

She and Mike rejoined Robert, Val, and Stephen at the table. Robert scowled. Val smiled, implike. "Where'd you two wander off to?"

Mike motioned toward Alison. "Keep an eye on this one. I need to have a quick chat with Mrs. Walston." He jerked his head over to where Ginny Walston, regal in a bustled lavender silk dress, stood alone, scanning the crowd.

Alison bristled. "I don't need a keeper."

"Sure you do, honey." Val picked at the strawberry trifle Stephen handed her.

Robert started around the table to her. The band played another gentle waltz. Uh-oh. How would she handle—?

"Mind if I steal your partner for one teensy dance?" Winnie, in a sheer white Greek toga that complemented her Greek heritage, slipped out of the darkness between Alison and the approaching Robert. His smile never disappeared completely, although it wavered.

"Not at all." She bit back a smile, wondering if Professor Dandridge in his tell-all book about Weathersby realized the Greeks had, in "History According to Winnie," settled Weathersby and America long before the English colonists.

Gallant to a fault, Robert offered Winnie his arm and gave Alison a regretful look. "Next time," he mouthed over his shoulder.

With Robert's back turned, Alison gave an audible sigh of relief.

Stephen cleared his throat and mentioned something about seeing a former patient of his before sidling off.

"You should take a load off those fancy gold slippers of yours"— Val dipped her spoon deep into the layers of the trifle—"and try this. If it was chocolate, it'd be sinful." She licked the spoon. "Now wipe that moonstruck look off your face—I expect mega details tomorrow—and help me eat this before I lose control and gain ten pounds I don't need and you do." She held out an extra spoon.

Reaching for it, Alison felt a tiny tap-tap on her shoulder.

Ivy stood, hands on hips, glaring, her hoop-skirted brown taffeta dress swaying from the abruptness of her motions. "Instead of partying like a teenager, I expect my staff and the board members to supervise the tours our real guests with the deep pockets expect of the true star of this evening." She swept a dramatic hand across the broad expanse of the house behind her, "Weathersby."

Before she or Val knew what was happening, Ivy grabbed her by the exposed tender flesh on the back of her arm and tugged her along toward the house. Val rose to her feet, but one foot got caught in the lower rung of the chair. She half fell into the rest of her trifle. "Ali!"

She looked over her shoulder and shrugged as Ivy prodded her like a herd of cattle along the path. "Tell Mike I'm in the—Ow!" Ivy pinched the back of her arm. "I'm coming, Ivy. Stop pushing me around." And for once, glad of her nine-inch advantage, shook herself like a wet dog free of Ivy's grabby little hands.

Once inside, passing by the dining room, she got a hurried glimpse of a formal painting of Prudence Weathersby, wife of the creepy-eyed Oliver, and realized Ivy had styled her hair and dress in direct imitation of the first Weathersby matriarch. A Victorian lace cap topped Ivy's brassy curls. Ivy's garnet earrings and a silver locket glimmered in the multifaceted crystal pendants of the 150-year-old chandelier.

Something tugged at her memory, but before she could capture it, Ivy yanked on her sleeve, propelling her deeper into the house, past the gaggle of guests strolling through the dining room and parlor. They headed for the older, pre-Revolution part of the house that led to the modern kitchen area. Overhead, taffeta rustled and floorboards creaked.

Ivy tightened her half-fingered, lacy-gloved grip on her arm as she stopped at the base of the stairs. "As for you . . ." Her sallow complexion glowed in the vibrancy of the electrically converted wall sconces, her great, golden green eyes gleaming.

"There she is, Henry. Safe and sound as I told you." Ginny appeared from the connecting door of the docent area with Henry Dandridge on her arm. He was in full turn-of-the-century splendor.

Releasing her hold on Alison, Ivy let out an exasperated breath.

His hand trembled on the silver-headed cane he carried. "Ivy? I didn't know where you'd gotten to."

"I'm working, Henry."

"When are we going to do the dance we've been practicing? I've been waiting for hours."

Ivy pulled at Henry. A brief tug-of-war ensued. "After my speech welcoming everyone, Henry. A few more minutes, I promise. I'll get you some punch." She patted him on the back and glared at Ginny. Ginny glared back.

Alison shivered, realizing how cold she was. The air-conditioning must be roaring, and she'd left her wrap on the back of her chair.

A long shadow fell between her and the others. Mike stood on the threshold separating the antebellum addition from the colonial portion of the house. Her wrap hung like spun gold from his fingers. A frown creased his forehead.

"Thought you might need this." He panted, as if he'd been running.

Had he been tailing Ginny?

Alison reached for the stole.

Ivy's gaze ping-ponged between Alison and Mike. "Perhaps Ginny can help me instead, by encouraging our guests in the house to gather by the dance pavilion for my welcome address."

"And the Mayor's." Ginny stroked the rose-tinted cameo pinned to the antique lace edging her pale throat with her forefinger as if soothing a fractious child.

Ivy narrowed her eyes to slits.

Ginny's ginger kiss curls on the top of her forehead—reminding Alison of a picture she'd seen once of the doomed Empress Alexandra Romanov—quivered with a strange vibe. Was Ginny inebriated again?

"Of course." Alison reached for Mike's arm, glad to escape the house and get out into the warm April air with its music and company.

At their unoccupied table, a waiter handed her a fluted glass of bubbling liquidity from the tray he balanced on his shoulder. Curling her lip with distaste, she set it beside her plate.

With a dismissive wave of his hand, Mike refused one for himself. "You don't drink?"

She laughed, a mirthless sound. "Not likely I'd ever want to with a raging alcoholic for a mother."

He pursed his lips. "I never drink, either."

She tilted her head, a question on her face.

"I know the stereotype about the hard-drinking cop, but like you, I have genetic reasons to avoid it like the plague. Alcohol was my dad's solace before the mine caved in and killed him. My older sister drank herself to death before she was thirty."

She was about to comment on their shared misery, but there was a sudden lull in the music as the mayor and Hilary mounted the small platform and approached the podium. Val, Stephen, and a partnerless Robert rejoined them at the table. As the closest table to the house, Ivy gently steered Henry into an available seat at their table.

Hilary directed the wait staff to ensure everyone had a drink in hand and offered a toast to honor the long and worthy history of Weathersby, to the mayor, and to the fair city of Raleigh. Applause spattered the night.

Erica and Todd stood at the edge of the circle of light behind her. She didn't see Ginny. Winnie plopped herself, chiffon all aflutter, into an extra seat.

"Alison?" Winnie whispered across the table. "I know I was late with my travel reimbursement form, but I've," lowering her eyes to the tablecloth, "overextended my credit card this month. How soon do you think you could have a check ready for me?"

Seriously?

Was she never off the Weathersby clock?

"Sorry, Winnie. I meant to take care of that today, but last-minute crises for the ball took my day. I promise to have it for you first thing Monday."

Winnie frowned, her full lips in a pout, "Well, if that's the best you can do, I suppose I'll have to wait for Monday."

And to Alison's dismay, Natalie loped up and put a predatory arm on first Robert and then Mike. Mike brushed her off like a worrisome wasp.

She smiled her man-eating tigress smile at Alison, leaned back, and said for Alison's ears only, "How you keep all the eligible men by your side, I'll never understand. But then, I forgot," she laughed. "As we both know, Frank was prone to wander."

Clenching the sides of her dress in her fists, she turned her back on Natalie. She'd read a verse from Ephesians about anger. She repeated it silently.

Twice.

Robert snagged a passing waiter and commandeered a glass of water for her. He was, she'd noticed, an observant and thoughtful man. Was Robert for real, as Claire would say? Or, too good to be true?

The mayor called everyone's attention to the small fireworks display set up by the professionals who oversaw the city's annual Fourth of July show. The crowd gasped at the sudden burst of sound as a rocket with its white tail of smoke flung blue, red, and white diamonds of light into the night sky. Everyone turned as one entity, eyes gazing heavenward, at the next spectacular display of spiraling blue pinwheels and flashes of white.

At the conclusion, the crowd burst into applause, and Ivy stood at the podium. Henry sat where he'd been left, clutching the head of his cane with his head sunk forward over both hands. Waiters moved about gathering empty glasses or refilling others upon request.

Ivy did her bit for Weathersby, thanking the honored guests assembled, explaining future plans for expansion, and encouraging hearty donations while members of the board roamed through the crowd collecting premailed donor pledge envelopes.

The envelopes were deposited with Bill and Linda, seated at a small table to the left of the platform. Mike stood with his feet spread even with his hips, tense and at attention. He never took his eyes off Bonnie and Clyde while they recorded the entries in an accounting log by the glow of the hurricane lantern at their table.

Robert and, unfortunately, Natalie returned to their table.

"Thirsty work collecting money for our worthy cause." Natalie grabbed for her glass on the table, but it had been taken away. She swiped one of the two glasses gracing Alison's place and not the one filled with water.

"Since you don't appear to want this, I'll help myself." Throwing her head back, the dark feather in the cloche hat bobbed. She downed the contents in one swift gulp. Natalie plunked the goblet on the table where it gave off a tiny crystal ping.

Natalie gave a nasty laugh, low in her throat. "But then, I seem to make a habit of that, don't I Alison, of taking what should belong to you."

38

Val rose to her feet, her fists curled. Alison shook her head and motioned for her to stay put. Looking around, she realized no one else had heard the malicious comment since the band had started up again.

Erica and Todd were on the dance floor. The merry Greek widow, Winnie, had found another victim. Stephen was engaged in a discussion with his department head, Dr. Reynolds, and Robert had caught sight of a friend across the dance pavilion, a much younger man about Mike's age.

"Go back into that web you crawled out of tonight," Val sputtered.

Natalie didn't answer. She gazed at Val, her eyes unfocused. Swaying on her feet, she pitched herself over to the nearest male she could find, which happened to be Stephen and Dr. Reynolds.

Realizing Natalie's next target, Val started after her, but Stephen saw Natalie coming and had the foresight to slink into the shadows. The hapless and rotund Dr. Reynolds wasn't so agile.

Natalie grabbed his arm and lugged him, much against his will, onto the dance floor as the orchestra played a fox-trot. Her movements became overblown and off kilter, her steps erratic. Dr. Reynold's balding head shone with moisture, and his face was a vivid puce of embarrassment.

Stephen shook his head as if surviving a near-fatal accident.

Val's fists coiled like a cobra about to strike. "That woman makes me forget my mama raised me to be a Christian woman."

"Let it go." Alison sighed. "Don't let her poison infect you. We all have to answer for our own words and actions."

"How did you get to be so wise so fast?" Val peered into her face. "You have truly changed in the last few months."

She laughed to lighten the moment. "A good change, I hope?"

"Definitely." Val let out a big sigh. "I let my temper and my tongue get away from me again," she told Stephen as he came alongside. "But that woman needs to be put in her place."

Stephen put his hands across the back of Val's shoulders. "Not your job, though, sweetheart. It's God's. Let it go." He massaged her tight muscles and winked at Alison. "Trained by my wife, the best physical therapist in Raleigh."

Val rolled her head in a clockwise fashion, releasing her tension. "I see Mike found his old buddy, Tom Richardson. Mike and Tom were at college together before Mike dropped out due to a lack of finances and joined the Rangers."

Alison crossed her arms. "And how do you know so much about Mike?"

Stephen laughed. "When have you ever known my intrepid wife not to know everything there was to know about anybody?"

Val wriggled free of his clasp. "Thanks for the massage, though you make me sound like a gossip. How much longer is this shindig going to take?" She yawned. "It's way past this working girl's usual shut-eye time."

"Not much longer, I imagine." Alison grabbed Stephen's wrist, the only one wearing a watch, to read the time from its green luminescent dial. "The band will be winding down in less than thirty minutes. People are already drifting home."

The dance ended, and Natalie staggered toward them, her breath coming in ragged gasps. She half-fell into the table, a wild, glazed look in her eyes. Stephen caught her arm before she succeeded in wiping out three chairs.

"Maybe you should call it a night, Ms. Singleton." Stephen's voice displayed both compassion and disgust.

Natalie jerked her arm free as if scalded but rubbed her bare arms with both hands as if cold. "I'm fine. Haven't had that much to drink." Her words slurred.

Stephen cocked an eyebrow. "Let me call you a taxi to get you home."

Natalie laughed, the sound giddy and overdone. Wobbly on her feet, she caught the back of a chair for support. "Don't worry"—Natalie blew Alison an audacious kiss—"I always manage to find someone to take me home." Brushing off Stephen's hand, she lurched down the path toward the front of the house and the parking lot.

"What a piece of work," Val fumed.

Stephen frowned after Natalie's retreating form, soon lost to the darkness of the night. "I'm not sure . . ."

"Where are the facilities in this place?" Val swiveled her head. "I'd like to make a pit stop before we go home and relieve our babysitter."

"Yet another expansion project still to be completed," Alison informed her. "There are the port-a-potties . . ." At Val's groan, she grinned. "Or I could give you my employee's key and you could go through the back of the house into the restroom the staff uses."

"You are a true friend." Val grabbed the small key chain from her as Alison removed it from her beaded purse on the table.

"I'll walk with you, but what about you, Ali?" Stephen looked around for Mike.

"Don't worry." She jerked her head over to the dance floor where Mike, Tom Richardson, and Robert stood deep in conversation. "My date's not far. I'd guess I'm not going home for a while." She laughed. "And you guys have the nerve to talk about women."

Val and Stephen disappeared toward the back of the house.

She went over to Henry, still slumped over his cane. "Henry." She kept her voice low, hoping not to startle him.

He lifted his head, his eyes cloudy and rheumy. He was certainly not in as good a shape as she'd seen him the other afternoon. But he was old, and the old had good and bad days.

Like the rest of us, but only more so.

"I want to go home," he whispered and clasped her hands like a child. "Can you find Ivy and tell her I want to go home now?"

She patted his hand. "I'll find her, I promise."

Hoping to spot the diminutive Ivy in her hoop skirt, she inspected the dwindling crowd. The Lawrences were packing the envelopes into a small brown satchel. Mike had positioned himself so he could keep a watchful eye on their movements while seemingly absorbed in a conversation with Richardson and Robert, whose backs faced the Lawrences.

The caterers packed the Bunsen burners and serving pieces onto trolleys to transport them to their van in the parking lot. The rental company would be there early Saturday morning to take down the tents. The band gathered music stands and sheet music. Erica and Todd had disappeared into the night. Winnie departed on the arm of another eligible Raleigh bachelor.

Well, Alison grimaced. There was nothing for it, but to go find Ivy.

She was probably in the house making sure all of the lights were off and the alarm secured. Lifting her skirt, she left Henry and picked her way up the path to the front of the house, retracing the route she and Mike had followed previously.

Rounding the curve, she stepped away from the pools of light cast by the Chinese lanterns and into the inky darkness lit only by the reflected glow from the lights that shone from the interior of the house.

Her nose filled with the scent of the "Miss Kim" lilac, its purple blossoms not visible in the darkness but fresh in her memory. She and Polly had planted that shrub a few years ago to replace the withered one that had inhabited the spot for years.

She caught the whiff of something less pleasant, putrid. Wrinkling her nose, she noticed a small, jerky movement on the ground underneath the lilac. She stopped dead in her tracks, afraid of a repeat performance of her experience on Wednesday night.

What had possessed her to take off alone, in the dark, no less? Perhaps Mike was right. Maybe she was stupid.

In a cold sweat, her arms tight around her body, she backed up a step at a time until she heard the sound of retching. Despite every nerve in her body telling her to get out of there, she inched toward the huddled form under the bush.

The figure writhed, face down on the ground. "Oh, Lord, help me please," she whispered as she knelt beside the form. The shape convulsed, its body wracked by tremors.

She was a horticulturalist by training, not a doctor. She didn't know what to do. She was afraid to do anything, afraid she'd make things worse. Where were Stephen and Val? Where was Mike? He was bound to have medical training.

"Help! I need help!"

The person wheezed and coughed. Afraid he or she was choking, she instinctively rolled the figure on its back and propped an arm under the unknown person's head to clear the air passageway.

A shaft of light from the parlor window fell upon the form, and a single black feather bobbed in the light. Natalie Singleton's eyes were dilated, her breath ragged with shallow and painful gasps. Alison drew back, but Natalie seized her hand in a death grip.

Natalie struggled to speak, her words bubbling. She bent her head low over Natalie, close to her face, trying to avoid the spittle and vomit that encircled Natalie's lips. Whatever it was she was trying to say, Alison could make no sense of it.

Natalie thrust a small object into the palm of her gloved hand. It was the small rose cameo Ginny Walston had been wearing that evening.

There was a rattle, deep in Natalie's chest, and one last convulsive heave before her head—the single black feather on the cloche hat—lolled backward where it lay stilled forever in the sandy gravel of the path at Weathersby.

Alison screamed.

39

MIKE HUNCHED HIS SHOULDERS AND CRAMMED HIS HANDS INTO THE POCKets of his tuxedo jacket. The paramedics had finished their routine procedures, although Natalie Singleton was far beyond help by the time the first ambulance arrived. The medical examiner and a forensics team had taken over. The florescent white of the halogen spotlights, reflecting off their white bodysuits and faces, rendered a surreal atmosphere to the antebellum setting.

Crime scene investigators combed through the Weathersby grounds, conducting interviews among the twenty-odd guests and catering staff still on site at the time of Alison's discovery.

He grimaced. What a discovery to come upon in the fairy-tale atmosphere of the hitherto successful Weathersby costume ball.

Mike flicked a glance over to where Alison huddled on the wide-planked steps of the front entrance, Robert Kendall's white tuxedo coat draped across her shoulders. Val sat beside her, holding one of Alison's hands. The fierce Rottweiler look on Val's face was back.

Unbuttoning his dinner jacket, he walked over to where Robert and Stephen stood beside one of the massive pillars. Another Friday night marred by murder and mayhem. And it had to be murder based on Alison's description of the victim in her initial statement to the police, barring any long-standing health issues to be uncovered by the autopsy.

Natalie Singleton had been the picture of health, a vibrant woman in her mid-thirties. Hardly the type to suffer from a life-threatening illness. But then again—he loosened his bow tie, leaving his dress shirt open at the collar—you never knew. The medical examiner had promised to perform the high-profile autopsy tonight.

Mike took a good look at the night sky, what remained of this night. "Any thoughts, Stephen?"

Stephen straightened. "Just a guess, mind you. Until blood work is done and the contents of her stomach tested, we can't know for sure. But according to Alison's description of her condition and the symptoms I observed before Natalie left the party, I would hazard a guess her death was caused by either a drug overdose or . . ." He paused, rubbing his chin between his thumb and forefinger.

"Go on," Mike prompted.

"Poison."

"That's what I was afraid you were going to say." He gestured over to the women. "Both of you are free to leave at this point."

"And you?" Mike cocked his head at Alison. "Don't even think about coming to the airport tomorrow."

She rose, clutching the front of Robert's coat with one satin-gloved hand, shivering despite its protective warmth. He was glad that, for once, she didn't argue.

His heart had skipped a beat when he heard the sound of her screams coming from the front of the house. His stomach clenched again, queasy and churning at the memory.

"Do you think this is connected to what happened to Frank or what's going down tomorrow?" She swallowed convulsively.

The rose cameo in its plastic baggie within his trouser pocket crinkled as he placed a foot on the step. "Too early to tell, but Ginny Walston is missing. Her car is in the lot, but we can't locate her. She can't have gotten far on foot, but I have a BOLO out on her. I have questions for Mrs. Walston she didn't want to answer before. She'll have to talk now."

"If you find her," Val corrected. "She may have had an accomplice and could be far away by this time."

"We'll find her." His teeth clenched. "Ms. Singleton, I believe, was trying to point us in her direction before she died by giving Alison that cameo."

"I always believed Natalie was involved with Frank's murder, but maybe I was biased against her for other reasons." Twin reflections of misery and shock darkened Alison's chocolate eyes. "She was my top suspect as the woman in San Francisco and as his killer." She shuddered. "I think poison is the most likely scenario, too. But Ginny?"

"A second victim." He shrugged. "Motive for killing Natalie? Maybe she saw something or knew something that was a threat. Means? Opportunity?"

Alison remained silent.

"Well, if you are not going to tell him, I am." Val's steely gaze told them she meant what she said.

Alison shook her head at Val in warning. "I don't believe that's relevant."

He stirred. "Let me decide what is and is not relevant."

Val looked at Stephen for corroboration. "The lab results will confirm the means. But as for opportunity, the last time I saw Natalie drink anything was a glass of champagne about one hour before Alison found her."

Stephen nodded. "Depending on the poison and the quantity, if our theorizing is correct, the poison would've been relatively fast-acting, resulting in death within an hour of ingestion."

Assessing the scene, Mike looked out across the south lawn where groups of guests and wait staff, for once equal in station, sat grim and shaken around the now bare white tables. Hilary Munro shivered with shock. A subdued Winnie Allen. Dr. Henry Dandridge appeared confused, and Ivy, her head in her hands, quietly wept. Erica Chambers and Todd Driver huddled into each other for comfort.

The Lawrences left the scene before Alison discovered the body. But they were tailed all the way home. If it was premeditated and poison to boot, they could be as guilty as anyone else. He whipped out his cell phone.

In the distance, a young, attractive woman—in black trousers and a white long-sleeved Oxford shirt—plucked a cell phone out of an apron tied around her waist. He barked out a command and she jumped to her feet.

Alison's eyes widened. "You had undercover officers here?"

"You didn't think I was keeping tabs on Bonnie and Clyde by myself, did you? My officer is going to round up the unwashed glasses the caterers have loaded in their van and take them for analysis."

"Like finding a needle in the haystack." Stephen whistled, softly. "There must have been five hundred guests floating in and out of the food tent eating and drinking over the course of the evening."

He sighed. "I know."

"Look for the tangerine lipstick stains," suggested Robert.

Surprised, Mike darted his eyes at him. Robert was so quiet most of the time it was easy to forget he was around.

Or maybe that was just wishful thinking on his part.

"I noticed that's what she tended to wear for every occasion. Must have been her favorite," Robert answered Mike's questioning look.

"Tangerine." Alison sent Mike a knowing glance.

"You're right, Robert." Val nodded. "I remember now there were stains on the glass when she set it on the table."

"Yes, how observant, Mr. Kendall." Mike laced his voice with sarcasm and doubt. Robert flushed.

Val's gaze toward Alison turned to steel once again. "If you aren't going to tell him the rest, I will."

He removed the phone from his ear. "What?"

Alison flushed and shuffled her feet on the step. She refused to meet his gaze, a sure sign in his experience with her that she was unwilling to face the truth. His eyes bored into her until she was forced to look at him.

"That last glass Val and I saw her drink," her voice choked, "was my untouched champagne. Sitting by my place at the table. Was the poison meant for me?" She snatched at Mike's sleeve. "It doesn't make any sense. I can't believe Ginny Walston would want me dead. Why?"

"Perhaps," Val's mouth tightened. "She was unhinged by her own grief and guilt."

Seeing Alison's distress, Mike touched her arm in an effort to calm her. "Coupled with what you've told me about her dependence on alcohol in the last months since her husband's death."

Alison shook her head. "Putting the poison in that glass was the final act of a vicious, well thought-out plan. That doesn't sound like Ginny or any alcoholics I've ever known who tend to act on impulse."

"It was an impulse to seize the opportunity afforded by the unguarded glass at your place at the table," Robert insisted.

Tears welled in Alison's eyes. Her voice dropped to a whisper. "Who hates me enough to want me to die like that?"

Mike couldn't answer her. His jaw ached from gritting his teeth together. He'd lost objectivity a long time ago. This was personal now. He cared far too much about Alison, Claire, and Justin Monaghan for his own peace of mind.

Who was he kidding?

He loved Alison and wanted those children to be his own. His feelings, usually so carefully clamped down into that region beyond the reach of his conscious mind, betrayed him.

Since Iraq, he'd kept a distance between himself and all other relationships out of sheer self-preservation. Now his feelings for Alison clouded his mind and impaired his judgment.

He gripped Alison's hand, crushing the purple orchid corsage, which, despite starting the evening with such bright hope, wilted in the humid April night. "Who would hate Natalie Singleton enough to want her to die like that? I'll find her killer, hers and Frank's. I won't rest till I do, I promise you."

"Tell me, Detective Barefoot." Robert's eyes glinted in the night. "Do you think you'll be able to solve either murder before you take off for your new job in D.C.?"

40

Alison's head snapped up.

"Robert," Val cautioned. "Don't."

Mike clenched his fists, taking a step toward Robert. Stephen put a restraining hand on his arm.

"What's going on? What does everyone apparently know that I don't?" Alison looked at Val and Robert. "D.C.? What are you talking about Robert?" She swiveled. "Mike?"

He gritted his teeth. "I was trying to tell you earlier, but—"

"According to our mutual friend, Tom, who stopped by the table while you and the Detective were . . ." Robert paused, suggestively.

"Stop, Robert," warned Stephen.

". . . were doing whatever, Tom told us Mike had a not-to-be-passed-up promotion to a federal job in D.C."

Stephen shot Mike an apologetic look. "Tom came over hoping to meet Alison, the woman he'd heard so much about these last months. He let it slip about D.C., but we all promised," Stephen fixed Robert with a glance, "not to say anything until you'd had a chance to tell Alison about it."

Mike shook off Stephen's hand. "Did he also tell you I haven't decided whether I'm taking it or not?"

Robert hooted. "Haven't decided what? Weighing your options first to see whether there's enough here to make you stay? Or do you have trouble putting down roots and staying any place long?"

Mike leaned toward Robert, but he caught sight of the reservoir of unshed tears in Alison's eyes. "Alison. Let me—"

She stiffened, pulling off Robert's coat. She thrust the coat toward Robert. "I'm going home with or without your permission, Detective Barefoot."

He sighed, closing his eyes.

"I'll be happy to escort you home," offered his rival.

His eyes flew open. Mike seared Robert with a silver hot glare. "Oh, no. I think not." Scowling, he barked further instructions into his phone. "An officer is on her way to question you regarding your movements this evening, Mr. Kendall."

Val gazed at him, sympathy written across her features. He swallowed. "Stephen, you and Val need to get home." He grasped Alison by the forearm. "I brought Alison to this party and I'll be—" He stopped, remembering he didn't use those kinds of words anymore.

Not since he'd started hanging around Alison and the Prescotts. Not since he'd finally opened his heart to God.

He took a deep breath. "I'll take Alison home."

Alison resisted the pull of his hand. "I'm not going anywhere with you, Mike Barefoot."

He clamped his jaw. "Oh, yes you are. And you," he jerked his head toward Robert reaching for Alison. "Don't you move."

"Val? Stephen?" Alison's voice rose.

Stephen coughed and caught his wife's hand. Val waggled her fingers at them. "I'll call you tomorrow, Ali."

"Traitors," she called over her shoulder.

The anger was seething from Alison's body, but she allowed him to lead her to his truck without further protest. The air between them crackled with electricity. In a nasty mood, he wished he could punch something.

Or someone, namely Robert Kendall.

He opened the door and bundled her into the passenger side. She leaned into his ear.

"I'm not afraid of you, Mike Barefoot."

He shoved the folds of her costume into the vehicle. "Well, right now, you should be."

He slammed the door closed.

"Are you going to take the job?" she demanded as soon as he scooted into the driver's side.

"If you'd let me explain . . ." He hoped she'd beg him to stay.

So, while he drove the short distance to her house, he explained. But she didn't. Beg him to stay.

Parked in the driveway, he glanced at the darkened windows, glad the kids had obeyed Alison's instructions to go to bed after she'd called them from Weathersby while waiting for the CSI investigators to arrive.

"Still weighing your options, Mike?" She curled her fists. "Getting too close to real emotion for you? Time to tuck tail and run? Again?"

He leaned over her. "No, that's your M.O., not mine. When are you going to get it through your head, I'm not Frank?"

"Just goes to show what a great judge of character I am with the both of you. Robert's right—"

"Robert ain't right about nothing—pardon my grammar—when it comes to you. He's eat up with jealousy and filling your head with addlepated notions." He touched her cheek with his finger. "Love by its definition can never be safe. Takes courage to trust and be vulnerable with another person. Nice and safe with Kendall," he snarled, "just don't cut it."

"How dare you talk about Robert that way? He's twice the man you'll ever be."

"Maybe so, but he'll never be your dad, and if you'd ever be honest with yourself, that's what attracts you to Robert."

Shrinking into the upholstery of the seat, her body went rigid. "If you are implying that I'm trying to replace my father?" Her nostrils flared. "You sick, dirty-minded—" She growled, low in her throat. "I hate you, Mike Barefoot."

"No, you love me. You just won't admit it yet."

Her hand came within inches of his face, but shaking, she dropped it to her side. Fumbling for the door handle, she wrenched it open and stumbled onto the driveway. "I don't ever want to see you again. Get out of our lives." Clutching her purse to her chest, she spun on her heel, reaching her front porch at a run.

Smacking his hand against the steering wheel, he watched her slam the door shut against the night and him. His jaw ached with the effort of not running after her. If that's how she felt—

He had a job to do. A job that would require the utmost of his attention for the next twenty-four hours if he hoped to catch the Lawrences off guard at the airport. Turning the key in the ignition, he moved the gearshift to drive and pulled out onto the street and back to Weathersby.

Maybe Robert was perfect for her.

She'd never have to—as his granny used to say—hit another lick at a stick as Mrs. Robert Kendall.

Not that Alison was afraid to work. Frank never allowed Alison to stretch her creative wings. He remembered the excitement in her voice after successfully designing and implementing the Lamberts' yard project last month, the thrill of accomplishment in her eyes.

Robert—he somehow knew—wouldn't want her to work at her new landscaping business. His first wife, Joan, hadn't worked, after all. He could hear Robert's reasoning in his head. It wasn't like Alison would need the money married to *him*.

Let Robert take care of her. Let him treat her the way Robert firmly believed Alison deserved to be treated—like the exquisite, fragile, hothouse orchid she was in his adoring sight.

Forget independence. Prepare to be a shining example of a trophy wife, he thought with a bitter glance in the rearview mirror at the Monaghan residence. She'd been there once already.

Some people never learned except the hard way.

Like you.

Easing his foot off the accelerator, he tried to slow his breathing and his speed.

"Handled that well, didn't I God?"

Some bodyguard he'd turned out to be. Stars in his eyes had nearly gotten Alison killed tonight. He had no doubt that Alison had been the poison's intended target. But as to why, he wasn't sure.

He wondered if God was as disgusted with him as he was with himself.

"What do I do now? Maybe she does hate me."

Silence, but he felt an urging to be still and trust.

Even if it meant he'd lost her for good?

Even then.

This faith stuff—as he was learning—wasn't for wimps. Fighting the heaviness sitting like a boulder on his chest, he whispered to the night, "I love her so much." His voice shook. "But Your will, God." Wasn't that like the hardest prayer in the world? "Not mine."

Crumpled against the stairs, Alison struggled to stifle the sobs racking her frame, so as not to awaken the children. She couldn't face their questions tonight. Had the world gone crazy? Two declarations of love from two totally different men, offering two totally different futures.

Wait.

Make that one declaration. Mike never said he loved her.

Just that she loved him.

They all left her in the end. And if she put her trust in Robert . . . ? They all disappointed. Her dad dead, her mom lost to an alcoholic stupor. Frank had left her years before his body actually did.

And now Mike. She buried her face in the crook of her arm.

Only God didn't betray or forsake.

Maybe that was the heart of her problem. Looking for things from people only God could ultimately provide. Was God truly enough for her every need? Was He enough for the hurts of the past, the heartache of the present, and the uncertainty of her future?

Enough for a future—without Mike in it?

41

ALISON SHUT OFF THE PHONE AND LET IT FALL AMONG THE FOLDS OF THE
comforter in which she lay wrapped on the sofa. Weary, she leaned
her head on the cushions and closed her eyes. It was over at last.

Out of obligation, Mike had called, giving her a terse up-date on
his successful apprehension of Bill and Linda Lawrence, caught red-
handed with the monies from the Weathersby fundraiser, as they
were about to board the plane for George Town. Their children
were now in the protective custody of the Child Services division.
The pain in Mike's voice reflected the pain in her heart.

Alison opened one eye to look at the wall clock. Eleven o'clock
in the morning. The day already felt as if she'd been living it twice
over.

Sunlight streamed through the French doors. She hoped the
phone hadn't woken the children, asleep in their beds after a long
evening the night before. Still in her pj's, she had been unable and
unwilling to fall into a deep sleep, her restless thoughts with the
investigation and the long-anticipated arrests.

Easier than dwelling on Mike Barefoot and the might-
have-beens.

She'd set up camp in the downstairs living room, fitfully doz-
ing off and on in the early hours of the morning as she tried to

reconstruct conversations over the last week with people she'd interviewed at Weathersby.

Her notes lay on the floor within arm's reach, but her brain was frazzled and her emotions fried with her efforts to recreate in her mind the events leading to Frank and Natalie's murders. For it was now confirmed, Natalie Singleton had been murdered last night.

Murdered by a poison called taxine, found in the juice of the yew, also known as the tree of death by the ancient Celts, with its toxic leaves, berries, and bark. The lab found traces of the toxin in the only champagne glass rimmed with tangerine lipstick.

With her landscaper's internal eye, she recalled the immense yew hedge that surrounded three-quarters of Weathersby, a boundary marker and easily accessible to anyone who knew what to do with its deadly horticultural secrets. Her info led Mike, who didn't know a yew from a hole in the head, to send a team to scour the hedges for clues.

Had Natalie been the intended victim all along? Or had the poison been meant for her? That disturbing thought refused to stop rolling over and over through her sluggish brain. Why would the Lawrences want Natalie dead?

Or her, Alison Monaghan, widow and mother of two teenage children? Was someone else still out there?

Maybe coffee would help. She untangled herself from the cocoon of flannel comfort and, swinging her legs onto the floor, clambered from her nest. Coffee always helped.

In the kitchen, she rubbed one hand across her eyes as she filled the coffeepot. The whirring buzz of the coffee grinder broke the silence of the morning. She glanced at the ceiling. Feet would be hitting the floor soon as the aroma of coffee permeated the house. She made a mental note to replenish her coffee stash today.

She was missing something. But what? There had to be a clue camouflaged somewhere she'd overlooked.

Alison refused to accept a perfect murder. The killer had to have slipped up at some point. But where? And was she intelligent enough to figure it out?

Probably not.

Tired and in desperate need of caffeine, she leaned her elbows on the counter, her head in her hands. Between her wide splayed fingers, the Kona brewed, saturating the room and filling her nostrils. She inhaled deeply, letting the fragrance begin its magic.

What had Frank done to invite such murderous hostility?

She recalled the strained conversation with Mike, as he caught her up on the progress of the investigation after his grilling of Bill and Linda Lawrence in separate jail cells.

"We've matched Bill's size-twelve shoe to the print found outside your house," he told her. "We've charged him with breaking and entering and assault for his attack on you. That's why the turtleneck at the meeting. Afraid you'd see the scratches. The DNA results we collected from underneath your nails finally came back as a match. After threatening him with a murder charge, and a word to the wise how Linda might cop a plea and turn state's evidence against him, he sang like a bird."

"Linda's ratting him out?"

Mike gave a short laugh. "No, I just let that possible implication sink in. And he bought it. Says a lot about the state of their union, doesn't it now?"

Alison's breath hitched. "He's admitted to killing Frank and Natalie?"

"I wish. He's confessed to everything else but emphatically denies any involvement on his or Linda's part in the murders."

"And Linda? What does she say?"

"She's saying nothing. Got her lawyer with her and keeping her mouth shut," he said, with a bitter tone. "She insists she was the dutiful wife and knew nothing about any of this until recently."

"Of course, she does. Typical Linda. And yet," Alison had cupped the phone in the curve of her neck, "as a mother, I imagine she's worried about what will happen to her children if she and Bill both end up in jail."

"You give her too much credit." Mike snorted. "She's in this up to her eyeballs. The Feds are involved, too. Seems dear old Bill is wanted in California for fleeing prosecution on embezzlement and fraud charges. He bilked investors out of millions with his phony

CompuVision company. He's actually Ira Wallace, or at least that's the name he was using five years ago in San Francisco. The Feds are following that trail. He's run no telling how many aliases and cons over the years and in as many states. I'm not buying Linda's innocence. Take a heck of a lot of naïveté on her part to accept changing identities every time you change states. She's not that dumb, and neither am I."

"Why was he searching my house?"

He sighed. She could hear the fatigue in his voice. He had to be more strung out than her. He'd gotten no rest that night. He sounded unhappy.

Good. Just how she felt.

"Bill or Ira, or whatever his name is, was running a similar Ponzi-type pyramid scheme here in Raleigh for his fictional computer company. I believe he solicited Frank and others through his connections in the community for thousands of dollars. He was probably looking for any incriminating records Frank might have left behind of their flight plan to the Caymans. The IRS and the Feds found their offshore accounts, thanks to your brilliant heads-up," he said. "They've seized all foreign and domestic accounts."

"Our money." She'd closed her eyes. "Frank must have realized too late he'd been swindled."

"Again a perfect motive for murder in my opinion. And I'm not letting up on that guy till I get a confession. Although, my money's on that cold fish of a wife of his. Even if she isn't the killer, she was probably the last person to see Frank alive and left a cigarette butt to prove it."

"They almost got away with it."

"They were stupid. We have an extradition policy now with the Caymans. If they'd made it to George Town, law enforcement there would have gladly turned them over to us eventually. They were also greedy."

"How so?"

"Linda wanted to play dress-up and grab the measly thousands from the spring fundraiser to add to their stolen millions. It gave us time to figure out their scheme."

"We're lucky Dennis happened to call me and tipped us off."

"Not luck. God."

She'd blinked at the phone. Since when were Mike Barefoot and God on a first name basis? If only . . . She hardened her heart.

"Alison, we need to—"

"Save it, Detective, for someone who cares."

A long silence. Broken only by the rasping of his breath.

"Would you tell Claire and Justin good-bye for me?"

She'd bit back a sob.

"And stay out of trouble. If you can."

42

THREE CUPS LATER, ALISON WAS DRESSED AND THE CHILDREN AWAKE AND fed. Saturday, no school or work, Mike had Bonnie and Clyde, and she breathed a small prayer of thanksgiving all was well. Or, as well as could be expected considering the status of her heart. But as she'd learned after Frank's murder, life moved on.

Robert left a message on her voice mail informing her that a prospective buyer for her house wanted to tour the residence this afternoon. Claire gave a huge sigh but didn't say anything. Justin excused himself, retrieving the driver that seemed permanently attached to his hand these days to hit some balls in the backyard. Before she lost her nerve, she e-mailed Robert, giving her permission with a request they have a talk either sometime today or Sunday.

She felt like curling into a ball and crying. But she was the adult. She needed to be strong for her children. Losing their home was going to be excruciating for the children on top of everything else they'd been through with the loss of their dad. And when they found out they'd lost Mike, too . . . ?

Maybe she was the adult, but at the moment, she didn't feel up to that conversation with them. To distract herself, she looked out to her flowerbeds, mentally starting the process of saying good-bye. Justin poked his head through the door.

"Something's wrong with Mrs. Lambert next door. She left her car in the driveway and got out of it all hunched over. She's crying like crazy."

Alison didn't hide her alarm. "Are the kids strapped in the car?"

Justin leaned out the door and darted a quick glance over the fence. "Yeah. The baby and Kelsey are in the backseat. The baby's shrieking her head off. Mr. Lambert's out of town again this week."

Claire, who babysat regularly for the Lamberts, got off the couch. "He's always out of town, like Dad . . ." Claire bit her lip. "I'll see if I can help."

The phone rang. If this was a solicitation . . . But it could be Mike with more news. Maybe he'd found Ginny Walston. She waved the kids toward the Lamberts.

"Let me deal with this, and I'll be right over."

She snatched up the phone just before the last ring would've routed it over to voicemail. "Hello? Hello?"

"Al-Alison?" A voice, vaguely familiar, trembled on the other end. "I didn't know who else to call."

She gripped the phone. "Miss Lula? What's wrong? Where are you?"

"I'm at Weathersby." Lula tried to swallow her tears and failed, her gravelly voice clogged like a storm drain after a tropical depression. "I'm a foolish old woman, but I can't find Miss Patty. Her bed's not been slept in, and she ain't touched her food since yesterday."

Miss Patty? Alison rubbed her forehead in confusion.

Ah. The cat.

"Maybe she's on the prowl. Cats, from what little I know, are pretty independent creatures. I'm sure she'll turn up right as rain soon."

Lula cleared her throat. "Miss Patty's too old, like me, to go on a prowl. She likes to stick close to home, and with those terrible goings-on last night, I'm afraid she got hold of that poison that killed Natalie Singleton. Miss Patty could be sick and dying somewhere." Her voice ended with a whimper.

She had a feeling she knew what was coming.

"I didn't know who else to call." Lula sounded old and pitiful.

"Okay, I'll be there in thirty minutes, and we can hunt for Miss Patty together."

"You're a kind woman, Alison. I always knew it."

A sucker was more like it. She hung up the phone after making arrangements to meet Lula at the main house.

She looked down at her attire. Blue jean denim capris and an old baggy white T-shirt, the short sleeves rolled Fonzie-style. She had on her grungy, let's-clean-the-house-it's-Saturday wardrobe.

But hey? How fancy did you need to be to hunt for a missing cat?

And it *was* her day off. The spring festival in full swing, the grounds would be loaded with visitors.

So why the niggling slivers of doubt? Too many bad memories?

She ran a quick hand through her hair. Mike, with her help, had done his job. The killers were behind bars. It was perfectly safe to go to Weathersby again though there was still no sign of Ginny Walston. A loose thread that continued to nag at the edges of her mind.

Alison needed this job and the goodwill of all who worked there. Besides, she *was* a sucker for the needy, whether elderly or feline.

Slipping her feet into a nearby pair of matching denim flip-flops, the band edges frayed and stonewashed, she ran over to the Lamberts where Claire stood next to the Lamberts' car yakking on her cell phone. Justin scurried past, carrying bags of groceries into the house.

"What's going on?" She panted with her small effort at running across the lawn. She needed to get back to exercising regularly.

Bright and early Monday.

Claire held up a hand. "Great, Sandy," she said into her phone. "You don't know how much this will mean to the Lamberts." There was a silence as she listened. "Make sure everyone remembers to wear white shirts and black pants. More professional looking. I'll see you guys in ten." She snapped her pink phone shut with a flourish. "Right," Claire nodded to herself as much as anyone. "We have a plan," she said as if metaphorically rolling up her shirtsleeves.

"A plan for what?"

"Mrs. Lambert's hurt her back." Justin reached for another bag in the trunk. "Today's Kelsey's fourth birthday party. Fifteen other little squirts will be here in three hours."

She frowned. "And?"

"The caterer called as Mrs. Lambert pulled into the driveway. He's got the flu and he canceled. Mrs. Lambert is flat on her back, and Claire and I are going to put on the party for her." Justin disappeared into the house.

"Mrs. Lambert had already bought the decorations, and I think I can throw something together for the children to eat. It's a cowgirl party, and I have a few ideas to jazz it up." Claire seemed energized by the thought.

She hoped Mrs. Lambert knew what she was getting herself into with Claire and her ideas. Not to mention needing a big wallet.

"Sandy, Julie, and the rest of the girls are going to come over and help serve the food, babysit the baby, and run the gaming portion of the event."

Had she missed something significant?

Claire scanned the front yard, oblivious to the frown lines forming between her mother's brows. "My main concern is getting the cake decorated in time. It's humid today." She patted her mother on the arm, not expecting her to understand but making the attempt nonetheless. "And the other issue that needs to be resolved is where we can put the ponies."

"Ponies? Are you sure, Mrs. Lambert—?"

"Chill-lax, Mother. I have everything under control. Mrs. Lambert is totally on board with my ideas. I've been watching the Food Channel, and I know just the thing to put this party over the top." She shaded her eyes with one hand as she continued to scope out the front lawn.

Justin ambled up. "I'm going to take Western-style studio portraits of each kid on horseback with Dad's old camera and put together a pictorial scrapbook for each one to take home with their goody bag."

"Pictorial scrapbook?"

She remembered one particular Ladybug party for three-year-old Claire, the pressure in her high society world to impress not just the children, but their moms, too. The ladybugs, real ones, had escaped and swarmed over her three-hundred-dollar, Let Them Eat Cake, edible centerpiece. She shuddered at the memory.

"Don't worry, Mom." Justin patted her shoulder. "We've got it under control, and reinforcements are on their way. It will be fan-tabulous."

"Uh-huh," nodded Claire. "Who was on the phone?"

She explained the mystery of the missing cat. "I'm going to stop by Fresh Market for a few supplies and then help Miss Lula search. The cat's probably already come home by now." She glanced at her watch. "I'll be home before Kelsey's party to help."

"No worries." Justin pretended to putt an imaginary golf ball. "We can handle it. Enjoy your day."

Right. Searching for a finicky feline was definitely her idea of fun. Still. Anything for a distraction.

She grabbed her keys and purse from the house. In her rush, she noticed her cell phone batteries were low and would need charging when she returned. Making a quick dash into the grocery, she didn't bother to bag it after checking out, just stuck the coffee bag into her purse.

Miss Lula waited for her on the front porch of Weathersby, wringing her hands in her apron. She raced through the deadly yew hedge, careful to avoid eye contact with the spot at the corner of the house where she'd found Natalie's body the night before.

"Still no luck?"

"If that cat is hiding from me deliberate, I'm going to take a broomstick to that creature."

"Let's search the house one more time." Alison helped Miss Lula up the steps. They quietly moved around the cluster of visitors taking the house tour conducted by Erica, who gave a small wave of acknowledgment as Lula and Alison slid by. Miss Lula went left into the massive dining room. She went right into the front parlor.

Over the mantel, Oliver's portrait hung. He *was* creepy. She'd never spent much time in the house before. Venturing behind the tourist ropes to look under the French Empire red stripe silk settee, she also peered around the baby grand piano. Erica's group moved into the dining room, and she heard the heavy, labored tread of Miss Lula ascend the staircase to the second story.

Oliver's beady eyes in that corpulent face did seem to follow you wherever you happened to stand, and she deliberately turned her back on the long-dead Weathersby progenitor. Under the portrait, the fragrance of dried rose petals in a blue Cantonese bowl filled the room.

Cordoned off, silver-framed photographs of weddings and family gatherings, sepia toned and aged, stood scattered artfully across the piano. She smiled, remembering the colorful history of fashion represented in the moonlight last evening. The side table held a stereoscope, the 1800s definition of vacation slides. And a silver jet locket. One of the mourning kind—macabre and gothically fashionable in the Victorian age—where a lock of the beloved's hair was kept in remembrance after their deaths.

Not her idea of preserving memories of the dead, but to each age its own customs. With the same irresistible ghoulish urge that caused people to watch horror movies, she found herself drawn to the locket. She stepped over the rope.

Opening it, she found a small, plaited braid of hair with strands of pure white, a salt-and-pepper gray, several ginger colored ones, an auburn as red as Claire's, and a solid strand of black interwoven together.

The black strand reminded her of Natalie Singleton's silky crow locks. In her mind's eye, she saw Natalie again as she had appeared last night. First, in her dazzling flapper dress, the black feather defiant of convention. And then, of Natalie writhing on the ground.

The red one looked like it belonged to Claire.

Or to Frank.

Goose pimples broke out on her arms. With the sound of laughter and shuffling feet, Erica and her group entered the parlor. Spinning around, she clutched the locket and shoved it into her purse beside the coffee beans.

Erica frowned. Had Erica seen her take the locket? Perhaps she already knew the contents of the locket.

She must look deranged. She felt deranged.

Had someone been collecting locks of hair from his or her victims? People didn't act that way, did they?

Even murderers? Who was that psychotic?

Jasper, definitely. But this smacked of a deranged female mind.

And Erica had set up the clothing and jewelry exhibits.

She offered an apologetic smile to Erica and the visitors. She slunk quickly out of the room and away from Erica's quizzical looks. Miss Lula was downstairs again in the docent office, her apron over her head. At the sound of Alison's tread upon the squeaky oak floorboard, Lula lifted her face and swiped at her eyes.

"I'm always careful to make sure the cat's in the house before dark. Too many wild creatures roam the night, animal and human. I've had Winnie and Erica searching the outbuildings and gardens on their tours this morning. Nobody's seen hide or hair of her. I don't understand it. I can't believe she's gone."

She tried to focus on what Miss Lula was saying, but all she could think about were scissors clipping at Natalie's silky black tresses while she lay suffocating in her own vomit.

And Frank, his head turned sideways on the headrest of his car, the breeze from the open window of the driver side ruffling his side-parted bangs into the fiery red dot of blood that marked his temple.

She closed her eyes.

"I hear some animals, maybe cats, go curl up and hide when death comes a-knocking." Lula sighed. "Maybe it's time for this old girl to hang it up, too."

She swayed on her feet.

"Are you all right, Alison? You look mighty strange."

She licked her lips and opened her eyes. Lula grabbed her forearm as the room started to tilt. She found her weight supported by the iron grip of the old woman. Who was the pitiful one now? She hadn't thought an old woman could be so strong. How strong did you have to be to shoot someone, poison another, and cut tresses from their hair?

"I'm okay," she whispered. "Just too much . . ." She stopped and gestured around the room. She needed to get away from this place and these people.

"You need to go home. You had a terrible shock last night." Lula tsked-tsked herself. "I shouldn't have called you away from your children."

She patted Lula's hand covering her arm. Better keep that open-book face of hers guileless. "I'm sorry we didn't find Miss Patty. Are you going to be okay?" Alison's fear mixed with feelings of guilt over her suspicions about Miss Lula.

Lula grimaced. "Life. Seasons change. And what doesn't kill us, the good Lord intends to cure us, I suppose. Nothing ever stands still. I don't know if you've lived long enough to notice," with a quick glimpse of Alison's set face, she amended, "but I reckon after the last few months, you knows exactly what I mean." She laughed hoarsely. "Trees that can't bend with the wind, honey chile, break. Don't let life break you."

She nodded. "You are one wise woman, Miss Lula."

Not Miss Lula? Surely not? Erica, maybe.

Lula's wrinkled, brown face creased into a smile. "Wisdom won the hard, old-fashioned way. Through blood, sweat, and a bucket of tears."

43

Alison stepped out onto the docent porch. She took a deep breath, inhaling and exhaling, trying to clear her mind of horrific images. Too much imagination could be a curse. Mike would want to look at this locket. She dreaded having to face him one more time.

Wood smoke curled from the detached kitchen chimney, tantalizing and tingling the nose. A small bonfire blazed in front of the kitchen stoop, a Dutch oven hung over a crane, the contents bubbling. Food historian and volunteer, Kathy Briggs, in the farmhouse garb of the last century, stood over the fire, stoking its flames with wood chips.

North Carolina artisans and craftspeople lined the path around the house all the way to the office with reed baskets, lace tatting, and cornhusk dolls for sale. The world famous Seagrove potters had a booth. If you closed your eyes, you could imagine a bustling plantation, one hundred and fifty years ago.

The gardens were fully restored, the orchards stretching into the distance, loaded with apple blossoms. The fields—where apartments and subdivisions now stood—were furrowed and planted with new corn and dotted with the red roofs of the barns.

Rows of slave cabins.

Her eyes snapped open. The hallowed and romantic past?

A better place—said the tourist tripe Ivy liked to shovel onto the guests—unless you happened to be a slave.

"Yoo hoo! Alison!"

Shaken out of her musings, she spotted Winnie waving energetically from the gift shop door.

Well, that sinks it.

Tempted to flee, she knew it was already too late. She'd been captured. There was only one possible reason for Winnie's pursuit: she wanted Alison to write that reimbursement check.

Winnie arrived, breathless from her unaccustomed sprint.

Alison held up one hand in surrender. "Fine, Winnie. I'll write you that check while I'm here. I'll drop it by the shop on my way out."

Winnie clapped her hands. "You're a doll."

She shook her head, sidestepping Winnie, and headed in the direction of the office. "No, I'm a sucker." She waved as she passed Velma and the quilters under their tent.

The office lay dark and deserted. She jerked the tiny golden chain of the green banker's lamp. Pulling her chair closer to her desk, she reached for the travel reimbursement form buried at the bottom of her in-box under another voluminous mass of Ivy's correspondence. Firing up the computer and with the machine gently humming as she waited for it to wake up, she grabbed her cell phone.

She wasn't going to make the party at this rate. Claire's cell was busy. Justin must not have his turned on. She left a message.

"Got caught doing paperwork. I'll be home by the time you buckeroos and dudettes are done. Hope everything went well. Love ya. See you soon."

She located the travel reimbursement folder on the desktop hard drive and opened it. The individual files were labeled by the month, date, and year of travel. She glanced over to Winnie's handwritten form. March 2, 2013. Sure enough, the file number was 0302013. She created a record of Winnie's reimbursement and entered the correct data.

Withdrawing her key chain, she unlocked the middle drawer where she kept the Weathersby checkbook. Surprisingly, Ivy, the ultimate control freak, didn't have a head for numbers and wanted no part of accounts payable or receivable. That job, one of many, fell to her assistant to deal with. In other words, Alison.

As she was writing Winnie's name and signing the check with the Weathersby rubber stamp of Ivy's signature, it hit her. The numbers.

She dropped the pen and rummaged through her purse. As her fingers reached the bottom, she felt the folder that held the photocopies of Frank's calendar. Four series of numbers. One denoted the latitude and longitude of Grand Cayman. The Feds had discovered another set were the offshore bank accounts opened by Bill Lawrence. The third belonged to the hotel in San Francisco.

And the fourth?

She scrolled down the list of travel reimbursement files on the computer screen. Yes, it was there. September 22, 2012 or 0922012. Someone from Weathersby had filed for travel expenses for that date.

One click and she would know who stood in that picture with Frank in San Francisco. She would know who had murdered Frank and maybe why. She wasn't buying Mike's all-encompassing Lawrence theory.

She'd felt all along Frank's murderer had been the woman he'd betrayed her with in San Francisco. A woman in a long line of women over the years. But the woman, who finally, for whatever twisted reason, had ended Frank's sorry existence.

She bit her lip. That was the anger talking. No one had the right to kill Frank, Natalie, or anyone else. No matter how deeply he'd betrayed her and the children.

This woman was someone she knew. Someone she'd worked with for years probably, first as a volunteer and now as staff. This woman had murdered Frank. Maybe because—despite the emotional and spiritual abandonment stretching back into the early years of their marriage—Frank would've never physically left her and the children.

Because of the scandal? Because he loved the children? Because Alison was safe and comfortable?

Maybe because they'd once had their Hawaii.

With all her heart, she'd like to be able to believe that. Maybe one day she would.

Swallowing a sob, she clicked on the file, two short jabs with her finger. The pieces fell into place.

She sat for a long time at her desk, her thoughts going over the last few months. The last time she'd seen Frank alive. Her conversations with his murderer. The subtle clues she'd missed somehow.

Picking up the phone, she dialed Mike's office. She was told he'd finally gone home. She left a message for him to contact her. She dialed his personal cell phone. He had it turned off, no doubt getting some well-deserved shut-eye. She left a message there also.

She stuffed the coffee beans, the folder, and her phone into her purse. She fingered the macabre silver locket. What should she do now?

Leaning back into the chair to think, she removed the photo of Frank in San Francisco from the folder and placed it under the glow of the lamp to study.

Now she knew the identity of his companion, and she wanted to examine Frank's face one more time for her own peace of mind. Up until now, she'd focused solely on the woman at his side.

Steeling herself to be objective, she stared long and hard at Frank's familiar profile. He'd been trying to capture the moment. Was he even then trying to provide them with a clue? Had he, weeks before his death, had a premonition of menacing disaster?

A phrase from Frank's letter came to her.

"I stared into the Abyss, and I saw myself falling forever. I was forced to examine my life, saw myself for what I was and all I had done, and I fell instead into the outstretched arms of my Savior."

What had Frank discovered about this woman that had resulted in his death? There was a look in his eyes, she noticed now, no longer merry, no longer defiant, but sad, afraid, yet determined.

She let out the slow breath she hadn't realized she was holding. The warmth of her breath tickled the fine hairs on the back of her hand holding the photo.

The sensation brought another inexplicable experience to mind.

Miss Patty.

She stood, scraping her chair across the wooden floor.

Reaching for the phone again, she dialed the main house. No answer. Miss Lula must have gone home. Flashes of heat lightning lit an ever-darkening sky as the predicted storm front rolled into the city.

Jasper was long gone. Or so she hoped. She debated whether to call for reinforcements, glancing at her watch. But, if what she suspected were true, Miss Patty was trapped and time was of the essence.

She had the foresight to grab a small black flashlight from her desk, and she shoved the locket into the back pocket of her jeans. She'd dash over to the toolshed, pry open the board with the mysterious air current, and free Miss Patty.

Visitors and artisans scrambled for the parking lot as she cut across the herb garden, the cell phone strapped to her ear. "Claire? Justin? Pick up if you're there." Silence. "I think Miss Patty is trapped in the toolshed. I'm going there now to mount a rescue. See if you can get hold of Mike. I have something important to show him. See you soon, I promise."

The phone emitted a small beeping. She banged it against her leg.

The battery was dying. Just what she needed today, of all days. Hopefully, the children would get her message and wouldn't worry.

She was extra careful as she hurried over the terrain, sidestepping the gargoylelike roots of the apple orchard and jumping over the ruts made by farm wagons a hundred years ago. In a moment, the half-light of the forest surrounded her, cutting her off once again from the comforting noise of modern life.

To be on the safe side, she walked around the perimeter of the ring of trees that encircled the small clearing where the toolshed stood. Nothing and no one.

Funny how not a single bird sang in this clearing. Funny, weird. Not funny, ha ha. Here, all was silent. Silent as death.

She shook herself. No time for ghost stories. Regretting every ax murder movie she'd ever seen, she poked her head in the shed door, the flashlight grasped with both hands pointed up and against her chest like she'd seen police officers do with their guns on TV.

Jasper was probably long gone. Good news not just for her, but for all of Raleigh. She scrunched under the workbench and removed one foot from a flip-flop. She edged her bare foot across the floor, hoping she didn't get splinters.

At a tiny trickle of air, she paused, her foot hovering over a miniscule crevice. She'd found the gap between the boards. She shone the beam of light directly in front of her. On her hands and knees, she fumbled around trying to find the outline of the board. She found three sides and the light caught the glint of metal. A hinge, rusty and old by the looks of it.

The board wouldn't budge.

Figuring there must be a hidden spring mechanism, she gingerly applied pressure with her bare foot at first one spot and then another.

The sound of a catch releasing, the table moved sideways and the board popped open about three inches. Smiling with satisfaction, she bent down to open it, revealing a set of stairs that disappeared into the darkness below.

With a small meow, Miss Patty bounded out, purring and rubbing her thanks against her ankles.

"No problem, old girl." She petted Miss Patty's sable-colored coat. "What's that in your mouth?" Miss Patty dropped a small glittering object at her feet.

A small rose-colored cameo earring. Like the cameo Natalie had pressed into her hand before she died. Like the one Ginny Walston had been wearing before she disappeared.

With a low purr, Miss Patty nudged open the flap of her purse. Her teeth sinking into the bag of coffee beans, Miss Patty chewed open the bag and cuffed a bean with her paw. A handful of beans rolled across the floor.

She stroked Miss Patty's back. "Are you a coffee lover, too, or just hungry? We'll get you something right—"

Angry voices erupted outside the shed. Miss Patty arched her back and, with an apologetic flick of her tail, dashed out the opened door and into the freedom of the woods. The voices moved closer, arguing.

Her heart pounding, she grabbed the flashlight and her purse. Descending the stairs, she yanked the secret door down. She prayed for the mechanism to engage, sliding the table to its original position.

The voices were outside the door now. Too close. No time.

With a sudden lurch, the door slid shut over her head, plunging her into darkness.

44

FOR A MOMENT, ALISON THOUGHT SHE'D GONE BLIND. THE DARKNESS WAS all-encompassing, a living entity. Oppressive and smothering. Tentacles of fear assaulted her, pressing upon her chest. It wasn't merely the absence of light. No hope here. No escape. Only gloom and the pungent aroma of an ancient, earthy mold, suffocating in its stench, pervaded this unholy place.

Fighting every instinct, she resisted the urge to scream. She dared not make a sound for fear the intruders above would hear her cries. She could hear them arguing, a woman's voice and a young man's. The boards above her head creaked as they paced back and forth across the floor of the cabin.

She wasn't sure of whom she was more afraid. Both of them were psychopaths. She was afraid to turn on the flashlight.

Her muscles strained with the tension of not moving. She'd caught sight of a set of stairs before she scrambled down into this abyss. Disoriented, she perched on one step. In the utter darkness of this pit, she was afraid to move, much less breathe, for fear of tumbling the rest of that yet to be determined length of staircase to the bottom. She could be two feet from the ground or a mile for all she knew.

She played a deadly game of Freeze, willing her joints to lock and stay frozen in position. She had the insane urge to sneeze just because she couldn't. One foot felt the edge of the stair, and she realized, with a sinking heart, she'd left the other flip-flop in the corner under the workbench above.

What if they discovered that?

Recalling Jasper's artwork, she fought an excruciating battle within her mind not to give in to the fear, the despair.

And because she'd lost the use of her eyes, her other faculties kicked in more strongly. In the darkness below her, sounds. Something small and furry scurried over her bare foot. To keep from shrieking, she bit her lip and tasted the salty tang of her own blood.

God, I need You.

The voices drifted out of the range of her hearing. Praying they'd left the vicinity of the cabin, with her bare foot, she felt for the edge of the step. An inch at a time, she lowered her foot. What seemed like an eternity was only the usual distance between treads, she soon discovered. She brought her other foot down and started over again with the next step, counting her progress.

One-two-three. Mike's arms encircling her as they danced . . . 1-2-3. As she reached the tenth wooden stair, her foot encountered hard-packed earth. Only then did she dare to turn on the flashlight. She held it in front of her, her body bent over it shielding the rays of light from reaching the cabin above.

She sucked in the light like oxygen.

The light revealed a cramped, subterranean chamber smaller in width than the average hallway. Mike's shoulders would brush the sides.

She took a step forward and swiped at the cobweb fastened onto her face. Strands of webs dangled from the ceiling of the ghostly passageway. Lichen covered the packed earth walls. She shuddered. Her slight movements had quieted the creatures that dwelled here. An eerie silence hovered.

Forcing herself onward, she crept along, both hands locked around the metal canister of the flashlight. She prayed the batteries wouldn't die. Alone in the darkness, she wasn't sure she could keep from screaming.

The passageway ahead curved, and she found an opening along one wall. The pitch-blackness yielded to the beam of her light. A room.

She placed her foot over the threshold. What was it? A crypt? A catacomb?

There was a bed and a table. A lantern, Frank's missing briefcase, and several objects littered the surface of the table. The sound of a whisper, more like a sigh, floated out into the air.

Her hands shook, but she shone the light at the source of the sound. A shrouded form occupied the bed.

Someone or something.

Wanting to turn and run, she walked over to the bed and, before she lost her nerve, shone the light on the bed and its occupant.

"Ginny!"

Ginny Walston lay spread-eagle upon the narrow wooden bedstead still robed in the lavender silk ball gown she'd worn the night before. Her eyelids closed, her face pale. She was unconscious, and her breathing was heavy and labored. What looked like the remains of a petticoat bound her hands and feet to the wooden posts of the cot.

"Oh, Jesus," Alison prayed. "Help us."

"Mom's not home yet," Justin announced as he helped Claire clean up the party debris from the Lamberts' yard.

Claire stuffed the discarded paper birthday plates and cups into the oversized trashcan.

"That cake was amazing." Sandy removed the makeshift hula-hoop lasso from the rocking horse.

Julie, flipping her straight black hair over her shoulder, gathered the broomstick horses from the Giddy Up Horse Relay. "You have a real talent for this kind of thing, Claire. The cowgirl boot cake was great, and the moms liked the flowers from your mother's garden."

Claire bent over to hide her smile. She'd borrowed Justin's cowboy boots and clipped a few sprigs from the dogwood tree, making the boots her floral centerpiece. She stood and leaned sideways, stretching her back.

These girls weren't as bad as she'd thought. They were hard workers and intelligent. She wouldn't call them friends exactly, but who knows? In her gone crazy world, anything was possible.

Lily tossed plastic horseshoes into a duffel bag, munching on the fake jerky Claire had created from licorice. "They liked the grub for sure."

Sandy smiled at Justin. "I think the biggest hit was when Justin took each of their photos on the ponies."

Julie nodded. "The scrapbooks were way cool."

She'd sent Justin over to their house midway through the party to put together a scrapbook of party memories, personalized for each child, with the new software he'd been itching to try.

Claire shrugged. "You guys didn't have to help me or Mrs. Lambert. Like you said the other day, you don't owe us a thing." She ducked her head to hide the sudden trembling of her lips.

"No, we don't." Anna put her hand on Claire's arm. "But we help our brothers and sisters, our neighbors, as Jesus said to do."

It was easy to forget someone quiet like Anna occupied space, she realized with a pang. It was too easy to overlook these kinds of people, the invisible ones, the geeks, the brains, the socially awkward, invisible to her before the world went crazy.

Visible now to the more sensitive—at least she hoped so—Claire. And actually, these people were more interesting than her old crowd whose primary concerns revolved around fashion, who had dumped whom, and the latest party.

A Volvo station wagon pulled up beside the curb and tooted the horn. Justin waved.

"My dad." Sandy waved at the driver.

"Our ride," said Lily and Julie.

She reached for the bags they were holding. "Thanks, you guys. I couldn't have pulled this off without you. And I know Mrs. Lambert and especially Kelsey were . . ." She struggled for the right word.

"Blessed?" Anna tilted her head.

She smiled. "That's the word. Justin and I can finish here."

"We'll see you tomorrow at church," Justin called as the girls took off for Sandy's car.

"This is the last of it." With a mighty heave, a garbage bag in each hand, she started for her own yard.

Justin followed. "Mom's left another message."

Overhead, Claire could hear the sounds of Robert giving the homebuyers the grand tour.

Washing her hands in the kitchen sink, she frowned as Justin played the message. "Something's not right." She glanced at the clock on the wall. "She should've been home by now."

Justin picked up the phone and dialed his mom's number. "No answer. She's got it turned off."

"Or"—she made a face—"she forgot to charge the cell battery again." Sometimes she worried about her mom and her mom's entire generation when it came to technology.

Justin dialed the Weathersby number. "No one's picking up."

"Look at the time." She pointed to the clock. "They're closed till Sunday afternoon. Call Mike." A prickly sensation ran up and down her arms.

"We'll look like a bunch of big doofuses calling him and then Mom walking through the door. She'll be livid."

"Good word, but call him. I don't like this."

Justin thrust the phone in her direction. "You call him."

"Do I have to do everything in this family?" She dialed Mike's number. "He's got it turned off, too." She stared at the phone in her hand. "What is it with the grown-ups today?"

Justin clenched and unclenched his hands. "Uncle Stephen?"

"They're off to Wilmington to visit Aunt Val's brother at the beach."

She didn't know what to do, feeling helpless and hating it. "I'm scared. Something bad is happening to Mom." She knew it in her gut. What if they lost her, too?

Justin squared his shoulders and shot a look at the ceiling. "I know who can help us. And we're going to pray. Pray, Claire, pray hard for Mom."

45

THEY HAD TO GET OUT OF HERE AND FAST. BUT HOW? HER HUSBAND'S murderers blocked the exit.

Alison bent over Ginny and with trembling fingers tried to loosen the corded knots binding Ginny's red, chafed wrists.

She shook her shoulder, trying to rouse her. "Ginny."

Ginny writhed, but her eyes remained closed. A faint sound emerged from her mouth.

She leaned closer, her ear to Ginny's lips.

"Pat—pat."

"Miss Patty's okay, Ginny. I found her. Miss Patty's already safe at the house by now."

"Not safe," whispered Ginny. She moaned. "House not . . ."

Picking up the flashlight where she'd laid it on the bed beside Ginny, she noticed a few cat hairs in a spot below Ginny's chest. Miss Patty must have wandered in when Ginny was kidnapped. And, curled into a ball, Miss Patty stayed behind to comfort one of her favorite human friends.

The darkness. How had Ginny been able to keep from losing her mind all these hours?

She swung the light over to the table. The oil lantern had been used recently. A brown glass prescription bottle and a syringe lay beside it. And, a large brass key.

Frank's missing Weathersby key? Had he discovered the room that last evening of his life?

She picked up the bottle with the edge of her T-shirt to examine the label. Mike would have her head if she smudged any fingerprint evidence. Wishing Mike were here, she shone the flashlight closer to the label.

The patient's name ripped off. The name of the medication remained. Baclofen. Whatever this was, if it had kept Ginny out of it all these hours, it had probably been a blessing.

Which also meant something else had been planned for Ginny, and someone would be coming back.

She placed the flashlight beside Ginny, where its beam would give her the most light as she fought with renewed determination to free Ginny from her bonds. As the minutes passed and her desperation mounted, she stopped and jostled Ginny.

She'd succeeded in freeing Ginny's legs and her left hand when she felt a subtle movement of air upon the calves of her legs.

Whirling around, she grabbed for the flashlight.

Jasper stood on the threshold, another lighted lantern in his hand, his brow furrowed in its perpetual scowl. His beady eyes gleamed, so like the portrait above the mantel in the front parlor.

Recoiling against the bedpost, she placed herself between Ginny and him, pressing back as hard as she could as wooden splinters pricked into the tender flesh underneath her T-shirt.

"You left this behind in the cabin." He hurled her missing flip-flop in the direction of her foot. "Careless."

She snaked out her foot, capturing the shoe, and eased her foot into it. Running would be better with two shoes.

If she ever got the chance to run.

"Why did you do this to Ginny? To my husband and Natalie Singleton?"

Jasper snickered. "I didn't do anything to those people. But I thank you for the compliment." He laughed, as unpleasant as the sound of a hyena. "You are a smart, though nosy, lady. I've tried to scare you off for your own good, but now you've gone and done it." He stepped closer.

Her fists clenched, she shrank back until she was practically on the bed with Ginny. But he veered off into the opposite corner of the room, stuffing an armful of clothing into his backpack.

"You've been hiding out down here. If you didn't kill Frank, then why that picture in Claire's locker?"

He kept his head down, gathering further personal items from the floor of the room. "I told you, lady. I was trying to warn you. It was easy to blend in with the other students. I figured if I put it in your girl's locker you'd take me seriously."

"If you didn't pull the trigger yourself, then you saw who did, didn't you, Jasper?" She gulped. "You saw her do it. So you drew the picture of what you'd seen the day Frank was killed. Like the other pictures. They weren't something you've actually done, right?"

He started toward her, a small pocketknife in his hand. She tensed against Ginny's silent form.

"Not yet. The others were . . . " he brushed her out of the way to slide the knife between Ginny's wrist and the cord. "Those were more like what I'd like to do to that mother—"

He used an expletive so vile she cringed.

With a single thrust, he sliced the remaining cord tying Ginny to the bed. "I tried to cover your shoe with my backpack so she wouldn't see, but she's evil smart." He snickered again. "In a weird way, I admire her."

She tried pulling Ginny to a sitting position. But she was dead weight. "But you hate her, too, don't you?"

An ugly look creased his face. "She left me with that monster. Walked away and never looked back. Left me to endure the cigarette burns, the middle-of-the-night visits . . ." His voice trailed off.

She swallowed, pity and disgust mingling, unsure how to respond.

He swept his dingy black locks out of his eyes. "Don't waste your sympathy on me. I don't need it. I settled with him a long time ago, and now it's her turn. For what it's worth, I'm sorry I waited too long to save your husband from her. She was obsessed with him, although he never gave her the time of day."

He shrugged. "No matter what she's made up in that fantasy world of hers, when he rejected her," he stuck one finger up to his head like a cocked pistol, "it was curtains for him."

She tugged harder trying to get Ginny to her feet. "Can you help me get Ginny out of here, Jasper? Please?"

He sighed. "I'm not so comfortable with the good-deed thing, Mrs. Monaghan. Out of character for me, you know." He smirked.

She put one arm under Ginny's rag-doll shoulder. "And Natalie? Why her?" She staggered as Ginny's feet trailed across the floor.

He laid his bag on the table and zipped the contents shut. "Number one: she had the unfortunate habit of being obnoxious. Two," he ticked off, holding up two fingers. "Frank liked her." He gave Alison an irreverent wink. "Three: she saw Ginny being drugged and dragged through the secret panel in the house down here."

He nodded at her startled look. "Oh, yeah. There's another way out. It was all about easy access for my illustrious forebears. And four," with a grimy forefinger, he brushed the tip of her nose for emphasis.

She drew back. He laughed at her repulsion.

"Four: Natalie Singleton was the last living Weathersby relation, Herself's other big obsession besides your husband. And by the way, you're on her hit list, too."

At her puzzled look, he laughed. "Frank wouldn't leave you for her. That knife in the tire was a promise for the future. She followed you out of the house that night while I watched from the bushes. If that Kendall guy hadn't shown up, you'd have bought it then. And you might want to warn Miss Lula, too. Not safe to leave any living reminders of past failures and a pedigree she'd just as soon keep a secret."

She stopped beside the table for a breather. Ginny's head lolled around. "Pedigree?" She panted.

He waved his arm, encompassing the room. "This little pre-abolition love nest of my great-great-granddaddy. That's how I'm going to get her. I'll give you ten minutes and then I'm burning

Weathersby to the ground. I can't wait for the look on her face. She'll be in the psych ward by morning." He howled at the thought.

"No, Jasper. There's a better way. We can go to the authorities. They'll put an end to her killing."

He cocked his head in her direction as if considering her proposition. Like a gnomish version of a vulture, he smiled, showing his teeth. She was beginning to see the family resemblance.

"I'll have to make that a no for me. My plan is way more fun. Now, you two better get a move on. I don't know how long she'll be in the house. She likes to play dress-up with the Weathersby clothes when the tourists have gone home for the day. Pretend she's the lady of the manor and not just the bastard born on the wrong side of the Weathersby blanket." He swung his pack in place and reached for the lantern.

With further protest on her part futile, she put her back into it as she settled a still comatose Ginny more comfortably onto her shoulder.

"How delightful," a silken voice called out from the darkness of the corridor.

He whipped around, panic streaking his face.

"All my loose ends in one place."

Ivy emerged from the shadows into the tiny pool of light cast by the lantern on the table. She was dressed in a long, sweeping, blue-velvet traveling dress, a matching hat perched jauntily atop her head. Her face was drawn, a caricature of the clownish Ivy Dandridge she'd known before. Her eyes were amused and hard as agates.

There was the glint of metal as Ivy slowly drew her arm straight up from the side of her skirt. She gripped a small, pearl-handled pistol.

Ivy advanced slowly and deliberately until only a distance of about six feet separated them. Enough distance to prevent one of them from wresting the gun from her grasp.

The barrel pointed straight at Alison's heart.

46

NOW MOVE!" IVY DEMANDED.

Jasper left his backpack on the table and took his place as instructed on Ginny's other side, helping Alison bear Ginny's weight. Moving behind them, Ivy retrieved the lantern from the table and jabbed the gun for emphasis into the hollow of Alison's back.

"We're going on a little journey." Ivy nudged them out the door and into the corridor. She held the light aloft, high over her head. "Up the stairs."

Another set of stairs at the far distant end of the tunnel disappeared into the darkness above. Slowly, one painful foot at a time, she and Jasper dragged Ginny up the stairs. She counted the steps silently, her lips set in a grim, straight line.

Ivy was too relaxed, too confident. She obviously feared no interruption of her plan, whatever it was. Jasper paused on the sixth step, as if on cue, and for a split second Alison surged forward, caught off guard.

Ivy jabbed the gun into her spine. "No bright ideas from you." She pulled a metal lever protruding from the packed earth wall of the chamber. With a sound reminiscent of rusty hinges, there was a clanging and scraping, and the dead-end wall at the top of the stairs slid over and out revealing the small electric sconce that hung below the main staircase in the house.

Thank God for electric lights.

Jasper lurched forward. Mounting the remaining steps with Ginny in tow, she stepped over the threshold into not safety but at least civilization again. Alison couldn't help taking a deep, steadying breath, glad beyond all reason to be out of that chamber of despair below the earth.

Looking back, she noted the massive grandfather clock had swerved to the right as if on an invisible track concealing the secret passageway beneath. Thunder boomed in the distance.

Right behind them, Ivy dogged their footsteps. "Take her into the parlor. Dump her on the settee. The police detective," Ivy turned with feverish eyes to Alison, "can find her there in the morning. Dead with the same gun that killed Frank."

Alison trudged with Jasper past the grand staircase and into the foyer turning into the front parlor. Glancing out the sidelights of the front door, she saw darkness had fallen across Raleigh due to the approaching storm. Another rumble of thunder rattled the glass panes in the windows.

She thought of her children. And Mike. Strange how she felt no fear for herself. Ivy had killed at least two people. And if she were not stopped, she would kill at least two more tonight. No one knew Alison's whereabouts. No one was going to rush in and save her and Ginny.

Only God could help them now. The thought, instead of reducing her to cowering terror, was oddly empowering. As she and Jasper lowered Ginny onto the settee, her eyes darted about the room for a weapon to utilize against Ivy.

As if reading her mind, Ivy planted herself between Alison and the fire irons under the mantel. Mute, Jasper's braggadocio had faded fast in Ivy's presence.

"It's the eyes." Alison pointed at the portrait in an attempt to distract Ivy. "I see it now. The resemblance. Green like your great-granddaddy."

Jasper scowled and Ivy frowned. "Think yourself clever, don't you? Well, too clever for your own good as I think you'll soon discover. Jasper," she gestured. "We'll not have further need of your services tonight."

He crammed his hands into his trouser pockets and slunk away into the foyer.

"You, too." Ivy motioned for her to follow.

With a backward glance over her shoulder to Ginny, slumped sideways on the settee, she was forced to comply.

"You," Ivy waved the gun at Alison, "stand on the bottom step and wait."

"I need to get my pack," mumbled Jasper. He turned his back to them, putting one foot on the descending stair step.

Ivy smiled at his retreating form.

That smile . . .

She opened her mouth to call a warning, but as the words formed on her tongue, it was already too late.

"You do that." Ivy grinned. "Son."

He whirled at the tone in her voice. Ivy brought the gun forward at lightning speed, pulling the trigger. Alison had no time to react as the bullet slammed into Jasper's chest.

A tiny spot of blood seeped through his grubby shirt. The force of the impact caused him to stagger farther into the recess of the hole. He stretched out one hand as if to catch himself.

Or perhaps, as if toward Ivy. Afterward, she was never sure which.

"Mother . . ."

With a manic push, Ivy shoved him backward into the pit of darkness and out of sight. There was a dull thud as his body hit the bottom of the hidden staircase.

Alison screamed.

"Shut your mouth," Ivy snarled.

Her hands over her mouth, she sank down and leaned against the curved banister of the stairwell. Had Ivy actually killed her own son?

Ivy reached up to the grandfather clock, adjusting both hands to the twelve o'clock hour and setting the moon dial to its crescent position. With a metallic grinding sound, the clock swung to the left, once more in its proper place, concealing the secret chamber beneath the house.

A rumble of thunder shook the house to its foundations. Lightning crackled.

"Do you fear God, Ivy?"

Gun in hand, Ivy motioned for her to climb the stairs to the second story. "There is no God." Her lips tightened. "We have to be our own gods. It's up to us to make our own destiny. I told Frank as much that day on Orchard Farm Road when he said the same to me."

Her heart pounding, Alison pulled herself to her feet. "Well, you should believe. God exists, and He's not going to allow you to hurt me."

Ivy laughed again. "Frank's God didn't help him that day in his car. And your God isn't going to help you, either. Who is going to stop me? You?"

With a confidence she didn't know she possessed, Alison mounted the stairs. "Yes, I believe I am."

For her bravado, Ivy shoved her forward, causing her to stumble up two of the treads and scrape her knee. "Shut up and do what I tell you. Move it."

At the top of the stairs, she found herself propelled toward the master bedroom and the sleeping porch overlooking the front portico.

Advancing gun in hand, Ivy backed her to the edge of the railing until her heels could retreat no further. The wind blew strands of hair across her face. The night air was sticky with moisture, pregnant with the coming violence the storm would unleash.

"Why the attack upon Ginny Walston?"

Ivy sighed. "So nosy. Right to the end. How Frank stood living with you all those years, I'll never know."

"Let's talk about Frank then."

Anything to delay and distract.

An odd look flickered across Ivy's face. "No. I don't want to talk about Frank. You want to know answers before you face this make-believe God of yours? All right."

Ivy took a deep breath, waving the gun as she spoke. "Ginny was getting too close to the truth. Too suspicious. I was careful. I've always had to be careful, but somehow she started to suspect I was involved with her husband's death."

"Dr. Walston?" Alison's eyes widened. Waving the gun around made her nervous.

"He was my boyfriend first at UNC." Ivy's voice took on a musing tone. "How different my life would have turned out if he'd only married me. He was in med school. Ginny and I were in nurses' training together." She laughed, a sound as unpleasant as her dead son's. "I actually introduced them to each other. Biggest mistake of my life."

In light of what she knew about Ivy's history, she doubted the validity of that statement.

Ivy's voice grew younger, as if she were once again that twenty-something version of herself. "She had everything, the daughter of a Raleigh surgeon. Her life has always been so easy." Her tone hardened. "And she took him. The only man I ever loved."

"Until Frank?"

Ivy looked at her, a frown creasing her brow. "Until Frank." She tossed her head. "Leo married Ginny the day we graduated from training. I kind of lost it."

Another vast understatement.

"The next thing I remember is waking up married six months later to that cretin, Jasper's father, and I was pregnant and trapped." Her eyes glittered. "I don't like being trapped. I bided my time. I made my plans. Then, I walked into my new life."

"As if Jasper had never happened."

Ivy sniffed. "It was him or me."

Alison suspected it had—when it came right down to it—always been all about Ivy when push came to shove.

"You've been clever."

Ivy's ramrod posture eased.

To Alison's relief, Ivy took the bait. She had counted on Ivy being unable to resist the urge to brag.

"Yes, I have." Ivy smiled. "It took many years, but I finally got that shrew Ginny." She gave an ugly laugh. "Leo and Ginny, so sickeningly devoted to each other. I saw Ginny leave the board meeting with Frank one night." Ivy shook her head in disbelief. "I couldn't believe she'd try to steal my man a second time, but she did."

As Jasper had said, Ivy's grasp of reality was tenuous at best. Lightning sizzled the air, causing Ivy and her both to jump.

In that split second before the streaks lit the sky, she thought she heard the sound of car doors slamming from the direction of the parking lot. She prayed Ivy had been too distracted to hear it.

"So, I went to see Leo late one night and told him what I'd seen." Her face took on a grotesque purple hue. "He laughed at me. He didn't believe his darling wife would do such a thing. Luckily, I came prepared."

"You killed him and made it appear a suicide."

Ivy gave a small smile of satisfaction. "If you could have seen the look on his face when I held the gun to his temple?" Her voice purred. "Priceless."

She rubbed sweaty palms down the sides of her capris. Crazy didn't begin to cover Ivy.

"And that's how it will appear to the detective when he finds your body on the ground below. After being overwhelmed by grief and shame at killing Ginny, your husband's lover, you leap to your death."

"I'm not leaping anywhere, Ivy. And Ginny was never Frank's lover. Just like he was never yours."

Ivy waved the gun as if waving the annoying mosquitoes of sanity away. Her voice grated like dry bones rubbing together. "Whatever. Ginny kills you and then kills herself or vice versa. Same result."

47

Alison shivered. Ivy had her cornered. She was tired, so tired, of being the cowering, trapped little mouse. Her fingers encountered a small round object stuck in her pocket.

"Your ensemble becomes you, Ivy." Alison's voice sounded oily even to her own ears. "But aren't you missing an accessory?"

Ivy narrowed her eyes.

She cautiously, so as not to alarm Ivy, put a shaky hand to her throat.

Ivy put her own hand to the lacy white chemise shirt under her traveling jacket. "My locket," she whispered.

"I found it. Would you like it back?"

She-Who-Must-Be-Obeyed extended an imperious hand. "Give it to me."

Alison pointed to her pocket. "Shall I get it? Or do you want to get it yourself?" If Ivy insisted on retrieving it herself, she wanted to be ready to make a grab for the gun.

She'd read that security experts advised to rid oneself of the notion of getting hurt. Survivors did whatever it took to get out of their situation, even if it meant getting shot in the process. Shot was not necessarily dead.

At this point—on a two-story balcony with no other options—she was willing to play the odds.

Ivy took a step forward and stopped. "No. You get it and hand it to me. Slowly."

Disappointed, she bent her head to fish out the silver locket. "Quite a collection you have here. Like trophy scalps." She hoped to irritate Ivy into a mistake. Stalling, she opened the macabre piece.

"I recognize Natalie's black do. I think I remember Leo's as salt and pepper." She cocked her head, gauging Ivy's reaction.

Pride warred with impatience.

Good.

"The ginger I assume is Ginny's. The red one I know matches Frank."

"I told you I don't want to talk about Frank." Impatience was winning. Ivy frowned. "Frank accidentally found out about my connection to Leo, and he put two and two together." Ivy reached for the locket Alison held just beyond her grasp.

"The white strands?"

Another smile creased Ivy's face, gargoyle-ish in the white-hot brilliance of another lightning flash. "Doris Dandridge, another snooty Weathersby cousin of mine. All her life, so easy, so carefree. Her husband was my ticket to the inner circle of Weathersby. I was only too eager to play nursemaid to his ailing wife."

"The MS and the Alzheimer's?"

Ivy sniffed. "The MS was real. But if there was anything I learned from my mother, the Weathersby drudge, plants, even ones with medicinal purposes, if overdosed can prove fatal."

"The baclofen."

"Prescribed for Doris's MS," said Ivy. "But if given too often or in sufficiently large quantities can mimic symptoms of dementia."

"Which further drove a grieving Professor Dandridge into your waiting arms," she deduced. "And no one thought to request an autopsy."

Ivy smiled again. "Why would they? And now like Jasper, dear Henry has about outlived his usefulness." She waved the gun.

Time was running out, Alison sensed. Ivy was ready to move on with the next stage of her plan.

With her free hand, Ivy fumbled in the small reticule, which hung from one arm. She withdrew a pair of embroidery scissors shaped like the head of a crane.

As Ivy tossed them on the floor, Alison's bare toes scrunched back self-protectively. The scissors landed on point inches away.

"No sense in waiting till that silver bird's nest you call hair is bloody. Pick up the scissors and kindly cut a lock of your hair. Place it next to the others in the locket."

At her incredulous look, Ivy pointed the gun. "Or not. Either way, I'll get it eventually."

Never taking her eyes off Ivy, she slowly lowered herself to the floor. She laid the locket down. With a twist, she pulled the scissors from the wooden floorboards. Rising again just as slowly, she grabbed a small hunk of hair where the ends brushed her jawline.

"I was thinking I needed a new style, anyway." She opened the scissors and closed them, slicing quickly. The snippet came free into her hand.

Holding both hands up, she squatted down once more to retrieve the locket. There was a creak from the staircase. Intent, Ivy didn't seem to notice.

"Slide the scissors over. Don't try anything funny," Ivy warned.

Alison complied, skidding the scissors across the floor to rest at Ivy's laced, black-booted foot. She placed her own hair with the others, and as she closed the locket, she vowed to not allow their deaths to have been in vain. She stood to her feet, all five foot nine inches of her.

She wasn't going to go quietly into the night. Not her. Not this time.

"Give it to me."

Alison dangled the locket over the edge of the railing out of Ivy's reach. Ivy stretched for it, but just as it seemed Ivy would grab hold of it, Alison drew it farther away knocking Ivy off balance.

"Perhaps I'll let it fall to the ground."

"No!" screamed Ivy and lunged for it with both hands.

This was her moment. Surrendering the locket to Ivy's eager grasp, without pausing to think, she karate-chopped Ivy's arm, causing the gun to fall from her fingers to the ground two stories below, where it settled on the porch with a crash.

"You—" shrieked Ivy, mad with rage. Seizing Alison by the throat, the locket looped around one wrist, Ivy pushed the top portion of Alison's body backward over the balustrade.

She hung on for dear life, kicking off her flip-flops, wrapping her bare feet like a monkey's tail around the spindles. She tried to pry Ivy's bony fingers from her throat.

Ivy tightened her hold. Alison fought madly, praying she wouldn't lose consciousness. She was done for, if she did. Despite Ivy's diminutive size and Alison's superior stature, Ivy's maniacal strength was winning the day.

She could hear gurgling attempts from her closed throat as it sought desperately for air, her body slipping.

A dark streak launched itself from the shadows to land with claws extended into Ivy's back.

With a screech of animal-like pain, Ivy dropped her hold on Alison, frantic to free herself from Miss Patty's hissing and spitting. Alison grabbed for the railing to keep from plunging over.

The cat wrapped herself around to Ivy's face and seized onto the white lacy front of Ivy's throat. Miss Patty slashed at Ivy's face with one paw, leaving streaks of blood. Ivy screamed and cursed.

Taking great heaving gulps of air, Alison leaned over the balustrade, clutching her throat. The melee behind her was high-pitched and deafening. Down below, the welcome sight of bobbing flashlights emerged from the gap in the yew trees.

"Here!" she called, her throat scratchy and her eyes burning. "Up here!" A coughing fit seized her as she rasped, "Hurry."

But, it was too late. Too late for Ivy.

With one mighty swoop, Miss Patty managed to yank the locket free of Ivy's grasp, breaking the silver chain and leaving a long, scraping, four-claw furrow down Ivy's hand. The cat jumped nimbly to the top of the railing and over.

"My locket!" screamed Ivy, her hat askew, her face a bloody mess.

Her hand outstretched, Ivy dived over the railing after Miss Patty. A look of panic crossed her face when she realized what she'd done. Ivy reached for Alison, but she had no time to react. In an instant, Ivy was gone, the insane, unearthly shrieking silenced as her body hit the ground.

She leaned over as far as she dared. Ivy lay sprawled, her legs and arms at strange angles, a pool of blood seeping into the Weathersby ground she'd so longed to possess. Miss Patty lay curled in a ball on the bottom step licking her paws. The locket lay beside her, glittering in a flash of lightning.

"You take care of your friends, don't you, Miss Patty?" she whispered.

A beam of light shone up to her perch.

"Alison?" Winnie sounded a touch hysterical.

"Alison? Are you okay?" called Robert.

Mike rushed past them to the porch and kicked in the door. His feet pounded up the staircase.

She sagged to her knees with sweet relief. Mike.

"Yes," she called. "I'm okay." She looked at the raging sky overhead. "It's over, Frank," she whispered. "It's over."

And that was how Mike found her. One final boom of thunder and the rain, pent up too long, burst forth from its dam in the sky, soaking her and Mike to the skin, cleansing the ground once and for all of Ivy's blood.

48

HAT CAT DESERVES A MEDAL IN MY HUMBLE BUT ACCURATE OPINION," joked Robert. "Winnie went to the office to chase down her check and found Miss Patty batting a coffee bean around on the porch. Miss Patty kept rubbing against Winnie, meowing like crazy and tugging on her trouser leg with her teeth as if she wanted Winnie to follow." He leaned back in the deck chair, taking a sip from the steaming mug on the patio table.

One week after Alison's narrow escape from death, he, Val, and Alison lounged on the deck overlooking her yard. Rays of sunshine filtered through the tall oak trees. She took a deep breath of air, glad to be outside and alive. It wouldn't be long before the moist blanket of humidity would drop once more upon them.

That night, a week ago now, Mike had called the paramedics for Ginny. He'd debriefed Ginny at Rex Hospital, relaying to her—via Alison—what had transpired the night Leo died. He'd left her softly weeping for Leo and relieved of the burden of guilt she'd been carrying.

The paramedics rushed to Henry's home. They'd done what they could, but Henry died in the ER of a drug overdose in the early morning hours, Ivy's final victim.

Folding her within the solid buttress of his arms, Mike carried her down the stairs. Despite her shock, she'd managed to show Mike and his officers how to work the hidden apparatus that opened the secret passageway behind the grandfather clock.

Jasper and his backpack were gone.

Only a small pool of blood remained at the bottom of the stairs to testify to the validity of what she'd witnessed. At the other end of the tunnel, the entrance stood wide open, the storm scattering leaves and debris across the cabin. The police were still looking for Jasper.

She didn't for one moment believe they'd ever find him. He'd crawled back under whatever rock he'd emerged from five years ago. She only hoped she never had to lay eyes on him again.

An eventful week had followed with scores of paparazzi descending on them once more. A week during which she'd had time for regrets over her knee-jerk reaction toward Mike. She and the children were exhausted, physically and emotionally. Claire was in the house whipping up a "rocking" Sunday lunch, and over in the grass, Justin quietly practiced his putting strokes. Claire, she'd observed, liked to cook and cook big when feeling stressed. Alison wasn't the only one feeling the loss of Mike.

She closed her eyes, allowing the sunshine to warm her upturned face. Feeling the sunshine on her face eased the ache in her heart. A little. As soon as he could decently get away, Mike boarded a plane for D.C. without her ever getting the chance to . . . What? She fought against the lump in her throat.

"Winnie ran across the orchard and into the woods trying to keep up with Miss Patty," Robert explained to Val. "She found the cabin door open and coffee beans spilled across the floor. She immediately thought of Alison and her coffee addiction."

Alison nodded. "Winnie didn't know about the secret tunnel entrance, but she told me she had a bad feeling with all that had been happening. She called the police from her parked car, and they reached Mike at home." Her voice quivered, remembering the rough stubble that covered his chin as he held her close to his chest while she sobbed that night.

"That's how we managed to arrive at Weathersby at the same time. Not that you needed our help in the end." Robert sent an admiring glance in Alison's direction.

Val frowned. "She could've gotten herself killed."

"I got all the help I needed from a Siamese cat and God. Otherwise, I'd be dead, too." Alison cleared her throat. "Lula Burke filled in most of the blanks. Seems that tunnel was built by Oliver Weathersby, well before the Civil War, for his little trysts with the favored slave girls."

"Not so favorable for them." Val took a quick swig from her mug.

Alison inclined her head in agreement. "It was also well known among the slave population whoever was assigned that particular slave cabin had 'extra' duties."

Robert grimaced.

"Anyway," she exhaled. "One day during the war, or so the legend according to Miss Lula goes, the mistress of Weathersby found out about her husband's clandestine activities. Lula's great-great-grandmother was the cook and known as an herb woman among her own people. Oliver was starting to pay too much attention to the cook's own daughter so together she and the mistress conspired to rid themselves of their problem."

Robert's eyes widened. "They poisoned him?"

"You got it. They passed it off saying he'd died while serving his country in battle. Raleigh was smaller then and the farm far from the outskirts of town. More isolated. No one questioned his disappearance or death."

"Scores of men dying in those days," observed Val.

"The Weathersby women were nothing if not enterprising. After the war, the Weathersby daughter, Opal, married a Yankee carpetbagger, Horace Tidwell, to pay off the debts. He, too, discovered the tunnel and found," Alison coughed, "it to be useful for similar purposes."

"Good heavens," Robert sputtered in his coffee.

"Nothing good about this bunch of murderers and sexual predators." Alison shuddered. "You need a genealogical chart to follow this one, but Tidwell raped one of the sharecropper's daughters—

one of his father-in-law's bastard children—Ivy's ancestor. Tidwell's mother-in-law, Prudence, his wife, Opal, pregnant at the time with their own child, and Miss Lula's great-granny dealt with him in like kind. Though I still don't figure how nobody reported him missing."

Robert sighed. "You haven't lived here long enough if you don't know the answer to that one, Alison. He was a despised invader and economic opportunist. He was never missed, I'm sure."

Val shrugged. "All ancient history."

"Not so, I fear." Alison shook her head. "That unborn Weathersby child became Ursula Weathersby's father, Malcolm, a highly decorated World War I colonel. By now, Ivy's ancestors were, I believe the term is 'passing' white, though they lived on the wrong side of the tracks. Her people, to keep them quiet, had been kept on as house servants, as had Miss Lula's."

"So she grew up bitterly resentful of the upstairs Weathersbys and their numerous legitimate relatives like Doris Dandridge and Natalie Singleton," Val elaborated.

"But that's not all. Seems Ivy's mother also caught the much older colonel's eye. By Miss Lula's account, it was a love match on both sides."

"You mean," Robert's eyebrows rose. "Ivy was actually Ursula Weathersby's half-sister?"

"Exactly, though she could never be acknowledged. Or inherit the house she longed to possess."

"It shows you what chain of events anger and bitterness can lead to, doesn't it?" Robert dropped his gaze. "Or what jealousy will cause an otherwise devoted follower of Christ to say." He sighed, the sound full of regret and apology.

Alison took another sip to give herself something to do. "We need to talk, Robert—"

"So that's how Ivy got Ursula to deed over the property to TAP," Robert surmised.

"Ivy certainly blackmailed Ursula, according to Miss Lula. Ivy knew in these modern times she could never hope to restore the old home to its former standard of splendor, and so she thought this would be the best way to preserve the home she loved so dearly and then cleverly used the Dandridges to solidify her place as executive director."

"Two obsessions." Val glanced over her shoulder to make sure the children were out of earshot. "Weathersby and Frank."

Robert made a face. "What about the press hounding Alison and the kids for a statement about Raleigh's female serial killer?"

Val stiffened. "Mike's got Ross and the others on a rotating schedule to keep those jackals out of Alison's hair."

She winced, recalling the contents of the locket. It hurt too much to think of Mike. And it would be a long time before she would stop reliving the hours she'd fought Ivy with the wits God had given her to save her own life.

"The hotel clerk in San Francisco positively ID'd Ivy. According to Winnie, whose son is with the Raleigh PD, Ivy's passion," Robert flushed, "for Frank appears to have been unrequited on his part. She followed him there unbeknownst to him on the pretext of a historic preservation conference also taking place in the city. A clerk remembers overhearing them argue."

Alison deposited her mug on the table with a thud. "He took that picture as a clue if something happened to him."

Robert grimaced. "He left a batch of incriminating documents on the Lawrences and their Ponzi scheme in the sleazy hotel safe. I think he was there on a fact-finding mission. It's going to help my friend, Tom, nail them both." He looked over at Alison. "Their illegally obtained assets have been seized by the Feds. There'll be an auction, and you and the other victims will receive a settlement."

"Anything we get at this point will be a help." Her eyes roved about the quiet beauty of her garden. "And the house?"

"The buyers I found loved the house. Their offer still stands, and if all goes well, we should close in a couple of weeks."

Val rose. "I'm going to help Claire with that—and I quote—'gi-normous' Sunday lunch. Stephen and the boys should be here soon."

As soon as Val disappeared through the French doors, Alison swiveled in her chair to face Robert. "Will you stay for lunch?

There's something I need to do before we eat, but afterward, you and I need to talk."

Robert patted her hand. "Anything you ask I'll do. No excuse for my deliberately trying to hurt you and Mike—"

Pushing back her chair, she touched his arm. "It's okay. Please stay. I promise I'll be back as quick as I can." Mike—a topic she didn't care to discuss with Robert. Moot point now. If only life offered do-overs.

With Claire and Val refusing offers of help and Justin and Robert occupied with the never-ending delight of the little white ball, Alison, slipping her feet into a gold-sequined pair of flip-flops, told Claire her intentions.

Claire laid the spatula on the counter. "You want to be alone?"

She nodded, trying to keep her eyes from brimming over.

"Okay, but don't be long. Justin and I need you. Here," Claire pointed at the terra firma.

Alison grabbed her purse, sticking a small white envelope inside. Time to say good-bye. And she had things to say the children could not hear.

Should not hear.

At the cemetery, she made her way over to Frank's grave. Her flip-flops made a crunching sound over the graveled path. She glanced around. Her solitude was complete.

Workmen delivered the headstone a few days ago. This was her first visit since the burial. The changed Frank was in a place where the now-changed Alison believed she would see him again one day.

Her despair had given way to faint stirrings of hope for the future. With Frank's killer dead, it was time for closure with Frank. Time for the anger to fade and forgiveness to start its healing work.

And there'd be no healing until she could let go of the rage and embrace the balm of forgiveness. Not for Frank's sake. He was beyond the need for her forgiveness. But for herself.

Frank had lived most of his life in the mistaken belief he could do whatever he wanted, whenever he desired, and get away with it. He lived his life as if there'd never be any consequences. God had shown him at the last what a lie he had embraced. Living life your own way and not God's always resulted in consequences. There was always a reckoning.

To hold on to the anger against Frank would result in a reckoning of her own. It wasn't how God wanted her to live. And God's way was the best way.

She dropped to her knees. Drawing the white envelope out of her purse, she removed a small object.

A memory of hateful words, demeaning remarks, flashed across her mind. She bit her lip with the effort to force out what she wanted—needed—to say. She was free-falling once more, spiraling out of control with no one there to catch her. Tears ran down her cheeks.

But there is Someone now to catch you, a gentle voice said. *Just ask*.

She prayed for help with the words she couldn't choke out for Frank. A peace gradually replaced her turmoil.

And, strength to do the impossible.

"I'm sorry, Frank," she whispered. "I failed you as surely as you failed me." She paused and looked skyward. "God, I give You this anger. I don't know what else to do with it. I'm tired of carrying it."

A weight lifted from her, floating skyward. "And Frank . . ." Sobs racked her frame. "I forgive you."

She had the sensation of her feet at last touching the ground as gently as a butterfly landing on a leaf. The free fall was over.

Dashing the tears from her face, she placed the dried plumeria petal in the center of the headstone.

"When I think of you, Frank, I'll remember Hawaii. Thank you, Frank, for Hawaii and two of the most wonderful children on earth."

Brushing the loose soil from her hands, she rose.

"We'll see each other again." She sighed. "I'll make sure Justin and Claire never forget you. With God's help, we're going to be okay."

And for the first time, she believed it. Even if Mike was forever gone from their lives. God would be enough.

They were going to have to move. She had to get a real job. The future was unknown.

But they were in the best place they could be. Held in the palm of God's hand, the future sifted through His fingers of love. He would ensure they all landed safely on their feet.

It was time, she reflected, as she made her way to the car, to begin the next stage of her life journey and embrace all God had for her.

49

Pulling into the garage, she passed Mike's truck parked alongside the curb.

He'd come back.

Her heart racing, she ran up the garage steps into the kitchen and smack into Robert on his way out the door.

Claire and Val stood awkwardly at the island. Halfway across the threshold to the dining room, Mike paused as if mid-flight, his eyes searching hers, uncertainty of his welcome etched across his face.

Val looked from Robert to Alison and back to Mike. "Mike Barefoot, you handsome thing. Come hug my neck."

Mike blushed—there was one for the books, boys and girls—but he appeared pleased. And self-conscious.

Robert cleared his throat. "I'm on my way out, Alison."

"Don't leave on my account. I probably shouldn't be here anyway." Mike made a move toward the front of the house.

"Wait, Mike," Alison called after his rapidly retreating form. He didn't slow down.

Robert brushed past her and into the garage. "Sorry, Alison."

Val tugged at Claire. "We'll take care of Mike." Untying the apron strings around her waist, she and Claire disappeared from their sight.

"Not going to work, is it?" Robert tilted his head to the side. "Us, I mean."

Her face constricted. "Robert, I'm sorry, but—"

Robert gave her a sad smile. "A nice dream, but kind of hard for you to marry me when you're already in love with someone else." He squeezed her arm. "Go on after him. And I wish both of you the best."

He always felt so hyperaware of her when they were in a room together. Her every move. Her every emotion. He needed to get out of there before he embarrassed himself.

Stuffing his hands in his jean pockets, he ended up in Alison's backyard and kicked a cloud of dirt with the toe of his sneaker. She'd told him she never wanted to see him again. What was he doing here?

His mind returned, as it often had during the past week he'd been in D.C., to that kiss at Weathersby. Surprised the heck out of him. Delighted the heck out of him.

But he'd had the sense not to push it farther or her. A few more minutes . . . His response would've scared her into Jupiter's orbit. That's why he'd backed away, broken it off.

Kind of scared him, too, the rush of feeling like nothing he'd ever felt for any woman. A bittersweet glimpse of a life he'd never get to live. Love. A vastly overused word. But in this case, it fit the condition of his heart.

Picking up an acorn, he threw it as hard as he could into the hedges. No way would this thing between him and Alison work out to be anything but painful for him.

Sure, she'd choose Robert. It was only a matter of time. The question was, did he have the guts to stand by and watch it happen knowing, as he did, its inevitable outcome?

He thought of Ray's tempting job offer. D.C., with its hand on the pulse of a nation, as exciting to him as any drug. He'd spent the last week letting Ray try to talk him into taking the job.

Walk away from her, he told himself again for the thousandth time this week. Don't look back. Chalk it up to the one who got away and move on with your life.

Trouble was, he didn't want to walk away. He'd stepped in it this time. Stepped in it big. There was no going back and not much use in going forward.

Crouching down, he made a heart in the mulch with his finger. And no Alison meant no Claire and Justin. Robert deserved a fair chance with the kids, too.

He sighed.

Maybe a clean break would be better for all of them.

Had she left things with Mike too late? She'd seen the look of hurt on his face as she stood next to Robert. Hurtling into the dining room, the hair on her arms tingled as she took in Val, the lone occupant of the room, setting out silverware on the table.

"Where's Mike?" Alison's voice rose. Her eyes searched the corners of the room as if he might be hiding.

"He left."

She gasped. "He left? What do you mean he left?"

"Needed some air, he said." Val shook her head. "Couldn't stop him. Maybe Claire knows—"

Rushing past Val, she found Claire in the breakfast area folding napkins. A quick glance confirmed Claire was alone. Panic flared and streaked through her body.

"Where's Mike?"

Inhale. Exhale, she reminded herself.

Claire looked up, unconcerned. "Went that way." She nodded toward the back. "Tell him lunch is almost ready."

Her brow furrowed, Alison caught hold of Claire. "Lunch?"

Claire turned sheepish. "Yeah. I called him this week and asked him to come. Didn't know you were inviting Robert, too. What's a girl gotta do around here to help her mother out? The two of you running around this week like you didn't have the sense God gave small animals."

Alison leaned over and planted a kiss on Claire's cheek. "Thank you, Claire, for trying. You've obviously got more sense than your mother."

Claire hugged her. "Don't be so hard on yourself, Mom. The good ones aren't exactly strewn around like rose petals after a storm. Got to grab 'em up when you see 'em."

Rose petals? Good to know her attempts to pass on her gardening know-how had not been in vain.

Claire concentrated her attention on the napkins. "And I know it's hard to think straight and be in love at the same time."

"And you would know this how?"

"Go, Mom. Why are you wasting time talking to me? Go talk to him." She shoved her mother toward the back of the house.

Alison flung open the door and spotted Mike in his black polo, a lonely figure facing her roses. Pausing on the deck, she removed her flip-flops, lacing them through her fingers. Dew squished through her toes, yet she moved as swiftly and silently as the barefoot beach baby she'd always been.

His back stiffened when she was a few feet from him. That legendary Cherokee gene he was always bragging about? Or was he as aware of her as she was of him?

"You found me."

She couldn't tell from his tone if he was pleased or not.

"How did you know it was me?"

Sighing, he backed up to the garden bench and took a seat. "I just knew."

Plopping down, the flip-flops landing beside the bench, she pulled her knees up to her chin, wrapping her arms around her legs. "I thought you'd left. Left me. For good. All my fault."

He said nothing.

Feeling the weight of words unspoken hanging between them, she cleared her throat. "Are you taking the job in D.C.?" And if you are—she dared not say it out loud—will you take us with you?

His eyes locked on her bare feet. "Do you want me to?"

The gap between their bodies, though only inches, seemed an unreachable gulf. "The children—"

He pivoted, facing her at last. "I asked what *you* wanted me to do?"

She gave a harsh laugh. "I'm not exactly noted for the wisdom of my major life choices, Mike. I don't want to be selfish and interfere with your career."

"Be selfish, Alison."

She stared at him, at the intensity in his eyes. And thought hard about what he was not saying. About what he might never say.

Jump, she told herself. Jump.

"No." She took a deep breath. "I don't want you to go. Ever."

A small smile flitted across his face, the noonday light casting great shadows along the hollows of his cheekbones. "Good. I don't want to go anywhere you won't be."

He touched her then, his fingertip brushing her cheek. "I love you, Alison. And if you'll have me, I want to spend the rest of my life loving you."

"I love you, too." The confession left her feeling freer to breathe. "And the answer is yes. Yes. Yes." She sagged against him, hugging the strong, solid side of him. "I missed you so much this week." She buried her face in the woodsy smell of his sleeve. "Next to Val and God, you're the best friend I've ever had."

She felt his chest rumble with a laugh.

"That's high cotton company for me."

She gazed at his beloved face. "Like you say, much better company than the hookers and serial killers you usually hang out with."

Cupping her face with his hands, his lips sought hers. An incredible rush of sweetness filled her being. A rightness, God-ordained this time.

"You won't leave us behind?" she whispered into his ear as he cradled her.

Mike drew back, looking her full in the face. "God willing, never again."

Placing her arms around his neck, once more she savored the fullness of his mouth on hers. His lips trailed, exploring the contours of her throat. He broke contact first with a sigh full of promise.

"I'd just as soon stay with the Raleigh PD. Make a new home with you and the children. Keep them at Stonebriar, expand your landscaping business, and give you a new space to create the garden of your dreams."

"Oh, Mike . . ." How she loved him for loving her children, loving her. For his gentleness of spirit and the strength of his soul. Her eyes devoured him. "You are my dream. The heart of any garden I will ever create."

She watched his face transform. His breath hitched. "And you are everything I ever wanted. More than I dared to dream possible."

He rose, offering her his hand. "Think we should go tell the kids our news?"

She took his hand. "News? Claire's probably got the invitations already preordered minus the date."

Mike grinned. "Well, let's not keep them in suspense any longer. Nor the engravers. Sooner rather than later would suit me fine."

Alison smiled, closing her eyes, her face tilted toward the sun.

God, You are enough. But thank You for Mike and all that's yet to be.

She picked up her flip-flops. Grass studded her pink manicured toes.

"Did I ever tell you those pink toes of yours were the first thing I noticed about you? And after the better part of a year with Claire, I've been educated enough to know official girly names like Shell Pink, Tropical Coral Reef, and Purple Passion. Not to mention Justin's contribution with words like *birdie* and *bogie*."

She laughed. "Glad we've been able to do our part in supplementing your sadly neglected education." Sticking her arm through the crook of his elbow, she found his hand, twining her fingers into his. "And if I know Claire, you could be accessorized in one of those colors on the Big Day, God preserve us."

Mike kissed her fingers. "He will, my love. God will."

Discussion Questions

1. With which character did you most identify? Why?

2. Has someone ever betrayed you? How did you deal with it? Would you have handled the betrayal the same way Alison did? Would you have forgiven Frank?

3. Why did Claire have a hard time embracing her mother's newfound faith? Have you ever struggled with faith during a time of loss, crisis, or death? Why was she so angry with God? Have you ever been angry with God? What did you do about it?

4. What was the biggest surprise to you in *Carolina Reckoning*?

5. Why was it important for Alison to solve her husband's murder?

6. What final step did Alison have to make before she was ready to let go of the past and move on to all God had for her in a new life and with a new love?

7. Have you ever had to let go of something or someone in order to move ahead with your life? Was it hard? What steps did you take to accomplish this?

8. Have you ever been the recipient of the healing power of forgiveness and God's love? Have you ever had to bestow forgiveness? Which was harder?

9. Why do you think there is such a healing power in the act of forgiveness?

10. Through a family crisis and tragedy, Alison and her children experience a spiritual awakening. What have you experienced that has brought you into a closer relationship with God?

11. From the pain of her past to the wounds of her present to the uncertainty of her future, how did Alison learn to rely on God for her every need? Have you experienced the presence of the God of all comfort and wisdom in your past and

present situation? Is He your hope for the future despite your circumstances today?

12. Have you ever received a second chance? Did you take it?

13. Why does Mike feel he has no chance with Alison? Why doesn't he feel good enough for her? Have you ever felt that way?

14. Alison learns that true security and safety cannot be found in money or relationships. What have you discovered that satisfies?

15. Alison had a choice between the love of two men. One represented to her safety and security. The other felt like "jumping off a cliff into nothingness" and symbolized a leap of faith. Would you have made the same choice as Alison? Why or why not?

16. For years, fear kept Alison from living the life God meant her to have all along. What do you need to confront to become the person you are meant to be? What barriers in your life need to come down?

17. How did Alison experience the truth of Romans 8:38-39? How have you?

Want to learn more about author
Lisa Carter and check out other great
fiction from Abingdon Press?

Sign up for our fiction newsletter at
www.AbingdonPress.com
to read interviews with your favorite authors, find tips
for starting a reading group, and stay posted on what
new titles are on the horizon. It's a place to connect
with other fiction readers or post a
comment about this book.

Be sure to visit Lisa online!

www.LisaCarterAuthor.com

What They're Saying About...

The Glory of Green, by Judy Christie
"Once again, Christie draws her readers into the town, the life, the humor, and the drama in Green. *The Glory of Green* is a wonderful narrative of small-town America, pulling together in tragedy. A great read!"
—Ane Mulligan, editor of *Novel Journey*

Always the Baker, Never the Bride, by Sandra Bricker
"[It] had just the right touch of humor, and I loved the characters. Emma Rae is a character who will stay with me. Highly recommended!"
—Colleen Coble, author of *The Lightkeeper's Daughter* and the *Rock Harbor* series

Diagnosis Death, by Richard Mabry
"Realistic medical flavor graces a story rich with characters I loved and with enough twists and turns to keep the sleuth in me off-center. Keep 'em coming!"—Dr. Harry Krauss, author of *Salty Like Blood* and *The Six-Liter Club*

Sweet Baklava, by Debby Mayne
"A sweet romance, a feel-good ending, and a surprise cache of yummy Greek recipes at the book's end? I'm sold!"—Trish Perry, author of *Unforgettable* and *Tea for Two*

The Dead Saint, by Marilyn Brown Oden
"An intriguing story of international espionage with just the right amount of inspirational seasoning."—*Fresh Fiction*

Shrouded in Silence, by Robert L. Wise
"It's a story fraught with death, danger, and deception—of never knowing whom to trust, and with a twist of an ending I didn't see coming. Great read!"—Sharon Sala, author of *The Searcher's Trilogy: Blood Stains, Blood Ties,* and *Blood Trails.*

Delivered with Love, by Sherry Kyle
"Sherry Kyle has created an engaging story of forgiveness, sweet romance, and faith reawakened—and I looked forward to every page. A fun and charming debut!"—Julie Carobini, author of *A Shore Thing* and *Fade to Blue.*

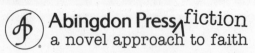

Abingdon Press fiction
a novel approach to faith

AbingdonPress.com | 800.251.3320

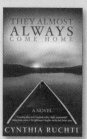